To Cur

Henrietta Altenkes

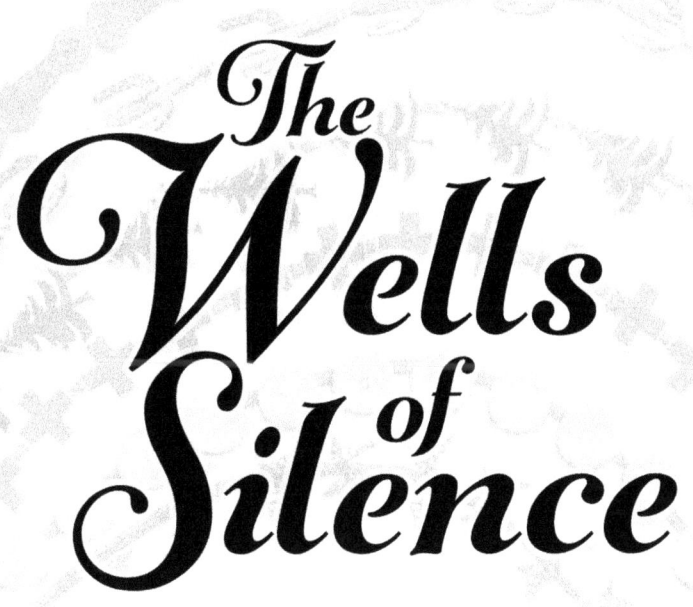

The Wells of Silence

Henrietta Alten West

LLOURETTIA GATES BOOKS • MARYLAND

This book is a work of fiction. Many of the names, places, characters, and incidents are products of the author's imagination or are used fictitiously. Any resemblance to actual events or locales or person living or dead is entirely coincidental.

Copyright © 2023 Llourettia Gates Books, LLC
All rights reserved. This book or any portion thereof may not be reproduced or used in any manner whatsoever without the express written permission of the publisher.

Llourettia Gates Books, LLC
P.O. Box #411
Fruitland, Maryland 21826

Hardcover ISBN: 978-1-953082-24-4
Paperback ISBN: 978-1-953082-25-1
eBook ISBN: 978-1-953082-26-8
Library of Congress Control Number: 2023915487

Photography by Andrea Lōpez Burns
Cover art by Thaxted Smith
Cover and interior design by Jamie Tipton, Open Heart Designs

This book is dedicated to the people of Poland who are free at last and to others who struggle to free themselves from oppression of all kinds.

Contents

Cast of Characters vii
Prologue xiii

Arizona, 2022 1

Chapter 1 3
Chapter 2 13
Chapter 3 22
Chapter 4 28
Chapter 5 34
Chapter 6 53
Chapter 7 66
Chapter 8 89
Chapter 9 101

The Katyn Forest Massacre, 1940 . . . 111

Chapter 10 113
Chapter 11 126
Chapter 12 136
Chapter 13 151
Chapter 14 160
Chapter 15 172
Chapter 16 179

Arizona, 2022 199
   Chapter 17 201
   Chapter 18 206
   Chapter 19 216

Moscow To Guadalajara, 1945–2018 231
   Chapter 20 233

Arizona, 2022–2023 249
   Chapter 21 251
   Chapter 22 258
   Chapter 23 280
   Chapter 24 285
   Chapter 25 298
   Chapter 26 312
   Chapter 27 320
   Chapter 28 331
   Chapter 29 338
   Chapter 30 352

Epilogue 357
When Did I Grow Old? 358
Author's Note 361
Complete Biographies Of The Reunion Chronicles Mysteries Characters 365
Acknowledgments 397

CAST OF CHARACTERS

Elizabeth and Richard Carpenter
Elizabeth and Richard live in a small town on the Eastern Shore of Maryland. Richard is a retired pathologist who did some work for the Philadelphia Medical Examiner's office many years ago. Elizabeth is a former college professor and CIA analyst. She began writing mystery novels after she had her 70th birthday. They spend the winters at their home in Tucson, Arizona.

Gretchen and Bailey MacDermott
Gretchen and Bailey live in Dallas, Texas. Bailey is a former IBM salesman, oil company executive, and Department of Defense intelligence agent. He currently is making another fortune selling commercial real estate. Gretchen works in the corporate world as the head of an HR department. Because she is so competent at everything she does, she actually runs the company she works for.

Tyler Merriman
Tyler lives in southern Colorado. Everyone suspects that Tyler flew the SR-71 Blackbird for the U.S. Air Force during his younger years. After he retired from the military, he made millions in commercial real estate. He flew his own plane around the country. He is an avid skier and hiker and rides his bicycle everywhere.

Sidney and Cameron Richardson
Sidney and Cameron have several homes and their own private plane. Cameron is a former IBM wunderkind who went out on his own to start several globally-known computer companies. Sidney is a retired profiling consultant who owned an innovative, successful, and very profitable home organization business before she married Cameron.

Isabelle and Matthew Ritter
Isabelle and Matthew live in Palm Springs, California. Matthew is a retired urologist, an avid quail hunter, and a movie buff. Isabelle has retired from her career as a clinical psychologist and now owns a popular high-end interior furnishings store and design business. Her creative skills are in great demand, and she works way too hard to please her demanding clientele.

Olivia and J.D. Steele
Olivia and J.D. live in Saint Louis. J.D. is a lawyer who gave up his job as a prosecuting attorney to found his own extremely successful trucking company. He is a logistics expert. Olivia is a former homecoming queen and valedictorian of her high school class. She is a brilliant woman who worked for many years as a mathematician and cypher specialist for the NSA.

Pia Karlsson
Pia is a psychologist and long-time friend of Isabelle Ritter. Her daughter is Annika.

Cast of Characters

Annika Karlsson/Catherine Murray
Annika is Pia Karlsson's daughter. She is married to Igor Arturo Castillo. Annika's life is in danger, and she has to go into hiding.

Detective Cecilia Mendoza
Cecilia Mendoza is a homicide detective with the Phoenix Police Department. She is in charge of investigating the crimes that are committed at the Mimosa Inn.

Igor Arturo Castillo / El Russo
El Russo is a drug kingpin who lives in Scottsdale, Arizona and in Mexico. His mother was connected to the Russian Mafia, and his father was connected to the Mexican drug trade. He controls the manufacture of fentanyl in Mexico as well as its distribution in large parts of the western United States. He is married to Annika Karlsson. He is the grandson of Lavrentiy Beria.

Hector Gutierrez
Hector is Igor Arturo Castillo's first cousin. He helps Igor run their family drug business. He struggles to keep his volatile and violent cousin under control.

Dr. Freddy Kernigan
Freddy is a friend of Matthew Ritter's from medical school. He is a trauma surgeon and an entrepreneur who developed the mobile hospital. He works in areas of the world that are underserved by medical care.

Beata Wojciech Boucher
Beata is the wife of Casimir Wojciech who was taken to a Soviet prison camp in the early spring of 1940. He was never seen again. Beata left Poland after her husband disappeared. She is the mother of Margot Boucher.

Father Jakub Janusz
Father Janusz is Catholic priest in Poland. He is a childhood friend of Beata and Casimir Wojciech.

Dr. Preston Boucher
Preston Boucher is a Canadian physician who works at a hospital in Malmo, Sweden during World War II. He is also an Allied intelligence officer who reports nightly via short wave radio to his colleagues in London. He is an organizer of resistance fighters who work against the Nazis in Denmark. He is Beata's second husband and Margot's stepfather.

Dr. Margot Wojciech Boucher
Margot is the daughter of Beata and Casimir Wojciech. She is the stepdaughter of Dr. Preston Boucher and the mother of Monique Simone Gauthier.

Dr. Monique Simone Gauthier
Monique Simone is the daughter of Margot Boucher. She is forced to leave her home in Montreal and go into hiding when her fiancé tries to kill her.

Mona Damours
Mona is a painter, a former physician, and recluse who lives in a secluded cabin in the White Mountains of Arizona. Mona can do anything.

Cast of Characters

Lavrentiy Pavlovich Beria
Beria was the head of the Soviet Union's NKVD from 1938–1945. He was Joseph Stalin's hit man. He was responsible for implementing the Katyn Forest murders. He is the lover of Tatiana Volkov and the father of Irina Volkov.

Tatiana Volkov/ Olga Lebedev/ Marina Baranov
Tatiana is Lavrentiy Beria's lover and the mother of Irina Volkov.

Irina Volkov/ Pavel Lebedev/ Anya Baranov
Irina is the love child of Lavrentiy Beria and Tatiana Volkov. She is the mother of Igor Arturo Castillo.

Prologue

It was the fourteenth Camp Shoemaker yearly reunion. This was the year that the "boys" would embark on the ninth decade of their lives. The group of friends had reservations to stay at the Mimosa Inn in Paradise Valley, Arizona, a very upscale resort in a very upscale zip code. The food was said to be excellent, but what would one expect... in Paradise?

This was the year the former campers from Cabin #1 would celebrate their 80th birthdays. The men in the group had been friends since they were little boys. They'd met when they were eight years old at Camp Shoemaker in the Ozark Mountains. They'd all been assigned to Cabin #1. In their minds, they had never stopped being #1. They made wonderful, happy memories together during the many summers that followed, but they had drifted apart as they'd grown older, and the demands of work and family responsibilities consumed their lives.

In 2009, Matthew Ritter had organized a reunion for the group of former campers. The boys from Camp Shoemaker, then in their sixties and accompanied by their current wives and partners, spent a long weekend in Palm Springs, California. They'd all had the time of their lives. The group had been meeting for a fun-filled long weekend together every year since.

They treasured their friendships, and the women who loved the Camp Shoemaker boys had formed their own bond. Everyone looked forward to the special reunion trips. They chose to visit places that had stimulating things to do and great food. As the years went by, the places where they chose to have the reunion became less important, and spending time together became more important. They never, however, stopped insisting on having great food. They talked about the past and hoped for the future. They cherished the memories from their younger years, and they were having a wonderful time making new memories as older people.

2022

One

The Mimosa Inn was everything it had been advertised to be...elegant, expensive, and exclusive. Located in one of the most coveted neighborhoods in the United States, if not in the world, the Paradise Valley resort had been in business since the 1930s. There was no "hotel" building in the usual sense of the word. There was a central check-in reception cottage that featured a fireplace with welcoming couches and chairs. An ornately carved desk held a computer and a phone. An antique refectory table that offered platters of homemade muffins in the morning and snickerdoodle cookies in the afternoon, along with coffee and tea, held pride of place along one wall. Guests' rooms were all cottages, arranged around the gorgeously-landscaped grounds. This was the Southwest, so the cottages are called casitas. All the casitas were one story, and each had its own patio with a table and chairs. This year's reunion promised to be just about the closest thing to paradise the Camp Shoemaker crowd could hope for.

The Mimosa Inn was beautiful and welcoming. It was quiet. The greeters, who unloaded the luggage and parked cars for guests who had driven to Paradise Valley, were friendly and accommodating. These helpful people who take your luggage to your casita and park your car for you used to be called bellboys and valets. Now they are known as greeters. This promised to be the perfect spot for rest and relaxation and catching up on a year's worth of news for this group of friends and their wives. They always said they wanted a stress-free and leisurely long weekend, but in recent years drama and mayhem had persisted in making their way into the carefully structured plans. Maybe this would be the year they would actually have a relaxing vacation with no untoward excitement to intrude on their days together.

Richard and Elizabeth Carpenter arrived a day early. Because Elizabeth sometimes required a wheelchair, the Carpenters found it was helpful if they arrived ahead of the rest of the group to sort out any problems that might arise over their reservation of a handicap room with an accessible shower. Even though the trip from their winter home in Tucson was not usually an exhausting drive, today's traffic around Phoenix had conspired to make the trip longer than they'd anticipated. They had arrived at 3:30 on Wednesday afternoon. Everyone else would arrive on Thursday. Richard and Elizabeth helped themselves to snickerdoodles while they waited in the lobby to check into their casita.

The two very hospitable young women who were in charge of the computerized check-in offered them bottles of cold water. Richard accepted his thankfully. Driving in traffic can make a person thirsty. One of the check-in hostesses offered them additional cookies. Elizabeth realized that, for some reason, they were stalling. As often happened when one requested an accessible handicap room, there was a problem. For some reason that Elizabeth had never been able to figure out, there was almost always a problem with the accessible room. Elizabeth had seen these expressions of consternation on the faces of the people behind the desk more than once before. Something had gone wrong.

Elizabeth hoped they had not given away her room with the accessible bathroom to someone else. That had happened to her too many times in the past to even begin to count them. Most hotels, motels, and resorts were not used to dealing with those who had special needs. The Carpenters were planning to stay at the Mimosa Inn for ten days. Elizabeth held her breath. She could go a night or two without a shower, but they had reserved their casita for ten days. She could not go without a shower for ten days.

Every October the Carpenters drove from their home on the East Coast to their winter home in Tucson, Arizona. It was a five-day trip. They spent four nights in various motels and hotels along the way. Both Richard and Elizabeth loved the drive. It was invigorating and inspiring to travel through so much of the United States and have a chance to see the beauty and variety of the scenery along the way, as they traveled almost from sea to shining sea. The problems arose with their accommodations. Because Elizabeth needed a shower that she could get into and out of easily rather than a bathtub, the Carpenters made their reservations months in advance. They always asked to reserve the handicap accessible room.

Every hotel and motel is required by federal law to have at least one handicap accessible room that can be reserved. But, too often, when the Carpenters arrived at the place where they'd held a reservation for many weeks, the handicap accessible room was not available to them. Even if they'd had their room reservation guaranteed for weeks or months and even if they had called that same day to confirm its availability, on many, many occasions and all of a sudden, they could not have the room. This had happened to them frequently and at all the major motel and hotel chains. Elizabeth hoped, with fingers crossed, that would not be the case today.

Both young women were staring at the screen of the computer that was on the check-in desk. They were conversing in quiet tones. One of them made a phone call on the landline phone that was beside the computer, and with her forehead wrinkled in concern, she explained something to someone. The explanation was long. She kept her voice low. She did not want the Carpenters to hear what she was saying. She consulted the computer again. She spoke quietly into the phone again. Elizabeth was watching her face as she spoke. This scenario was not new to her, but Elizabeth never enjoyed the complications that requesting a handicap accessible room inevitably seemed to bring.

Finally, the young woman on the phone relaxed the furrows in her brow and put on her best smile as she faced the Carpenters. "All right. Let me explain to you what was holding up the check-in process for your casita." She smiled her biggest smile again. Elizabeth knew very well that too much smiling might not bode well for the ultimate outcome in this or any situation. "You reserved one of our two standard handicap accessible casitas. One of those casitas has been undergoing a renovation for the past several days. The shower is being redone in that bathroom. You were scheduled to stay in our other standard handicap accessible casita. However, just this morning, our maintenance people discovered that the HVAC in that casita, as well as in the casitas on either side of the one that was reserved for you, is not working. The room you reserved is not available." Elizabeth's heart sank. She had heard this excuse before, many times, and it was not pretty.

"The good news for you, Dr. and Mrs. Carpenter," the young woman said as she smiled her big smile again, "is that our casita that is designed as a luxury handicap accessible suite *is* available. It is not located as close to everything as your standard room would have been. It is a little more remote, a bit farther away from the dining room and the swimming pool. But it is a much larger and more spacious accommodation with a very luxurious spa bathroom and shower. We are delighted to be able to offer you that suite for the next ten days."

Ms. Big Smile could see that the Carpenters were somewhat relieved but still anxious. She continued. "And you will be happy to know that we are offering you the upgrade at no extra charge. Your standard room was to be billed at $450 per night. The larger suite is usually billed at $975 per night. Because this inconvenience and the change of accommodations is our fault and not a result of anything you requested, you will be charged only the rate for the standard accessible casita that you originally booked. It is a bargain, if you are willing to take the suite."

Elizabeth thought all the rooms at the Mimosa Inn were overpriced. There really were no "bargains" here, but she and Richard had agreed to pay the outrageous amount for the standard handicap accessible casita. Elizabeth acknowledged that they would be willing to pay the same outrageous amount for the upgraded suite. "That sounds fine. I'm just relieved you had an additional accessible casita available for us. Thank you."

Richard looked as if he were about to launch into a tirade, but Elizabeth had set the tone by being gracious. Richard said nothing but put his credit card on the desk with a thump.

"Housekeeping is putting the finishing touches on your suite right now, and your luggage will be there when you arrive at your casita. We just ask that you be patient and wait a few more minutes until your suite is ready."

The Carpenters were anxious to be in their room. Richard had already missed his afternoon nap and was out of sorts. Elizabeth was tired and ready to unpack and get settled in the casita...wherever it was. They each had a cup of hot tea and two more cookies. Finally, the phone on the desk rang, and one of the welcome hostesses answered it. When she hung up, she smiled her big smile again and announced that the Carpenter's casita was ready. She was going to personally walk them to the suite. She gave Richard and Elizabeth each a real key on a large key ring that would lock and unlock the door of the cottage. It was so old school, Elizabeth had to smile. It had been years since she'd stayed anywhere that didn't have electronic door locks and key cards.

The walkways were stone. The flagstones had been precisely laid and made for a smooth surface that was easy going for Richard to push Elizabeth's wheelchair. She decided that the perfect outdoor spaces were really what they were paying for. The few minutes' walk required to reach their suite took them past the outdoor patio dining area and the resort's restaurant. The Mimosa Inn's gardens were first class, and the flowers that bloomed everywhere were stunning—even in November. The landscaping and the profusion of flowers helped to explain the high room rates. Guests were paying for the wonderful plants and the elaborate horticulture display as well as for the flagstone walkways. Meticulously cared for and a riot of color, the grounds really were akin to paradise. Elizabeth decided maybe the high room rate was worth it...maybe.

The suite was not that remote, and it had a large, covered patio in the front. A table with a top made of colorful tiles, two chairs, and an upholstered bench made the patio a desirable place to spend time. The wooden French doors opening into the room were wide enough to easily accommodate the wheelchair. The room was luxurious, just as the woman at the desk had promised. It was beautifully furnished in high-end Southwestern décor, and all the amenities were in place. The large sitting area had an adobe fireplace with an arched opening. Whoever had prepared their room had turned on the gas fireplace. The fire was welcoming and was doing an excellent job of warming the chilly space and dispelling the very slight but noticeable odor of mildew. One of the Mimosa Inn's greeters had delivered their luggage to the casita. Luggage racks had been set up, and coats had been hung in the closet.

Elizabeth peeked into the bathroom and saw that the shower was indeed a spa-like design that filled one entire end of the large room. There was a built-in bench positioned in just the right spot. The next ten days were going to be fine. She smiled her own biggest smile at the welcome woman who had accompanied them to their quarters. "This is a lovely room. The shower looks especially inviting, from my point of view. Thank you for arranging this for us."

Richard had dropped his keys and wallet and phone on the table beside the bed and was looking longingly at the duvet folded at its foot. It was all he could do not to toss the decorative pillows onto the floor and climb in for his nap. The young hostess, mission accomplished, left some paperwork on the table beside the door. "Because you had to wait to get into your room, dinner tonight is on us. I have left the coupon on this table beside the door, but we have also entered the coupon into the computer. Enjoy your stay." She let herself out of the room.

Richard was asleep before the door had been closed for thirty seconds. Elizabeth transferred from her wheelchair to her rollator and began to unpack her clothes and plug in her electronics. There was a good-sized desk in front of a window that looked out on a cheerful display of flowers. She intended to do some writing in the room when she was alone for a few days. After the reunion was over, Richard and Matthew planned to go quail hunting in the area of the San Carlos Apache Indian Reservation located in the mountains a few hours east of Phoenix. Isabelle was flying home because she had several pressing appointments with clients at her store in Palm Springs. The desk facing the window would be perfect. Elizabeth set up her computer at the desk. She put away a few more things and plugged in her phone and her Kindle. It had been a long day, and she sighed with contentment as she sank into a very comfortable leather armchair in front of the fire.

The Carpenters were tired after packing, taking care of closing up their Tucson house, and remembering to load everything they were going to need into Richard's truck—including all of his hunting gear. Driving to Phoenix bogged down by traffic was always a challenge. Arriving at the Mimosa Inn and being subjected to the fuss and delay about the change in rooms had been stressful.

When Richard roused himself from his nap, they decided they would order room service for dinner. Richard ordered the sugar pumpkin bisque, the Caesar salad, and the filet of beef. Elizabeth ordered the shrimp remoulade and the New York strip medium rare with mashed potatoes and sautéed spinach. They split a bottle of Zinfandel from Paso Robles in central California. They were too tired and too full to eat most of the molten chocolate cake they'd ordered for dessert. They stored the leftovers in the refrigerator that was cleverly disguised under the coffee bar. They were on vacation. They were thankful they had arrived a day early...especially given the confusion over their casita. Their friends would be arriving the next day.

There was a shadow of despondency over the reunion this year. Olivia Steele was gravely ill, and neither she nor J.D. would be making the trip to Paradise Valley. Cameron Richardson had offered to send his plane to St. Louis to pick them up and fly one or both of them to the Mimosa for the day or even just for a few hours. But Olivia was much too sick to make the trip, and J.D. wanted to stay by her side. The reunion goers who had been able to make the trip to Arizona were filled with apprehension and sorrow about Olivia's illness, but they were determined to have some fun in spite of the fact that every one of them was thinking constantly about Olivia. The group of friends knew that Olivia would want them to laugh and enjoy each other...and to toast her when they all sat down at the table together.

Olivia had taken a turn for the worse on the last day of the Steele's cruise of the Greek Islands. She and J.D. had flown home to St. Louis, and Olivia had immediately been admitted to the hospital. The prognosis wasn't good, and the Camp Shoemaker group was keeping both the Steeles in their prayers. J.D. promised daily updates to his friends regarding Olivia's condition.

Elizabeth said a prayer for Olivia and sent her warmest and most healing thoughts in her friend's direction. She adored Olivia and would greatly miss her gregarious personality. The reunion this year would not be the same without Olivia's smile and joie de vivre. J.D. likewise had a fun-loving and outgoing personality. His enthusiasm and his stories would also be missed.

Elizabeth had to use the small set of steps she always took with her when she traveled. Whenever she took a trip, she knew she would be sleeping in a strange bed, a bed that was inevitably too high for her to get into easily. The steps helped her to comfortably climb into the king-sized bed. She had not realized how tired she was until she had spent twenty minutes in the spa shower. It had been a delight, and she was not at all disappointed that their standard accessible room had been afflicted with an HVAC problem. The luxury suite would be her home for the next ten days. She looked forward to seeing her friends the next day and to having new surroundings in which to create a story. She was asleep in minutes.

Two

Sidney and Cameron Richardson flew in their private plane to Sky Harbor Airport and took an Uber to the Mimosa Inn. They'd tried to arrange for the inn's airport bus to pick them up at the private terminal, but the bus was engaged elsewhere. Gretchen and Bailey MacDermott flew from Dallas. Tyler Merriman arrived after a more than eight-hour drive from Colorado. Isabelle and Matthew Ritter arrived last. They had lived in Phoenix for two years when Matthew was fulfilling his government obligation in the Public Health Service. They knew the city better than anyone else in the group. They'd suggested the Mimosa Inn, and they had made all the lunch and dinner reservations. Matthew had arranged for the group to have a special private tour at the Heard Museum, and of course he had several movie montages ready to show. Everyone was missing Olivia and J.D., but J.D. had promised to join the reunion via a Zoom call that would be placed at dinner that night.

Cocktails would be on the Mimosa Inn's outside patio where the group would gather to watch the sun go down and then huddle around the fire to stay warm. Because most of those in the group had spent the day traveling, they'd opted to stay at the Mimosa Inn for dinner on their first night together.

Although the reunion was inevitably overshadowed by concern for Olivia and J.D., the group knew their absent friends would want them to have a good time and enjoy being together. Seating on the Mimosa's sprawling outdoor patio was grouped around individual southwestern-style fireplaces. The reunion group found a spot that could accommodate their crowd. Everyone knew to bundle up in warm clothes, and in addition to the gas fireplaces, outdoor heaters kept them comfortable. They were all thrilled to be together again, and there were many stories and much catching up to do. Elizabeth ordered a hot buttered rum, the only warm drink the Mimosa had on its cocktail menu. The first toast of the evening was to Olivia...accompanied by prayers.

The fire in the fireplace on the patio was a delight, but they were all glad when the maître d' from the restaurant arrived to let them know their table inside was ready. The men in the group would all be celebrating their 80th birthdays in the coming twelve months. They were all in good shape, so walking a few steps from the patio to the restaurant was easy. The women in the group were considerably younger, except for Elizabeth. She rode the distance in her wheelchair, and for her, that was easy, too.

Elizabeth had been very busy in recent weeks as she stayed on top of her complicated plans to rescue Henley Breckenridge. The Camp Shoemaker crowd had rallied around to help save Henley, even though they really didn't know her. Each person in the group had contributed considerable time and effort to successfully helping Henley leave the Balkans and return to the United States. It had not been an easy thing to accomplish. Tonight at dinner, Elizabeth intended to bring the group up to date on Henley's status and thank them again for everything they had done to bring Henley home from her covert mission.

The Mimosa Inn had given the group their own private room at the back of the restaurant. They had a wonderful round table and their own waiter. The menu looked interesting... a combination of classic Southwestern fare and gourmet organic farm-to-table cuisine. Matthew offered another toast to Olivia, and he set up his computer on the table so that J.D. could participate in the discussion.

J.D. appeared on the screen and gave his friends an update on Olivia's condition. He said how much he wished he and Olivia could be with everyone. J.D. said he was going to stay on the Zoom call a little longer. Drinks were ordered, and Elizabeth began to give her report about Henley Breckenridge to the group. She announced that Henley was at last in good health and had returned to her family and her ranch in Paso Robles, California. She was once again living the life she had always loved. She was back to running things and bossing everybody around as only Henley could do. The Camp Shoemaker crowd all clapped when Elizabeth made this announcement. Sidney clapped the loudest when she heard this news, along with J.D. who could be heard clapping loudly over the Zoom call. Sidney and J.D. had both personally interacted with Henley as she'd made her way home from halfway around the world and finally returned to Paso Robles, California.

All were happy they'd been able to participate in helping to save Elizabeth's friend and bring her back to the United States. No one, including Elizabeth, knew exactly what Henley's mission had been, but they suspected her actions should have earned her a prominent place in history. All had their suspicions, and most of these suspicions were probably on target. Henley would never tell, and even though Elizabeth was almost one hundred percent certain she had figured it out, she would never tell either. There would never be any kind of definitive verification of Henley's mission, but the world was a better place because of Henley's success.

J.D. promised to give everyone's love to Olivia, and he had tears in his eyes as he ended his participation in the Zoom call. The group was silent for a few minutes as all missed Olivia and J.D. tremendously. Cameron broke the silence and called for the waiter to serve another round of drinks. Appetizers were ordered, and the fun and the talk, albeit somewhat sobered, continued. Elizabeth had one more announcement and promised that she would keep her mouth shut for a while after that.

"Henley knows what each of you did for her. I told her everything. She was very touched that you would volunteer to help her, even though most of you don't really know her and especially since her relationship with J.D. got off to a rocky start." Elizabeth smiled and laughed. "Henley is grateful to every one of you. She is so grateful that she has insisted on picking up the tab for all of us for this entire weekend...rooms, meals, drinks, everything. I told her she was much too generous and that it was not necessary for her to pay for any of it. I also told her the Mimosa Inn was a very expensive place to stay. I told her we would be having several outrageously expensive meals while we are here. I tried to talk her out of doing this, but she is standing firm. She said she intended to stick by her guns and pay the entire bill. And we all know better than to argue with Henley and her guns."

Murmurs of surprise and protest were heard from around the table. Elizabeth had one more comment to add. "Henley says she has more money than she knows what to do with. She says we saved her life. She says she can afford to pay the bill for all of our rooms and all of our meals. She says we should just be grateful and accept her gift. That's all I am going to say for now. Oh, and she wants us to come back to Paso Robles sometime. I told her maybe we would." Elizabeth let the rest of the group grapple with how to handle the generous gesture from Henley. Elizabeth had heard that, in spite of the way Henley dressed and the life she lived, her friend was enormously wealthy. You certainly would never guess that Henley was worth hundreds of millions of dollars, and maybe the rumor wasn't even true.

The steaks were outstanding. Pistachio-encrusted halibut with a special Meyer lemon sauce was the fish of the day. Two members of the group ordered the spaghetti squash entrée. Roasted vegetables were considered a specialty of the house, and the short ribs were the most popular entrée on the menu. So many decisions. Richard ordered the quinoa salad. He loved quinoa, but he could not for the life of him understand why something so delicious had such a ridiculous name that was not spelled anything at all like the way it was pronounced. When he ordered quinoa salad, which was whenever it was on the menu, he never missed an opportunity to point out his annoyance about this matter to the waiter.

Tonight the waiter explained that he thought quinoa was an ancient word derived, along with the grain itself, from native peoples who long ago had lived in the Andes Mountains in South America. Bailey Googled the word and explained that quinoa was a Spanish word and should be pronounced KEEN-wah. Matthew said, "EKT, everybody knows that." Other spellings of the delicious and healthy grain were offered...quinua...kinwa...and on and on. Finally, all the orders were placed, and the wine was poured. Another rousing reunion of the Camp Shoemaker boys and their partners was underway.

By the time dessert and coffee and an after-dinner port for Richard had been consumed, everyone was tired and ready to return to their casitas and to their beds. The next morning was unscheduled, but a table had been reserved for breakfast. The breakfast buffet was free to guests of the inn, but one could also order a la carte. Elizabeth and Richard had ordered breakfast from room service that morning and attested to the many delicious pancake offerings and the omelets that the Mimosa made to order. Surprise! Two mimosas had arrived on their breakfast trays that had been delivered to their casita exactly on time as requested. Breakfast in bed, or at least in the casita, sounded like the way to go for the women in the group. The men wanted to have breakfast together and indulge in the buffet.

Several spa appointments had been scheduled for the next morning, and plans were made to leave at 2 p.m. for all those who wanted to visit the Desert Botanical Garden in Phoenix. Dale Chihuly's creations were there. Several in the group had visited the Desert Botanical Garden more than once, but seeing the way this brilliant glass artist incorporated his uniquely fabulous work with the desert plants invited multiple viewings. If there were gravel paths, Elizabeth's wheelchair would not be able to make the trip. Someone asked if there would be time during the day set aside for naps.

It was late, and everyone was ready to end the evening. Richard pushed Elizabeth's wheelchair back to their casita. They now had the last casita at the far end of the Mimosa Inn's grounds, and it backed up to a tall Arizona rosewood hedge. Behind the hedge there was an even higher adobe wall that surrounded the entire resort property. Paradise Valley was...paradise to those who had spent millions on their houses to be able to live in this very special community. The Mimosa Inn and its grounds seemed like a very secure and safe place.

When they unlocked the door to their casita, Elizabeth's sharply instinctive radar engaged and immediately sent her a signal that something was off. She sensed that someone had been in the room while they'd been at dinner, but she could not find any actual evidence that there had been an intruder. Housekeeping had completed their tasks much earlier in the day, and there was no turn-down service at the Mimosa. Chocolate-covered mints could be had in the lobby, but nobody came around and put any on the pillows. Elizabeth could not put her finger on exactly what was wrong, but Richard had learned, after being married to the woman for more than fifty-five years, that she was almost always right about these things. He dared not doubt her although he was unaware that anything about the room wasn't right.

Elizabeth knew that someone had been in their room, but she could not immediately determine that anything had been stolen or even moved. As far as she was able to remember, everything was pretty much where it had been when they had left to go to dinner, and nothing seemed to be missing. She checked her jewelry, and it was all accounted for. Maybe it was the barely discernible change in the smell of the room. Elizabeth's sense of smell was very acute, and sometimes a new scent in a room was so subtle it only worked on her subconscious.

The slightly uncomfortable feeling she had and the flash of anger she experienced let her know that an uninvited person had indeed invaded her privacy. She knew someone had been in the room but could not find that they had disturbed anything. However, she was almost certain that the little set of steps she used to climb up into the bed were no longer in exactly the same spot where she had placed them. But she couldn't be absolutely sure about that. Maybe the papers on the desk had been moved a little bit, but she was not sure about that either. Maybe one of the maintenance staff had come into the room to check the thermostat and the HVAC system. The inn was older, and there had been a problem with the HVAC in their original standard accessible accommodations.

As long as nothing had been taken, she would try to ignore her radar's alerts. But when she got closer to the bed, she felt even more certain that another person had been in the room. But she saw nothing that was obviously amiss. The duvet was folded exactly where it had been folded before they had left for dinner. On a closer inspection, Elizabeth was convinced her steps had been moved to a somewhat different position, as if someone had pushed them slightly out of the way to look under the bed. Why would someone have been looking under the bed? This was a mystery she could not spend any more time worrying about.

Elizabeth had done pretty much nothing that day, but the emotion of being with the group of friends all evening had worn her out. She was terribly distraught about Olivia but had tried hard not to dwell on sad thoughts. She looked forward to enjoying the luxurious spa shower once again.

When she went into the bathroom, her suspicions about an intruder were confirmed. She knew without question that her toiletries had been slightly rearranged on the marble surround of the sink. She knew exactly how she had positioned everything. Because of her excellent visual memory, she realized that someone had been in the bathroom and had moved her shampoo and her soaps. They had not taken anything, and they had not left a mess. She decided she would just have to live with it...whatever it was. She was too tired to devote any more time to worrying about what apparition had invaded her space. She didn't like it but there was nothing she could do about it. The apparition had been too careful.

Three

Everyone wanted to go to the Desert Botanical Garden to see the Chihuly glass sculptures and the plants. Most had been there before, but it was such a magnificent exhibit, it was worth more than one visit. Gretchen and Bailey MacDermott rode to the Desert Botanical Garden with Elizabeth and Richard in the Carpenter's pickup truck. The Ford truck had all the bells and whistles a vehicle could hope to possess, and everyone wanted to ride in it.

Of course, the MacDermotts had the latest news about what was happening at the Mimosa Inn. Bailey always knew what was going on...wherever he was. Gretchen and Bailey were eager to share what they knew with the Carpenters. According to the Mimosa Inn gossip, there had been a break-in at one of the casitas the night before. The casita that had been vandalized was located in the same area where the MacDermott's and the Carpenter's suites were located. Elizabeth had been listening closely to the story anyway, but she paid even more attention because of her feeling that someone had been in Richard's and her room the night before.

The woman who was staying in the unlucky cottage had been out for the evening when her place had been ransacked. It seemed that the thieves had been looking for something, and they had left the room in such a shambles, the woman had not yet been able to determine if anything had been stolen. The casita that had been vandalized was Room #167. Elizabeth gulped when she heard this piece of information. The Carpenters' room number was #161. Elizabeth thought about the way people in some countries wrote their ones. Ones sometimes looked like sevens. She had to wonder which casita the burglars had actually intended to rob. She knew someone had been in their room the night before, and she was extremely grateful that they had not left it in disarray. She wanted all the details about the break-in from the MacDermotts.

The MacDermotts knew only what the woman from housekeeping who'd cleaned their casita had told them. Housekeeping staff, no matter what hotel or resort one is visiting, know pretty much everything that is going on. This was certainly the case at the Mimosa Inn, particularly because it was a relatively small resort. Gretchen was convinced that the information about the break-in, which she had learned from the woman who cleaned their room, was reliable. Gretchen spoke fluent Spanish and was able to engage the cleaning people in complex conversations. The police had been called. The guest had been moved to a different room, and the CSI people were trying to get fingerprints from surfaces in the room that had been burglarized. The chatty cleaner from housekeeping had told the MacDermotts that the staff was sure whoever had done the vandalizing had been smart enough to wear gloves.

Elizabeth didn't say anything about her own suspicions from the night before. She had no proof, other than her own observations, that anyone had been in her room, and she didn't feel as if she could go to the authorities based on what little real evidence she had. The extent of her real evidence was basically that she had none. She hoped the intruders would not return while she and Richard were away from the room and across town for dinner that night.

The tour of the Desert Botanical Garden was the delight it always promised and always delivered. Elizabeth, along with millions of other people in the world, adored Dale Chihuly's work. She had been a fan for decades. The paths at the gardens were paved, so Elizabeth's wheelchair had been able to go everywhere, and she had been able to see everything. She loved this place and always felt enriched and renewed whenever she experienced anything Chihuly had created. The day had been relatively warm for November. The sun had been shining, and most of the people in their group had worn hats. Everyone was ready for an iced cold drink and a nap when they returned to their casitas at the Mimosa.

Later that evening, the group met on the patio for drinks. November nights in the desert are chilly, and Elizabeth ordered another hot buttered rum. The first toast of the evening was of course to Olivia...again accompanied by prayers. The fire in the fireplace on the patio was always a delight, but they were ready when their drivers arrived to transport them to Chez Auguste. Most of those with older bones asked that the heat be turned up when they climbed into the SUV.

The group was having dinner that night at the Ritter's favorite French restaurant. The Ritters had previously lived in Phoenix and had maintained a relationship with the chef and owner of Chez Auguste, even after they'd moved to California. They always ate at least one meal at the French restaurant whenever they were back in town. Auguste had arranged for the Camp Shoemaker crowd to have a private room and a large round table. The food at Chez Auguste was famous, and the upscale bistro had an extensive wine selection. Everyone was looking forward to the evening.

Two vehicles had been rented to transport the group to the restaurant. No one wanted to drive back to the Mimosa Inn after having indulged in the wines that Auguste had to offer. Paying someone else to drive them was a must for the night. But finding drivers had not been as easy as they'd imagined it would be.

The Mimosa Inn had promised, when the Camp Shoemaker group had made their reservations, that there was a luxury airport bus that would drive them wherever they wanted to go. But when they tried to engage the bus to drive them to Chez Auguste, they were told that the bus was not available.

And, although no one in the group had been aware of it, Elton John was giving a concert at Diamondback Stadium for two nights that exactly coincided with the Camp Shoemaker reunion. Because of the concert's popularity, sedan services and limousines were in high demand and in short supply. However, the Camp Shoemaker group had managed to find a Chevy Suburban and an Uber with enough seats between the two vehicles to accommodate their numbers.

Chez Auguste specialized in classic French cuisine, and the chef was proud to let diners know that seafood from both the east and west coasts was flown in daily. Lobster bisque with a southwestern twist was offered as the first course. French bread and French butter were served with the bisque. Poached Alaskan salmon with hollandaise sauce accompanied by a vegetable and lemon wild rice medley was offered as the fish course. Two magnificent crown roasts of lamb were brought to the table and carved with great fanfare. The lamb rib bones were even dressed with the old-fashioned frilly paper caps that many of these older people remembered from years gone by. The crown roasts were stuffed with creamed spinach. Duchesse potatoes were served on the side, and julienne carrots in a mint-flavored glaze rounded out the entrée. In the finest European tradition, a romaine and butter lettuce salad with a garlicky, mustardy dressing was served after the entre. Desserts of Grand Marnier and chocolate soufflés left everyone at the table groaning. The meal had extended over several hours, and the laughter and the conversation, accompanied by glasses of Auguste's delicious wine selections, lasted until midnight.

The drivers from the sedan service returned to pick up their sated passengers to deliver them back to the Mimosa Inn. The driver of the Chevy Suburban recounted a few wild tales about the revelers who had attended the Elton John concert. Traffic had subsided, and half the people in the SUV were asleep by the time they arrived at the resort. It had been another successful evening. Elizabeth had not fallen asleep on the return trip from Chez Auguste. She was somewhat anxious about what she would find when she returned to her room.

The Camp Shoemaker reunion goers headed for their casitas. The MacDermotts and the Carpenters, however, were dismayed to find that there was a considerable police presence in the area where their rooms were located. The law enforcement contingent was low key, but an official in uniform as well as significant amounts of yellow crime scene tape blocked their way. A coroner's van from the Phoenix

Police Department was parked at the scene. They could not get to their casitas. In a place as exclusive and expensive as the Mimosa Inn, it would have been imperative to have the police maintain as low a profile as possible, no matter what might have happened. Both couples knew there had been a break-in at the Mimosa Inn the night before, but they certainly had not expected another incident so soon, especially one that required a coroner's van.

It was almost one o'clock in the morning, and it was cold standing outside in the November wind. Elizabeth was sitting in her wheelchair, but the other three older people were standing. None of them were used to being up this late, and no one is ever prepared to see a body bag on a wheeled stretcher as it is rolled out of one of the casitas. A policewoman and a representative of the Mimosa Inn approached them. The senior citizens were of course more than curious about what had happened. They also hoped with all their hearts that they were not going to be kept out of their casitas for the night. They waited nervously to hear what these official people had to say about what was going on and what was going to happen.

Four

The policewoman was very tall and had red hair. She was dressed in a uniform. She was young but very confident and very much in charge at the crime scene. The policewoman started to speak but was interrupted by the woman who, the four tired Camp Shoemaker reunion goers guessed, was the night manager at the Mimosa Inn. The night manager was into damage control, not into information sharing. Her message was basically "nothing to see here."

"I'm Lucinda Duncan. We've had an incident in one of the casitas. There is no danger to any of the other guests, and everything is under control. You will be allowed to return to your rooms as soon as the police have cleared them. In the meantime, we would like to invite you to join us in the lobby. We have hot tea and coffee there and some pastries we know you will enjoy." The young woman was clearly out of her depth in the current situation, and she was intent on minimizing what had happened. She wanted to sweep it all under the rug and pretend it hadn't happened at all. Whatever it was.

She was into hospitality, not into solving the crime. She looked frightened and inexperienced. Maybe she thought these older folks could be distracted and their attention diverted with pastries and tea. She did not know the Camp Shoemaker crowd.

Gretchen McDermott was not one to hold back when circumstances demanded a sensible response. "What are you talking about? We can see, right in front of our eyes, that there is a dead person on that coroner's gurney. The body bag says Phoenix Coroner...printed right on it. Someone has died here, and because there is a police presence, I can only assume the death has not been from natural causes. I am going to want to know a lot more about what has happened, if I am going to believe you when you say there is no danger to the other guests. You just brought a dead body out of the casita that is right next to my own. Of course I am upset. Of course I am concerned. Of course I want answers."

The night manager had not expected this kind of a response from an older female guest. "We have a nice warm fire going in the reception area. You must be freezing." She was already heading towards the lobby and those delicious pastries. But until they had been told the truth about what was going on, the four people who were waiting outside at the crime scene in the wind and cold were not going to be easily convinced to go to the promised place of cozy warmth to wait to be allowed back into their rooms,.

The tall, redheaded law enforcement officer stepped forward to diffuse the situation. "I'm Detective Cecilia Mendoza, Phoenix P.D....homicide. This is my crime scene. There has been a murder here tonight. Ms. Duncan, Lucinda, is correct that we do not believe there is any danger to any of the other guests. We are certain that this death is the result of a domestic dispute. We regret that we have to keep you out of your rooms for a while longer, but we will have uniformed officers checking out all the other rooms in this part of the resort. We think the perpetrator of this crime is long gone, but we want to be sure he is not hiding out in any of these casitas. After my people have completed their search, you can rest assured that you will be safe. You will be able to sleep tonight without any worries. Crime scene investigators will be working all night in the room where the crime was committed. There will be a significant law enforcement presence around this block of casitas all night. But there is nothing for you to be concerned about. You are not in danger. It will be another twenty minutes or so before you can get to your rooms, so feel free to go to the lobby to warm up if you want to."

Gretchen was grateful for the information. "Thank you Detective Mendoza for your explanation about what is happening here. We really appreciate your candor." Gretchen glared at Lucinda Duncan. "It is always better and more reassuring to be told the truth, even if it is an unpleasant truth." She glared at Ms. Duncan again.

The Phoenix P.D. detective consulted a clipboard. "What are your room numbers?"

Gretchen was doing the talking, and she continued. "The MacDermotts are in casita #164, and the Carpenters are in casita #161." Bailey was nearly asleep on his feet, and Richard, who was never cold, was worried that Elizabeth was soon going to be chilled to the bone.

"I need to take my wife to the lobby where she can get warm. Will someone please let us know when we can return to our rooms? Thank you."

Detective Mendoza wanted to get back to her crime scene. She was desperate to get her severely injured witness, now hovering between life and death, to a place where she could receive the medical care she needed. The detective struggled to stay calm and take her time. She handed each of the four displaced guests her business card. "I've already told you more about what's going on here than I probably should have. I know you are tired and that it's an inconvenience for you not to be able to go to your casitas. Please call me if you have any more questions, or if you see or hear about anything you think I should know. Again, you don't need to have any concerns about your safety. I know this has been very disturbing, to have something violent happen so close to where you are staying. This was a very specific domestic crime. The victim was targeted. This is not random violence. You are safe. I hope you will be able to get a good night's sleep tonight without any concerns."

Bailey muttered under his breath. "If I can ever get into my room and into my bed, I might be able to get a good night's sleep."

Elizabeth thought Detective Mendoza looked stressed. She'd been polite and even friendly when she'd explained what was going on, but at the same time, she had seemed as if she was under a lot of pressure. Elizabeth thought the policewoman had definitely looked relieved when the Carpenters and the MacDermotts left the crime scene and decided to go with Lucinda to the lobby to have hot tea.

The four walked to the reception area and sat around the fire. They were almost too tired to talk, and Lucinda Duncan flitted around the room, trying to take their minds off the murder that had occurred on her watch. Everyone was a little bit in shock because of what had happened. Gretchen and Elizabeth each had a cup of tea. Bailey helped himself to several pastries.

Richard was quiet, and the creases in his forehead revealed that he was quite concerned about what had happened.

He was paying big bucks to stay at this fancy resort. He'd so far spent two nights here, and he was about to spend a third. He'd heard about a casita that had been broken into and vandalized the night before, and now he'd just seen a dead body rolled out of the casita that was right across the walkway from his own. What kind of a place was this?

🌲

Elizabeth and Richard were finally allowed to go back into their casita. Richard was completely worn out, but Elizabeth's adrenalin had kicked in and she had somehow rallied with a second wind. Her mind was racing with a hundred questions. She'd wanted to quiz the police detective, but Cecilia Mendoza had not been around when they made their way back to the casita. Elizabeth knew that law enforcement personnel had searched their casita earlier, looking for the perpetrator of the crime. She was relieved that nothing set off her personal radar when she entered the room. As far as she could tell, no intruders other than the police had been inside their cottage that night.

Elizabeth told Richard to take the first shower. She was still too energized to relax. Eventually her adrenalin surge would subside, and when it did, she'd realize that her best course of action would be to pursue the answers to her questions the following day. Finally, she was able to calm down and appreciate the hot shower which warmed her body's core and also forced her brain to relax. She fell into bed at 3:30 in the morning.

🌲

Arizona, 2022

A personal tour of the Heard Museum, dedicated to the preservation of American Indian art, was on the schedule for the next morning. It was a wonderful museum, a fascinating repository of pottery, textiles, and other Native American artifacts. Elizabeth and Richard had visited the museum several times in the past, but they had never had a personal tour. Matthew and Isabelle Ritter donated money to the museum, and they had arranged for the reunion group to have a special guided tour and talk from the museum's head docent.

Elizabeth hated to miss what she knew would be a special and outstanding presentation, but she was too worn out from the excitement and the late hours of the night before to make it to the eleven o'clock tour. She needed more sleep. Richard had promised to drive several in the group, so he fortified himself with coffee and sugar and dragged himself to the parking lot by 10:15. In addition to the guided tour, the group had arranged to eat lunch at the museum's café. Richard would take some photos with his phone, if that was allowed. He would give Elizabeth a full report when he came back from the Heard. In the meantime, she would sleep late and order lunch from room service.

Five

Detective Mendoza was at the scene of the crime, speaking on her cell phone with her FBI contact. This FBI agent was the only other law enforcement person who knew all about what was happening with their witness. The detective and the FBI agent were running the operation jointly. They had decided that, for many reasons, no one else in either the Phoenix Police department or in the FBI needed to know anything about what was going on. Detective Mendoza did not try to minimize the trouble they were in. "This is not at all the way we had hoped things would turn out tonight. Our witness has been severely beaten, and she needs immediate medical attention. She might die. I think I've managed to stop most of the bleeding, but she will certainly need surgery or a blood transfusion. I'm not a doctor, but I'm pretty sure she's going to need both. We've had to improvise, and she is, as we speak, lying inside a body bag on the PPD coroner's stretcher. She's breathing, thank God, and I am trying to decide where to put her and how to get her there. I don't know how I am going to get a doctor to see her and treat her? She can't go to a hospital. We know that."

The two older couples, who were out way past their bedtimes, had finally left and gone to the lobby of the Mimosa Inn with the extraordinarily unhelpful night manager, Lucinda Duncan. Thank goodness for that. Having witnesses to the presence of the body bag was not good for the Mimosa Inn, but it actually was serendipitous for Detective Mendoza's purposes. That is, if the witness, who was inside the body bag and barely clinging to life, lived. The story about the coroner's body bag on the stretcher would be everywhere at the Mimosa Inn by morning.

The most important thing right now was to save the life of her valuable witness. That this woman had given secret testimony against a major drug cartel that operated between Mexico and the Phoenix area was known to only a handful of people. Protecting the witness was the highest priority, and law enforcement had waited one day too long. Mendoza was mentally kicking herself because she knew she should have moved the schedule forward after the woman's room had been broken into the night before. The detective should have trusted her own instincts and defied the orders her FBI contact and partner on this joint task force had given her.

It was too late for that now. Her witness had been brutally beaten and left for dead. She had also been attacked with a knife or knives, one of which had been left at the scene. Mendoza had worked quickly to try to save the life of the witness as well as to keep under wraps everything else that had gone haywire. The carefully laid plans to get the witness someplace safe and hide her before anyone from her past was able to find her... all of that had completely fallen apart. Mendoza was going to have to ad lib a plan and cross her fingers that she could save the life of her witness and salvage some part of the complicated operation.

The original plan had been for there to be a pretend attack and a pretend murder in the victim's casita at the Mimosa Inn. A pretend dead body would be rolled out of the murder scene to the coroner's van. Because the victim was a federal witness, the FBI was in charge. The FBI alone would decide who would be allowed in on the investigation. Detective Cecilia Mendoza was allowed in. The witness would be declared dead. A body bag on a gurney would be taken away from the scene of the pretend murder at the Mimosa Inn.

An obituary would appear in the Phoenix newspaper. Because the witness would no longer be able to testify against anyone because she was dead, she would no longer be a threat to anyone. Because she was no longer a threat to anyone, she would no longer be in danger. She could disappear. If everyone could be convinced that the witness was no longer alive, there would not be anyone trying to find her.

The witness, who was staying as a guest at the Mimosa Inn, should have already left the casita where she'd been staying and made her way to another casita. Only a few people knew she would be spending the night in a different casita. She was to have remained hidden in that second casita until the next step in her disappearance could be undertaken.

Detective Cecilia Mendoza had driven the coroner's van to the Mimosa Inn. The original plan had been that the detective would pretend to load a body bag with a body inside into the van. Detective Mendoza had planned to push the stretcher to the coroner's van from the casita where the brutal crime was supposed to have been committed. Mendoza would drive the empty van back to the PPD morgue and explain that the FBI had taken possession of the dead body. In fact there would never have been a dead body, in the van or anywhere else. It was an unconventional plan and an unconventional use of law enforcement resources. The FBI agent in charge of this witness was desperate to keep secret as many of these machinations as possible.

Detective Mendoza had come up with the plan, and she had insisted on being included in every step of the operation. As a member of the Phoenix Police Department's homicide division, it made sense that someone from the local police department be included in the bizarre enterprise. The FBI agent who was in charge of helping the witness disappear agreed that they needed a local police presence involved in what was ostensibly a homicide case. When Detective Mendoza returned the coroner's van to the Phoenix PD morgue without a body ever having been in it, she would report that she had turned the body over to the FBI.

Detective Cecilia Mendoza had been confident she could control the situation with her boss at Phoenix PD. Mendoza had a convincing explanation about why she had driven the coroner's van and about how things had happened the way they had. She thought she could sell the story to her boss at PPD homicide. The FBI was often at odds with local police and sheriff's departments about who was going to be in charge of a case. The FBI would make the Phoenix Police Department angry by pretending to abscond with their body, but the PPD would get over it.

Detective Mendoza would explain to her boss that the person who had been murdered was an FBI witness. Because the victim was a federal witness, the FBI had insisted that the body be turned over to them for the autopsy. Detective Mendoza would pretend that the FBI had taken possession of the body in the body bag. The Phoenix Police Department would protest and be angry for a while that the FBI had intruded into their case. And then everything would be over with. Eventually it would all be forgotten.

When Detective Mendoza had arrived at the witness' casita that night, she had expected to find an empty room in which she would be able to stage her fictitious murder of the important federal witness. Instead, when Mendoza had entered the casita, she'd found Annika Karlsson Castillo, the actual federal witness, lying on the floor in a pool of blood. Something had gone terribly wrong. This uniquely vital witness had been tortured. She had been severely beaten, stabbed repeatedly, and left for dead.

The detective's first concern, of course, was to save the woman's life. But Mendoza also had to get her quickly out of sight and hidden away in a safe place. The witness was still alive, but barely. Her breathing was shallow, and her pulse was weak. She looked as if she had been attacked by both a baseball bat as well as some kind of knife, maybe two kinds of knives. The baseball bat was no longer in the room, but whoever had attempted to murder Annika Castillo had left a machete behind.

Annika had lost a lot of blood, but Cecilia could not call the PPD EMTs to the scene. According to their planned scenario, the witness was already dead. The detective worked hard on her own and drew on all of her knowledge about first aid to stop the bleeding. Thank goodness she had arrived on the scene as soon as she had. Her witness would have bled to death in another several minutes. Cecilia Mendoza had completed several EMT classes in the past, and she had some first aid skills. But adequately taking care of the horrendous injuries that had been inflicted on her witness was way out of the detective's league.

Detective Mendoza was determined that this valuable source of information, this young woman who had been willing to tell the FBI everything she knew, would not bleed out on her watch. Mendoza had to find help, and she had to find it fast. Mendoza worked as quickly as she could, and at the same time tried to be as gentle as she could, with the severely injured woman. The detective single-handedly managed to get the still-breathing woman zipped into the body bag and onto the wheeled stretcher. It had not been easy.

Then the night manager at the Mimosa Inn had unexpectedly arrived on the scene, followed almost immediately by four older guests, one of whom was in a wheelchair. The detective was panicked about what was going to happen with her witness who was in critical condition and unconscious inside the body bag, but she managed to remain calm and cool enough to answer questions as well as get rid of the guests and the night manager. Now she had to save her witness' life.

Mendoza was good at thinking on her feet, and she had to come up with an alternate solution that she hoped might keep alive the brave young woman who was now so close to death. The detective decided she would try to continue with some parts of the original plan. She would push the wheeled stretcher with the body bag on it to the casita where her witness was supposed to already be hiding. The witness was supposed to already be in the casita—alive and well and uninjured. But that was not the reality of the moment. The witness was currently inside a body bag on a coroner's stretcher. She might not live. Detective Mendoza knew that a doctor and his wife from California were staying in the casita next door to the one where Annika Karlsson Castillo was supposed to spend the night.

Arrangements had been made with this doctor and his wife who had some kind of a special relationship to the witness. Their role in the original plan had been that they were to be to be responsible for the next steps in the woman's disappearance. They would make sure it was all accomplished safely and in secret. Detective Mendoza had not wanted to know where the witness was going to be hidden. She just wanted to be sure her woman was safe and would show up to testify in court, if and when that time came. Now the doctor and his wife were going to have a much more serious role to play. They were going to have to be responsible for saving the young woman's life.

Detective Mendoza called her contact at the FBI again and briefly told her what was going to happen. It was not a good plan, but what else could anybody do at this point? Mendoza wanted to save the life of her witness, and she wanted her to be able to testify. Whatever it took to accomplish those goals was what Mendoza intended to do.

Fortunately, it was the middle of the night, and Cecilia Mendoza did not have very far to push the stretcher. No one was outside on the path she took to the witness' new casita. Lucinda Duncan was busy keeping the quartet of elderly guests occupied elsewhere, and Cecilia quickly reached the empty casita. Mendoza had what she thought was the key to the room. She'd found the key lying on the floor covered with blood as if it had fallen out of her witness's hand. Mendoza sent a text to the doctor and his wife asking them to meet her in the casita next door to theirs.

The Ritters would not be happy to see what condition their friend was in. They would also not be happy to learn that they were going to have to be the ones to step up and find a way to get her the medical treatment she needed. Matthew Ritter, the husband, was a doctor, but he had been retired for almost ten years. And he had never been a trauma surgeon. That's what Cecilia was certain her witness was going to need at this point.

When she reached the empty casita, Cecilia Mendoza unzipped the body bag and checked the woman's pulse again. It was weak and thready, but at least she still had a pulse. Dr. Ritter was the first one through the door. His wife Isabelle followed closely behind. The doctor was furious. "What in the world has happened? She was supposed to be here more than an hour ago." Dr. Ritter stepped close to the body bag and pulled it away from the woman's body. He looked at the police detective with a scowl.

"At some point, I am going to want to know exactly what happened to her, but first we have to do everything we can to save her life. Isabelle, get Freddy Kernigan on the phone and tell him to get his mobile operating room over here right now. Tell him it's a matter of life and death. Tell him if he isn't here in fifteen minutes, I won't ever let him use my hunting cabin in Sonoita again. Tell him he has to be discreet. No one can be allowed to see him driving that enormous mobile hospital. He has to come in the back way and park behind here, in the employee parking lot. Tell him we're going to need several pints of O negative blood."

Matthew Ritter got to work examining the woman's injuries and shouting orders at Isabelle. Isabelle did her best trying to make bandages out of towels and washcloths and two pillowcases with a pair of nail scissors she'd hunted down in her suitcase in the room next door. Matthew Ritter was determined to keep his patient alive until his friend with the mobile operating suite showed up.

Detective Mendoza stayed quiet while Matthew Ritter was shouting orders and working on the critically injured woman.

Cecilia had no idea how big the life-saving vehicle was, but she tried to imagine where a mobile operating room could park without attracting attention. She didn't want anybody to see it, but she was resigned to the fact that something as big as the mobile operating room sounded as if it would be impossible to keep out of sight. Mendoza also wondered if she would be the one who would have to move the wheeled stretcher to wherever the mobile hospital vehicle would be trying to hide.

The detective was feeling tremendous pressure to keep pace with the schedule she had set for herself. She had to get the coroner's van back to the Phoenix PD. Several CSI people from the FBI were already on their way to the Mimosa Inn. A real crime had been committed there, and she had to maintain the subterfuge about the alleged homicide. She would have to explain to the FBI investigators why the body was gone. Because there was no dead body, she could not allow the CSIs to look in the van. She would have to get the van away from the scene as soon as possible in order to maintain the deception. She needed to return the van to the PPD morgue. The wheeled stretcher would not be in the van when it was returned. The detective would have to explain to the people in the PPD coroner's office that the stretcher was with the body, and the body was with the FBI. It was confusing and complicated. There were many oranges she was struggling to keep in the air.

She'd already called two Phoenix police officers to the scene to check the other casitas in this group to be sure the perpetrator of the crime was not hiding in one of the other rooms. Mendoza was concerned that the person or persons who had attacked Annika might still be at the Mimosa Inn. She had to be certain this was not the case.

The FBI's crime scene investigators would arrive at any minute to investigate the casita where Annika had been attacked. Supposedly there had been a homicide in the room, and Detective Mendoza had only just been able to prevent the Phoenix Police Department's CSIs from coming to the scene. There was plenty of blood, but who knew what else the FBI might find. Detective Mendoza was worried that the FBI crime scene people might find something in the casita that she could not explain away. There was too much subterfuge going on. Things were getting way too convoluted, and it felt to Cecilia Mendoza as if the whole thing, this crazy plan, that had been hers to begin with, was coming unraveled.

Mendoza realized she was going to have to leave her severely injured witness with the retired doctor and his wife and get on with her own role in the plan. She told Dr. Ritter and Isabelle what little she knew. "I don't know what all has happened here, but I am almost certain a machete was used. It was left at the scene. Another kind of knife was also used, I think, and somebody beat her badly, probably with a baseball bat. She was tortured. If we are going to salvage anything from this debacle, I need to leave immediately and follow through with the many things I have to do to make that happen. I'm in a time crunch. Can you manage by yourselves from now on, or do you still need my help?"

Dr. Ritter was preoccupied tending to his patient. He wasn't paying any attention to what the detective was saying to him. Isabelle had been listening and told Mendoza to go ahead and do what she had to do. This was Isabelle's friend's daughter, and Isabelle would take responsibility. "We promised to take Annika off your hands after you delivered her here, and we will do that. My husband has called his friend, Freddy Kernigan, who works with international humanitarian medical organizations. He's an ER doctor and trauma surgeon and works mostly in Africa, but he goes everywhere. He has been a pioneer in taking medical care to those who need it, rather than requiring those who need care to go to a hospital. His fully-equipped mobile operating rooms are being used in primitive areas all over the world. He keeps one of these mobile operating rooms in his garage...right here in Paradise Valley. It may not be quite as big as a Greyhound bus, but it has everything in it anyone could possibly need. Freddy is very proud of it and likes to show it off to his friends and colleagues. He is a good surgeon, especially with gunshot wounds and knife wounds. He will be able to help Annika if he can get here in time."

"Where will he park this bus? And how will you get Annika to the mobile hospital?" The detective was very skeptical when she heard about the mobile hospital, but there was no good alternative solution to the current crisis.

Isabelle had at least part of an answer for Detective Mendoza. "Matthew and I took a walk around the grounds yesterday. We discovered that there's a gate in the wall behind the rosewood hedge. The gate isn't locked." Isabelle pointed in the direction of the wall and the gate. "It isn't far from here. I told Freddy to come through the service entrance of the Mimosa Inn and pull his bus into the staff parking lot back there, as close to the gate as he can manage. We will take the stretcher out through the gate and just cross our fingers that no one will see us pushing a woman in a body bag out the back entrance. Freddy has a lift system on the bus, so he will be able to get her into the mobile unit without any problem. Once we get her to the mobile unit and if she is still alive, Matthew will go with Freddy, and they will drive the bus away from the Mimosa Inn."

Isabelle sighed a deep, discouraged sigh and almost started to cry. "Of course, Annika may not survive. I will text you and let you know what her condition is after Freddy has worked on her. I won't tell him her name or anything about her. He has been friends with Matthew since medical school. We trust him. He's a bit of a showboat, but he's a first-rate doctor. You go ahead and do whatever you have to do. We will do our best to take care of Annika and try to save her."

Detective Mendoza hated to abandon her witness. She didn't want to leave the young woman in the hands of other people. But she knew she had to leave Annika with the Ritters for her to be able to receive the medical care she needed. Mendoza told herself she had to have some faith that Annika would be all right.

When Detective Mendoza returned to the casita that was soaked in blood, the CSI people from the FBI were outside, waiting for Cecilia to let them into the room where "the murder" had taken place. The CSIs would work all night in the room where the attack had occurred. The detective briefly explained that the body had already been removed from the scene...orders from the higher-ups at the FBI. Before the CSIs could protest, Cecilia Mendoza left the casita and drove the coroner's van away from the scene.

The two uniformed officers from PPD that the detective had called would arrive at any minute. They had their orders to search the group of casitas for the person or persons who had tried to kill Annika. The detective was on the police radio in the van giving them their instructions. After the casitas had been cleared, Cecilia would notify Lucinda Duncan that the two older couples could return to their rooms. She hoped they would be reassured that their casitas were safe. All she could really think about was whether or not Annika would make it and what a mess this had all turned out to be.

Matthew insisted that both he and Isabelle were needed to push the wheeled stretcher through the gate into the Mimosa Inn's staff parking lot. Isabelle would hold the gate open, and Matthew would push the patient into the rear lot behind the casitas. Freddy Kernigan texted them that he was two minutes away, and they arrived with Annika at the gate in the back wall at the same time the mobile hospital arrived. Freddy knew his vehicle well, and in less than two minutes, he had the patient on the lift and inside the mobile unit. Matthew was going along to assist Freddy in whatever surgery had to be performed.

Isabelle was heading back to her room to try to get some sleep. She would be the one in charge of taking care of Annika after the surgery, if the woman lived through it. Isabelle was not a nurse, and she felt unprepared to have to take on such a critical task. Annika's casita would become, not only a surgical recovery room, but also an ICU. Annika was that seriously hurt. Matthew would be exhausted when he got back and would have to get some sleep. Freddy would have to get his mobile hospital back to his house and out of sight inside his specially constructed oversized garage. It would all be on Isabelle to take care of Annika in the make-do ICU.

While Freddy began frantically working to save Annika, Matthew drove the mobile hospital to a secluded spot just off the road and into a wash. The wash was an area that held water when it rained but was dry most of the time. No water was in the wash, and it hardly ever rained in Phoenix. No rain was predicted, so it made sense to park the mobile hospital in the wash while they did the surgery. They were not very far away from the Mimosa Inn.

Freddy had told Mathew where to go so the enormous vehicle would be relatively obscured while they gave their patient the life-saving surgery she had to have. During the day, hikers and joggers would be all over the place, but in the middle of the night, no one was anywhere around. There were no street lights in the area. Only the coyotes and the javelinas would see the enormous mobile hospital sitting in the wash. Matthew parked the bus, and Freddy was scrubbed and already tackling the difficult task of putting Annika back together again.

The mobile hospital was a miraculous invention. The problem was that it did not include a recovery room. It was a big bus and would have to be safely hidden, back in Freddy Kernigan's garage, before dawn. It would be much too conspicuous if it were out on the street, in a park, in a wash, or in a parking lot during the day. The two doctors had to finish their surgery and return Annika to the Mimosa Inn as soon as possible. They had to be sure she was safely back in the casita, not only before the sun came up, but also before there was any activity at the service entrance of the Mimosa Inn. Annika would have to recover from her surgery in the casita next to the Ritter's. The casita was a hotel room, not a hospital room, and Isabelle was not trained to care for a critically ill post-op patient. This was definitely an ad hoc medical emergency.

Isabelle was awakened by a text from Matthew letting her know that he and Freddy and Annika were five minutes from the gate in the wall at the rear of the Mimosa Inn property. Annika had come through the surgery, and Matthew would tell Isabelle all about it. Matthew needed to sleep, and Freddy needed to get his mobile hospital back into his garage ASAP. Isabelle would have to push the wheeled stretcher, on which the patient would be lying, still unconscious, back to the casita. Matthew would be carrying all the equipment necessary to set up a very minimal recovery room in the casita next to the Ritter's... including pints of whole blood, everything required to continue Annika's IV fluids, a heart monitor, antibiotics, and a myriad of other medical supplies that were required to aid Annika in her recovery.

Isabelle had been expecting the text message that the mobile hospital was close to arriving at the parking lot, so she had gone to sleep dressed in her clothes. She unlocked the door of the room next to hers and hurried to the rosewood hedge and the gate in the wall. She made it there just as Matthew and Freddy arrived in the bus with Annika. The sun was already coming up but it was still dark enough behind the wall at the Mimosa Inn. The lift on the hospital bus made quick work of lowering the stretcher on wheels to the ground. Matthew motioned for Isabelle to get moving. An early morning jogger would find it very odd to see a woman on a coroner's stretcher, hooked up to an IV, being pushed along the pathways of the Mimosa Inn. Isabelle had to get the patient inside the casita and out of sight before early-rising guests and runners and staff were up and about. Sunrise was threatening. Freddy left immediately to drive his hospital back home and secure it inside his garage.

As Isabelle pushed the wheeled stretcher that held the recovering Annika Castillo, Matthew followed, loaded down with supplies and equipment. Isabelle was trying to go slowly and carefully. Mathew was telling her to hurry up and get to the casita. Freddy would be bringing more paraphernalia for the makeshift recovery room after he had returned the mobile hospital to his house. Matthew was bringing the minimum that Annika needed right now...until Freddy could arrive with the more sophisticated medical equipment.

Two delivery trucks were coming in through the service entrance of the Mimosa Inn as Freddy's bus was leaving. The drivers had to question what in the world would be making a delivery at the resort in a vehicle like that. They had never seen anything quite like it. Freddy would have his mobile hospital safely hidden in less than ten minutes. The drivers of the delivery trucks that passed him exiting the resort's service entrance would wonder if they had imagined seeing the large, strange bus-like vehicle.

It had been years since Matthew Ritter had been in a hospital recovery room, but he found it was a bit like riding a bicycle. He remembered mostly everything he needed to know to keep his patient alive. His patient had lost a lot of blood, and he and Freddy had given her two transfusions, one during and one immediately after the surgery in the mobile unit. They were continuing to give her more blood through her IV. Freddy Kernigan always had a surprise for Matthew. This time the surprise had been finding out that Freddy kept units of O negative blood in the refrigerator of his mobile hospital. Matthew didn't know how that was even possible, but he was thankful that Freddy had managed to do it, however he had managed it.

Matthew hooked up the heart monitor. Annika seemed to have made the transition from the mobile surgical suite to the slapdash recovery room casita without any major trauma. Matthew could not believe he was doing what he was doing, years after he'd retired from practicing medicine, and at age seventy-nine! One of these days he was really going to have to retire for good.

Isabelle wanted to know how the surgery had gone. She wanted to know how seriously Annika had been injured and if she was going to live. Matthew was exhausted. He just wanted to go to sleep. He didn't want to talk about the surgery, but he gave Isabelle a quick run-down on Annika's condition.

"Freddy was brilliant...as always. Annika had been beaten with a baseball bat or a piece of wood or something like that. She has a head injury...a pretty severe one. The first thing we had to do was stop the bleeding. She'd suffered what could have been a fatal laceration of her liver. There was so much blood. Freddy fixed that. He's sure she was attacked with a machete as well as with some kind of smaller knife. That's why we think there were two people who attacked her. A machete is a vicious weapon. It's what inflicted most of the wounds that caused her serious bleeding. Annika had a serious laceration of her shoulder. Lots of blood there. It took a bunch of stitches to repair it. It was bad. It looked like whatever SOB did this had tried to get to her neck, probably trying to cut her head off. But it was obvious she had fought them very hard. They didn't get her carotid artery. She had many smaller deep cuts from a different kind of knife. These were almost like puncture wounds and had to be stitched up or glued back together. I took care of a lot of those smaller wounds while Freddy worked on the really serious stuff...on her liver and her legs." Matthew paused, remembering how severely beaten this young woman had been.

He took a deep breath and went on telling his wife what had happened. "One of her legs was broken... both the left tibia and fibula were crushed. Freddy's good with broken bones. He set and casted the leg, but it's still in terrible shape. If she'd gone to a hospital, they probably would have amputated the leg below the knee, but you know Freddy. He was determined to save it. She had several cracked ribs. He taped those. One hand was smashed. She really needed a hand surgeon for that. Freddy spent a long time on the hand."

Matthew hesitated before he continued. "We're both worried that she may have sustained a spinal cord injury. Freddy doesn't think it's permanent. He has all that imaging equipment in the bus, and he took quite a few pictures of her spine. He thinks it's swelling from an injury that's causing the temporary paralysis. But it's a concern, and we have to keep an eye on it. In short, she's a mess, and she may never walk again. She was left for dead, and it's truly a miracle that she's still alive. We worked on her for more than five hours. I have to sleep now."

There wasn't much left of the night, but Matthew needed to get some sleep. The Heard Museum tour was that morning, and he was in charge of organizing it and getting his friends there on time. No one could know anything about Annika, so cancelling the special tour was not an option. Matthew would have to act as if he'd had a full night's sleep and as if nothing out of the ordinary had happened during the previous twelve hours. He would be exhausted, but he would have to behave as normally as possible.

The original plan had been, if Annika had been in good health and had not been attacked and almost bled to death, that she would spend the night sleeping in the casita next to the Ritter's. Isabelle had always intended to skip the tour at the Heard Museum because she'd planned to be driving Annika to the safe house in the White Mountains that day. All of the careful planning for that to happen had now been turned on its head. Now Isabelle would be taking care of Annika, the critically injured post-op patient, in a makeshift recovery room that was in fact a casita at the Mimosa Inn. Their drive to the safe house would have to be postponed for several days...or maybe even for weeks.

Six

In spite of the attack on Annika and all the unexpected complications that had resulted from her injuries, Isabelle had no regrets that she had volunteered to help her friend's daughter. When the Ritters had lived in Phoenix during Matthew's stint in the US Public Health Service, Isabelle had been working on her master's degree in clinical psychology at Arizona State University. Isabelle had become good friends with her fellow psychology student, Pia Karlsson. The two had studied together and eaten lunch together. Isabelle was a newlywed and didn't have any children. Pia hadn't yet married. They both received their graduate degrees in clinical psychology at the same time.

Pia had immediately set up her own counseling practice in Tempe, Arizona. Isabelle and Matthew had moved to Palm Springs, California, but Isabelle and Pia had remained friends. They'd stayed in touch with each other through the years. Isabelle and Matthew made frequent trips to Phoenix. Matthew returned to Arizona often to hunt quail, and he spent time in his hunting cabin near Sonoita, south of Tucson. Isabelle sometimes accompanied her husband, and she always got together with Pia whenever she was in the Phoenix area.

Pia married and then divorced a few years later. The only good thing to come out of the marriage was Pia's daughter Annika. Pia was devoted to her only child, but Annika had a wild streak. As Annika became a teenager and moved into her high school years, she became impossible for her mother to handle. Many teens act out and rebel against their parents' rules and lifestyles, but Annika was unusually stubborn and defiant. Annika was a talented artist, but she did not seem to be able to apply herself or pursue a career with her art.

After she graduated from high school, Annika refused to go to college. Pia recognized that Annika had a great deal of artistic talent. If Annika didn't want to go to college, that was all right with Pia. She tried to get her daughter to go to art school, but Annika refused to do anything her mother wanted her to do. Pia was at her wits end and called Isabelle occasionally to discuss her difficult relationship with her difficult daughter.

Annika was a beautiful young woman. Pia was also quite beautiful, and Annika's father, who was no longer a part of her life, had been very good looking. Annika had been involved with a number of men. Some of them had been fairly respectable, but others had made their money dealing drugs and engaging in questionable and illegal activities. Even though Annika had gone through a period of attending drunken parties when she was in high school, as far as Pia knew, her daughter had never been into drugs. Annika's relationships were always with wealthy men, usually considerably older than herself.

It was not really a surprise to Pia when Annika finally settled down and married a man who was ten years older than she was. Pia didn't approve of her daughter's choice of a husband, but she tried to keep her mouth shut. Annika knew her mother didn't approve of Igor. Mother and daughter stopped seeing each other. Annika had made her choice, and she no longer wanted to have her mother in her life. They were estranged and remained estranged for years.

Igor Castillo was Annika's choice, and he was very rich. Castillo was also very handsome. He had been married before, and his first wife had died in Mexico under somewhat suspicious circumstances. Igor met Annika Karlsson when she was working as a bartender at a steakhouse in Tempe. He was captivated by her Scandinavian looks, especially her thick blond hair that hung down past her waist. She had a slim but curvaceous body. She was charming and flirtatious. She was an excellent bartender, and she was smart. Igor was entranced and thought he was in love for the first time in his life. He had to have her.

Igor could be very charming when he made the effort. He courted Annika and promised her a luxurious lifestyle. She would no longer have to tend bar to make ends meet. Igor assured her she would have everything she'd ever wanted. Annika was at a point in her life where she was tired of working. She had ended her education after high school, and she'd made do with low-paying, menial jobs ever since. Because she had become estranged from her mother, Annika refused to take any financial help from Pia. Annika struggled to support herself. Igor seemed like the answer to all of her prayers.

Annika never bothered to ask Igor how he earned his money. She married him without knowing much of anything at all about him, including what he did all day every day. He wined her and dined her, and he kept his best face forward during the first few months of their marriage. He bought a large house in the old part of Scottsdale and allowed Annika to furnish and decorate it without any constraints on how much she spent. She was in her late thirties when Igor began to beat her on a regular basis.

Igor's mother was Russian. Her family had control of the Russian mafia's illegal drug distribution networks west of the Mississippi River. Igor's father, El Sagrado, was Mexican. El Sagrado was a tremendously powerful and secretive Mexican drug lord. His cartel manufactured most of the drugs in several states in Mexico and then sent the drugs to the United States. The union of these two drug families had resulted in the birth of Igor Arturo Castillo. Together, Igor's parents were a powerful force and controlled most of the aspects of the drug trade in a large part of the United States. Igor inherited this massive drug manufacturing and distribution empire when his parents died.

Igor was spending more and more time away from his home in Scottsdale. He had businesses and real estate holdings in Mexico. When the novelty of having Annika in his life began to wear off, he devoted more and more of his time to doing deals outside the country. Annika had figured out long ago what Igor did for a living and why he spent so much time in Mexico. She knew that drug lords from Sinaloa and other places in Mexico kept their wives and families, including their mistresses, safe in Phoenix... far from the dangerous cartels who killed each other on a daily basis south of the border. Annika realized she was being kept safe in Scottsdale and that her husband was a drug kingpin.

Igor began to slap her when they were having an argument. At first he didn't really hurt her very badly. He slapped her because he was asserting his control and dominance over what he regarded as his personal property. Igor had kept his dark side hidden for the first few years of their marriage, but when Annika was no longer a compliant and youthful bride, Igor was no longer able to keep his anger in check. He was a violent man in the other aspects of his life, and it had been only a matter of time until that cruelty and viciousness spilled over into his marriage.

One time Igor beat Annika so badly he broke her jaw. He would not allow her to go to the hospital to be treated. He knew the police would be called, and he had to avoid involvement with the authorities at all costs. Igor called his cousin, Hector Gutierrez. Hector found an oral surgeon, who was beholden to him, to come to the house to repair Annika's jaw. Hector was used to stepping in and fixing Igor's messes.

After several years of marriage, Annika was unhappy and restless. She feared Igor when he lost control. She had a broken jaw and many other scars on her body that attested to what a cruel and violent man she had married. She was bored with her fancy, indolent life. Annika decided she wanted a college education. Annika enrolled in ASU and found she was a good student. She decided to study art because she'd finally admitted to herself that it was her passion. She also studied psychology because it interested her. She did not like it that she was following in her mother's footsteps with her choice of major, but she loved her classes. The double major of art and psychology would prepare Annika for a career as an art therapist. As she studied more and more about abnormal psychology, she gained insight into herself and into her relationship with her husband. Annika's fear and her resentment were building, and she knew her relationship with Igor was not going to get any better.

Because Annika now had an interest in something other than her husband and their fancy house, Igor became jealous. He said he supported her attending classes and working towards a degree, but that was all lip service on his part. In fact he felt threatened by her accomplishments and growing independence. They argued about everything. He wanted her to stay home. She wanted to finish her degree and get a job. He wanted her to cook his meals and wash his clothes. She wanted to attend classes and hire a housekeeper to take care of the domestic chores. Annika studied hard to finish her college courses in three years. She'd already begun to hide cash from the household accounts. She sequestered even more money.

Annika knew that escaping from the Russian Mafia as well as from any family connected with a Mexican drug cartel would be impossible. If she was going to escape from Igor, she needed the help of someone she could trust. The only person she felt she could really trust was her mother. Although she had not spoken to her mother for years, Annika called her mother on Pia's 70th birthday and asked if they could meet for lunch. Of course, Pia would always be there for her daughter. They met, and Annika told her mother everything. She showed her mother the scars from the beatings she had received from Igor. Pia cried when she saw what Annika's husband had done to her. The mother and daughter began to make plans for Annika to disappear.

Pia wondered if it would even be possible for Annika to free herself from Igor. Men like Igor had connections everywhere. They had crews of men who enforced their will. They employed hit men to take care of those who refused to comply with their orders. Annika had stepped into a very dangerous world when she had married Igor Castillo.

She had stepped into the middle of the Mexican cartels and their drug smuggling, and she had stepped into the middle of the Russian Mafia and their powerful dominance of the drug distribution networks in the western part of the United States.

Annika explained to her mother that Igor, with the mix of Russian Mafia and Mexican drug lord in his background, was connected to both the drugs that came into the United States from Mexico and the drugs that found their way to the streets and playgrounds of cities and small towns throughout the U.S. Igor was a very connected and a very rich man. He was now the Western drug kingpin of both the organization that brought drugs in from Mexico and the organization that distributed those drugs inside the United States. People were always challenging the near-monopolies that both of these organizations enjoyed. The only way for a drug lord to hold on to his drug territory was to kill the competition. Igor was a very dangerous man. He was a killer.

Annika told her mother she wished she had never met Igor. She wished she had never married him. She had been young and vulnerable and tired of working at crappy jobs to support herself. Igor had seduced her and promised her the world. Annika had fallen for him and for the many material things he offered her. She'd thought she was in love. Although she had never become involved with his drug businesses, she had been complicit in enjoying the luxurious lifestyle those businesses had provided to her.

After Annika had reconciled with her mother, they decided there was no other choice. Annika had to disappear. Her former life with Igor Castillo was finished, at least in Annika's mind. Her efforts from this point on were focused on finding a way to flee the brutal and unhappy existence she now endured with Igor. She had to become someone else. She knew she had to disappear so completely that Igor would never be able to find her. She had to disappear from the face of the earth. She had to die.

Pia agreed with her daughter. They agreed that Annika would have to establish an entirely new identity. She might have to have plastic surgery to change her appearance. Pia hated to consider this possibility as she looked at the beautiful face of her only daughter. But it would be better to say goodbye to that lovely face than to say goodbye to all of Annika. Both women knew that if Annika stayed with Igor, he would end up killing her. They also knew that when Annika left Igor and disappeared, he would do everything he could to hunt her down. He would kill her in an instant if he was ever able to find her. They decided that the only way for her to ever be safe was for Annika Karlsson Castillo to die.

"Killing" someone and at the same time making sure they lived was not an easy thing to do. A new place to live, a new identity, plastic surgery to change her appearance...all of these things would cost a great deal of money. Pia had some savings and had put money into a retirement account. She was willing to give it all to Annika to help her escape from her current situation and establish a new life. But Annika and Pia knew the retirement fund would not be enough to allow Annika to successfully disappear...essentially forever. Annika might never be able to work again. She could never use her own social security number because her husband would be able to find her if she did. Annika would have to be able to buy an entirely new identity and an entirely new existence. Annika had to secure enough money so that she would have enough to live on for the rest of her life, if she had to stay in hiding that long.

Annika was able to find out where Igor hid his money. Igor thought his home in Scottsdale with Annika was his secure place. He had a safe concealed behind a false wall as part of the bookcases that lined his office. He never suspected that Annika might attempt to discover this hiding place or be able to find the index card taped to the bottom of one of his desk drawers. The combination to the safe was written on that index card. But Annika had found it all. She knew the combination to the safe. Inside the safe, along with the cash, the weapons, and the drugs, she found the passwords for his computer and the numbers of and passwords for his numerous bank accounts around the world. Annika was not a computer whiz, but she had been able to find the information she thought she needed.

Pia knew more about computers than Annika did. It was usually the other way around. Kids almost always knew more about computers than their parents did. But Pia had been fascinated with computers when they'd first become available. She had learned to write software programs when she was in graduate school—more as a hobby and for fun than for anything that had to do with her graduate work. Because Annika knew where Igor's funds were located and had the relevant passwords, Pia promised her daughter that, when the time came, Annika would be able to steal Igor's money and make it her own. Pia had the skills to accomplish this transfer of Igor's wealth to Annika. Pia established secret bank accounts for her daughter, all in various false names.

With a few key strokes on her computer, the last thing Annika would do, just before she disappeared, would be to transfer her husband's ill-gotten drug wealth into her own secret bank accounts. Pia set it all up, and she told Annika exactly what she had to do to clear out Igor's millions. Annika needed some of Igor's money to live on, but she also wanted to punish the man who had hurt her so many times. She didn't need all the money that she and her mother were planning to take from Igor, but she was going to take every cent she could get her hands on. There was a tremendous amount of satisfaction in taking something from the hateful and dangerous man who was forcing her to have to give up her life and go into hiding.

Pia promised to help Annika, but in return, she wanted Annika to give to the authorities all the information her daughter had about Igor's drug dealings. Annika protested that she didn't really know much of anything about Igor's businesses. She had purposely not asked questions and had avoided involvement in that aspect of Igor's life. She honestly didn't think she knew very much. But after she and Pia talked about it, Annika realized she knew a lot more about what Igor was up to that she'd realized.

Annika began to write down everything she remembered from the past and everything that happened going forward. She wrote down the names of people who had been to the house. She wrote down dates. Because she was an artist and had an excellent visual memory, she was able to sketch the faces of the people who had come to the Castillo's home to conduct illicit business. Soon she had a sketch book full of drawings and a notebook full of other kinds of information. She copied onto thumb drives everything that was on Igor's computer. She took photographs of all the papers he kept in his office desk and filing cabinets. She realized that he kept a great many important papers and a great many secrets in their Phoenix home. Annika made it her mission to find out everything and document everything. Finally she felt as if she had something to offer the FBI or the DEA or whoever was going to receive her treasure trove of information.

Pia knew a fellow psychologist who had been a profiler for the FBI. The woman had retired from government service several years earlier and now had a private counseling practice. Annika and Pia met with the former profiler and another female agent who still worked for the FBI. They made some plans. They came to some agreements. They brought in Detective Cecilia Mendoza of PPD homicide because there was going to be a dead body involved in their plan. They set up a timetable for Annika to disappear from her life in Scottsdale.

Annika was scared, but she was also excited about being able to leave behind her life with Igor. She was willing to live a much more circumspect and frugal life than she had led with her drug lord husband. Now that she fully understood who and what Igor was, she was sickened by him and his big house and expensive cars and all the rest of it. She was not only ready but eager to leave all of Igor's excess and largess behind and become a different person.

Annika and Pia, Detective Mendoza, and the FBI agent finalized their plans. Everything was in place. Then tragedy struck. Pia had a serious stroke and was unable to speak. She could not move the right side of her body and couldn't walk. Annika was devastated by her mother's stroke. Mother and daughter had finally reconciled after being estranged for too many years. Annika had found her mother again, and now she was afraid she was going to lose her.

Even though she was unable to speak, Pia was able to communicate to her daughter that she wanted her to continue with the plans that had been made for Annika's escape to a new life. Pia was able to communicate that she wanted Annika to arrange for her old friend Isabelle Ritter to visit her in the facility where Pia was recovering from her stroke and trying to learn to walk and talk again. Pia realized she could no longer assist in her daughter's disappearance. She needed help. The advantage of asking Isabelle to become involved was that hardly anyone knew about Pia's relationship with Isabelle. Pia hated to impose on her long-time friend, but she trusted Isabelle. She knew Isabelle would not let her down.

Annika contacted Isabelle in Palm Springs. Isabelle was surprised to hear from Annika. She was shocked and saddened to hear about Pia's stroke. Annika told her everything…about her mother's medical condition and about their previous estrangement and reconciliation. Annika told Isabelle about the man she was married to. She told her about what kind of a person Igor was and what he did for a living. She told her about the injuries her husband had inflicted on her. She told Isabelle about the plans for Annika to turn over evidence against her husband to the FBI and then to disappear.

Isabelle immediately flew to Phoenix and went with Annika to visit Pia. Pia was able to communicate, with Annika's help, that she wanted Isabelle to help her daughter with her disappearance. Pia wanted Isabelle to take over and do the things Pia had hoped to do for Annika but was no longer able to do. Time was of the essence. Pia was pushing herself to come back, to be able to function normally again. But there was not time for that to happen before Annika had to make her escape. Annika was reluctant to admit to herself that Pia's recovery might never happen, but she knew she had to go ahead with what they had planned to do. Pia wanted that to happen. The schedule and the planning with the FBI had to continue to move forward, without interruption and without regard to the stroke that Pia had suffered.

Isabelle agreed to participate in the arrangements to help Annika disappear. Isabelle was devastated that her old friend

Pia was in such bad shape, but she was happy that Pia and Annika had reconciled before Pia had become disabled. Isabelle understood exactly what she was required to do, and she agreed to do it all. She was honored that her friend Pia wanted her to stand in for her to help rescue Annika. Isabelle would be acting in Pia's place to get Annika to her hiding place to start a new life.

Before she'd suffered the stroke, Pia had already set up all the steps that were necessary for Annika to be able to transfer Igor's millions to herself. Pia had given Annika careful instructions, so Annika knew exactly what to do once everything was in place for her disappearance. She would transfer the money just before she took her first steps to disappear. Timing was critical. No money could disappear from Igor's accounts until Annika was safe. Annika was afraid that when he found out someone had stolen his money, Igor would immediately suspect her. He would become enraged. Annika had to be completely gone by then. The timing had to be perfect. Annika would have to already be on her way to her new life before she began the money transfers. But she could not wait until Igor knew she was gone before she took his money. She would have to time her disappearance and the computer transfers of Igor's money exactly. She would have to accomplish both her escape and the secret financial transactions when Igor was on one of his trips to Mexico.

Seven

The original plan had been for Annika to reserve a casita at the Mimosa Inn for several days of rest and relaxation. The Mimosa had a full-service spa, and Annika was a regular customer. Occasionally, when Igor was going to be away for a period of time, Annika would check into the Mimosa Inn under her assumed name and schedule several days of massages, facials, pedicures, and other indulgent spa services designed to keep her feeling good and looking young. The Mimosa knew her well. The Mimosa Inn was not very far from her home in Scottsdale. Annika reserved her casita and scheduled her spa appointments. She had done this often enough that no one had any idea that this time would be any different than the other times Annika had checked into the Mimosa Inn for pampering.

The Ritters had organized the reunion with their Camp Shoemaker group and their visit to Phoenix so they could accommodate Annika's plans. The choice of the Mimosa Inn and the dates when the Ritters would be staying there had been carefully scheduled. None of the reunion participants, except the Ritters, knew anything about Annika Castillo or her plans to escape. No one except Isabelle and Matthew had any idea that there was anything going on other than the group of old friends getting together for the weekend. The Ritters were juggling two schedules on this trip, but they knew exactly what they were supposed to do and exactly when they were supposed to do it.

Annika would not sleep in her own casita on the night she disappeared forever. Earlier that day, and with the help of the hotel's luggage cart, Isabelle would load Annika's suitcases and a few boxes of belongings into the back of the silver Jeep that was parked in the Mimosa Inn's parking lot. Before she'd suffered the stroke, Pia Karlsson had bought the used Jeep for Annika to keep at her cabin hideaway. She wanted Annika to have wheels in case she needed to flee and disappear again.

Annika would go to dinner as usual, return to her casita, transfer Igor's money, put her laptop and a few toiletries into her oversized tote bag, turn out the lights in her room as if she were retiring for the night, lock the door of her casita behind her, and slip outside into the darkness. She would walk a few hundred yards to a different casita at the Mimosa Inn. As soon as Annika had completed the money transfers her mother had set up, she would have cleaned out Igor's accounts in Panama, in Mexico City, in the Cayman Islands, in Lichtenstein, and in Zurich. With a few strokes on her computer, Igor's fortune would all now be Annika's, but once the money had been moved, there was no going back.

Annika had reserved and paid for her casita for a week so no one would know when she left or suspect that she was no longer staying there. Once she had moved to the casita next to the one where Isabelle and Matthew Ritter were staying, she would no longer be Annika Karlsson Castillo. She had reserved that casita in a different name. She would spend the night in the room where no one knew she was sleeping, and she would be safe there. Detective Cecilia Mendoza, with help from the FBI, had a plan in place to make it look as if Annika had been murdered.

Very early the next morning, Annika would put on a wig and disguise herself with clothes she didn't normally wear. Before the sun came up, she would walk to the parking lot of the Mimosa Inn where Isabelle Ritter would be waiting in a rental car. Annika, who was no longer Annika, would drive the Jeep, and Isabelle would follow her. They would drive away from Annika's old life and leave the Mimosa Inn and Paradise Valley behind forever. Isabelle and Annika would drive to the White Mountains where Pia had set up a safe house for her daughter. The house had been ready for Annika since before Pia had been crippled by her stroke. No one else except Isabelle and Matthew Ritter, Mona Damours, and Annika knew anything about the cabin in the woods.

Pia's father, Ingmar Karlsson, had owned several investment properties which had brought him rental income throughout his life. All of them were owned through various LLCs, and none actually had Ingmar Karlsson's name on them. When he had died a few years ago at the age of ninety-six, Pia had inherited everything.

Ingmar Karlsson had bought the property near Pinetop, Arizona decades earlier and had rented it out to the same person for more than twenty years. The mountain cabin was owned by an LLC under the ambiguous and innocuous name of Lifestyle Seasons 365. Pia's father told Pia that he had designated an old friend of his as the director or the LLC, but the truth was that Ingmar Karlsson had been the only person who had known anything about the LLC or the cabins in the White Mountains.

Ingmar Karlsson had occasionally spoken to Pia about Mona Damours, the artist who rented the secluded cabin in the mountains. Pia had heard Mona's name, but until after her father died, Pia had not really connected Mona directly with the place in Pinetop, Arizona. The female tenant in the cabin was French Canadian and seemed to have plenty of money. She was never late with the rent which arrived without fail in the Lifestyle Seasons 365, LLC, post office box on the first of every month. The rent was always in the form of a check drawn on a bank in Montreal, LBD Banque de la Cité.

When her father had gone into an assisted living facility, the rent checks had been forwarded to his accountant's office. Now the checks, made out as always to Lifestyle Seasons 365, LLC, arrived at a post office box Pia had set up in Chandler, Arizona. All mail for her father's various LLCs was sent to this post office box. At the time Pia had set up the post office box, she'd not been trying to hide anything. It was just easier to keep things simple and not change the names and all the other things her father had so carefully constructed.

Pia had known almost nothing about either the LLCs or the properties until her father had died and left it all to her. She was grateful for the inheritance and enjoyed having the additional income from the investments. But she had never actually seen any of the properties or met any of the people who rented them. Pia had never known the name of or met the person who had been renting and living in the cabin on the property in the White Mountains for the past twenty-two years. Pia thought that sometime down the road, she might decide to actually live in the cabin herself, at least part-time. If she decided she liked living in Pinetop, Arizona, she might decide to make it her permanent residence when she gave up her counseling practice.

When Annika's situation had become critical and Pia realized her daughter was going to have to disappear, she thought the property in the White Mountains might be a possible hideaway for Annika. She worried that it might be too close to Scottsdale. She worried that she might have to dislodge the tenant who had lived there and paid her rent faithfully for so many years. Pia decided she would have to finally drive to Pinetop and look at the place herself. She would have to meet the eccentric woman who had lived there in the primitive cabin for more than two decades.

🌲

According to scuttlebutt in the small town of Pinetop, the reclusive woman, who lived at the end of the dirt road that nobody ever approached, only left the remote cabin twice a month. Rumors speculated that she drove to Phoenix in her old truck to pick up mail that arrived for her at her post office box. Or maybe she had a post office box someplace else? No one was really sure. Maybe she drove to Whole Foods and AJ's in Scottsdale. She had occasionally been seen visiting the grocery store in Show Low. She sometimes purchased things at the local pharmacy in Pinetop. She paid cash for everything. Hardly anyone paid cash for anything anymore, so she was noticed for that reason. She never used a credit card, and no one in either Pinetop or Show Low really knew what the reclusive woman's name was. That was the way Mona Damours wanted things to stay.

She was completely anti-social and never engaged in a conversation with anyone in Show Low or in Pinetop. She was a true hermit, and those with whom she came in contact apparently respected her desire to be left alone. She had no landline and no internet, as far as anyone knew. She conducted her business and communicated via snail mail. No one knew if she drove her old truck anywhere other than into Show Low and Pinetop, but the truck supposedly had been spotted a few times on the road to Phoenix. If she did drive to other places, she didn't drive through town or allow anyone to see her when she left or when she arrived back home. She had been an enigma, an intriguing mystery ever since she had first moved to the mountain cabin. She had now lived in seclusion for so long and other local residents were so used to her odd ways, she was pretty much a fixture that nobody paid much attention to any more.

Pia had Mona's mailing address. Pia wrote a letter to Mona to tell her she was coming to Pinetop for a visit and wanted to meet with her. Mona had written back a very nice letter and said she would be happy to meet with Ingmar Karlsson's daughter. They confirmed a date through the mail. Pia drove to the White Mountains to meet her tenant and to see for the first time the remote property Pia had owned for several years. Pia made arrangements to stay at a bed and breakfast in Pinetop for the weekend.

Their meeting was awkward for the first few minutes. Mona Damours was actually quite attractive and presentable. Pia had expected the worst...a deranged, wild-haired hoarder who had trashed the cabin her father had decided to rent to her twenty-two years earlier. But none of that turned out to be the case. Mona had long, white hair which she wore braided and wound around her head. Her skin was slightly tanned as if she spent time outdoors. Although the woman had to be in her sixties at least, she did not have a single wrinkle on her lovely face. She wore black leggings and an artist's smock. The smock looked clean enough, but it was covered with permanent smudges of oil paint in all the colors of the rainbow. Oil paint does not come out in the washing machine.

The house was spotlessly clean and contained only a few pieces of furniture. The woman clearly lived a minimalist and even an ascetic life, except for her painting. The entire main room of the cabin was her artist's studio. She spent most of her time here...working on her enormous and colorful masterpieces. Pia was stunned when she saw Mona's work. It was striking. It was abstract and colorful. Pia knew Mona's art work was exceptional. She knew Mona must sell it. But where did she sell it, and how did she get it there to wherever she sold it? Why had Pia never heard of this talented artist? Pia's awe was evident when she first entered Mona's cabin. The artist was obviously pleased that she had made an impression on her landlady. Mona actually smiled. She asked Pia if she would like a cup of tea. Pia answered yes but was otherwise totally entranced and occupied with her admiration of Mona's amazing work.

Mona brought the apricot tea, a pitcher of real cream, and a pot of honey. There were only two chairs in the room.

Pia sat in one of them and put her cup of tea in its saucer on her knees. She had considered asking Mona to move out of the cabin so that Annika could live there, but after meeting Mona and seeing her art work, she knew she did not have the heart to ask the woman to leave this place that had been her home for so many years.

"I know what you have come here to say to me. I was afraid, when Ingmar died, that this day would come. But then I never heard anything from you, and I began to think I was going to be allowed to stay. You own this house. I rent it. I will move out if that is what you want. I don't know what has changed in your life, but I know you want my house."

"You are right. I've come here on a mission. I wanted to see if this house might be the right place for a very special project of mine. I have to tell you that after seeing your magnificent paintings, I have completely changed my mind and given up the idea of asking you to move elsewhere. I will look for my cabin in the woods someplace else."

"Tell me why you are seeking a cabin in the woods. Maybe I can help you with that." Mona had a twinkle in her eye that did not go unnoticed.

Pia had sworn she would not tell anyone else about Annika's situation or her daughter's need to disappear. But being here in this cabin with Mona and Mona's work had changed her mind. Something about the artist and the paintings had moved Pia. Pia was not easily moved. She was suspicious of others. She had seen too many sociopaths in her own psychology practice to trust others readily. Even though she had just met Mona and did not really know the woman at all, she knew she could trust Mona. She knew this in her heart and soul without any reservations. She spent the next few hours telling Mona everything...about

Annika, about Igor Castillo, about the FBI, and about why she needed a safe house for her daughter.

Mona asked a few questions. "I can help you, Pia. I can help Annika. You probably don't know that there is another cabin, very much like this one, farther back in the woods. Almost no one has ever known it was there. No one ever comes on this property, because I want it that way. To get to the other cabin, you have to travel on my road and go through my driveway. No one ever comes, so no one remembers that the other house is here. Your father knew, of course, but it is antiquated. He didn't want to rent it out to anyone."

"Another cabin? Here on this property? I looked around when I drove up and didn't see anything. Where is it and what kind of condition is it in?"

"You can't see it from here, or really from anywhere. It was built at the same time this cabin was built. Years ago, somebody stayed there, but the last people stopped coming to the other cabin about thirty years ago. One previous owner built a corral at the side of that cabin for his horses. He liked to ride on the trails in the mountains. Then he got old and died. A couple bought the property and lived here in my cabin for a few years. Your father bought the place, including both cabins, from them."

"If nobody has stayed there for thirty years, it must be in terrible shape."

"Not really. I've made it kind of a project of mine to keep it from falling down. It was well built to begin with, and I have tried to maintain it. Your father and I have been at odds from time to time over the costs of keeping the second cabin in good repair. I think he would have preferred to let it fall down, but I kept after him...about the roof and about the windows."

"I remember him talking about that roof. You told him the place needed a new roof, and he didn't want to pay to have it done. Didn't you put the new roof on yourself... or something like that? My dad had several rental properties, but I didn't put the roof story together with you and with the White Mountains until now."

"I told him the other cabin needed a new roof. He said he didn't want to spend the money. I think he had just written off the other cabin and was willing to let it go. I told him I would put the roof on for him. I had learned how to do everything for myself, or at least almost everything that needed to be done here, in my own place. We always agreed ahead of time on a budget for each project, including the new roof for this cabin. I paid for the materials and deducted those costs from my monthly rent. I charged him for the hours of labor I put in and deducted that, too. Because I did pretty much everything myself, and didn't overcharge him, he'd decided the improvements I'd made to my own place all passed muster. He balked when I wanted to save the other cabin. But I kept after him. I took some photos and sent them to him. He finally agreed to allow me to repair the roof. After I'd finally convinced him the roof project was worth doing on the cabin in the woods, we came to terms on the budget and agreed on what I would be allowed to spend. I drove to a Lowe's in Phoenix and bought the plywood, the tar paper, the roof shingles, and the nails. I already had a good ladder because I'd put a new roof on my cabin a few years earlier. Fortunately both places are just one story. I was older when I put on the second roof, but I could still get up the ladder and crawl around on the roof. I did a bang-up job on the new roof for the second cabin, and I finished the project under budget." Mona chucked, remembering her negotiations with Pia's father, Ingmar, who had been a hard-nosed businessman.

"With the money I had left over from fixing the roof, I decided I would replace the windows in the other cabin. I got a great discount on the price of those replacement windows. They were high-end Marvin windows that somebody had special ordered. They were custom made and really good quality. Maybe when they arrived it turned out they were the wrong thing or the wrong size. In any case, it seemed these wonderfully constructed windows were an odd size that nobody could use. For whatever reason, the price on those nice windows was marked way down. The home improvement store in Show Low was almost giving them away. They said the windows were taking up space in their warehouse. No one wanted them, and they were thrilled when I offered to take all the windows off their hands. So I bought all of them and put them in myself. I was lucky to find such a bargain. I didn't tell your father about the windows until after they were already installed. When I told him I'd finished the roof under budget, he thought I should have turned the money I'd saved back over to him. He wasn't happy to hear about the windows. But I enjoyed putting in the new windows and didn't charge him anything for the labor to do that. Anyway, the cabin is in pretty good shape. The floors will look good after I've cleaned them up, and I have been able to keep the critters and the various bugs out of here. It's fairly clean, but it needs some work. The kitchen needs new appliances, and the bathroom is really old. Your daughter needs a place to hide. I understand that better than you can imagine. I'll tell you about it sometime. If you will buy the new kitchen appliances, the tile for the bathroom, and new bathroom fixtures, I will do the work.

What kind of a timetable are we looking at? It will take me several weeks, once I have everything I need. I work on my paintings in the mornings and in the evenings. I do home repairs and work in my garden in the afternoons."

"I'm very thankful you were able to talk my dad into having the roof repaired. Thank you so much for doing that. And thank you for replacing the windows. I want to see the place, of course, but I am grateful in advance that you have taken such good care of the other cabin. Especially since nobody can see it and nobody remembers that it's even there, it sounds like it will be the perfect place for Annika. She is desperate to get away from her life as it now exists. She is ready to live a simpler lifestyle. Do you think you can get the work done in two months? She has a window of opportunity to get away from Igor in November. Every day she stays with that monster, I worry about her safety. He is leaving for some kind of an extended trip in November, and she knows she will have several days to make her escape. Do you think the other cabin can be ready by late fall? I didn't realize you also have plumbing and electrical skills, too, but I am very grateful that you do."

Mona laughed a little. "I have had to learn to do many things for myself while I have been living alone and really pretty much off the grid for so many years. And, yes, I can do the work in two months or less, as soon as I have everything I need."

They walked along Mona's driveway and then down a narrow dirt road into the woods to the hidden cabin. On the way, they walked by Mona's garden. In August, the summer's display of vegetables and herbs was bountiful. Mona loved to garden. She was clearly pleased with the harvest she'd been able to produce in the forbidding mountain climate. She admitted that in the spring she had more leafy greens than she could use. She canned her own tomatoes and green beans. She bought peaches at Whole Foods in Phoenix when they were in season and canned those, too. She froze the squash and the broccoli. She dried and froze the herbs she couldn't use when they were fresh. Mona was proud of her garden and proud of being able to provide herself with her own vegetables.

"The growing season is short up here in the mountains, but I cover my plants when we have a freeze. I've figured out how to stretch out the number of good gardening days. Growing one's own food is very satisfying. I have an excellent well that provides my garden, as well as both cabins, with plenty of water."

The cabin farther back in the woods was about two hundred yards from Mona's cabin. It looked almost identical to Mona's house on the outside. It was the same size and had the same arrangement of rooms. There was an addition on the north side of the cabin that now looked like it was a small sunroom. Pia asked about it. Mona told Pia the addition had been built originally as a corral for a previous owner's horses. Neither woman could understand why anyone would want their horses sleeping and eating right next to the living room, but the addition was obviously no longer a corral or a horse barn. The house was a bit dusty inside, but Mona had been taking care of this second cabin. It was clean and smelled like new wood.

"The people who were here before your father bought the cabins made the corral into a screened-in porch. They were probably from the city or the seashore, but screened-in porches don't work around here because there are so many trees. Pollen collects on the porch and on the screens. It covers everything and sticks like glue. You have to constantly wipe it down, and if you have allergies, a screened-in porch here in the woods is your worst nightmare. I made the decision that the screened-in porch had to go. The screens were all torn up anyway. I'd bought all these nice windows with the money I had left over from the roof project's budget. I had windows left over after replacing the windows in the cabin, so I decided to make the screened-in porch into a sunroom. It was easy. The roof was already on and the structure was sound. I tore out what was left of the screens and put in the extra windows I had left. The size of the new windows wasn't perfect, but I made them work. The screened-in porch had a cement slab floor. I put down a plywood sub floor. There was some lumber in the garage that was similar to the flooring in the cabin...wide-plank boards. The sunroom isn't large, so I laid a rather rough-looking floor, sanded it down, and put on several coats of polyurethane. The floor in the sunroom isn't exactly like the floor in the rest of the cabin, but it all goes together nicely. I added the bookshelves and cupboards for storage along this back wall. That was the fun part. I think it looks pretty good." Pia thought it looked better than pretty good. She was incredibly impressed with Mona's many skills and the quality of her renovation work.

Mona had updated her own kitchen and bathroom, but none of that had been done in this cabin. This cabin also looked different from Mona's on the inside because it was completely empty of any furniture. Pia was thrilled with the place—especially with its remote location in the woods. Thankfully, Mona and Pia were on the same page with how to modernize the cabin, and Pia was already figuring out how to furnish it for her daughter.

It was past dinnertime when all the decisions and the lists had been made. They had both agreed that an on-demand hot water heater was a must. Mona had one, and she loved it. Pia promised to drive to Pinetop again in two weeks to be sure Mona had everything she needed for the renovations. Pia was completely confident that the artist and self-taught handywoman would not let her down. Pia hugged Mona when she left. Mona stood on the porch of her cabin and waved goodbye to Pia as she drove to the bed and breakfast.

Two weeks later, Pia rented a truck and packed it with furniture she thought would fit into the cabin. Quite a few of the pieces she was bringing to furnish Annika's cabin were things she hadn't been able to part with when she'd cleaned out her father's house a few years earlier. Pia was glad to have a use for them and to be able to retrieve them from a storage unit. When she arrived at Mona's cabin, Mona's truck was there, but the artist wasn't at home.

Pia found Mona on her knees, hard at work, tiling the bathroom floor in the cabin in the woods. Mona had driven to Phoenix to pick up the new kitchen appliances, the new hot water heater, the stackable washer and dryer, and the new bathroom tile and fixtures. Somehow, with the help of a dolly, she had been able to move the old refrigerator into the garage and move the new one into the kitchen. There was a new wall oven and a new stovetop. A small dishwasher had been installed. Mona had scrubbed down and waxed the solid wood cabinets inside and out. They had been sturdily built by a talented cabinetmaker many years ago, and now they almost looked like they were new. The kitchen was done, and Pia was in awe of how clean and modern and inviting it all was.

Mona was expecting Pia and called out, "Hello. I'm in here." Pia walked to the bathroom and stood in the doorway as she watched Mona lay the blue and white tiles in a beautiful pattern on the floor. "Artists like to lay tile. It's like making a painting out of ceramics...like a mosaic. This is the tile you picked, and I decided to make it a little bit special for Annika." Mona was obviously enjoying the renovation project. The bathroom was fairly large and had space for the existing tub and a good-sized separate shower. Mona had already replaced the antiquated pipes in the floor and had tiled the shower. When she finished tiling the floor, the only thing left to do was put in the new bathroom fixtures.

"It's gorgeous. I want to move in here myself." Pia walked around the cabin and looked at everything Mona had done. The washer and dryer were tucked away in the back hall between the kitchen and the garage. Mona had installed the hot water heater and had created a small pantry with narrow shelves on the opposite wall of the hallway. "It's perfect, Mona. Everything she needs is here. I brought furniture. I couldn't wait until you'd done all your work, but it looks like you are way ahead of schedule."

"I admit I've neglected my painting these past two weeks, but I have really enjoyed doing this work. I'm excited to meet Annika, and I want her to have a nice place to escape to." Mona's forehead wrinkled with concern. "Is everything on schedule for Annika? Is she going to be able to leave it all behind and make it to Pinetop in November?"

"As far as I know, everything is still on schedule. She has given her videotaped statement to the FBI. It took several days for her to do all of that. They still want her to be able to appear in court...if things get to that point. I'd just as soon she didn't have to go to court. That will put her in a very vulnerable spot... getting away from here, getting to the courthouse, getting back here. I also worry about what might happen to her while she is in court, giving her testimony. These drug people... nothing is sacred to them. They would come into a courtroom with guns blazing and blow everybody and everything away. They would shoot the judge without a second thought, and they would certainly target Annika who has given away their secrets." Pia shuddered when she thought of her daughter having to leave the safe house and travel to a courtroom to testify against her snake of a husband and his disgusting drug cronies.

Mona finished her tile work and began to clean up. "Grout tomorrow. Then the new fixtures go in. That won't take long. I put a new finish on the old-fashioned claw-foot bathtub—inside and outside. The tub is a classic and just too wonderful to get rid of. I have to admit I couldn't move that heavy thing myself. It looks great in the bathroom, and the shower is ready, as you can see. I just have to put in the new sink and countertop and the new toilet. It won't take long to install all the new faucets. A coat of paint on the walls, and we are almost there. This bathroom has been a fun project. I love blue and white together, and I guess Annika does too, since you picked out these beautiful tiles for the shower and the floor. Let's get your truck unloaded."

The antique walnut writing desk was the heaviest thing they had to get off the truck and into the house. The new double-bed mattress and box springs were the most awkward things they had to handle. The couch for the living area was surprisingly lightweight. Although both women were older, they were both strong. With the help of two furniture-moving dollies, they were able to get everything out of the truck and into the cabin. The best-looking piece of furniture was the antique table for the kitchen. It would double as a work space, and its scrubbed pine surface and thick turned legs made a great contrast to the dark wood cabinets. The last thing off the truck were boxes of nonperishable food, canned goods, and staples. Pia began putting the cans of tuna, boxes of pasta, and canned plum tomatoes on the shelves in the pantry. "I love this pantry with its narrow shelves. What a great idea."

Mona smiled a rare smile. "Everybody needs a pantry. Even if it's a really small one. I wiped out the freezer in the garage and plugged it in. I wasn't sure if it would run. It must have been years since anyone has used it. I don't think it was ever used very much. It doesn't look great on the outside, but the inside is spotless. It seems to be running fine. They don't make freezers, or anything else, like they used to. That freezer will probably still be clunking along years after this new washer and dryer have given up the ghost. I'm sure the old freezer is not climate change friendly, but who gives a rip about that up here in the middle of nowhere."

Pia had brought towels and sheets and dishes and pots and pans. She'd even brought a few lamps and decorative items. "On my next trip, I am bringing Annika's clothes and books and a few things she can't bear to leave behind at the house she shares with her husband. She never again wants to see most of the things she bought for that house, but there are a few special things she wants to keep. I will leave those boxes for her to unpack. The closet here is about one-twentieth the size of her closet in Scottsdale, but she won't be bringing most of her fancy cocktail dresses and evening gowns anyway. She doesn't want to see those clothes anymore...especially the shoes. She was never a fan of high heels, but Igor loved to see her wearing them and insisted that she buy them and wear them for him." Pia sighed and shook her head. "I hope this all works out like we've planned. I am so worried about Annika. Can she possibly hope to escape from that monster she's married to? Will he be able to find her here? We are doing everything we can to make sure he can't find her, but there are no guarantees that all of our preparations and secretiveness will work out."

Mona was nodding her head. "I completely understand. You know I will shop for her groceries and anything else she needs. The people in Pinetop and Show Low are used to seeing me around. It won't be a problem. She doesn't have to go to town or show her face anywhere. But I wonder if she will be able to adjust to living such a solitary life. It will be very different, living here alone in the middle of the woods. I will be the only person she will see...if she is smart and can tolerate hiding out way up here in the mountains."

Mona wanted to say something more but was hesitating. "I have been hiding here in the White Mountains for more than twenty years. It's a long story, but I left Canada many years ago. I left an abusive relationship with a very important and well-known Canadian politician. I knew he would never let me go. So I disappeared. I have never been back, and he has never been able to find me. I left my family behind. I lived in New York City for almost twenty years. I painted, and the sale of my paintings provided me with enough income to live quite well. Then one day, the man I was hiding from came to the gallery that sold my paintings. He demanded to know, from the gallery's owner, where I was living. She didn't know where I lived, but he beat her up anyway. I knew it was time for me to move on. Also, the winters and the weather in the Northeast finally got to me as I grew older. I have some arthritis in my knees and ankles. I knew I wanted to move to the Southwest where the weather was milder and drier. I eventually found this cabin in the woods, and I moved here. I feel completely safe in this place. I still paint, and I send my paintings to the gallery in New York City. My paintings command high prices these days, and I don't have to keep on painting to support myself. But I love to paint, so I keep on doing what I love, even though I have plenty of money in the bank to finance my lifestyle. It's a very simple lifestyle to be sure." Mona smiled another small, rare smile at her statement of the obvious.

"So essentially, now I am painting for fun. I still make a lot of money selling my work. The most important thing is that I am safe here. I know the politician with whom I was involved in Quebec has tried to find me. He has attempted to hunt me down. He periodically threatens the owner of the gallery that sells my paintings, and she eventually had to get a restraining order against him. He is basically bat shit crazy, but that's another story. The gallery owner has never known where I was living, and she has no idea where I am living now. She doesn't know my real name...only the name I sign on my paintings and the name she puts on the checks she sends to a bank account in Florida. Now it's electronic transfers, of course. She doesn't want to know anything more about me than where to send the money. I go to great lengths to drive a long way from here to ship my paintings to her. I crate them myself and pack them into my truck. Every couple of months, I drive to various locations in California and send the paintings from California to Key West. I pay an agent who lives in Key West to send the paintings on to New York. He drives the paintings to various places in the South and sends them to New York...never from the same city. It's a very expensive and convoluted process, but it keeps me safe. Nobody knows where I am. My former fiancé, who would still like to track me down, would send a hit squad after me if he could find me. But he will never find me here. I will be sure Annika doesn't make any mistakes that might reveal where she is hiding. One of the reasons I have worked so hard on her cabin and have finished almost everything ahead of schedule is because I understand her flight. I have been there. I know something about what she has been through, and I know she will have an adjustment when she makes the final break and gives up her previous life. I can help her make that adjustment, and I'll be sure she doesn't do anything to give herself away. Staying completely hidden isn't easy... especially if someone is actively hunting for you."

Pia was not entirely shocked to hear Mona's story. She'd had the feeling that Mona was hiding from something. No one opts to live in seclusion and mostly cut off from the world as entirely as Mona had chosen to do unless they have a very compelling reason. Pia was glad to know Mona's story, and she was even more reassured that Mona would be looking out for Annika and guiding her during her first weeks and months on the run.

"I will be back in about two weeks with the rest of the things Annika wants to keep with her. I am also going to bring her painting supplies and some of her finished and unfinished paintings. Several of these have been in a storage room in the basement of the condo where I live. Annika has trained as an art therapist, but she will probably never be able to work in that field. I was after her for years about going to college or going to art school. I finally gave up. Then, all on her own, she decided to go to college, and now she has a new degree from ASU. She double-majored in art and psychology. She wanted to get into a master's program so she could be an art therapist, but that is probably never going to happen for her. I hope she will learn from you and be inspired to pursue her painting more seriously. She has talent. I think the sunroom that used to be a horse corral and then was turned into a screened-in porch for a while will be perfect for her to use as a studio. It has the northern light exposure that artists treasure. All of her life, my daughter has been difficult to deal with. But I think she has finally grown up. I hope she will be able to stay on track and stay alive. She became involved with some terribly dangerous people. To her great credit, she has gone to the FBI and told them all the secrets she knows about the Mexican drug cartel her husband controls and about the Russian Mafia's drug dealings...which he also controls. She has placed herself in an untenable position. I almost hate to put you at risk by having her move up here close to you, but after having met you and having heard a little about your own escape story, I know you can take care of yourself."

Mona and Pia walked to the rented truck that had brought the furniture and household goods to the remote cabin in the White Mountains. Pia climbed into the driver's seat of the truck and reached out to grab Mona's hand. "Thank you for everything you've done for Annika and for me."

Mona smiled another rare smile and squeezed Pia's hand. "I will see you in two weeks when you bring Annika's things. You have keys to the cabin in case I'm not here. I'm almost always here, but you never know. I'll take good care of your girl."

🌲

Two weeks later, when Pia returned with Annika's boxes, Mona's truck was not parked outside her cabin. Mona wasn't home. Pia let herself into the cabin in the woods and unloaded the boxes into the living room. The bathroom was finished and looked like something from a fancy house on HGTV. Pia had brought a few more things for Annika's freezer and pantry. She'd brought some decorative items and some family scrapbooks and heirlooms she thought Annika would enjoy having. She hung some clothes in the closet. She looked around with satisfaction at the home she and Mona had created for Annika. She said a silent prayer that her daughter would somehow be safe and sound living in this place.

Pia drove back to Tempe and had the best night's sleep she'd had in years. It was still a few weeks before Annika was scheduled to leave her husband and her home in Scottsdale. Now that the cabin was ready, Pia wished Annika could leave immediately.

Pia was meeting a friend for lunch. That day when she unlocked her car, her vision blurred, and she knew something was terribly wrong. She collapsed on the ground before she could get into the driver's seat. She'd had a stroke. Her next-door neighbor found her lying beside her car and called 911. Pia's life was saved, but she was left severely disabled by the stroke. She knew she would have to call on someone to help her if Annika was going to be able to make it successfully to her new home in the White Mountains. She decided she would have Annika contact her old friend Isabelle Ritter and ask her to take over the complicated task of getting Annika to her hiding place.

Eight

Elizabeth kept telling herself she needed to get out of bed and get going, but she kept falling back asleep. She finally allowed herself to rest, figuring that after all the excitement of the night before, her body was telling her she needed the extra sleep. It was after noon when she finally made herself call room service and order lunch. She asked for unsweetened iced tea and the turkey club sandwich on toasted sourdough bread with a side of Thousand Island dressing.

The room was cool, and she decided to turn on the gas fireplace to warm things up. The fireplace had a raised hearth and was made of adobe. It had an arched opening in the traditional southwestern style. It was charming. When she turned on the fire, Elizabeth noticed that the fireplace had originally been built to hold a wood-burning fire. The burn marks from the wood fires were still on the hearth, even though it had been converted to a low-maintenance gas fireplace. Some of the cottages at the Mimosa had been here since the 1930s. Back then they might have had wood fires.

Elizabeth could imagine that when the fireplaces had burned wood, housekeeping would have had to clear the ashes and the charred wood out of the fireplaces every day when they cleaned the cottages. It would have been a lot of work. The staff would have had to lay fresh logs, ready for the room's occupant to be able to easily light the next fire. And then there would have been the wood to chop to the right size so that it would fit into the relatively small fireplace opening. Wood would have had to be replenished almost daily. She wondered how many people the Mimosa Inn would have had to hire, back in the day, just to clean and supply and take care of the fireplaces. She was sure everyone had been greatly relieved, especially the staff, when the inn had decided to convert the quaint adobe fireplaces to gas.

Next to the fireplace opening, there was still a large storage space for the wood that had been necessary to feed those long-ago fires. Built into the fireplace surround, the niche that had once held logs now held a beautifully crafted ceramic vase. The colorful piece was really more the shape of a pot than it was the shape of a vase. It was the perfect shape to fit in the spot that had been built for firewood. Wider and shorter than a vase, the ceramic pot had a fairly narrow neck. But it was large and would hold a lot of something. It was a perfect addition to the room, and the blues and greens and reds of its design added a bright spot to the earth-colored clay tones of the fireplace. There was a knock on the door of the cottage. Elizabeth's lunch had arrived. She hurried to pull her warm wool dressing gown with a hood over her nightgown.

The room service waiter set up her lunch table in front of the gas fire. The kitchen had included an entire quart of delicious homemade iced tea...some of the best Elizabeth had ever tasted. She was happy to have this time to herself, but she also was sorry to miss the program she knew her friends were enjoying at the Heard Museum.

As she sat in front of the fire, she studied the colorful pot that stood in the alcove that had previously been a repository for wood. It was obvious that the colors of the pot had been chosen to complement and enhance the overall décor of the room. Whoever had chosen it had made sure it fit perfectly into its spot. The piece looked old, but Elizabeth doubted it was actually an antique. Antique pots belonged at the Heard. Antique pots could be so easily dropped and broken by a curious guest or damaged by an overenthusiastic house-keeping person. Elizabeth decided this beautiful ceramic pot was probably a reproduction and had probably been made in China. Everything else was made in China these days. She decided that even if it had been made in China, it was lovely. She was happy to have it in her room.

Of course, curiosity was going to get the better of her eventually, and she knew she was going to have to look more closely at the pot that was securely tucked into the alcove next the fire. Because of her arthritic fingers, she did not entirely trust her hands to pick up the somewhat bulky piece and turn it over, but she was going to be extremely careful and do it anyway. The pot had several decorative dried saguaro ribs sticking out of the top. Elizabeth would have to remove these before she turned the piece upside down to see where it had been made.

She sat on the raised hearth and removed the saguaro ribs. She grasped the pot with both hands and lifted it out of its resting place. She almost dropped it. It was very heavy, much heavier than she was expecting it to be and much heavier than it should have been. It was awkward and she was afraid she would drop it when she turned it over. She realized there was something inside the pot that was very heavy. It was too heavy. It felt as if stones had been placed inside — maybe to anchor it and make it more difficult to tip over. But when Elizabeth lifted it, it didn't sound as if there were any stones inside.

When she looked into the pot, she could see there were no rocks or stones inside. There were several packages wrapped in plastic which had been stuffed down into the pot. There were four large packages wedged in the bottom. Elizabeth didn't know if she would be able to get them out or not, but she was going to try. Her curiosity was now in charge. She thought she had figured out what was inside the pot, but she had to know.

Turning the vase upside down was not going to dislodge the packages. Elizabeth knew that Richard always traveled with a long shoehorn that helped him put on his shoes. She thought the shoehorn might help her pry the plastic bags out of the vase. Finding the shoehorn was another story, but she finally had it in her hands. She decided what she really needed was spaghetti tongs. Whatever was wedged inside was stuck in the wider bottom part of the vessel. She was going to have to somehow work the packages, one at a time, out through the narrow neck of the pot. She worked carefully. She did not want to break the pot or drop it.

At last the pot gave up one of its plastic packages. Elizabeth had been suspicious about what was in the package, and she was extra careful to extract the bundle with the shoehorn. She didn't want to touch any of the packages with her hands. Each bundle was securely wrapped and was about the size of a quart box of chicken broth. But these packages were heavier than chicken broth. Elizabeth thought each one must weigh close to five pounds.

When she pulled the first one out of the pot, she was immediately able to confirm what she'd suspected, that these were packages of drugs. She'd never before seen drugs in bulk like this, but this is how she'd imagined drugs would be packed. The more she looked at the packages, the more she was convinced her conclusion was correct. She estimated that she had about twenty pounds of some kind of drugs on her hands.

She considered removing the other three plastic packages that were still in the pot but decided to leave them where they were. Seeing one of the packages up close was enough. She didn't need to remove the other three plastic packages to know what they contained. She left the pot and the one package of drugs she'd removed from it on the fireplace hearth.

But her curiosity got the better of her. Elizabeth picked up the one package and carefully pulled the plastic away from the top. When she look inside, she knew immediately that the package held fentanyl. She wished she hadn't touched the plastic that held the fentanyl, but she had. She didn't have any gloves to put on. She was glad she had left the other three bags alone. She knew she was going to have to confront the truth about what she had found.

Halloween had been less than two weeks earlier. Elizabeth had read an article on her phone that warned parents and their kids who went out to trick or treat that they might be given the lethal drug in place of candy. Authorities were warning the public about fentanyl pills that had come into the U.S. from Mexico. The potentially lethal drug had been pressed into colorful tablets that resembled a popular candy that might be handed out as a door-to-door treat for children. The picture on her phone had shown what these colorful fentanyl tablets looked like, and they had looked exactly like a kind of candy her own kids used to eat. She couldn't remember the name of the candy, but she remembered sending it in care packages to her children when they attended summer camp. The tablets inside this plastic bag looked exactly like the drugs in the phone photo. They looked exactly like candy.

Her throat went dry. What was she going to do with all of this? From her reading, she figured that this much fentanyl was probably worth a great deal of money. She also realized that, depending on the strength of the tablets, this many pounds of the powerful drug could kill a great many people. Elizabeth knew she had a serious problem on her hands. She was going to need help from law enforcement to deal with this discovery. Were these fentanyl tablets the prize that the person, who she was almost certain had been in her casita the night before last, had been trying to find? There had been two break-ins in one night…one in her own casita and another one in the casita that had been ransacked. And then there was a dead body in the casita across the walkway the next night. This luxury resort was becoming more dangerous by the hour.

Elizabeth had saved the policewoman's card from the night before and decided she would call Detective Cecilia Mendoza. Even though she knew the detective was assigned to homicide, Elizabeth was betting that Cecilia would know what to do. If Mendoza were unable to handle the drug issue herself, Elizabeth was confident she would put her in touch with someone who could help.

Elizabeth didn't want the room service people to come into the room and see a bag of drugs beside the fireplace. She wouldn't call them to pick up her lunch tray until after she had talked with Mendoza. But what if they came on their own while she was on the phone? Or what if housekeeping decided it was time to clean the room?

Elizabeth was able to hang the privacy card on the outside of the door to the casita. She put the room service tray on her rollator. It was precariously balanced, but she was able to push the rollator through the exterior doors and place her lunch tray outside the room on the patio table. After all of this, she felt as if she would not be interrupted and could safely call Detective Mendoza.

Elizabeth called Cecilia Mendoza's cell phone, and thankfully she picked up immediately. Mendoza sounded tired, but she said she remembered Elizabeth from the night before. The detective listened while Elizabeth explained about how she had found the drugs in her casita. She told Mendoza that everyone else in their group, including her husband Richard, had gone to the Heard Museum for a special tour and lunch. She told the detective that she'd been too tired to go to the museum with the others.

"I don't normally do drug cases." Detective Mendoza was quick to set the record straight. "Officially, I'm homicide, but the murder investigation here at the Mimosa Inn from last night is already my case. I think your discovery of the fentanyl might be related to the other things that have happened there. I'm coming right over. Don't let anyone else in the room until I get there. Just don't touch anything at all if you can help it. Especially don't touch any of the packages of drugs. Please text or call your husband and ask him not to come to the room when he returns from his trip to the Heard Museum. Suggest he wait in the lobby or wait in the room of another couple in your group. I will text you when I am outside the door to your room. Don't answer the door for anyone else. I will be there in about fifteen minutes."

Elizabeth hadn't told Mendoza that she had already touched one of the bags of drugs, but she would tell her about that when she arrived at the casita. Elizabeth scrubbed her hands with soap and hot water. Then she doused them in hydrogen peroxide. She did not really think the fentanyl was any danger to her, but she washed her hands with a vengeance, just to be sure. The plastic bags the drugs had been wrapped in seemed thick and sturdy enough. She had opened one plastic bag, but she had not touched the tablets. She knew that just a few grains of fentanyl could be lethal.

The fifteen minutes until Cecilia Mendoza arrived were just about the longest fifteen minutes of Elizabeth's life. Cecilia had said not to touch anything, but Elizabeth had taken off her robe and nightgown and pulled on a turtleneck and a dark gray warm-up suit. She sat on the opposite side of the suite from the fireplace, as far away from the drugs as she could get. But she kept her eyes on the colorful pot and on the package of fentanyl.

Richard was going to be furious, especially when Elizabeth told him he couldn't come back to the room. He said she was always getting herself into something that was none of her concern. He said she needed to mind her own business and stay out of other people's problems. He didn't say too much, but she could tell when he was angry and worried about her. He had been supportive when she had gone all out to rescue Henley, but he'd been hugely relieved when Elizabeth had finally finished bringing Henley home. Richard wanted the two of them to have a nice quiet retirement, but Elizabeth's life just wasn't working out that way.

After a morning traipsing through a museum and then a long lunch with the reunion group, Richard would be more than ready for his nap when he got back to the Mimosa Inn. Now she was going to have to text him and tell him that he couldn't come back to their room. He wouldn't understand,

and he would be fussing. She sent a carefully worded text in which she told her husband not to worry, but that he could not come to their room for a while. Elizabeth assured him that she was perfectly fine.

Finally Cecilia Mendoza texted Elizabeth that she was outside the door of her room. Elizabeth opened the door and was incredibly happy to see the redheaded detective. The detective looked exhausted, as if she had not slept at all the night before. Elizabeth felt guilty that she'd called her. She realized the detective had probably been up most of the previous night.

Mendoza had brought another young woman with her, a CSI whose specialty was handling drug busts. Cecilia introduced her as Marcia Onacona. She nodded to Elizabeth. Marcia was wearing a white protective suit over her clothing and looked as if she would be on top of every detail there was to find at a crime scene. Elizabeth was very glad to have both of these women here in her room to take charge of things. Hopefully they would take the fentanyl off her hands and far away.

Marcia immediately spotted the package of drugs on the raised hearth of the fireplace and began her work. She'd brought a large kit with her, and in a few seconds and without a word, she had set up what looked like a mini laboratory. Cecilia suggested that she and Elizabeth talk outside on the patio while Marcia worked in the room. Elizabeth put on her shoes and her jacket and joined Cecilia outside.

The detective took Elizabeth through her story again. She told Elizabeth she was recording everything. This time, Elizabeth added the information that she thought someone had been inside their casita the night before last. She explained that she didn't have any proof, but she was pretty sure several things in the casita had been moved. She told Cecilia that she'd noticed her toiletries in the bathroom had been rearranged. Elizabeth told her that the steps she used to get into the bed were in a slightly different location when she and Richard had returned to the room that night. The steps had been pushed to one side as if someone might have looked under the bed. Elizabeth had the distinct feeling that there had been someone in the casita while they'd been at the Mimosa Inn's restaurant for dinner. Elizabeth also told Cecilia she had wondered if whoever was breaking into the resort's guest rooms and looking for something had mixed up rooms #167 and #161.

"When I found the drugs in the room today, I began to wonder how long it had been since anyone had occupied this suite. It's a handicap accessible casita, and the Mimosa would probably not give this room to a non-handicapped guest. It's also a very expensive room. Most people who want a handicapped room don't want to pay the $875 per night room fee. That's what the Mimosa normally charges for this casita. We only have this luxurious suite because neither one of the other two standard handicapped accessible rooms was available to us. One of the standard handicap rooms is undergoing an extensive renovation, and the other one, the one we were supposed to be in, had a problem with the HVAC at the last minute. The Mimosa Inn gave us this suite at the rate we would have paid for the standard accessible casita." Elizabeth paused to see if the detective was giving any credence to her theories.

"I hear what you are saying. Please continue."

Elizabeth's information was based strictly on her own impressions, but Cecilia seemed to be paying attention. "We had to wait until the staff got the room ready for us. I had the distinct feeling this room wasn't used very often, and they had to mobilize the cleaning people and rush around to clean it and get it ready for us. I think they may have had to put sheets on the bed and otherwise make the casita presentable for somebody to stay here. When we finally got to the suite, it smelled musty...unused. I was sure they'd not turned the heat on in here for quite a while. The cleaning people turned on the gas fireplace to warm the room up more quickly and to get rid of the musty smell. Everything was perfectly clean by the time the staff finally brought us here, but I could tell that no one else had stayed in this room for weeks or even months."

Elizabeth continued. "Everyone on the staff at the Mimosa and everyone in housekeeping would know this room was vacant most of the time. It would have been the perfect place to hide the drugs and the perfect drop for one drug trafficker to leave his wares for the next drug trafficker to pick up. Or, one dealer might leave the drugs and come back later to pick up his money. Who knows? What I am certain about it that no other guests have been staying in this room for a while. Housekeeping never came in to clean because hardly anyone ever stayed in this casita. It would have been the ideal place to use as a drug drop. Nobody was supposed to be in this room at all, and nobody was until the Mimosa Inn put us in here because they didn't have any place else to put us. Only a couple of people would have known that we'd been moved to this room. It was a very last-minute thing."

Elizabeth was glad she had shared all of her hypotheses with the law enforcement officer. "This is just speculation on my part, of course. But I wanted you to know that someone was definitely in the room the second night we were here. And I wanted you to know that I don't think anyone had slept in this casita for a long time until they gave it to us. It's been empty for a while. No one would have known we were going to move into this suite. It all happened quickly... and at the last minute. We got this room because the HVAC in the room we were supposed to have was unexpectedly on the fritz. Of course, you can easily check how often this room has had anyone staying in it by asking the people at the front desk about the occupancy of the casita."

Nine

Marcia, the crime scene technician, stuck her head out the door. "I'm done in here for now. I have quite a few things to take back to the lab. I'm taking this beautiful vase with me, of course."

Cecilia had been paying attention to what Elizabeth had been telling her because she told Marcia to check the steps beside the bed for fingerprints. She explained that Elizabeth thought there had been someone in the room the night before last. Elizabeth thought they might have moved the steps she used to get up into the king-sized bed. Cecilia told Marcia someone might have moved the steps in order to look under the bed. Marcia went back into the room to see if she could lift some fingerprints from the set of steps.

Cecilia spoke to Elizabeth. "Of course, you know that you and your husband will have to have your fingerprints taken...for elimination purposes. We will take yours now and catch your husband when he gets back from his trip to the Heard." Elizabeth cringed. Richard would be furious when he was told he had to have his fingerprints taken.

When they went back inside the suite, Marcia was packing up her gear. "I tried to clean up the fingerprint powder. I know it's really inconvenient and difficult to have to scrub that off of everything."

Elizabeth sat in the chair by the fireplace while Marcia took her fingerprints. She handed Elizabeth something like a wet wipe that did a pretty good job of removing the ink from her fingers. "You'll also want to give your hands a good scrubbing." She told Elizabeth.

Marcia put away the last of her mobile laboratory and carried her bags and boxes to the patio. "I'll load all of this up in the golf cart and take it to the van. I'll come back for you, detective, when I've locked everything up." Elizabeth had been so focused on telling her story to the detective, she hadn't noticed they'd arrived in a golf cart.

"We borrowed a cart from the Mimosa. They would rather we ride around in their golf carts like everybody else does. We are less conspicuous that way. It makes them nervous to have cops around. And that's understandable. When people are paying as much as they are paying to stay here, nobody wants to hear about break-ins or drugs, let alone murders. This is Paradise Valley after all." Cecilia gave Elizabeth a small smile. "I don't think we've left you with a big mess, but I am going to talk to the manager and have housekeeping come and give the place a good going over. I think we have everything we're going to get from your room...in terms of fingerprints. Marcia checked all the other possible hiding places in the casita, and we didn't find anything...no drugs and no money."

Elizabeth nodded. She was so relieved that the bags of fentanyl were going to be gone from the room. Now all she had to worry about was explaining to Richard what had happened, why he hadn't been allowed back in their room, and why he had to have his fingerprints taken. At least the drugs were out of the room. Richard wouldn't have to look at them, but he would still be upset that Elizabeth had found them.

The group was meeting in the Ritter's cottage for a showing of Matthew's movie montages this evening before dinner. The Ritters had reserved a large suite because they had anticipated the group would gather in their casita for the movie showings. Tonight Matthew had, in addition to his famous montages, slides of his favorite works of art. He would show the art work and talk a little bit about that, and then he would move on to the movie montages.

Of course, no one else in the group knew anything about what had happened with Matthew and Isabelle and the person in the body bag. No one knew anything about the mobile hospital vehicle that had arrived the night before. No one suspected that there was a patient in critical condition recovering from surgery in the casita next door to the Ritter's.

Freddy Kernigan had returned to the Mimosa in his car to take over caring for the woman he'd just operated on. He'd made several trips with the luggage cart, bringing supplies to fully equip the recovery room he was setting up. Because Freddy was confident and a bit of an actor, no one questioned him when he commandeered the luggage cart, filled it with odd looking containers, and pushed it along the pathways to the cottage next door to the Ritter's. Isabelle was enormously relieved that the patient hadn't died on her watch, and she was more than ready to turn things over to Freddy when he arrived with his life-saving equipment.

The Camp Shoemaker group was ordering pizzas and salads and subs for dinner that night. Matthew had a case of IPA beers and several bottles of red and white wines on ice. The group would watch Matthew's movie montages and eat pizza and enjoy each other's company. It would be an informal night spent in the Ritter's suite. Elizabeth thought Matthew looked very tired and was not his usual exuberant self when he talked about his movies. He was trying hard to exhibit his well-known Captain Sunshine enthusiasm, but he seemed tired to the bone. He also seemed preoccupied. None of the others in the group, only the Ritters, had any idea what was going on in the casita right next door to the pizza party. After the movie montages and the Italian meal, everyone helped clean up and went back to their casitas early. Matthew and Isabelle checked in with Freddy and then collapsed into bed. Freddy Kernigan was sleeping on the couch in the casita next door so he could keep a close eye on his post-op patient.

🌲

Detective Mendoza had managed to drive the empty coroner's van away from the scene and return it to the Phoenix police department. She had managed to explain to her boss why it had been necessary for her to leave the body with the FBI. She'd had to lie about the timeline, about exactly how it had all happened, and about everything else. But she thought she'd successfully explained why the FBI was taking over the investigation. She let her boss know that she was to be included as part of the FBI team, and she promised to keep him fully informed. There were so many crimes to be investigated in the Phoenix area these days, Cecilia didn't get too much pushback from her superiors about allowing the FBI to take the lead in this particular homicide. It was a tricky situation anyway, dealing with a murder at an exclusive and expensive resort. The entire mess had to be handled with extra care and discretion. Cecilia sensed her captain was relieved that he didn't have to get involved in this one.

When she felt she'd managed things to the best of her ability with her own department, she again called the agent she was working with at the FBI. The situation was out of control, and they had some serious decisions to make.

"I've checked in with the Ritters, and they say they're pretty confident that our witness is going to pull through. She was badly beaten with something... probably a baseball bat. Then she was attacked with a machete and really badly cut. That's what caused most of the bleeding—the machete. She also had all these small lacerations and puncture wounds. Those were caused by some other kid of knife. It looked to me like the perpetrator or perpetrators had probably tortured her, trying to get her to tell them something. I am almost certain there were two of them. That's just my opinion. It appeared to me as if they hadn't finished the job... that they hadn't really searched the room. I think they were starting to search the room when they got spooked. Maybe there was a noise outside or next door, I don't know. But they left in a hurry, all of a sudden... before they finished their search. I think. I'm sure they believed Annika was dead. There was certainly enough blood on the floor and around the room that they could have thought they'd finished her off. And they almost had. They must not have checked her pulse carefully enough. Or maybe they didn't check it at all."

Cecilia listened closely to the questions the FBI agent had for her about the attack. She thought she had most of the answers.

"We have her computer and her phone. She'd put them both into a tote bag along with some toiletries. I think she was just getting ready to leave to go to the other casita, the one next door to where the doctor and his wife are staying. She was almost away. She'd almost made it. It looked to me as if she'd pushed the tote bag down between the bed and the wall—probably when her attackers came into the room. She didn't want whoever had come into her room to find that bag. It was pretty well hidden. If the attackers were moving quickly, and I think they were, they would not have been able to find the tote bag without a thorough search of the room. I'm sure that whoever did this would like to have taken her computer and her phone, but they didn't get them. Thank goodness they left when they did. Even though they probably thought they'd killed her, at least they left before they decided to put a bullet in her brain."

Cecilia listened to more questions from the FBI agent.

"That is the big question, of course. Given the enormous stash of fentanyl this other guest at the Mimosa Inn found hidden in her room today, we just don't know who it was who attacked Annika. It could have been the dealer who was desperate to find his supply of drugs. Somebody could be really angry that their bags of fentanyl have gone missing. Of course, Annika didn't know anything about that. She would not have been able to tell the people who attacked her anything at all about the drugs, no matter how much they tortured her. And of course, the drugs were not hidden in her casita at all…in either one of her casitas. Somebody messed up, I guess. Whoever was looking for the fentanyl was looking in all the wrong places and in all the wrong casitas."

Mendoza listened again. "Yes, the people in the room where the drugs were found were very lucky. The woman who found the drugs thinks someone was in their room two nights earlier looking for something. I believe her. She's old, but she seems sharp and very observant. If someone was in their casita looking for the drugs, they didn't find them, of course. This older woman found them today. I just hope that whoever searched Annika's casita and may have tortured her to try to force her to tell them where they were hidden — if that's what happened — doesn't decide to break into these other people's room again and either ransack the place or attack them. The people in that room are an older couple. The wife is a writer, and she has very bad arthritis. She is staying on at the Mimosa Inn for another week — in the room where she found the drugs. Her husband is going bird hunting with Dr. Ritter. They are old friends from years ago. Ritter is an avid quail hunter, and I do mean avid. He hunts quail several days a week, at least, during the quail hunting season. The other doctor's wife, Mrs. Carpenter, the writer, will be here alone in the casita... every day and every night. She's disabled, so she will probably stay in the room most of the time. She says she plans to spend the time she has alone working on her next book."

Cecilia continued. "If Annika wasn't attacked because someone was looking for the fentanyl stash, it probably was her husband who sent his men to torture and kill her. All along, Annika has maintained that she's positive Igor didn't have any idea she was planning to leave him. I tend to believe her. Of course, he might have suspected something. Maybe he'd detected something suspicious about her behavior that led him to think she was up to something. Of course, he never would have done this himself. I mean, he never would have committed the actual crime. He would have sent an underling or two to take care of the wife while he arranged a perfect alibi for himself. If he wanted to kill her, he would have hired an assassin. That's what all these drug guys do. Their hands are always impeccably clean when it comes to actually charging them with a crime. They pay big bucks to have their hit men take care of things. Having said that, I really don't think this was a hit arranged by her husband. Of course, I'm sure he knows by now that she was attacked, and hopefully, because of the way we've set things up, he thinks she was killed as a result."

The detective was looking ahead to what might result from the attack on Annika. "I don't know what is going on among the various drug lords right now. I'm homicide. My duties often overlap with our narcotics division and with the DEA's work, but I don't really know as much as I wish I did about the various drug dealers. Their hierarchies and their disputes over turf are pretty much a mystery to me. I know they are always killing each other and fighting over who is going to be in control of certain territory. There is so much money involved, it seems like they spend a lot of their time just protecting their piece of the action from other drug dealers. I know enough about how these drug gangs work that I'm guessing a war of some kind among them may result from the public report of Annika's death."

Detective Cecilia Mendoza was not convinced that Igor Castillo, as terrible a person as he was, had been responsible for his wife's murder. "A drug war might also get started because of the twenty pounds of fentanyl tablets we now have in our possession. Somebody, sooner or later, is going to miss those drugs. In fact, I think they already have. That might be why Annika was attacked. Drug wars have broken out for less. I don't know for sure, but my gut instinct is that the attack on Annika was not instigated by Igor and his gang of bad guys. We will have to see what shakes out, but I am betting the husband didn't order this done to her. He was spending more and more time in Mexico and away from his home with Annika. He probably has a new woman he's spending time with. Supposedly, Igor and Annika were fighting all the time, but I don't think the situation had reached the point where he was ready to kill her off. I may be completely wrong on this. The good thing is I think she is going to recover. I am going to urge the Ritters to get her to the safe house the minute it's okay for her to be moved. She needs to get away from the Mimosa Inn and away from Phoenix. I don't know where the safe house is, but I suspect it's in California... somewhere close to where the Ritters live in Palm Springs. That's just my best guess at this point."

Cecilia listened again to the comments and questions from the FBI agent.

"We all agreed that the best thing was for us not to know anything about where she was living when she went into hiding. We decided at the outset, because of all the leaks at the FBI as well as at Phoenix PD, only the Ritters and Annika would know where her safe house is located. Of course, her mother also knows, or did know, but her mother has now had a second stroke and is not expected to make it this time. So sad for Annika. Apparently they were estranged for years. After they finally worked things out and made all these plans for Annika to leave her husband, the mother had her first stroke. Now she's had a second stroke.

It's a tragic story all the way around. I hope Annika recovers from this horrible attack and the Ritters can get her to the safe house...wherever it is. I'll let you know if there is any fingerprint or DNA evidence when my CSI is finished with her tests."

The Katyn Forest Massacre

1940

Ten

If it is not one of the most remarkable stories of the twentieth century, it is certainly one of the most remarkable stories of World War II. The Katyn Forest massacre and the disappearance of thousands of Polish military men and leaders of Polish society in 1940 is astonishing for several reasons. The actual facts about the events that resulted in the murders of these Polish citizens are shocking and difficult to believe. The extremes to which the Soviet Union went to lie about and cover up their crimes, represented an unprecedented effort to deceive the world. The number and variety of investigations into this crime are surprising, especially when one considers how little is publicly known, to this day, about such a horrific genocide.

But perhaps the most amazing piece of the entire saga is the complicity of top level Allied leaders in keeping this secret, in keeping the truth from becoming known. Churchill and Roosevelt knew the truth about the Katyn massacre as early as 1943. To keep the Allied coalition together, they chose to ignore the atrocity, if not lie about it. To publicly or even privately acknowledge the true story of this horrible Soviet crime would have endangered, and possibly shattered, the relationship between the Western allies and the Soviet Union. Keeping the anti-Nazi alliance intact took precedence over acknowledging an atrocity that was committed by one of those allies. Holding the Allied coalition together took precedence over admitting the truth.

Both Roosevelt and Churchill knew the truth about the genocide, but both leaders chose to pretend it hadn't happened. The priority was to win the war against the Nazis. The crimes committed by the Soviet Union in the Katyn Forest are not close to being of the same magnitude as the atrocities committed by the Nazis against Europe's Jews. The Soviet Union committed crimes that were commensurate with what the Germans did in terms of wickedness, albeit on a much smaller scale. The Polish genocide was swept under the rug for decades.

There is no question that the Soviet Union committed the atrocities and murdered thousands of Polish citizens in cold blood in the Katyn Forest. The Germans discovered the murders and blamed them on the Soviet Union. The Soviets in turn tried to blame the murders on the Germans. Because the Nazis had committed so many atrocities of their own, it was easy and convenient to believe that they had also committed the atrocities of the Katyn Forest. German efforts to blame the Soviets for the mass murder, in fact to tell the truth about these crimes, were generally dismissed as German propaganda designed to create a schism between the Soviet Union and its allies.

The Soviet Union was desperate to hide the evil acts they had committed against the nation of Poland in the spring of

1940. The Western Allies were complicit in their desperation to hide the truth. If the Soviet Union turned against the Western Allies or if the Soviets made a separate peace with Germany, the Nazis might have won the war. This is what the leaders of the United States and Great Britain feared might happen. So they joined with Joseph Stalin in a conspiracy of silence to smother the story about the disappearance and murder of as many as 25,000 Polish citizens.

Even after the war, the Nuremberg Trials failed to acknowledge the truth of these horrendous war crimes committed by the Soviet Union. Even after countless investigations by various groups throughout the world, including an investigation by the Congress of the United States in the 1950s, there was no outcry against the guilty. Little is known about what really happened in the Katyn Forest, and nothing is known about what happened to the other Polish men who disappeared into thin air. The truth has continued to be buried.

🌲

A few days before Hitler invaded Poland on September 1, 1939, and began World War II, Nazi Germany and the Soviet Union signed a mutual non-aggression pact. Known as the Molotov-Ribbentrop Pact, the two countries reached the agreement on the 23rd of August 1939. Hitler's goal in convincing the Soviet Union to sign this agreement was to keep the Russians out of the war he was about to begin. The pact stated that the two countries would not attack each other for ten years, and Germany and the USSR secretly divided the countries that lay between them. Germany would claim Western Poland and part of Lithuania. The Soviet Union would claim Eastern Poland, Estonia, Latvia, and other territories as part of its sphere of influence.

This short-lived alliance allowed Hitler to begin World War II by attacking Poland without fear of Soviet intervention. Hitler invaded Poland from the west on September 1, 1939. The Soviet Union invaded Poland from the east on September 17, 1939. Poland was divided between the two aggressors. These invaders, Germany and the Soviet Union, declared that Poland was no longer a country. The prearranged territorial dismemberment of Poland gave Germany 72,806 square miles of Polish land (22 million people). The USSR gained 77,020 square miles of Polish territory (16 million people). This last-minute pact between the two countries held until the summer of 1941 when Hitler, without warning, turned on his former ally and invaded the Soviet Union by initiating Operation Barbarossa.

In June of 1941, during the early days of Operation Barbarossa, the German army invaded the USSR. The Soviet Union had occupied eastern Poland from the fall of 1939 until the late summer of 1941. In the late summer and early fall of 1941, after the launch of Operation Barbarossa, both the country of Poland as well as large parts of the western Soviet Union were attacked and occupied by Germany.

It is critical to determine which country occupied this Soviet territory where the mass graves were found and when they occupied it. Because previous to the late summer and early fall of 1941 the Soviet Union occupied the area where the mass graves were found in the Katyn Forest, all atrocities are, without question, entirely attributable to the Soviet

Union. The Germans did not arrive in and occupy the western Soviet Union until the late summer of 1941.

After the mass graves were discovered at Katyn in 1943, and for the ensuing many decades, the Soviet Union tried to blame the Germans for the massacre that the USSR's own NKVD had perpetrated in the Katyn Forest in April and May of 1940.

How can thousands of people disappear and leave no evidence of where they have gone? This may seem impossible, but it happened in Poland in 1940. The mass graves of some of those who disappeared have been found, but the majority of those who vanished left no traces whatsoever. The atrocity of the Katyn Forest massacre was covered up by the Soviet Union for nearly fifty years. The lies the Communist government told about this horrendous event were on a global scale. The lies began under Stalin but continued under all the subsequent demagogues who ruled the Soviet Union until Mikhail Gorbachev decided to reveal the truth on April 13, 1990.

In September of 1939, thousands of citizens who lived in eastern Poland were arrested by the advancing armies of the Soviet Union. When the Soviet Union invaded, they arrested and imprisoned thousands of Polish military officers and other Polish leaders. Many of these men had civilian occupations and had been called up from the reserves in 1939. In addition to almost half of the Polish military officer corps, the Soviets imprisoned members of the Polish intelligentsia.

Doctors, lawyers, high school teachers, university professors, scientists, artists, clerics, and others were taken from their homes and deported to prison camps that were inside the Soviet Union. These Polish leaders, who were mostly men and were taken to camps in the Soviet Union, have been described as the "flower of Polish society" and "the brain and heart of Poland."

The Soviets arrested and imprisoned these Polish citizens whom they believed would not, in the long run, be willing to accept and live under Communist rule. The Soviets were planning to stay in Poland for the long term. They had decided that Poland would no longer exist as a nation. According to the plans the USSR had for Poland, Polish territory had become and would remain a part of the Soviet Union.

With the arrests of the intelligentsia, the Soviets hoped to eliminate from the Polish population the leaders they believed would be most likely to resist Communist rule. The Soviets intended to impose communism on the people of Poland, and the Russians did not think the Polish intelligentsia would be willing to cooperate with an occupying Communist government and its ideology. These influential members of Polish society would be troublemakers, the protesters who would object and speak out against communism under the Soviet Union.

At least fifteen thousand Polish military officers and other Polish leaders were arrested and sent to three prison camps in Soviet territory. These three Soviet prison camps were Camp Kozelsk (5,000 Polish prisoners), Camp Ostashkov (6,570 Polish prisoners), and Camp Starobelsk (4,000 Polish prisoners). A total of 15,570 Polish prisoners of war were known to be imprisoned in these three Soviet camps by November of 1939.

The Katyn Forest Massacre, 1940

After the Soviets had arrested and imprisoned the Polish leaders, the Soviets conducted a significant indoctrination campaign within the prison camps to try to convince the inmates to become Communists. The Soviets had some hope they might be able to propagandize at least some members of the intelligentsia of Poland, to convince them of the superiority of communism. But the Soviet attempts to sell their totalitarian political system and state control of the economy to the Poles were a complete and utter failure. These Polish leaders said no to communism.

In the end, less than 448, of the more than 15,000 who had been arrested, would be deemed to be able to be manipulated into becoming Communists. The Soviets determined that some of these 448 were susceptible to manipulation or were already convinced that communism was the way, the truth, and the light. It was decided that the rest of the Poles who were held in the three prison camps, in fact the vast majority of the prisoners, were too dedicated to traditional values and the politics of freedom to ever accept communism as a way of life. The majority of Polish prisoners would never accept pro-Soviet attitudes.

In the eyes of the Communists, most of the prisoners who were interned in the three prison camps, the Polish military officers and the intellectual and professional elites, were bourgeoisie. The bourgeoisie were the enemies of the Communist state. The Soviets knew that the majority of these Polish leaders who were their prisoners would never accept or agree to live under communism.

Because the prisoners were the cream of the Polish nation, the Soviets feared that these leaders would be able to sway and convince the populace, the citizens of Poland, to oppose communism. That could not be allowed to happen. These leaders of the Polish people, these enemies of communism, which consisted of most of the prisoners in the Soviet prison camps, therefore had to be eliminated. These Polish leaders had to disappear forever.

Only the 448 prisoners, singled out from the more than fifteen thousand, were chosen to be allowed to live. Some estimates are that only 400 out of thousands were chosen to live. These few had been selected to be spared because the Soviets, after extensive interviews with the Polish prisoners in the camps, had determined that some of these 400+ prisoners might eventually make good Bolsheviks.

The rest of the thousands of Polish prisoners who had been incarcerated by the Soviet Union disappeared entirely. By early May of 1940 all three of the Soviet prison camps had been completely evacuated by the Soviet authorities. The camps were empty. Almost all of the human beings who had inhabited these Soviet prison camps were never heard from again. How could this happen? How was it possible for all of these men to just vanish?

The 448 prisoners who would not be murdered had been selected from the three Soviet camps. They were transferred to Camp Grazovec. They would be the only prisoners from the original 15,000 plus who would ever be found alive or ever be heard from again. Except for these 448, all of those imprisoned in the three Soviet camps had completely disappeared off the face of the earth by the early spring of 1940. In fact, they had been sentenced to death. They were exterminated. The Soviets murdered them and hid their bodies.

A few of the 448 chosen to live were spared execution because of special circumstances unrelated to their political beliefs. These few were spared for a variety of other reasons and were not thought to be candidates for conversion to communism. Thousands of Polish prisoners held in the Soviet prison camps had been interviewed and analyzed by their Soviet captors. The Soviets finally determined that fewer than 448 could be manipulated and might be convinced to accept Communist rule.

The Polish prisoners in the three Soviet camps had been writing letters to their families in Poland since December 1939. The letters stopped abruptly in April 1940. No letters were sent from these prison camps after the early spring of 1940. No family member or friend received a letter sent from any of these prison camps after the spring of 1940. Letters written to the prisoners from their families were being returned to sender by the Soviet Post Office as of April 1940. The letters were stamped "mail could not be delivered." All communications between the Polish prisoners and the outside world had ceased.

When the Polish prisoners held in these camps stopped writing letters home to their loved ones, the Polish Government in Exile in England and other humanitarian organizations began investigating to try to determine what had happened to these men. They could no longer be found in any prison camp in the Soviet Union. None of them could be found in any German prisoner-of-war camps. They could not be found anywhere. Only the 448 Polish citizens, those who had been chosen to be allowed to live, out of the thousands who had previously been in the three prison camps in the Soviet Union, were ever found alive.

The families of those who had disappeared were desperate to find out what had happened to their loved ones who had been imprisoned by the Soviets. Where were these people? What had happened to them? Not a word had been heard from any of them since April of 1940. Everyone knew the prisoners had been evacuated from the three Soviet prison camps in the spring of 1940, but no one seemed to have any idea where the men had gone.

The 448 prisoners who had been transferred to Camp Grazovec confirmed that all of their compatriots from the three Soviet camps had been evacuated in the early spring of 1940. These few remaining prisoners were able to reconstruct, from memory, lists of the names of the missing men. Among the more than fifteen thousand missing were 8,300 to 8,400 Polish military officers. There were 800 doctors who had gone missing. Every attempt to find these men failed. Polish, British, and American diplomats searched for them in vain for more than two years.

▲

When Hitler began Operation Barbarossa in June of 1941 and turned on his former ally, the Soviet Union did an about face and joined with the allied forces of Britain and France to fight the Germans. At this point in the war, the allies discussed the possibility that a Polish military force, commanded by Polish General Wladyslav Anders, might be formed to fight the Nazis. But scarcely any Polish officers could be found to lead this potential force. What had happened to all the military officers? Once the Soviet Union had become an ally of England and France, a number of investigations were initiated by General Wladyslaw Sikorski who led the Polish Government in Exile in England. Other investigations were begun by various ambassadors to the Soviet Union from Western countries, as well as by other organizations, including members of the press. All were desperate to locate the missing soldiers and other Polish leaders.

In May of 1942, Admiral William H. Standley, the American ambassador to the Soviet Union initiated an investigation into the whereabouts of the missing Polish citizens. The eminent and well-known Soviet writer, Ilya Ehrenburg, took up the cause. Searches for these men were undertaken at the informal level as well as at official and diplomatic levels, and these investigations were intense. All of these inquiries were met, on the part of the Soviet Union, with silence or with evasive and outlandish answers.

There were many questions, and none of the answers to the many inquiries were satisfactory. The Soviet Union's responses, to those who were asking questions about what had happened to the missing officers and members of the Polish intelligentsia, were all lies. The answers to the world's questions were diverse and even nonsensical. None of the answers were believable. Forced to say something about what had happened to these men who had disappeared from their prison camps, the Soviets invented a number of implausible, and mostly impossible, stories about what had happened to their prisoners.

The Soviets claimed the missing Poles were now in a German prison camp. One of the false stories the Soviets reported was that the missing prisoners had been engaged in roadwork and had been taken into custody by the Germans during the German advance into Soviet territory as part of Operation Barbarossa. Another answer given by the Soviet Union was that the men had been transferred from the Soviet prison camps and imprisoned in German POW camps as part of the German invasion of the Soviet Union.

These explanations were easily disproved because not a single one of the missing prisoners could be found anywhere in any German prison camp.

Soviet leaders claimed, in one response that is as embarrassing as it is puzzling, that these missing men had been transferred to an unknown Soviet camp somewhere and that their whereabouts were unknown. Had the Soviets really lost more than 15,000 of their own prisoners and had no idea where they had put them?

Another unlikely explanation given by the Soviets about why the men could not be located was that the prisoners had all been set free from the Soviet camps and had been returned to Poland. At one point, Soviet authorities claimed that the prisoners had all gone home to their families and communities in Poland. This was a ridiculous explanation as there was not a trace of even one of these supposedly "freed" men to be found in Poland or anywhere else on the face of the earth. This explanation was an obvious and even laughable lie.

Another explanation, given to the Poles by Stalin himself, was that every single one of the Polish military personnel and other Poles being held in the three Soviet prison camps, had escaped. When asked where they had escaped to, Stalin replied that they had escaped to Manchuria. Anyone who has ever looked at a map could see that Stalin's answer was completely ridiculous. One has to wonder if Stalin had any idea where in the world Manchuria was actually located. Had the man ever taken a geography class or ever looked at a map?

Not one of these explanations about the disappearance of thousands was the least bit adequate or the least bit believable. In spite of relentless inquiries and investigations as to what had happened to these thousands of human beings, officials of the Soviet government denied knowing anything at all about where they were.

🌲

More than fifty inquiries were initiated to try to find the missing prisoners. Not a clue about what had happened to these missing men was ever discovered...until 1943. The search continued. By April of 1943, the Germans had advanced into the Soviet Union and were in control of territory in western Russia, specifically territory in the area of the Katyn Forest. It was not until April 13, 1943, that any trace at all was discovered about any of the thousands of Polish leaders who had simply disappeared in 1940.

Eleven

In April of 1943, the German military occupied the Katyn Forest, an area which had formerly been a part of the Soviet Union. The Katyn Forest is located inside the country of Russia. Ten miles west of the Russian city of Smolensk, the first mass grave filled with the bodies of murdered Polish military officers was discovered by the German army. The Nazis subsequently discovered a number of mass graves in the Katyn Forest and unearthed the horrible crime that had been committed by the Soviet Union. By 1943, the Soviet Union had joined the Allied cause, and the Germans were more than anxious to blame the Soviets for the deaths they had uncovered at Katyn.

The Germans knew this was one atrocity they had not committed. They knew the Soviets had committed the genocide, and the Germans thought they could use the discovery of the mass graves and the deaths of thousands of Polish citizens to their advantage. In 1943, the Soviets were fighting alongside Britain, France, the United States, and others. The

Germans saw the Katyn Forest massacre, which they knew had been committed by the Soviet Union, as an opportunity to cause a rift in the Allied coalition. The Germans exaggerated the number of bodies that had been found in an attempt to dramatize the ferocity of the massacre. They used the discoveries in Katyn as propaganda to try to destroy the Soviets in the eyes of their coalition partners.

Because the Germans had a well-known record of atrocities, public opinion supported the view that the Germans had committed the Katyn Forest atrocity. It was just one more in a list of many. It was plausible and possible that the Germans had committed the murders in the Katyn Forest. But it was also plausible and possible that the Soviets had committed these murders. One side blamed the other. It was inevitable that any investigation would be manipulated by propagandists from all sides. The Katyn Forest massacre became a political football.

The Soviets and Stalin vociferously denied knowing anything about the Katyn Forest massacre. Western Allied leaders did not want to believe that the Soviets had committed these horrific crimes. It was much more convenient to blame it all on their common enemy, the Nazis. But the Nazis had not done this.

After the gruesome discovery was made in the Katyn forest in 1943 and for years afterwards, many international commissions were formed. Investigations were initiated with the goal of attempting to determine who had killed the thousands of Polish citizens who were interred in the mass graves found in the Katyn Forest. The German Government invited an independent international commission to investigate. The Polish Red Cross Commission did its own investigation, independent of all the others. They wanted to be certain this was not one of Herr Joseph Goebbels' hoaxes. The German Special Medical-Judiciary Commission and other independent commissions conducted investigations into the deaths.

The international commission, made up of distinguished scholars and specialists in forensic medicine from all over Europe, invited well-known forensic pathologists to examine the crime scene and the corpses. Bodies were exhumed and autopsied. Internationally recognized scientists from Switzerland, Italy, Hungary, Denmark, Belgium, Spain, Norway, Sweden, Croatia, Holland, and other countries all agreed on their findings. In fact, all of the non-Soviet commissions that investigated, even the ones that were virulently anti-Nazi, agreed unanimously that the Soviet Union was responsible for the massacre.

The International Red Cross offered to do its own independent investigation. But it would only do an investigation if all interested parties agreed to allow them to investigate. The Germans and the Poles immediately agreed, but the Soviet Union refused to give its approval for the investigation and in effect blocked the International Red Cross offer to investigate. The Germans offered every assistance to the International Red Cross. They were anxious to have an impartial organization investigate the Katyn murders. This was further circumstantial evidence that the Germans had not committed these crimes. The Germans knew that an unbiased investigation would exonerate them of the murders. But because the Soviet Union did not agree, the International Red Cross did not do an investigation.

From the time the bodies were discovered in the Katyn Forest graves in 1943, the Soviets tried to block any and all investigations by those other than themselves. They absolutely did not want any impartial observers or experts examining the Katyn site or the bodies in the graves. The Soviets initiated several bogus investigations of their own. The Soviets maintained that the Germans had committed the Katyn murders and were blaming the Soviet Union in an attempt to break apart the Allied coalition that was fighting against them in the war. In fact parties on all sides were exaggerating and lying and dramatizing. The Soviets, the Germans, and the Poles were all attempting to manipulate the situation for their own ends.

The Soviet Commission was formed and did an investigation of its own in an attempt to refute the findings of the legitimate investigations. The Soviet Commission report failed to address any of the real facts that had been found by others. The Communists ignored completely any and all of the things that could not be falsified. The Soviet Commission report failed to mention the evidence of the spruce trees, the rope that bound the hands of the corpses, the evidence left behind by the four-cornered bayonets, the winter coats the dead were wearing when they were killed, and a myriad of other evidence that proved the Soviets had committed the crimes. The Soviet Commission report simply ignored the facts altogether.

🌲

In April and May of 1940, when they committed their terrible crimes, the Soviet Union did not have a crystal ball. They could not have anticipated that their German allies would turn against them in June of 1941 with Operation Barbarossa. The Soviet Union could not have imagined that they would be forced to cede any of their own sovereign territory to an invading German army. They could not have imagined that they would not always be in control of land that was actually inside the country of Russia. They could not have known that in a little more than a year, the Germans would become their enemies, would attack the Soviet Union, would occupy large tracts of former Soviet territory, and would dig up bodies in the Katyn Forest. The Soviets believed that they would always rule over the Katyn Forest which is in Russia. They thought their terrible secrets which were buried there were safe forever. Their evil deeds would never be discovered. No one would ever be allowed to dig in the Russian forest.

The Soviets could not have known that the little spruce trees they had transplanted to try to cover up the graves of the thousands they had murdered would actually lead the way for German soldiers to discover where the mass graves were located. The Soviets did not know that they would lose control of parts of their country and that the evidence of their evil deeds would be uncovered for all the world to see.

It was important to determine how these dead men in the mass graves had died. But it was even more important to determine *when* these men had died. If they had died in 1940, as the Germans claimed, the Soviet Union was responsible for the massacre. If the men had died during or after the summer of 1941, after the Germans occupied the area of the Katyn Forest, the Germans were responsible for the deaths.

A number of legitimate investigations examined the bodies and the scene of the crime, the areas in and around the mass graves. All of the investigations, except for those undertaken by the Soviets, determined that, without question, the bodies found in the Katyn Forest mass graves had been there for at least three years. Therefore, the bodies had been in the

The Katyn Forest Massacre, 1940

ground since the spring of 1940. All the evidence that was found at the scene supported this opinion. With the exception of the duplicitous Soviet investigations and other fraudulent investigations set up by the Soviets to fool the participants, every legitimate and trustworthy independent investigation came to the conclusion that the thousands of Polish citizens had been murdered in the spring of 1940. The evidence was damning.

In spite of Soviet protests, the conclusions of all the independent investigators agreed and provided incontrovertible evidence that the Soviet Union, under the direction of Stalin and Beria and the NKVD (People's Commissariat for Internal Affairs), also known as the Soviet Security Police, had committed the murders. The NKVD was in fact Stalin's secret police force, and they did his dirty work under Lavrentiy Beria. The NKVD was responsible for carrying out the deaths of thousands of Polish citizens and for the mass graves in the Katyn Forest.

The facts that were discovered by the various non-Soviet investigations were all conclusive and in agreement. The Soviets had committed these war crimes. A great deal of circumstantial evidence and a number of eyewitness accounts attested to Soviet guilt. But it was the hard evidence that was discovered at the site of the mass graves and inside the mass graves on the bodies of the dead that could not be disputed. The facts told the incontestable truth of what had happened there.

The facts that could not and would not tell a lie were the spruce trees planted to cover the graves in the Katyn Forest, the origin of the rope that bound the hands of the dead men in the mass graves, the wounds inflicted on the bodies of the dead, the condition of the corpses and the clothing worn by the dead, the arrangement of the bodies in the ground, and the documents, personal items, and newspapers found on the bodies in the graves. This hard evidence made it impossible to lie about what had happened in the Katyn Forest and made it impossible to deny who had perpetrated this horror. All the evidence pointed conclusively to the guilt of the Soviet Union.

The Soviet Union claimed that the Germans had massacred the Polish prisoners in the late summer or early fall of 1941. But the heavy winter uniforms worn by the corpses with the buttons all fastened verified the fact that the men had not been shot during warm weather. Some of the men wore fur-lined coats, further testimony that it had been cold when they had been murdered and put into the graves. The total absence of any bugs or insects in the graves was further evidence that the crimes had not been committed during the warm late summer and early fall.

The boots worn by the officers in the graves were in excellent condition, proof that these men had never worked in either German or Soviet chain gangs doing road repairs, as the Soviets claimed.

The rope used to tie the hands of the prisoners who had been shot and were lying in the mass graves, was rope that had been made in the Soviet Union. All the knots were identical, and the pieces of rope that were used to tie the hands of the prisoners were the same length, a sure sign they had been pre-cut for that specific purpose. What more evidence could anyone ask? The prisoners' hands bound by rope that all agreed had come from the Soviet Union was iron-clad testimony to the fact that they were murdered by the Soviets and not by the Nazis.

The bodies of many of the prisoners found in the Katyn mass graves had been pierced by bayonets. Every one of the wounds, determined by multiple autopsies, was the result of an injury caused by a bayonet with a four-cornered tip. Only the Soviet Union was using that type of weapon, the four-cornered bayonet, at that time. This was further hard evidence that the Soviet Union that had done the killing.

No documents, letters, diaries and other papers found on any of the dead bodies were dated after April 1940. Soviet newspapers found with the bodies were dated up to April of 1940, with none at all dated after that. Likewise the grouping of the bodies in the graves corresponded exactly to the order in which the soldiers and others had been removed from the Soviet Camp Kozelsk. It was obvious, from the way the bodies lay in the ground, that the Polish prisoners had been taken directly from Camp Kozelsk to the Katyn Forest and murdered.

The young spruce trees that had been planted on top of the graves to cover them and to try to hide them were younger and smaller than the trees in the rest of the forest. The plots of young spruce trees were distinctive in the Katyn Forest and stood out. These stands of younger trees unintentionally marked the locations of the mass graves. This clear sign enabled the Germans, when they were searching for the graves, to dig where the smaller spruce trees were found. Mass graves were inevitably found underneath the plots of the younger spruce trees.

Cross sections of the trunks were cut from these spruce trees that had been transplanted over and around the mass graves to try to hide what was underneath. Microscopic examination of the tree rings proved without a doubt that the spruce trees had been transplanted no later than the spring of 1940. Experts in forestry analyzed the rings of the trees beginning in 1943. These analyses of the tree rings provided the most incontrovertible evidence that the murders had occurred in 1940. Mother Nature doesn't lie. The tree rings on these spruce trees told the truth which could not be ignored.

The conclusion that the mass graves found at Katyn were dug and filled with the bodies of Polish prisoners no later than the spring of 1940 provided conclusive and verifiable evidence that could not be evaded or refuted by political maneuvering. One anecdote indicates that Winston Churchill was considerably disturbed when he heard this news about the trees. This was evidence that could not be covered up by political manipulation.

All of the dead found in the mass graves in Katyn were prisoners from only *one* of the Soviet prison camps, Camp Kozelsk. The estimated 4,443 to 4,800 bodies of prisoners discovered in the Katyn Forest accounted for only one-third of the Soviet prisoners who had disappeared. Where were the men from the other two Soviet prison camps? The whereabouts of these Polish military officers and other Polish leaders who were imprisoned in Camp Ostashkov and in Camp Starobelsk has never been discovered. None of them, with the exception of the few who were included in the 448 who had been sent to Camp Grazovec, were ever located...either alive or dead. No other bodies have ever been found. No other graves have ever been found. No traces of what happened to the prisoners from the other two Soviet prisons, Camp Ostashkov and Camp Starobelsk, have ever been found.

It is suspected and has been stated by those who have, with integrity, investigated this atrocity, that there are probably many Katyn Forests in the Western part of the Soviet Union. There is a strong suspicion that there are many mass graves, which have yet to be discovered and which hold the bodies of prisoners from the Ostashkov and Starobelsk prison camps. These remains have never been found.

Twelve

After World War II ended, Poland was under the boot of the Soviet Union until 1991-1993 when Poland threw off the final vestiges of communism and became a free country. During the Cold War, it would have been impossible to search for the other killing fields. It is still impossible. The Soviet Union claimed to have nothing to do with the massacre. No excavations to search for more bodies would be allowed anywhere inside the Soviet Union. Under Vladimir Putin, no further excavations to search for the remainder of the Polish dead will ever be permitted in Russian territory as long as the current totalitarian regime is in power.

Anecdotal information from questionable eye witnesses has suggested that the prisoners who were held in the Ostashkov Soviet prison camp were put on several barges which were then sent off shore, out into the White Sea. These accounts claim that the barges were then sunk with massive artillery fire. This story has never been proven to be true, and no bodies have ever been recovered from the White Sea.

To have transported thousands of POWs from Ostashkov to put them on barges in the White Sea would have required a journey of more than a thousand kilometers. Other than the corpses found in the Katyn Forest, which were all bodies of men who had been imprisoned in the Soviet Camp Kozelsk, none of the bodies of men from either of the other two Soviet prison camps have ever been recovered.

Only the mass grave in the Katyn Forest can unquestionably substantiate the fact that the Soviet Union massacred thousands of Polish leaders. The Evil Empire spent decades desperately hiding from the world the fact of this horror perpetrated by Stalin and his henchman Lavrentiy Beria. Beria was the head of Stalin's secret police, the NKVD from 1938 until 1946, the time period during which the Katyn Forest atrocity was committed. During this same time period, the remaining Soviet prisoners of war disappeared forever. Any murders, both those that have been discovered and those that have not yet been discovered, would not have occurred without direct orders from Stalin and Beria.

🌲

In July of 1941, as the result of Operation Barbarossa when Hitler invaded the Rodina, the Soviet Union chose to join with the Allied powers who were fighting against the Nazis. The old adage "the enemy of my enemy is my friend" was proven once again when the strange bedfellows of the authoritarian Communist state led by the tyrannical dictator Stalin aligned itself with the democratic and free enterprise countries of Churchill's Britain and DeGaul's France. The United States joined the Allies in December of 1941 when the Japanese attacked Pearl Harbor.

Although leaders of all the Western Allied powers knew that the Soviet account about what had happened in the western Soviet Union was not the truth, the leaders of the Allied coalition chose to accept the Soviet Union's lies about the murders that had occurred in the Katyn Forest. In spite of absolute, hard evidence to the contrary, the world was told that the massacre in Poland was perpetrated by the Nazis. Known lies were accepted as truth in order for the Allies to win the war against the Germans.

▲

The Soviet Union continued to deny any knowledge of the massacre during World War II and long after the war was over. In spite of the fact that everyone knew the truth, the Soviets continued to blame the Germans for the murders and the mass graves. Both Britain's prime minister, Winston Churchill, and United States president, Franklin D. Roosevelt, were repeatedly presented with undeniable proof that the atrocity in Katyn was the work of the Soviet Union. But the Communist USSR and its vile and vicious leader Joseph Stalin were our allies in the fight. All Allied leaders of western countries chose to ignore the truth. These leaders were afraid, if they admitted to the world the truth about what had happened in Katyn, the Allied coalition would break apart. They feared that Hitler would make a separate peace with the USSR and that the Russians would no longer fight the war.

At the time, the most important thing, in fact the only thing that mattered, was to defeat the Nazis. Roosevelt went so far as to exile one United States diplomat and military leader who refused to be muzzled. This man also happened to be FDR's personal friend. This diplomat had served the United

States in Bulgaria and in Austria before the war. In 1943, he was the Special Emissary of President Roosevelt for Balkan Affairs, assigned to Turkey. This Special Emissary had gathered evidence, through contacts he made during his wartime travels in the Balkans, about the atrocity in the Katyn Forest. He presented the evidence he had collected directly to his friend, President Franklin Roosevelt. When his own personal special emissary and personal friend wanted to go to the press with the truth, Roosevelt forbade his going public with the information. When his friend persisted that the truth of this genocide needed to be told, the president ordered his friend sent to an obscure and remote diplomatic post in Samoa, an island in the Pacific Ocean for the duration of the war. The diplomat protested but was ordered to Samoa anyway.

In addition to his diplomatic post, this friend of the U.S. president held a commission in the United States Navy. After Roosevelt died, the United States Navy immediately recalled their officer from Samoa and apologized to him. The Chief of Personnel of the Navy and the president's naval aide both apologized to the officer and assured him that his being sent to Samoa had *not* been the decision of the United States Navy Department.

Roosevelt's attitude toward the Soviet government regarding the events in the Katyn Forest indicate that the president cared more about his relationship with the Soviets than he did about the truth. The truth about the evil that had been perpetrated by Stalin's Communist state was accepted and ignored. The Soviet leader and his henchmen at the NKVD were going to get away with their horrible crime against the Polish nation.

One of the post-World War II investigations about the murders in the Katyn Forest included the Nuremberg Trials.

War crimes were to be investigated and adjudicated at this eminent hearing, but because the USSR was one of the victors in the war, the Soviet Union was one of the nations that was responsible for prosecutions at the trial. The Germans were the accused. The Germans were the losers and the bad guys.

The four major victorious powers, the United States, Great Britain, France, and the Soviet Union, organized the Nuremberg Trials and divided the areas of responsibility for prosecution. The Soviet Union was assigned, no doubt at their own insistence, that they be given the responsibility for prosecuting "crimes against humanity." The Katyn Forest massacre of course fell under this classification. Consequently, as duties for the business of the trial were allocated, the Soviet Union was given the task of investigating Katyn. Only the Soviets would be allowed to prosecute Katyn. This a clear example of the fox being assigned to watch over the hen house. The Soviet Union did everything they could to stifle the truth and to prevent any mention of the Katyn Forest massacre from becoming public.

The Soviets, hoping to put the problem of Katyn to rest once and for all, brought witnesses to Nuremberg to testify against the Germans about the atrocity. These witnesses were all from the Communist countries the Soviet Union occupied after the war, countries that had been granted to them at Yalta, countries that were within the Soviet sphere of influence. These countries, from which the Soviet Union found their witnesses to testify in the Nuremberg Trials, were forced to subscribe to Communist doctrine under the iron fist of Joseph Stalin. The witnesses, who were brought to testify, were threatened and bullied into saying what the Communists wanted them to say. Their families were threatened and even imprisoned so that these Soviet "experts" would say only and exactly what the leaders of the USSR directed them to say.

No Polish participation was allowed at Nuremberg. Polish evidence that had been gathered about the war crimes in the Katyn Forest was offered at the trial, but it was not allowed to be presented. No Polish witnesses were allowed to testify. Eyewitnesses to the tragedy of the murders in the Katyn Forest were not allowed to speak. Much evidence was available, but it was all disallowed by the Soviets. Even evidence already in the hands of United States government was not allowed to be introduced at the trial. The British were likewise not able to present any of the evidence they had acquired about Katyn. All information about Katyn from the Allied camp was suppressed or omitted from any consideration because of political expediency. The Soviets had their way completely. It was a travesty of justice.

The Soviets were successful in making Katyn completely disappear from the Nuremberg Trials. The atrocities at Katyn were ignored. What little real evidence that was presented in court was left unanswered. When the final verdicts were read on September 30, 1946, the Katyn massacre was never mentioned. Any responsibility for the deaths there was simply disregarded. It was as if the massacre had never happened. The American prosecution staff said that the treatment of the Katyn massacre at the Nuremberg Trials "looked mighty funny." The Nazis were set up to be the criminals at this trial. And indeed they were. But there were other horrible crimes that should also have been adjudicated. Stalin and the Soviet Union were the victors in the war. To the victors goes the privilege of telling the most abhorrent lies.

Everyone knew the Soviets had committed the Katyn atrocities. A Lieutenant Colonel in the United States Army, who was captured by the Germans during the war, spent time in a German POW camp. While he was a prisoner in the camp, his Nazi captors took him to the Katyn Forest to show him the mass graves. After his liberation towards then end of the war, this United States Army officer presented his first-hand report about what he had observed with his own eyes at Katyn. He made his report in secret to American military intelligence, to his superior, General Clayton Bissell. The report was classified as Top Secret and subsequently buried. It would never see the light of day.

When General Bissell was later questioned in front of the United States Congress about why he had suppressed this vital and authentic first-hand report, Bissell said he had received specific instructions to do so from President Roosevelt. Supposedly, the hope was, in the spring of 1945, that the Russians could be convinced to join the fight against the Japanese. The reasoning behind the suppression of the report of the first-hand account about the Katyn Forest was that the Poles could not fight the Japanese but the Soviets could. Roosevelt did not want to antagonize the Russians if there was a chance they would be willing to participate in the fight that was still raging in the Pacific. For years after the war ended, the Lieutenant Colonel's report continued to be classified as Top Secret. The report that told the truth subsequently disappeared completely. It was obvious that this report had been lost, or maybe even destroyed, on purpose. But why?

🌲

For many years after the hostilities of World War II ended, the truth about Katyn continued to be suppressed. An argument can be made that even after the war was over and the Germans had surrendered, the Western allies still needed the cooperation of the Soviet Union to successfully conduct the Nuremberg Trials. It can likewise be argued that the Western allies still needed the cooperation of the Soviet Union to accomplish the establishment of the United Nations. These goals took precedence over truth for years.

Why, even after the Nuremberg Trials were finished and the United Nations became a reality, did the truth continue to be suppressed? For years after the war was over, and even after the Cold War was in full swing and the Soviet Union was our unequivocal and avowed political enemy in the world, the United States policy of suppressing the truth about Katyn continued. U. S. State Department policy, as late as 1950, forbade anyone from even being allowed to mention the word Katyn. Various United States agencies investigated the Katyn Forest massacre. All legitimate investigations were unanimous in finding the Soviet Union culpable. The information discovered in these investigations was classified, suppressed, and not allowed to become public. But why?

The truth continued to be hidden from the American people. When some Americans heard about the Katyn massacre, they abhorred the crimes that had been committed. They particularly resented the manner in which knowledge of who was responsible for the massacre was kept from the public. The American Committee for the Investigation of the Katyn Massacre, Inc. was formed by a group of distinguished and influential Americans from public life who wanted the truth to come out.

In 1951, a special congressional committee was formed to do its own investigation in an attempt to uncover he truth about what had happened in the Katyn Forest during World

War II. The congressional committee's report was made public in 1952, and it established beyond any doubt that the Soviet Union was responsible for the crimes. No action was taken regarding the recommendations of the congressional committee. This investigation, which had discovered the truth, was pretty much ignored by the public and by the United States government.

It is very troubling and of particular concern that the information gleaned in the Special Congressional Investigation was ignored. The Korean War began in June of 1950 and continued for more than three years until the armistice was signed in July of 1953. The North Koreans and the Chinese were taking American soldiers as prisoners of war. It seems that the treatment of captured soldiers and the importance of guaranteeing them humane treatment should have been a top priority for the United States Government... especially considering what everyone knew was happening to United States military personnel during the Korean War.

🌲

In the post-World War II era, Poland was a satellite state of the Soviet Union. It was lost to the West, lost to the free world. The Soviet Union, our former war-time ally, was now our Communist foe. The Soviet Union became our Cold War enemy in 1948. Considering the overwhelming enormity of the Holocaust and the murder of six million Jews in German concentration camps, Katyn was relegated to a minor event. The Nazis were indeed the evildoers. Compared to the Nazis, the Soviet Union's evil deeds were just minor evil deeds. What had happened in the Katyn Forest during World War II didn't seem to matter to anyone anymore.

The conspiracy of silence continued. Winston Churchill wrote his memoirs four years after the end of World War II. He admits in his memoirs that the victorious governments in the war decided that the issue of Katyn should be avoided. The crimes of Katyn have never been widely known. The truth in large part has remained unrevealed. The murders at Katyn have never been punished. They have scarcely been acknowledged.

The Soviet Union did not admit its culpability until 1990 when its leader Mikhail Gorbachev officially accepted blame for the Katyn Forest massacre that occurred during World War II. Under Gorbachev's attempts at Glasnost and Perestroika, the Russians made a commitment to be more honest about Soviet history. Gorbachev's admission of Soviet guilt about Katyn was one effort to correct the lies of the past.

At the time Gorbachev finally admitted Soviet responsibility for Katyn, the United States and other Western powers were trying to achieve detente with the Soviet Union. The world wanted a reduction in the nuclear weapons arsenals of both the United States and the Soviet Union. These enormous hordes of nuclear weapons had reached the point where the world's superpowers had the ability to destroy every living thing on earth several times over. The world wanted the United States and the Soviet Union to put away their atomic toys and play nice. It was more important to get along than it was to reveal and seek recriminations for a massacre that had occurred decades earlier. By 1990 most of the people who had actually participated in that massacre were already dead.

Then the Soviet Union fell, and the United States was friends with Russia. We supported their attempts at democracy and private enterprise. All the Western democracies cheered on Yeltsin. It was not the right time to talk about the terrible atrocities that the previous and disgusting Soviet Communist government, the now defunct USSR, had committed. It was a new day.

And then neo-Soviet and former KGB thug, Vladimir Putin came on the scene. He has committed his own war crimes, his own atrocities. It is time to tell the story of what the Soviet Union did during World War II and try to understand why those who knew the truth pretended they didn't know it.

The disappearance of 25,000 Polish citizens, including Polish military officers and other military personnel, doctors, lawyers, priests, educators and other important Polish leaders is still shrouded in mystery. Eight hundred doctors were killed. The graves of less than 5,000 of these missing men were discovered in the Katyn Forest. What happened to the other approximately 11,000 to 20,000 Polish men who had previously been kept in Soviet prison camps has never been determined. It is assumed that they were likewise murdered, but their bodies have never been found.

▲

Everyone who has studied the rise of Hitler and the Nazis in Germany accepts that this regime was the epitome of evil in the twentieth century. The Nazis committed horrible crimes, unbelievable crimes. Because the things the Nazis did have grabbed the headlines, as they should have, crimes committed by the Soviet Union have been hidden or ignored. But the Nazis did not commit the atrocities in the Katyn Forest. German authorities went to great lengths and took special care to preserve evidence found on the bodies of the dead in the graves at Katyn.

Thousands of letters, identity cards, photographs, diaries, and other personal possessions were removed from the corpses in the mass graves in the Katyn Forest. This evidence from the Katyn graves included hand-penned personal diaries found on the bodies. There were no entries in any of these diaries about anything after April and May of 1940. There were no letters found on the corpses with any dates later than the spring of 1940. This irrefutable, authentic, and valuable evidence provided undeniable proof of Soviet guilt in the Katyn murders.

This cache of documents and other evidence was preserved and carefully guarded by the Germans to prevent its being stolen and destroyed by the Soviets. In 1940, the Katyn Forest was located inside the territory of the USSR, inside the country of Russia. In 1941, the Germans invaded the Soviet Union during Operation Barbarossa and held significant parts of Soviet territory for a few years. It was during the German occupation of the Katyn Forest that the mass graves were uncovered in 1943. The documents retrieved from the dead bodies in these graves were the most important evidence and in fact the only tangible evidence the Germans had in their possession after the Katyn Forest was ceded to Soviet forces later in the war.

During the closing weeks and days of the war, the German authorities guarded this vital evidence from the Katyn Forest closely, as both the Polish Underground and the NKVD planned and attempted to steal it. The Polish underground wanted to know what had happened to their fellow citizens. The Poles knew the Soviets wanted to steal and destroy the documents. The Polish underground wanted to keep the Soviets from taking possession of the evidence. The Soviets, of course, were desperate to find the documents so they could destroy this evidence of their own wrong doing.

The Germans packed up the evidence, which comprised the documents and the personal possessions of the dead, in nine large wooden crates. In the closing months and weeks of World War II, the Soviets pushed relentlessly west and retook territory previously lost to the Germans. The Soviets were about to enter eastern Poland. The nine wooden crates of evidence, taken from the graves at Katyn, were initially moved out of the Soviet Union to the Polish Institute of Forensic Medicine in Krakow.

The chief of German Police issued an order to Dr. Beck who was the German director of the Institute of Forensic Medicine and Scientific Criminology in the German Government of Poland. Beck was to destroy the crates of documents rather than allow them to fall into Soviet hands. But Beck felt the evidence should be preserved, not destroyed. He had attempted to hide the boxes in private homes in Krakow, Poland, but the stench of death was too much for the citizens who were holding the wooden boxes. Beck decided to evacuate the precious evidence to Germany.

The documents were repacked in a number of smaller boxes and loaded on two trucks that headed west. Dr. Beck personally accompanied these trucks. The trucks were initially sent to Breslau, now Warsaw. Beck temporarily stored the crates at Breslau University. Towards the end of the war, when the Soviets took Poland and reached Warsaw, the NKVD searched desperately for this valuable evidence against the Soviets. But the boxes had once again slipped through the fingers of the Soviets and disappeared.

During the final days of the fighting when World War II was about to end, the German SS took Dr. Beck and the wooden crates of evidence from Breslau back to Germany. Beck recognized the political importance of the materials he had in his possession and was determined to save this evidence at all costs. As the Soviets advanced in the east, Beck decided he had to try to get the crates of documents to Berlin. In May of 1945, the German military truck, which had been carrying the crates, reached Dresden. Continuing to push on to the West, the truck made it as far as the town of Radebeul, Germany. Radebeul is a town located between Dresden and Meissen. Given the conditions of the war, it was impossible to proceed any further.

Dr. Beck was forced to leave the crates in the Radebeul, Germany train station in the hands of the station agent. Beck knew that the war in Europe would be over in a few days. He wanted to get the documents into the hands of the non-Soviet Allies. Beck told the station agent that the crates of documents he was leaving in the agent's care were very valuable. The station agent was explicitly instructed to burn the boxes rather than allow the advancing Soviets forces to take possession of them.

The Soviets arrived in Radebeul. It was assumed that the station agent had burned the boxes as he had been instructed to do. The station agent and his family were arrested by the Soviet police, and neither the agent nor anyone in his family was ever seen again. The Soviets were never able to get their hands on the valuable documents. They were always a few days behind Beck and his attempts to keep them from seizing the evidence.

The Soviets continued in their relentless attempts to track down Beck and the documents. Beck's parents' home was searched several times. The homes of his friends and family were searched. Even Beck's elderly mother was arrested and held in a Soviet prison for six months. During her incarceration, the Soviets questioned her as to the whereabouts of her son, but she refused the give them any information about him. She protected him, and he was able to make his way to West Germany. The Soviets never found the documents they'd so desperately searched for, the documents that would inevitably incriminate them in the Katyn Forest atrocity and reveal to the world what had happened there.

Thirteen

"I have not heard from Casimir since he wrote a letter to me in March. His last letter was dated March 28th. I didn't receive the letter until four weeks after that, but that last letter he wrote was definitely written by him. It was in his own handwriting, and what he wrote was in his usual style. I have heard nothing since." Beata Wojciech knew that war was hell, and she had been brave when her young doctor husband had been arrested the previous November and sent to a Soviet prison camp, Camp Kozelsk. They had exchanged letters while he was being held in the Soviet camp. It was now July, and she had heard nothing from him since the letter he'd written in March. She was beside herself with worry. The tears began to roll down her cheeks. "The last few letters I have written to him have been returned to me. They were marked 'whereabouts of this person are unknown.' What does that mean? Do you want to know what I think it means? I think it means they have killed him." She began to sob.

Father Jakub Janusz was in despair. He had heard this same story from too many of his flock. Wives and children had been left behind when the Soviets had invaded Poland the year before and arrested hundreds of military officers and doctors and other leaders of the community. These leaders would have resisted totalitarianism and might have caused trouble during a Communist occupation. The arrests and deportations to Soviet prison camps had been bad enough. At least for a while, the families had been able to exchange letters with their loved ones. But then suddenly, almost all of these incarcerated men had stopped communicating with their families or with anyone. No more letters arrived from the camps. Letters were not answered. Many letters were returned to the senders. The story was the same. After April and May of 1940, all of these prisoners had stopped writing. They were incommunicado. It seemed that they had disappeared. No one had seen them or heard anything from them or about them since early spring.

The priest knew in his heart that something very bad had happened. So many men could not just vanish. Father Janusz knew more than a local parish priest would know. He traveled from parish to parish, from town to town. He had heard the same story too many times and in too many places. He had begun an informal count in his own head, and the numbers of those who had disappeared were staggering.

"Does Casimir know that you are expecting his child? He was arrested in late October, and you would not yet have known yourself."

"I don't know if he knows or not. You are right. I did not know myself until after he was taken away, and I was not certain until just after Christmas. Then I was torn about whether or not to tell him in a letter. I was thrilled and frightened at the same time. We'd always wanted children, but then the Soviets and the Germans came to Poland. We'd decided we would wait. We didn't want to bring children into a world consumed by war or into a country occupied by evil foreign armies. When I finally accepted for myself that I was going to deliver our child in July, I held off telling him the news. My feelings were conflicted. I was thrilled to be carrying my husband's child, but we had agreed together that we would wait until after the war was over. Finally I decided it was not fair to keep an event of this importance from him. I wrote to him in March. It was a long letter, and I poured out my heart to him. I told him how much I wanted to have this child, this child of his, of ours. I don't know if he ever received my letter. He never answered that letter. I haven't heard anything in months. Now I am sorry I didn't tell him sooner. He deserved to know about the baby. It might have given him some hope that our lives would go on. I have pursued every possible path to try to find out where he is and why he has not written to me. I can only assume that he is dead." Beata began to cry again.

Beata, Casimir, and Father Jakub Janusz had known each other since they were children, and they had all grown up together in the small village of Brok in Eastern Poland. Jakub Janusz had loved Beata from the time he was six years old, but Beata had only ever had eyes for Casimir. She waited patiently while he finished his studies at the university and then his years at medical school. They had finally married after Casimir received his medical degree. Then Hitler crushed Poland from the west, and the Soviet Union crushed Poland from the east.

Janusz had entered the Catholic seminary after his graduation from university. The three had remained close friends during all those years. Now Casimir was gone, and Father

Janusz felt a heavy responsibility to do something to help Beata and to comfort her.

"Perhaps the Soviets are no longer allowing the prisoners to write or send letters. That may be why you have not heard anything from Casimir, and so many others have also not heard anything from their loved ones."

"No, Janusz, he would have found a way to get word to me. I know in my heart that he is dead. I cannot tell you how I know that, but I am now convinced that they have murdered him. It has taken me a long time to be able to admit this to myself, but I am quite certain he is no longer among the living."

"What will you do? I know you have some family money, but how long will it last and how will you manage on your own? Soviet soldiers are horribly brutal and violent. They take advantage of every woman they see. You will not be safe living alone as a single woman. Your parents are dead, and you are an only child. You have no family to protect you. Your friends are all facing the same difficulties, especially the women whose husbands have disappeared, like Casimir has disappeared. Most of these women have family to take them in, but you have no one."

"I know all of these things, Jakub Janusz, but what can I do? I am now heavy with child and will deliver in a few weeks. I have a good midwife who will stand by me. There are no doctors left in any of the towns nearby. The Soviets took all the doctors away to the work camps. I can only pray that nothing goes wrong with the birth and that the midwife can handle everything on her own without the help of a doctor."

"If you truly believe that Casimir is dead, would you consider leaving Brok and leaving Poland?"

"Of course I would consider leaving Poland. But that is a pipedream. Many people want to leave Poland now, but no one can. I would leave in a minute if I could."

"I may be able to find a way for you to leave Poland and go to Sweden. Would you be willing to do that, if I can arrange it? I am not certain that it will be possible, but if you are amenable to leaving, I might be able to arrange a way for you to escape this place."

"I would not want to leave until after I have the baby. I want my child to be born in Poland. Casimir would have wanted that, too. But as soon as the baby and I are able to travel, I would be ready to leave, to go to Sweden. Can you do this for me, Jakub?"

"I'm going to try. Casimir would have wanted me to keep you safe. The only way I can do that is to try to get you out of Soviet-occupied Poland. The journey to freedom will be an arduous one. You will also have to travel through German-occupied Poland to the Baltic seacoast, and then there will be a dangerous sea voyage to reach Sweden. If you think you can make this journey with a newborn infant, I will do everything in my power to make it possible for you and the baby to escape."

"You have given me hope where none existed. Dear Father Janusz."

"I will do my best for you."

🌲

Malgorzata Alina Wojciech entered the world on August 3, 1940, into the hands of an experienced midwife. The baby was healthy and screaming at the top of her lungs. She weighed a robust 3.5 kilograms and had a gorgeous head of black hair. Her mother and her godfather, the priest, Father Jakub Janusz, wept with joy when they saw her. They were both thinking of the baby's own absent father, Doctor Casimir Wojciech, and how much he would have adored his energetic and beautiful daughter.

During the final weeks of her confinement, Beata had quietly moved from the home she had shared with Casimir to a nearby Catholic convent. Father Janusz had arranged for her to live with the nuns. He felt it would be safer for her and the baby if she had already moved out of her house before the baby was born. Most of her furniture and household goods had to be left behind. A completely empty house would have attracted the kind of attention they didn't want. A few heirlooms and precious antiques, along with some valuable paintings, were stored in the caves beneath the convent. Beata knew she could not take anything with her except her infant and a few valuables when she left her beloved Poland and traveled to Sweden. She would have her baby, her new identity cards, and some money. She sewed her jewelry into the hems and pockets of the cloak she would wear on the journey. She would not be able to take most of her photographs, or clothes, or other valuables.

Father Janusz had arranged for some of her wealth to be transferred. Before the Soviet invasion, Casimir and Beata had sent some of their savings to banks in France. The priest, through the church, was able to transfer some of Beata's wealth to a bank in Stockholm. Beata donated money to the Church, and Father Janusz was able to move that money to Sweden and deposit it in an account in Beata's name. Beata's family had owned significant acres of property in Eastern Poland, but there was nothing Father Janusz could do to liquidate that land in Beata's favor. Beata and Malgorzata would have to leave their inherited landholdings behind when they fled the country. Being able to escape to freedom would make it worth the price.

Father Janusz felt it was better to move the newborn and her mother sooner rather than wait. The winds and rain on the Baltic Sea did not deter the men who fished for a living, but the priest worried that a new mother and a baby that was just a few weeks old would be vulnerable in their escape. It would be better if the voyage and the transfer at sea be undertaken in September or October when the weather was warmer. It would be a stressful exodus under any circumstances. To wait until November would be asking for trouble.

Father Janusz had obtained papers for the three of them to travel through Poland to a small town close to the Baltic Sea. None of them would actually be going to that small town, but their papers would enable them to travel close to where they would be able to embark on the Baltic. A herring fisherman would take Beata and her baby on board his boat. The fishing vessel would keep to its normal route and normal schedule so as not to attract any attention from the occupying Soviets who kept a close eye on fishing boats leaving the shores of Poland. The Germans and the Soviets patrolled the Baltic Sea, and especially its shores. They often stopped and boarded fishing vessels to search for contraband and for those they suspected were trying to escape from Nazi and Soviet occupation. These patrol boats also stopped and searched fishing vessels just to harass the Polish fisherman, to let them know in no uncertain terms who was now in charge of their lives.

The priest's plan for Beata and her baby was for the herring fisherman from Poland to meet with a Swedish fishing boat at night at a predetermined longitude and latitude in the middle of the Baltic Sea. Beata and her child would be transferred to the Swedish boat to continue their journey to neutral Sweden. These arrangements had not been easy to put together. It had taken weeks for the priest to organize the complicated plan, and it had cost a great deal of money. Beata knew she was one of the lucky ones. Hardly anyone in Poland at that time had friends who could arrange such an escape and had the financial means to pay for it.

🌲

Beata would be wearing a nun's habit when she made the railway journey through Poland to the Baltic coast. The cover story was that Sister Beata, the nun, and Father Jakub Janusz, the priest, were taking a recently-orphaned newborn to the Polish village of Szemud to be raised by relatives. If anyone inquired, the baby's father had disappeared, and the mother had died in childbirth. The deceased mother's sister, who lived in the rural village near Danzig, had agreed to take the newborn and raise the child in her own family. The two religious volunteers were on a mission of mercy, to deliver the orphaned child to a family member who would love and take care of her and bring her up as her own child. Who could possibly argue or stand in the way of such a good deed? Even the cruel and uncaring Soviet military would be hard-pressed to deny a priest and a nun safe passage on such a Samaritan's journey.

🌲

"We will travel by rail for much of the way. The first part of the long trip will be through Soviet-occupied Poland. Then we will travel through German-occupied Poland. As you know the Germans and the Soviets have divided our country between them. I don't anticipate that we will have any more trouble from the Germans than we do from the Soviets. If our papers and our story hold up with the Soviets for the first half of the journey, they will probably hold up for the second half of the journey...through German-occupied Poland." Father Janusz was explaining to Beata how he hoped their escape plan would work.

"We will be able to travel on the train almost all the way to Danzig. Of course, the train does not go all the way to the tiny fishing village on the Baltic from which you and the baby will leave the country by boat. That destination is purposely way off the beaten track from everything. And we do not intend to go anywhere near Szemud either. That is where our papers say we are going. In fact, we will leave the train several stops before we reach Danzig. We will travel by motor car for the rest of our journey. The Soviets have conscripted most of the motor cars that were previously owned by private individuals. But after much searching, I was able to find a vehicle to borrow to complete our journey. Hopefully the motor car will hold up for the remaining miles and be able to deliver us safely to the seacoast."

Because Beata was nursing her infant, feeding the baby during the journey on the train could also present a problem. Who would not be startled if they happened to see a nun nursing a baby? Beata and Janusz realized that if anyone saw Beata nursing the baby in her nun's habit, her disguise and her cover would be blown. This would make the two clerics appear very suspect at a time when they desperately wanted to attract as little attention as possible. This wrinkle made the planning of their trip even more complicated.

Fourteen

When they left the convent, Beata wore a nun's habit. She had a carryall that held supplies for the baby. Every one of the worldly possessions she would be able to take with her was either hidden in the carryall with the baby's things or sewn inside her clothing. Father Janusz carried a valise that held clothes and toiletries and things for the baby. Money and papers that Beata would need were secured in a hidden compartment inside the valise.

The priest had procured paperwork that stated the two clerics were transporting the newborn infant to be raised by a relative who lived in Szemud. Their story, that the baby's mother had died in childbirth and the baby was being taken, thanks to the goodwill of the nuns, to live with an aunt in the small village, was a somewhat plausible excuse for the two of them to be traveling with an infant. Even the atheistic Soviets occasionally deferred to representatives of the Catholic Church in Poland. The priest hoped that he and Beata could keep a low profile and attract as little official attention as possible while they made their way across their occupied country to the Baltic Sea.

Encumbered by the many things required to meet the needs of a newborn, Beata and Janusz left their small town of Brok in Eastern Poland on the first day of October in 1940. They traveled by train through Soviet-occupied Poland. They had to show their papers often. The Soviets were everywhere on the train, checking papers and interrogating travelers. Father Janusz did the talking for his small band. He knew how to deal with the Soviet occupiers who were suspicious of everything and everyone. He told the soldiers, who were questioning the train's occupants, the story about the orphaned baby and why he and the nun were making the journey.

Before they were allowed to continue on the train and travel through German-occupied Poland for the second part of their journey, they were questioned closely. Their papers were scrutinized again. Most people had their luggage and their persons searched by the Germans, but even the hard-boiled Nazis were reluctant to search the body of a nun or a priest. Without incident, Beata and Jakub made the transition from the Soviet controlled part of Poland to the German controlled part of Poland. They continued on the train in their solitary compartment.

Beata had fed her baby just before they'd left on the train. They managed to find a compartment and establish themselves in it for the trip through Poland. Most of the passengers who got on the train avoided them when they looked in the window of the compartment and saw a nun, a priest, a small baby who might scream for the entire length of the journey. Assorted baby paraphernalia was spread out on the seats of the compartment. Who would willingly chose to spend the hours of their journey in such a space? Passengers unanimously decided against joining this odd and potentially disruptive group and moved on to seek out other more comfortable seats to reach their destinations.

    Malgorzata slept most of the way but woke up hungry and crying several times before they reached their destination. Father Janusz pulled the curtains of the compartment closed, and Beata nervously fed the baby. When she was satisfied, Malgorzata went back to sleep. Every time Beata fed her child, she was terrified the conductor or some Soviet authority would knock on the door of the compartment and demand to be admitted.

    Father Janusz had purchased tickets for them to travel on the train all the way to Danzig. Traveling to Danzig would be the most logical place for them to disembark to reach the small town of Szemud, the place they said was their ultimate destination. But from the beginning, the priest had planned that they would exit the train before they reached Danzig. He'd arranged for the motorcar to be left for them at a train station that was several stops before they reached the port city.

    They exited the train in the pouring rain. The dark day's twilight was fading quickly into nighttime. Both Beata and Jakub were soaking wet after they'd stepped down from the train and gone in search of their motorcar. They shivered in the cold and wind and worried that the baby would become ill. Beata did everything she could to keep the baby covered and protected from the storm. The older vehicle was waiting for them behind the train station. Father Janusz was tremendously relieved when he found the motor car parked where he had arranged for it to be. He had been particularly worried that this crucial part of his plan would not work out.

The motorcar looked even older than Father Janusz had expected it would look. He said a fervent prayer that their transportation would hold together and would not break down until they reached the seacoast. Father Janusz also prayed that the petrol in the motorcar would be sufficient to get them to the fishing village and the boat that was waiting to carry Beata and the baby away from occupied Poland. It was wartime, and petrol was scarce and nearly impossible to buy for any amount of money. The wind howled, and they knew that many of the dirt roads on which they were going to have to travel would have turned to mud. The remote village that was their actual destination was purposely difficult to get to and did not have good roads.

Father Janusz drove, and Beata and the baby sat in the back seat. Both Beata and Janusz were exhausted, even before they began this last leg of their journey to the coast. Traveling with an infant is never easy. Most women who lived in Poland in 1940 would never have dared leave their homes to undertake a lengthy trip with a baby as young as Malgorzata. But extraordinary circumstances called for extraordinary efforts. They pushed on through the dark night and the thunderstorm. The priest prayed constantly that the car would not have a flat tire and that they would not become stuck in the mud or run off the road into a ditch. He prayed they would not run out of petrol before they reached the fishing village.

They had a deadline. The fishing boat would wait only so long for their unusual passengers to arrive at the dock. It had not been easy to find this fisherman who was willing to use his boat to take a woman and a baby on board, let alone a fisherman who was willing to illegally meet up with a Swedish fishing vessel in the middle of the Baltic Sea. The captain of the Polish fishing boat was risking his own life to take these secret travelers on this leg of their journey to freedom. Father Janusz had paid dearly to convince the fisherman that it was worth it. The priest hoped and prayed that neither his trust nor his money had been misplaced.

Father Janusz had driven faster on the dirt roads than he should have, but they managed to arrive in time for Beata and Malgorzata make it on board the fishing vessel. There was no time for lengthy goodbyes. The priest and the nun both cried when they said goodbye to each other. The two childhood friends knew in their hearts that they would probably never see each other again. Given the hazards of a world at war, they knew they would be lucky to live through the next few years. The captain of the fishing boat was anxious to leave. The priest helped load his precious human cargo onto the boat. Then he carried aboard the few things they had been able to bring with them on the journey. Father Janusz paid the fisherman the initial part of his fee. Beata would pay him the final part of his fee when she and the baby had safely boarded the Swedish fishing boat.

The Polish fishing boat had crude accommodations for the new mother and her infant. Everything on the boat smelled of fish. Beata clung to her baby as she lay on the narrow cot in a hidden compartment below the deck. There was scarcely room for her to stand, let alone change the baby's diapers. Beata felt sick to her stomach. It was going to be a rough trip to sail out into the turbulent, dark waters on this stormy night. But they were on their way to freedom. Beata kept whispering to her baby that it was all worth it, whatever they had to endure. Beata fed Malgorzata, and they both slept.

The captain knocked on the door of their hiding place. He shouted to Beata and the baby that they had to come on deck to make the transfer to the Swedish boat. Beata had fed Malgorzata twice during the night. The nursing mother had drifted off to sleep between feedings, worn out from traveling and worn out from taking care of a hungry infant. Beata roused herself and gathered her belongings. She made her way, still dressed in her nun's habit, out of her cramped quarters and out into the cold rain. Fishermen welcomed the rain. The fish were more plentiful when it rained. Mothers traveling with tiny babies did not welcome the rain. When she went out on deck, Beata was soaked to the skin again in minutes, and she tried desperately to keep Malgorzata from also becoming drenched. The baby's blankets were wet, and Beata could not wait to change her baby into dry clothes.

The transfer of the passengers from one fishing boat to the other was not without peril. Both boats were small, and they tossed and turned in the tumultuous swells of the waves. Beata paid the Polish fisherman his final sum and put herself and her child in the hands of the Swedish fishermen to transfer them to the other fishing boat. A small dinghy was used for the transfer. It was a precarious, if short, voyage to the fishing vessel waiting in the turbulent Baltic Sea. The Germans who patrolled this body of water could happen on them at any time. Several times, Beata was certain they were going to capsize and would not make it all the way to the Swedish fishing boat. The mother and baby made the transfer in the dinghy as quickly as they could.

Beata knew she was not well. Her exhaustion was one thing, but she knew she was now also running a fever. She began to have difficulty breathing. She struggled to stay alert. She had to take care of Malgorzata. She had to survive to take care of her child. The Swedish fishermen guided the mother and baby to another cramped sleeping quarters. They had to stay hidden until the Swedish fishing boat reached Sweden's territorial waters. Only then would they be safe from the Nazi's patrol boats which prowled the waters of the Baltic.

On the open sea, all fishing vessels were vulnerable. They were fair game, especially for the German patrol boats which stopped and searched every vessel they encountered. The Nazis occupied Denmark and Norway, and although Beata was aboard a Swedish vessel, she was not a Swedish citizen. Only when Beata was on Swedish soil would she be relatively safe. The Nazis frequently ignored laws about territorial waters, so Beata would have to stay hidden until the fishing boat had actually docked in Sweden. Beata used the last ounce of her rapidly failing energy to change and feed her baby and get her settled. Then Beata collapsed and gave in to her own illness.

She remembered only random pieces of her arrival in Sweden. It had been arranged that a representative from an order of Catholic nuns would meet her when she stepped from the fishing boat onto a tiny island off the coast of neutral Sweden. The island was connected to the mainland by a narrow causeway, more akin to a footbridge than it was to a roadway. The plan was that the nun would meet the fishing boat and take Beata and the baby to a convent in the Swedish countryside where the two refugees would be cared for.

But when the fishing boat arrived on the tiny Swedish island, Beata was unable to walk off the boat on her own. The captain of the boat tried to rouse her, but she was slipping in and out of consciousness. The man was beside himself. He had a very sick woman on board his fishing boat, and he also had a very young infant on his hands. Beata was too ill to do anything at all. There was no one to care for the baby. The captain had never married. He knew nothing about taking care of a child, especially an infant. He sent one of his crew to his sister's house. She had raised five children of her own. She would know what to do.

Beata was taken off the fishing boat on a crude stretcher made of wood and canvas. Four fishermen carried her to the captain's sister's house. Beata was quite seriously ill by this time. She was dehydrated and no longer able to feed Malgorzata. Fortunately, the woman of the house kept goats and was able to provide goat's milk for the baby. There was no doctor on the island. Fortunately, the captain's sister realized the young mother needed more medical attention than she could provide. Because the young woman was burning up with fever, the captain's sister worried that the young mother had contracted pneumonia. She was delirious. She needed to go to a hospital.

They loaded Beata and the baby into a wagon. The small fishing island was quite a few miles from Malmo. The captain's family had no motor vehicle. Even though the refugee mother and baby had finally reached Sweden, they still had to maintain a low profile. The wagon drawn by work horses was scarcely able to manage the trip across the primitive and not very well maintained causeway to the mainland. The wagon drove them to Malmo. It was a very rough journey for Beata and for the baby. Beata's belongings and the few things she had brought along for the baby were sent along with her in the horse-drawn conveyance. The fisherman's sister made sure that Beata reached the hospital in Malmo, but none of the fisherman's family stayed around after they were sure that Beata and the baby were in good hands.

The fisherman's family knew that Beata and her child were in the country illegally. There might be repercussions if anyone realized the fisherman was bringing in refugees. The fisherman's family could not take responsibility for them. It had been intended that Beata would disappear, as soon as she reached Sweden, into a convent where she could be safely hidden until she was able to procure the proper papers for herself and her child. The representative from the convent had been on hand to receive her when the fishing boat arrived at the island. But the nun had realized at once that Beata's condition was too serious and that the nuns in the convent would not be able to adequately care for her. The nun from the convent did not think Beata would survive her illness. Beata was abandoned by both the fisherman's family and by the nuns. The hospital in Malmo took her in.

Beata and her infant were left on a stretcher outside the front door of the hospital. Someone at the hospital took the responsibility for feeding and caring for the baby. The hospital staff took care of Beata. She was completely out of it, delirious with fever, and suffering from pneumonia and septicemia. Sulfa drugs, the only medicines that might save her life, were in short supply everywhere because of the war. But the hospital was able to procure some of these medications for Beata.

After a week of hovering on the edge between life and death, Beata began to heal. She fought for words as she experienced lucid moments in her delirium. She always asked about Malgorzata as she struggled for consciousness and tried to make sense of where she was and what was happening around her.

The Swedish city of Malmo was much too close to the border with Denmark. Denmark had fallen under the iron fist of the Nazis on April 9, 1940. As a neutral country, Sweden had seen its share of immigrants who swarmed its borders to escape the Nazis. Norwegian and Danish Jews escaped in droves to find refuge in Sweden. Finns who were escaping the Russian invasion of Finland, refugees from this Winter War, had also fled to Sweden. A few hapless but lucky souls who had crossed the Baltic Sea from Poland were able to make it to the shores of the neutral country.

It is challenging for a country to maintain neutrality when the rest of the world is at war. Sweden struggled to maintain its neutrality during World War II. It compromised itself by doing favors for the Nazis. It compromised itself by doing favors for the Allied forces. The attempts to juggle what was morally the right thing to do versus the political realities of the times ate away at the purity of the country's neutral position.

Malmo was technically a city in a neutral country. But it was just a few miles from Copenhagen, the capital city of a country occupied by the Nazis. It was inevitable that Malmo would become a city full of spies and agents from both sides in the conflict. Intrigue reigned. Malmo drew diplomats and secret agents from every corner of the world. They came from far and wide to discover the secrets of the other side. Information was bought and sold. Many were betrayed. There were murders. Fortunes were made.

🌲

Canada had declared war on Germany in September of 1939. As a member of the British Commonwealth, it was inevitable that Canada would support Britain in the fight. Canada also recognized that the Nazi scourge threatened the very existence of Western civilization. Soldiers from Canada joined the British Expeditionary Forces within weeks of Germany's invasion of Poland.

Major Preston Boucher, M.D., of the Royal Canadian Air Force was a pilot and a physician. Because of his linguistics skills, he was sent to Sweden to coordinate intelligence agents who brought information about the Nazis out of occupied Denmark and Norway. This information was vital to the Allies. Major Boucher was from Montreal, and both English and French were his native languages and spoken in his home and in his community. His mother was of Norwegian background, and from her he had learned to speak all of the Scandinavian languages. Boucher had studied German in school, and he spoke some Russian. He was an invaluable resource for the Allies as a linguist who was able to interview those who had escaped from Nazi occupied Scandinavian countries. He was working undercover as a physician when Beata reached the hospital in Malmo, stricken with two life-threatening illnesses.

As a doctor who was interested in infectious diseases, Boucher was the admitting physician when Beata arrived at the hospital. She was so ill that most of the staff on the ward did not think the young mother would make it. Dr. Boucher was determined that she would. He went to the black market to procure the necessary sulfa drugs that might save her life. He stopped by her bedside several times a day. She lay as still as a stone in her hospital bed, her blond hair in disarray like a messy halo around her head. The doctor knew she had an infant who was being cared for in the children's ward. No one knew the woman's name or where she had come from.

She could not speak, and of course, the baby could not give them any information. The young mother and her baby had been dropped off at the hospital without any explanation or any backstory. She was the beautiful mystery woman who had appeared out of nowhere.

Fifteen

As she began to regain consciousness, she mumbled words and phrases. Mostly she called out for Malgorzata. A member of the hospital staff thought he had heard her speaking in the Polish language. He said that Malgorzata was the Polish name for Margaret. Major Preston Boucher spoke quite a few languages, but Polish was not one of them. He asked that he be notified immediately when the woman regained consciousness and began to speak.

When Beata opened her eyes at the hospital in Malmo and saw Dr. Boucher leaning over her bed, she thought for a few seconds that Boucher was her own beloved husband, Casimir. She thought the doctor was her long-lost spouse who had been arrested and taken away to a prison camp by the Soviet army. She called out to him and told him she loved him and had missed him.

French was the international language of diplomacy before World War II. Many well-educated people in Poland spoke French. Beata had studied French in school and spoke it fluently. She knew very little English. French was one of the languages that was spoken in Preston Boucher's Canadian home. Beata and her physician found that they were able to communicate by speaking French. It was their common language.

One of the first things Beata was able to say when she regained the ability to speak was to ask for her baby. The hospital staff and Dr. Boucher reassured her that the infant was not only fine but thriving. Of course Beata wanted to see her child. As soon as she no longer had any fever, Dr. Boucher had a crib for the baby moved into Beata's hospital room. Being reunited with her child raised Beata's spirits and in that way facilitated the healing process. Dr. Boucher encouraged Beata to resume nursing her baby, and after some difficulties, that was accomplished.

Beata had been quite ill and had almost died. It took several weeks before she was able to regain her strength. She confided in some of the personnel at the hospital that she really had no place to go when she was discharged. Because she had been critically ill and had gone immediately to the hospital, the nun from the convent, who had been supposed to meet Beata when she arrived in Sweden, had returned to the convent in the countryside. The nun had left the young mother and baby on the island, believing that Beata was going to die. Beata had no way to contact the convent. Living with the nuns had never been a long-term solution for Beata and the baby anyway. Beata had some funds, but they would not last forever. Dr. Boucher had grown fond of Beata, and the relationship between doctor and patient grew closer as Beata recovered from her illness.

Beata had trusted him enough to share with her Canadian doctor that she had escaped from Poland. Major Preston

Boucher had realized from the outset that Beata and Malgorzata were in the country illegally. He took it upon himself to protect them. He claimed that they were relatives of his from Norway, distant cousins related to his Norwegian mother's side of the family. The doctor referred to the baby as Margaret. He had talked this over with Beata, and she understood that it was necessary for her daughter's safety that she would have to give up using the baby's Polish name and begin to use the name Margaret, the English version of Malgorzata. Preston Boucher began to discreetly inquire of his British and Canadian contacts how he could obtain papers for the refugee mother and her baby, Margaret.

Most of the hospital staff knew that Boucher's story about the mysterious patient was not true. They knew the woman had arrived in Malmo unconscious and unknown to anyone. A few thought they'd heard her speaking Polish in her delirium. They knew she was not Norwegian and was not really related to Dr. Boucher. In Malmo, of course, nothing was normal or necessarily true during this time of war. Boucher had become a favorite at the hospital, so the staff willingly played along with Boucher's story that the woman was his distant cousin from Norway.

When he had been sent by British intelligence to his post in Malmo, Preston Boucher had been provided with a cottage close to the hospital. He'd needed accommodations that would allow him to set up his short wave radio with which he could regularly communicate information to his MI6 colleagues in England. The cottage, which was owned by a Scottish businessman who was currently living and serving in London during the war, was more spacious than the doctor needed. But he had to live alone. He had to be able to use his radio in secret.

Ostensibly, he was a Canadian doctor who had volunteered his services to the hospital in Malmo. In reality, he was also an agent gathering intelligence for the Allies. He gathered information about Nazi troop movements and other actions from refugees who crossed the narrow channel of water from Denmark. He was a key contact for other Allied agents in Sweden and throughout Scandinavia. Boucher was the one who had the radio which transmitted the critical information to Allied military planners in England. It was essential that he keep his secret mission hidden from everyone, including all Swedish citizens and especially the Swedish authorities. Because he was operating in a neutral country, he would be in serious trouble if he were found to be sending information about Allied enemies to the British.

Boucher knew that Beata and her baby were essentially homeless, and he tried to find a place where they could live when she was able to leave the hospital. There was a one-room guest house in the rear garden of the cottage where the doctor was living. This small guest house was overgrown with vines and vegetation. It had been empty and abandoned for years. It was probably uninhabitable, and it would be cramped for Beata and the baby to live in its one room. Boucher worried that having someone living so close to him might compromise the clandestine nature of the war work he was doing. Boucher knew he had to keep secret his vital intelligence activities. It was essential that no one discover the fact that he regularly used his short-wave radio to communicate with London to convey to them the information he'd gathered.

Because Beata had escaped from Poland, the doctor assumed she was in sympathy with the Allied cause and opposed the Nazis and the Soviets. But he did not want to put Beata at risk because of his secret work. Housing was in short supply in Sweden, in part due to the flood of refugees that were pouring in from neighboring countries. In the end, Preston Boucher decided the only place that would be safe for Beata and her child was in the decrepit guest house at the rear of his garden.

Beata stayed in the hospital longer than she might have needed to stay. Dr. Boucher was trying to get the one-room guest quarters ready for her and the baby before she left the hospital. He obtained permission from the Scottish owner of his property to clean up and repair the one-room house. The roof was fixed. The broken bathroom fixtures were replaced. The owner didn't ask why Boucher wanted to fix up the place, but he agreed to allow the doctor to do whatever was necessary.

Boucher found a bed and a mattress, a crib for the baby, and a table and two chairs for the guest house. He moved a chest from one of the bedrooms in his own cottage. The guest house had electricity and running water, and a previous owner of the property had added a small WC and a bathtub at the rear of the one-room residence. There was a wood-burning Swedish fireplace that would adequately heat the small space. It would be a cramped and difficult accommodation in which to care for a baby. Boucher felt terrible about asking Beata to endure the hardships that living in the small guest house would require, but it was the best he was able to do.

It was the end of November when Beata and Margaret arrived at the guest house. Boucher brought a bouquet of flowers that he had found somewhere and put them in a vase on the small table to welcome the mother and daughter on the day they left the hospital and moved into the house at the back of his garden. Beata was still weak but assured the doctor that she would be able to manage on her own. She felt she could take care of her baby and take care of herself in their one-room home. She was grateful to have had good care at the hospital and beyond happy to now be able to take care of her precious child. She was tired and not fully recovered from her illness, and she was lonely. But she was no longer in a country that was controlled by Nazis or Communists. She was thankful to be alive and in a free country, even though she didn't speak a word of Swedish. She would learn.

Beata tried to think about only one day at a time. When she began to think of what she was going to do with the rest of her life, she became overwhelmed. She was still too tired to think that far ahead. Dr. Boucher had asked her if she was depressed. She had told him she thought she might be. She'd recently given birth to a baby, and she was still recovering from a near-death illness, so it was difficult to determine if she was still in the recovery phase or if her lack of energy was something more serious. After everything she had been through, it would not be any wonder if she was depressed. More than anything, she wanted to be a happy mother for her baby.

Dr. Preston Boucher had a housekeeper who came to his cottage three days a week. She cleaned, did his laundry, and cooked food for him which she left in his icebox. He told the housekeeper that his cousin had moved into the house in the garden and asked her to also buy food and cook for Beata. The housekeeper also agreed to do laundry for the doctor's cousin and her infant. The doctor paid the housekeeper generously for her additional work.

Boucher stopped by the one-room quarters every few days to check on Beata and the baby. He was worried because

Beata seemed so pale and tired. She was terribly thin, and the doctor wondered if she had enough to eat. It was war time, and everyone was short of everything. Food was scarce. Boucher worried about whether or not the little house where Beata and the baby were living would be warm enough during the coldest winter months.

Sixteen

Preston Boucher loved to cook. His father was French and also loved to cook. The elder Boucher had taught his son from the time he was able to stand on a stool at the kitchen counter and watch his father. Preston Boucher had his Swedish housekeeper cook for him because he did not have the time to cook for himself. He was so tired at the end of his long days at the hospital, he did not have the energy or the desire to cook when he returned home at night. His first priority, when he finally left the hospital and walked to his nearby cottage, was to make contact with London via his short-wave radio.

Some days, after his hours at the hospital, he drove to Helsingborg which was more than an hour's drive north of Malmo. The Oresund Strait, a very narrow strip of water that connected the North Sea with the Baltic Sea, separated the Nazi occupied country of Denmark from the free neutral country of Sweden. The two counties were very close together. Less than twenty-five miles of water separated Copenhagen, the capital of Nazi-occupied Denmark, from Malmo on the Swedish mainland. At its narrowest point, this ribbon of water separated Helsinger in Denmark from Helsingborg in Sweden by only 2.5 miles. In spite of everything the Nazis tried to do to keep people from escaping their clutches and leaving occupied Denmark, many were easily able to make the relatively short trip across the water from Denmark to Sweden. In all but the coldest months of the year, a strong swimmer in a wet suit could make it from one country to the other without the use of a boat.

Boucher frequently drove to Helsingborg to interview new arrivals who had made the short trip across the strait from Denmark. Those who had recently been in Nazi-occupied territory often had information about what the Germans were doing in Denmark and in Norway. The Germans were believed to be working on a secret heavy water project somewhere in Norway. To have the chance to learn the locations of important military assets and troop movements in countries occupied by the Germans was like discovering gold for the Allies. Boucher recruited agents who traveled back and forth between Denmark and Sweden on a regular basis. These agents often had assignments to find out specific information the Allies needed to know.

Increasingly, these Allied resistance fighters were beginning to engage in sabotage against Nazi military installations and personnel in neighboring Denmark. More and more, Boucher supplied his agents with explosives and weapons. Dr. Boucher was a significant link between the Allied forces and these brave warriors, men and women, who worked to defeat the Nazis in occupied Denmark. The information and boots on the ground these informants could provide was of great value to Britain and the other Allies.

As his agents took on more dangerous missions, Boucher was under increasing pressure to provide them with the materials they needed to fight their guerilla war against the Nazis. Procuring explosives and weapons and ammunition for these freedom fighters was time-consuming and dangerous. Boucher took enormous chances to obtain and transport these supplies that were essential to fight the Nazis. Because Sweden was a neutral country, Preston Boucher would be arrested and severely punished if the Swedes found out he was sending explosives and weapons across the strait. Preston knew he was taking tremendous risks, but the stakes were high. He was willing to put his life on the line to beat back Hitler's Nazi goons from the face of the earth, but he did not want to put anyone other than himself at risk.

Driving to Helsingborg and back to Malmo, after he had already put in a full day at the hospital, left the physician exhausted. Making an evening meal for himself was the last thing he could think about when he returned to his cottage. Sometimes, he was so tired, he could barely make himself eat the food his housekeeper had left for him. He knew how important the information was that he sent to England. Only after he had delivered his messages across the air waves did he allow himself to think of food.

🌲

However, for Christmas, Dr. Preston Boucher decided he wanted to prepare a special meal. He invited Beata and her baby to come to his cottage for Christmas dinner. Boucher cut down a Christmas tree and decorated it with the old-fashioned ornaments he'd found in a box in the attic of his cottage. He bought a wreath that had been fashioned out of pine boughs and added a red velvet ribbon. He hung it on the front door of the cottage. He bought wine and candles for the table. He realized he was looking forward to having Beata join him for dinner. He could see that she had been a beautiful woman before she had been ill and had become so thin. He hoped that in time she would be able to regain her strength and beauty.

Beata was both thrilled and nervous about going to the doctor's house for Christmas dinner. A good Catholic for most of her life, she had not been to church or to confession for many months. She had decided not to attend church in Sweden. She did not understand or speak the language, and she did not want to be noticed by anyone. Many of the churches in Sweden were Lutheran. Beata was content to stay quietly secure with Margaret in their small house. She was not able to summon the energy or the enthusiasm to do anything to celebrate the Christmas holiday this year, but she was looking forward to joining the doctor at his home for dinner.

Beata ventured out shopping one day and purchased a red dress at a secondhand store for very little money. The dress was entirely the wrong size, but the fabric was a fine, soft wool and a wonderful bright color. Beata remade the dress to fit herself. She knew the bright red of the dress would complement her blonde hair and bring some color to her pale cheeks. She had brought her grandmother's pearls with her from Poland, secreted in the bottom of the carryall she had filled with baby clothes and diapers. She would wear the pearls and her matching pearl earrings to dinner. These were among the few things she had been able to bring with her from her former life. She braided a red ribbon into her thick blonde hair. It had been such a long time since she had made any effort to try to make herself look nice. It was fun to look forward to something and to know she looked pretty.

Dr. Boucher caught his breath and almost gasped out loud when Beata and Margaret arrived at his cottage in the late afternoon. The baby had a red bow and a tiny silver bell tied into her hair, and Beata was transformed. She glowed in her red dress and smiled and laughed. She had brought homemade sugar cookies cut in shapes and decorated with colored icing, silver balls, and red cinnamon drops. She presented the doctor with the small box of baked goods that was her Christmas gift to him. He could not take his eyes off the beautiful woman who had appeared at his door. He struggled to make himself focus his attention on the elaborate dinner he was in the midst of preparing.

He lit the candles and poured wine into a crystal glass for each of them. They began with a seafood chowder made from the wonderful fresh seafood and shellfish that was available in Sweden, including prawns, crayfish, and langoustines. The cream and butter and the herbs and fish stock that went into the chowder made up the recipe Preston Boucher had learned as a boy growing up in French Canada. His Norwegian mother might have chosen a standing rib roast of beef as the main course for the holiday meal, but Preston Boucher decided to prepare a leg of lamb this year. He made roasted potatoes and glazed carrots and Brussels sprouts. In his copper saucepan, he made perfectly smooth, rich lamb gravy. He was proud of the yeast rolls he had made from scratch. There was butter and raspberry jam. He had spent hours preparing a gorgeous bûche de Noël for dessert.

It was a fabulous meal. They laughed and talked and realized they shared the same tastes in music and in books. They looked out the window as they ate and saw that it had begun to snow. Seeing the snowflakes in the air put them in the Christmas spirit. They sang Christmas carols after dinner as they cleaned up the kitchen. They both had exceptionally melodic voices. Beata sang soprano and sang in Polish. Preston sang baritone and harmonized with her as he sang in English. They sang a few carols in French together. After the dishes were put away, Preston served her a glass of brandy in his living room in front of the fireplace. Beata told her host the story of her husband's arrest by the Soviet soldiers more than a year earlier and about his disappearance. Preston asked some questions and found it puzzling, as everyone did, why Beata had never heard from Casimir again after the early spring of 1940.

Beata was not used to eating so much, and she was not used to drinking wine. She was definitely not used to drinking brandy. She fed Margaret, and then she fell asleep on the couch in front of the fire. The doctor let her sleep and rocked the baby as he watched the brave and beautiful Beata. She had been through hell. She had lost her husband, and she had lost her country. She had left behind most of her worldly possessions when she'd undertaken the journey to freedom with an infant across the Baltic Sea. She had almost lost her life to illness. She was raising a child alone. But today she had smiled and laughed and talked and sung Christmas carols. She had found within herself enough happiness to celebrate the nativity and the day and a meal with a friend. She was a remarkable woman. Dr. Boucher knew he admired her tremendously. On this Christmas Day he had caught a glimpse of the woman Beata had been before war and tragedy had temporarily crushed her spirit. He did not realize quite yet that he was falling in love with her.

Proximity, shared interests, and the loneliness of living in a country that was not one's own—as well as that indefinable something that causes a man and a woman to become attracted to each other—brought Beata and Preston together. Preston invited Beata to his home more often. They walked and talked in the garden when spring and summer arrived. Baby Margaret adored the doctor who came to visit, and he was enchanted by this child who lived in the house just across the garden from his. Her dark baby hair had fallen out and white blonde hair was growing in to replace it. Boucher began to refer to Beata's daughter as Margot, a French version of the name Margaret. The baby seemed to like the name Boucher used. Margaret, over time became Margot.

Beata and Preston shared with each other the stories of their past lives. They shared their hopes that the Nazi scourge would be defeated and that Poland and the rest of the world would someday be free again and at peace. Dr. Boucher eventually decided to tell Beata about his work as an agent for the Allies. He told her of the information he gathered about German activities in Denmark. He told her about the materials he supplied to the Danish underground. He told her about his trips to Helsingborg and his nightly communications via short wave radio with intelligence offices in Britain. He told her about how he admitted Jews, who had just arrived from other countries illegally and without any papers, to beds in the hospital wards. He hid them in plain sight, with the help of several of the nursing staff, until they could obtain papers and passports that would allow them to find homes in Sweden or to move on to other safe places.

Beata loved the good man for these things he did to work against the Nazis. She wanted to help. Boucher told her honestly that he intended to return to Montreal after the war was over. He told her he loved her. She told him she still grieved for her doctor husband whom she was now certain was dead, but she admitted that she had also grown to love the Canadian doctor. She told him that when the war was over, she wanted to move to Canada with him. They eventually married at a civil ceremony in Malmo, and Beata and Margot moved into Preston's cottage.

Beata became a critical part of Preston's work as an agent for the Allied cause. She learned to speak Swedish. She learned to drive a motorcar. She was the one who drove to out-of-the-way small towns along the coast of Sweden to make contact with Allied agents and pick up the deliveries of explosives and weapons that arrived by boat and submarine. Beata drove Preston's car to dangerous places so she could do this work. She took many chances. Because she was a woman, Swedish authorities never stopped her or questioned her. She usually had Margot in the car with her. The baby provided her with additional anonymity. She was a woman, a wife and mother, and an agent above reproach as she carried on important work for the Allies.

After the war, Beata, Preston, and Margot returned to Canada and had a long and wonderful life together in Montreal. Preston adopted Margot as his own daughter, and he loved her fiercely. Beata learned English, and Margot grew up speaking Swedish, French, English, and Polish. Both Beata and Preston lived to see their daughter Margot receive her M.D. degree and marry Claude Gauthier, the fellow medical student she had fallen in love with. Margot and her doctor husband had a daughter, Monique Simone

Gauthier, who likewise graduated from medical school. Monique Simone was also a talented artist. She was Preston and Beata's only grandchild.

Beata had never forgotten the early years of her life that she'd spent in Poland. She never forgot her first love and her first husband, Casimir Wojciech. Although he was Margot's biological father, she had been born after he had disappeared. Beata and Preston had never stopped looking for Casimir, but they were never able to find out anything about what had happened to him. Beata had long believed that Casimir had been killed when he was in Camp Kozelsk, the Soviet prison.

Beata and Preston closely followed the stories about and the investigations into the discovery of the mass graves in the Katyn Forest. Beata wondered if Casimir was among those who had been so brutally shot and buried beneath the spruce trees. She knew exactly when Casimir had stopped writing to her. She knew when he had disappeared. As despicable and evil as the Nazis had been and as many atrocities as they had committed, in her heart Beata knew the truth. She knew it was the Soviets who had slaughtered Casimir and his fellow prisoners and buried them in the Katyn Forest.

The sadness in their lives was that Monique Simone had been forced to leave Montreal. She had been happy in her work as a physician, but she had become romantically involved with a politician on the rise. The man had a popular and smiling public face, but he began to beat the beautiful Monique Simone. The man was obsessed with Monique Simone, and he was increasingly brutal in his abuse of this woman he said he loved. Finally, she could not take it anymore. Her family realized that eventually his abuse would kill her. Her abuser was wealthy and powerful, and he was a member of a well-known family dynasty in Canada.

The young woman's family helped her disappear and acquire a different identity. The politician threatened them because he wanted to know what had happened to Monique Simone, the woman he was abusing but claimed to love. Where had she gone? No one ever told the politician anything. They said they didn't know what had happened to her. They told him that one day she had left without a word, and they said they had never heard from her again.

They no longer dared even speak about Monique Simone, beloved daughter and beloved granddaughter. The parents and grandparents occasionally heard from Monique Simone, but they knew that any contact with her would put her in danger from the cruel and powerful man who wanted her back under his control. They knew she no longer could practice medicine because she could no longer use the name in which she had acquired her medical degree. They grieved for the loss of this beautiful woman with a beautiful soul. Their lives were never the same without her.

🌲

In 1990, the leader of the Soviet Union, Mikhail Gorbachev made a statement about the Katyn Forest massacre. He admitted that the Soviet Union had perpetrated the mass murder of Polish military leaders and other members of the Polish intelligentsia. Beata was eighty years old when the Soviet Union finally admitted its culpability at Katyn. The Soviet Union fell the following year, in December of 1991, and Beata and Preston were delighted that they had lived long enough to see this momentous and hoped-for event that had been a long time coming. Dr. Preston Boucher practiced medicine in Montreal until he died at the age of eighty-nine. Beata died later that same year.

The story of this family's search for Casimir might have ended with the deaths of Beata and Preston, but in 1993, Margot received a large envelope in the mail. It had been mailed from Brok, Poland. After World War II ended, the hated Soviets once again had Poland in their clutches. Margot's mother, Beata, had no desire whatsoever to visit the country of her birth or her home town of Brok, where she knew the people were being forced to live under a repressive Communist regime. The Soviets had taken her precious Casimir from Beata. They had taken her country from her. They had almost taken her life.

After the war, Beata had tried to find her old friend Father Jakob Janusz. She had written letters and had even hired a private investigator to try to locate him. But she was never able to find out anything about what had happened to him after he had put her on the fishing boat for Sweden. She wrote to the next-door neighbor who had lived beside the house in Brok, the small Polish village where she and Casimir had lived. The old woman had died, but the neighbor's daughter, Jolanta, still lived in her mother's house and wrote back to Beata. Although she had been only nine years old when the Soviets invaded Poland and destroyed their lives, Jolanta, remembered Beata and Casimir.

Beata and Jolanta had carried on a careful correspondence during the post-war years. Because Jolanta was still living in a brutal, totalitarian police state, they were careful because they did not know to what extent the Communists read mail sent from the United States or read the letters written by people in Poland and sent to the United States and other free countries.

When Beata died, Margot wrote to Jolanta, who was now an old woman herself, to tell her of Beata's passing.

Margot spoke Polish fairly well, but writing a letter in Polish was difficult for her. She apologized to Jolanta for her lack of writing skills when she wrote to her about Beata's death. Jolanta had written Margot a kind note of sympathy... in Polish, of course. Jolanta's handwriting had become difficult to read, but her letter was full of the joy she felt that she had been able to live long enough to see Poland exist again as a free country... at last.

Margot opened the large envelope from Poland that had Jolanta's return address on it. There were four items inside. One was a letter of many pages written in Jolanta's shaky script. The other three items were yellowed and damaged with age. Margot found a military card in the name of Casimir Wojciech. Casimir's black and white photo was on the card. Major Wojciech was so handsome. Margot had often seen the faded and ragged honeymoon photo of her father and mother taken in Paris, a photo that Beata had carried with her when she'd fled Poland.

But here was Casimir, young and strong and dressed in his Army uniform. He was a physician who had also been an Army reservist. When the Soviets invaded Poland in 1939, Casimir had reported for active duty to defend his country, along with thousands of other reservists. Also in the envelope was a Polish passport. It showed that Casimir had traveled to Paris in 1937. Margot knew that this was the year that he and her mother had married and spent their honeymoon in the City of Light.

The third item in the envelope was a letter, dated March 3, 1940, written from Beata to Casimir in which she'd told him she was pregnant. Beata had always wondered if Casimir had received that letter and if he had known they were going to have a child. Now Margot knew that indeed Casimir had known that she was going to be born the following summer. Being aware that her father had known about her brought Margot great comfort. Her biological father became more real for her. They had a connection. He had been able to anticipate, before he was brutally murdered by the NKVD, that he was going to become a father. Margot had never wanted to be anything but a physician, but she smiled an extra smile to herself because she knew her father, Casimir, would be proud of her career choice. She had followed in his footsteps. She had followed in the footsteps of both of her fathers.

Jolanta had included a very long and scrawling letter in the envelope with the three items from 1940. Margot had a difficult time making out Jolanta's Polish script as well as her words. She had to consult her Polish dictionary, and several of the words remained undecipherable. She was proud of herself when she had finally been able to translate Jolanta's long letter.

Dearest Malgorzata,

The items enclosed were brought by a courier to your parents' old house. The house has been vacant for some time now, so the courier knocked on my door when no one answered the door at the Wojciech home. The courier said he had a packet for Beata Wojciech whom he believed to be the surviving spouse of Major Casimir Wojciech, a Doctor of Medicine and an officer in the Polish armed forces reserves. I told him I had known them both, Beata and Casimir, even though I was a small child at the time Casimir had been arrested and sent to the Soviet prison camp. I told the courier that Beata had left the country many years ago. I told him that Beata was dead and that no one had seen or heard from Casimir since 1940. The courier told me he had been born in East Germany and had lived there until the wall came down. He said he understood completely how happy the Polish people must be that the Russians were finally gone from their country.

The German courier told me an odd story about these papers that he said had belonged to your father. He said these were relics from the Katyn Forest massacre. He said these papers were among those which had been taken from the bodies of the Polish men who had been murdered at Katyn and found in the mass graves there. Major Casimir Wojciech, formerly of Camp Kozelsk, a Soviet prison camp, was one of the men found murdered in a mass grave at Katyn. These papers, which had been removed from the bodies of the dead by the Germans who had discovered the graves in 1943, were proof that it had been the Soviets and not the Germans who were responsible for the murders in the Katyn Forest.

These documents were carefully preserved during the final years of World War II and after the war during the Cold War and the Soviet occupation of East Germany. These papers that belonged to your father, along with papers that belonged to the other Polish dead who were found at Katyn, had been secretly kept since 1945 by nuns who lived in East Germany. The courier said there were many boxes of documents that had been saved and hidden by the German nuns since the end of World War II.

Somehow, these boxes of papers had found their way, in the chaotic early spring days of 1945, to the town of Radebeul, Germany near Dresden. The courier told me an amazing story about how these documents were saved by a man who worked at the train station in Radebeul. For the duration of the Cold War, they were kept in the cellar of a Catholic convent in East Germany.

An important German doctor had boxes of these documents in his possession at the end of the war, in late April and early May of 1945. He'd put the boxes on a truck and intended to deliver the papers safely to Berlin. His truck ran out of petrol when he reached Radebeul, but he was able to make it to the train station. He instructed the station agent there to hold the documents for him. He wanted to be able to contact the Americans or the British and ask for their help to save the documents. These documents indicted the Soviet Union in a terrible crime. The German doctor was adamant that the contents of the boxes were very valuable and could not be allowed to be taken by the Soviets. The doctor said that if the Soviet army reached Radebeul before the Western Allies did, the station agent was to burn all the boxes. He insisted that the documents had to be destroyed rather than be allowed to fall into the hands of the Communists.

The station agent in Radebeul didn't know what the boxes contained, but he realized their contents were important. We all know that the Soviets reached the eastern part of Germany before the Allies did. The station agent, who had been given instructions that he was to burn the boxes of valuable documents rather than allow the Soviet army to take possession of them, could not bring himself to burn the boxes.

The station agent decided, all on his own, to take the boxes to a nearby convent. His sister was a nun at the convent, and the station agent was able to convey all the boxes to her safekeeping, just before the Soviet army reached Radebeul. The station agent returned to the station and burned some pieces of wood, as a way of pretending to show that he had indeed burned the crates of documents. When the Soviets arrived, they found only the smoldering wood. But they did not necessarily believe that the station master had burned the documents.

The nuns took possession of the boxes of documents and guarded them from the Stasi and from their Soviet masters for more than forty-five years. After the war and for the ensuing decades, the Soviets searched for these documents which were tangible and definitive evidence that they had committed the murders in the Katyn Forest. The Soviets were never able to find out what had happened to these boxes of evidence against them.

The courier told me that the many boxes of papers contained conclusive proof that the Polish citizens buried in the Katyn Forest were murdered by the Soviets in 1940. The nuns kept the papers hidden in the cellar of the convent during the years of the Soviet occupation of East Germany. If the documents had fallen into the hands of the Soviet Union or the Stasi, the secret police of the puppet East German Government, the nuns knew they would have been destroyed or altered in some way. The nuns knew that neither the East German Communist government nor the Soviets could be trusted. If they got their hands on these papers, they would disappear forever. The nuns carefully guarded and hid the papers from the Soviet authorities and their evil henchmen, the Stasi of East Germany. It was only after the Berlin wall came down and the Soviet Union collapsed, that the nuns were convinced that Poland would at last become free. Germany was reunited and became one country again.

Only then were the nuns, who had guarded these papers so religiously, willing to give them up. The nuns, who had saved the papers for the descendants of the murdered soldiers and the other Polish leaders at Katyn, felt it was finally safe to allow these personal items to be returned to the loved ones of the dead. It was decided that the documents should be returned to the families of those who had been murdered and buried at Katyn, even though they realized that most of these loved ones, who had actually known the men who were murdered in 1940, were now also dead.

The courier said that the nuns felt that the descendants of the men who had been murdered at Katyn would like to have these artifacts that had been found on their ancestors' bodies.

I knew you would want these things. I am just sad that Beata did not live long enough to have them returned to her directly.

My eyesight is declining...along with everything else in this ninety-three-year-old body of mine. It has been difficult for me to write all of this down for you, but I wanted you to know everything the courier said to me when he brought the packet of papers that belonged to your father. You may not hear from me again.

With much love to the child of my dear friends Beata and Casimir,

Jolanta, a neighbor

Arizona

2022

Seventeen

ATTACK IN PARADISE VALLEY

Annika K. Castillo, age 38, was brutally attacked and killed at a local luxury resort on Friday night. Castillo was a resident of Scottsdale and the wife of Igor Arturo Castillo, aka El Russo. Because of her husband's high profile and underworld connections, the investigation into her murder has been taken over by the FBI. The FBI will conduct the autopsy. According to the Phoenix Police Department's homicide division, Annika Castillo died at the scene. Authorities have been unable to locate the victim's husband to notify him of his wife's death.

El Russo is the son of the infamous Mexican drug lord, Ignacio Castillo, aka El Sagrado, and Anya Varvara Baranov, the so-called Bratva princess and heiress to one of the Russian Mafia's most extensive drug distribution networks in the United States. El Sagrado and Baranov died in 2018 when their home in Guadalajara was firebombed during the Mexican drug war in which several hundred people died. After his parents were murdered, El Russo took over both his mother's and his father's legacies as well as their drug distribution territories. Igor Castillo has become one of the most powerful drug kingpins in Mexico and in the western United States.

Drug bosses from Mexico are known to send their wives and children to live in the Phoenix area for security reasons. Families of cartel members live locally in the exclusive and wealthy neighborhoods of Phoenix. For decades it has been a common practice for cartel kingpins to send their loved ones, including their mistresses, to the United States where they can live relatively normal lives in luxurious, gated, and heavily-guarded compounds in cities close to the Mexican border. Relatives of these powerful drug lords live and attend school in the United States under assumed names, posing as American citizens. Sending their families north of the border is an attempt to keep their families safe from the constant drug violence and killing in Mexico.

Annika Castillo will be cremated. Her ashes will be scattered to the winds from an undisclosed mountain location in the Phoenix area. It will be a private ceremony. Mrs. Castillo is survived by her husband, Igor Castillo, and by her mother, Pia Karlsson.

▲

Igor Castillo first read about his wife's murder on his mobile phone. Then he bought a Phoenix newspaper and read the few details that the article disclosed about the crime. At first, he was in a state of shock. When his anger took over, he was uncontrollable. Usually, when no family is present at the time of death, law enforcement is able to notify the next of kin before any names are released to the media. In the case of El Russo's wife's murder, the usual notification procedures were not able to be followed. The Phoenix Police Department had not been able to locate Igor Castillo to inform him of his wife's death. Authorities have said they think that Igor Castillo has fled the United States. Because of her husband's high profile as the leader of a powerful drug cartel, it is believed that the news of Annika's death was leaked and reported prematurely to the local Phoenix television news stations and then to CNN cable news.

When Castillo saw his wife's photo and the information about himself and his parents disclosed on international television, he threw his mobile phone at the plasma flat screen. Then he threw a chair at the television and completely destroyed it. He threw lamps and furniture around the room. He screamed for his underlings to rush to do his bidding. He took his gun from the shoulder holster that he always wore and shot at the already destroyed television set and at the walls of the room until he was out of ammunition.

Igor Castillo had stopped being infatuated with Annika long ago, but she had been his most prized possession. She was beautiful. She was a good hostess. They'd had their disagreements, and he had to admit to himself that he had probably beaten her up too many times when they'd argued. He'd felt he had the right to beat her, but he knew that sometimes he'd been out of control. But she had been his. He had lost something of great value, and he was determined to find out who had taken Annika from him.

He screamed orders at his men. He had people inside both the FBI and the Phoenix Police Department. He wanted to know everything the FBI knew and everything that PPD knew. He wanted the autopsy report. He was certain that one of his rivals in the drug business had murdered Annika. He was sure her murder had been the opening salvo in a drug war in which his enemies were determined to destroy him and would try to take over his lucrative territories and networks. He was determined that would not happen. He demanded to know which of his many enemies was responsible for killing Annika. If he could not find out which competing cartel was to blame, he was committed to going after all of them. He was a madman on a crazed course of total revenge.

"I want all of them killed, and I want all of their families killed. I want them destroyed...the ones in Mexico and especially the ones who are hiding out in Arizona and in California. Put the ones in Phoenix and in Tucson at the top of the list. We know who these people are and where they are living. The gloves are off. I want them all murdered, and I want all of their houses burned to the ground. Blood will run in the streets, and the streets will burn. There will be no mercy whatsoever. They have challenged me. They have begun this war. I will finish it. I will finish it when they are all dead...including their women and their children."

El Russo had been at his home in Guadalajara when he'd learned the news. He refused to return to the United States. He blamed the entire country for Annika's death, for failing to protect her. He had thought she would be safe in the house he had provided for her. But she'd had to go off to the resort in Paradise Valley to indulge herself with their spa services. That was when she had been attacked. Annika always used an alias whenever she went anywhere. She had used her alias when she'd made her reservations to stay at the Mimosa Inn. She paid for her room and meals and for her spa services with a credit card issued in the false name that was not Castillo. She knew better than to use her husband's name. All of Igor's enemies kept track of his comings and goings. But Igor had not thought that anyone knew the name Annika used as an alias. Someone had been watching her, and they knew when she was not guarded. Someone had known she was alone at the Mimosa Inn.

Igor gave orders to have his house in Scottsdale burned down. He was going after nothing less than total scorched earth destruction. It wasn't that he grieved for the loss of the love of his life. It was that someone had stolen her from him. Someone had messed with him, messed with his lifestyle. Annika was his thing, and now she was gone. He could not allow that to happen. He was too rich and too powerful to allow anyone to do that to him. He would show them who was the boss.

Hector Gutierrez was Igor's first cousin on his father's side. The two boys had grown up together. Hector was El Russo's right-hand man, his confidant and bodyguard. Igor trusted only Hector. Igor sent Hector to Scottsdale to retrieve his laptop computer, his collection of expensive watches, and the contents of the safe that was hidden behind the wall in a secret compartment of the bookcases in his home office. When he had collected everything on Igor's list from the Scottsdale house, Hector was to burn the house to the ground. Igor didn't care if the fire marshal knew it was arson. He just wanted the house destroyed—gone from the earth. El Russo wanted no remnant of his life with Annika to be left standing. But before the house was destroyed, Igor had to have the information he thought was securely stored in his safe. He had to have the passwords and the account numbers in order to access the fortune he'd sent to banks in tax havens all over the world. Once the financial information and the other valuables in the house had been rescued, the house was to be torched.

Eighteen

It was their last night together, and the Camp Shoemaker reunion group was having a special dinner in the wine cellar of the Mimosa Inn. They had reserved the space for their party alone. It was an exceptional and private venue that had been in the lower level of the oldest part of the Mimosa Inn since it was built in the 1930s. They were always sad when the last day of their reunion arrived. Everyone had looked forward to the event in Paradise Valley, and they knew they probably would not be together again for another year.

All of the Camp Shoemaker boys would be celebrating their 80th birthdays during the ensuing twelve months, and each one planned to have some kind of party to mark the momentous occasion. Promises were made to fly to various corners of the U.S. to attend the birthday events. But as one entered the ninth decade of one's life, health and family considerations often interfered with the best-laid plans. Before they ended their yearly reunion, the group usually decided where the next reunion was going to be held. That hadn't happened yet, but everyone hoped there would be another get-together the following year. For this final night, they would laugh and drink some wine and appreciate their time together.

They enjoyed the charcuterie platters and the fry bread that arrived as their appetizers. A special menu with three choices had been part of the arrangement for having the dinner in the wine cellar. The choices all sounded so delicious; it was almost impossible to choose. The pork chop was stuffed with sourdough breadcrumbs, onions, celery, pecans, apples, and sage. An apple brandy, apple cider, and heavy cream gravy with mashed potatoes accompanied the chop. The grilled swordfish was served with a lemon and curry orzo pilaf, and the marinated, Spatchcock roasted chicken arrived, glazed and sizzling and scented with thyme, on a bed of colorful, roasted and caramelized vegetables. Hand-cut French green beans served al dente with mushrooms and butter was the vegetable of the day. All of the vegetables had been grown in the gardens of the Mimosa Inn. Or so the menu claimed. Dessert was flan covered with homemade butterscotch sauce and toasted almonds. Dark chocolate truffles were served as an after-dessert treat. The reunion goers were groaning after the fabulous Mimosa Inn wine cellar food and the wines that had accompanied their extraordinary repast.

They said their goodbyes with hugs and some tears. The Ritters, the Carpenters, and Bailey MacDermott would be meeting one last time the next day for brunch on the outside patio dining room at the Mimosa. Gretchen was leaving early the next morning for a conference she had to attend in Los Angeles. Bailey was staying an extra day at the Mimosa

Inn so he could make a second trip to the Desert Botanical Garden which he loved. Sidney and Cameron were flying on their private plane to Dallas where Sidney had an appointment with a specialist to do something about her kidney stones. After her health had been restored and she'd had a chance to rest, she and Cameron would fly to Turkey and Bulgaria where he had big business deals pending.

Tyler Merriman had already left to drive home to Colorado. Although he always hoped for early snow because he loved to ski, this morning he hoped the snow would hold off for one more day until he'd made it home. He was still an avid skier and always looked forward to his time on the slopes. But it was November, and he could run into bad weather driving through the mountains. He had to make it home before an approaching blizzard blocked the roads and delayed his drive. Everyone's thoughts and prayers were constantly with Olivia and J.D. Steele.

Matthew Ritter and Richard Carpenter were going quail hunting in an area that was close to the San Carlos Reservation. The reservation was a two-and-a-half-hour drive directly east of Phoenix to what the hunters hoped would be quail-rich country. If there were not many quail to be had in San Carlos, they would drive to Wilcox, Arizona, southeast of Tucson, to try to track down the delicious birds. Matthew still had his hunting cabin outside of Sonoita, and the two planned to spend a few days there.

Elizabeth was looking forward to spending time in her room at the Mimosa Inn. Late in life she'd discovered a passion for writing that kept her intellectually challenged as well as happy. She had always loved reading mystery novels and had read many thousands during her long life. When she'd turned seventy, she found that she could write mystery novels as well as read them. She let her imagination run wild, and her stories were complex and exciting. She fell in love with the characters she created for each book. She enjoyed her writing tremendously. Her endorphins flowed when she wrote, and she was never happier than when she was working on a new book.

Elizabeth had made some progress on her next book, but the discovery of several packages of fentanyl tablets in her casita had been an enormous distraction. The drug stash that she'd discovered had made her more than a little bit nervous. She didn't know much about illegal drugs. She had immediately called law enforcement and told Detective Cecilia Mendoza of the Phoenix Police Department the story of her discovery. The only other person with whom she had shared the information about what she'd found in the colorful ceramic pot was her husband Richard. No one else in the reunion group knew anything about her discovery of fentanyl in the Carpenter's casita. Elizabeth could only hope that the bad guys would not be coming back to the room to pick up their drugs or to look for their money.

Elizabeth knew something unusual was going on with the Ritters. She didn't know what it was, but neither one of them had been themselves for a couple of days. They both seemed unusually tired. Matthew and Isabelle Ritter were always two of the most energetic members of the group, but they now seemed preoccupied and lacked their usual enthusiasm. Elizabeth was puzzled and concerned, but she didn't want to ask intrusive questions.

Isabelle was always so glad to see everyone during the first days of the reunions, but she had a very demanding business that required her attention at home in Palm Springs. Towards the end of the reunion events, she usually seemed ready to get back to her store. She received countless texts and emails on her phone, even when she was on vacation. Isabelle had mentioned to Elizabeth on their first day in Paradise Valley that she was swamped with work. She had said she was planning to fly back to California the morning after the final dinner in the wine cellar. But something had changed.

It was a surprise to Elizabeth when Isabelle told her she had arranged to spend several extra days at the Mimosa Inn. Bookings at the resort were tight, and there had been some tense moments before Isabelle was able to convince the inn's staff to extend her reservation and allow her to stay in the same suite. Finally, it had been arranged, but Isabelle seemed agitated that she was staying in Arizona longer than she'd planned. She explained the longer stay by saying she was exhausted and needed the extra rest. She said she had been working much too hard in Palm Springs and was desperate to get away for a few days of unscheduled R and R. Always on the go, it was very unusual for Isabelle to stay for any extra days after the reunion had ended. Elizabeth had to admit that her friend looked worn out and seemed as if she really did need the rest.

The last five reunion goers in Paradise Valley met for brunch on the Mimosa's patio the following day. They ordered an international assortment from the eclectic menu. Richard had the Huevos Rancheros. Bailey chose a half-pound cheeseburger with everything and an order of fries. Matthew and Isabelle split the turkey club sandwich, and Elizabeth had the Swedish crepes with lingonberry syrup. Richard ordered a dessert of cinnamon churros, and it was a huge order, much more than he could handle on his own. He passed the churros around to the entire table. Everyone took a bite, and Matthew was delighted to finish off the entire thing. They said their goodbyes again.

Elizabeth suggested to Isabelle that, since she was also staying on at the Mimosa while her husband went hunting, the two of them might get together for dinner. Isabelle's answer was vague, and she seemed to have a lot on her mind. She said she needed to talk to Elizabeth after everyone else had left. She said she needed Elizabeth's help with something. Elizabeth hoped perhaps her talk with Isabelle would shed some light on what was going on. Elizabeth said she would be happy to help if she could and looked forward to their talk.

The men left after brunch as scheduled for their hunting trip, and Elizabeth worked the rest of the day on her writing. She took a short walk with her rollator outside on the Mimosa Inn's paths where she enjoyed the flowers and the fresh air. She spent some time sitting on her patio watching other guests walk by her cottage. She loved to people watch and gather material for her mystery stories from the people she observed. She didn't hear anything more from Isabelle about either talking or getting together for dinner.

Detective Cecilia Mendoza spoke often with the FBI agent who was in charge of Annika Karlsson Castillo's case. "I've been in touch with the Ritters daily. They have assured me that Annika is recovering. But she almost died, and her injuries were severe. The Ritters arranged for her to have miraculous and life-saving surgery, but it's going to take more than a few days for her to convalesce from the attack and from the surgery. I know it's vital that we get her out of the Mimosa Inn and out of the state of Arizona as soon as possible. It seems like it has been a long time, but it has really only been three days since the attempt on her life."

The FBI agent was nervous. "I'm just not sure I'm comfortable with not knowing where Annika is going...once she has recovered from her surgery. I know we agreed that no one in either the FBI or in Phoenix PD would have this information, but I'm not sure these people, the Ritters, can adequately provide her with the security she needs. Matthew and Isabelle Ritter are up there in years, although the wife is considerably younger than the husband. They both still have all their marbles, but can we really depend on them to get a severely injured and on-the-mend Annika to some secret hideout? I know you think they are taking her to someplace in California, but how can they get her all the way out there on their own? And if she is still recovering from her injuries, how can they possibly take care of her once she arrives there, wherever there is?"

Cecilia Mendoza was adamant. "I feel strongly that we have to honor our agreement with Annika. She does not want us to know where she is going into hiding, and I am going to trust the Ritters to get her there. Annika heard about her mother's second stroke a few days before she was attacked. She went to visit her mother and realized her mother was not going to be able to recover from this one. She told her mother goodbye. I heard from the nursing staff at the rehab hospital that it was incredibly sad. Annika knew she would never see her mother again." Cecilia paused, thinking how difficult it must have been for Annika to tell her mother goodbye.

Cecilia continued. "I met with Annika on the day she was attacked. That afternoon, she told me she knew her mother would want her to go ahead with the plans they'd made. Of course, the schedule has all changed now. But Annika again insisted that she did not want to share anything about her plans to disappear with me or with the FBI. I respect that. We all know there are way too many leaks to allow that information into either of our organizations. It's sad to have to admit that things are that way, but it's the truth."

"Of course, we already have Annika's deposition about everything she knows. That should be all we need to bring in a number of the bad guys. But you know as well as I do that the impact of having a live witness tell it all to the jury or to the judge is huge. Annika would be a compelling witness, and I would love to have her there in person if any of this ever comes to trial."

"Annika has promised to testify in person if we need her. I believe she will follow through with that." Cecilia hoped she could put an end to the FBI agent's insistence that the FBI know where Annika would be in hiding. "We know Annika's mother does not have long to live. Annika has assured me that her mother arranged everything that has to do with the safe house before Pia had her first stroke. If Annika trusts that her mother had everything set for her, I believe her. The Ritters have promised me again that they will be able to get Annika to the safe house, even though she has now been badly hurt. I've offered to help in any way I can, but Isabelle Ritter assures me they have it all arranged. The husband is a doctor. He's retired, but he knows what he's doing. And they have this mysterious friend Freddy, the trauma surgeon with the mobile hospital, who is helping them."

"This whole thing is so far removed from the way we usually operate. I am very uncomfortable with all of it." The FBI agent almost seemed to be more worried about Annika's husband than she was about Annika's hiding place. "We still have not been able to locate El Russo. I can only believe that he has heard the news that his wife has been murdered. Of course, we don't know and may never know if he was the one who ordered her death or if her death was planned by someone entirely unconnected with him or his drug business. The assault on Annika may be connected with whoever ransacked her room the night before she was attacked."

The FBI agent continued. "If the husband believes her death was caused by one of his rivals or someone who is trying to break into the drug trade by challenging him, he may consider Annika's death a personal affront. Even though he beats her up and has other women, he may still think he loves her. He may think of her as property that was stolen from him. These drug people have a distorted sense of morality, and the ones at the top are malignant narcissists. And El Russo is certainly one who is at the top. We can't get inside his head, so we don't know how he will react or if he will react at all. If he ordered the hit on his wife, there won't be any drug killings, no drug war. But, if he wasn't the one who had her killed, there could be serious consequences. We'll just have to wait and see. I would really like for the witness to be very far away from the Mimosa Inn before we have to find out what those consequences will be. El Russo is half Mexican and half Russian. He has a really explosive and unpredictable personality. We think he might be bipolar, given his manic-type eruptions. I wouldn't want to be married to him... or be around him at all. He really is a maniac."

"If he's so volatile, how has he been able to be so successful?" Cecilia was trying to understand this drug lord, but of course she knew that El Russo was such a bizarre and erratic character that figuring him out completely would be an impossible task.

"He inherited it all. He didn't have to build it. Building something takes some people skills and some organizational skills. He doesn't have either of those. The empire was already built when his parents died. At that point, it was all basically handed to him. He has become an enforcer, and he's very, very good at that. He is brutal. If someone gets out of line, he punishes them and everyone they know and care about. Everybody's afraid of him. The people in the drug business, even his own people, the people who work for him, are terrified he might come after them for some minor transgression. He rules his fiefdom through terror."

The FBI agent knew a great deal about El Russo, and Detective Mendoza was listening. The agent continued. "Another factor is that he has a right-hand man who seems to be able to talk him down when he gets crazy. This guy, Hector Gutierrez, is his first cousin on his father's side. Hector is smart and level-headed. He graduated from the University of Arizona with a degree in business. He's Hispanic, obviously. He doesn't seem to want to take over from El Russo. He doesn't want to be the boss of it all, and he seems to genuinely love his cousin, even as crazy and out of control as Igor can get. They grew up together. It's curious why Hector is so laid back. But thank goodness for him. He is the only voice of reason that El Russo will listen to. He's diffused more than one drug war that El Russo wanted to get into."

"Let's hope nothing happens to Hector."

"Hear! Hear!"

Nineteen

Matthew Ritter and his childhood friend, Richard Carpenter, left Paradise Valley to hunt quail on the San Carlos Reservation. Matthew had seriously considered cancelling the hunting trip to stay at the Mimosa Inn so he could help take care of Annika. He and Isabelle had talked it over, and they had decided he needed to follow through with his previously made plans to go hunting. It wouldn't make sense to Richard or to anybody if Matthew cancelled the hunting trip and then stayed around at the Mimosa Inn for another week. Isabelle and Freddy would have to be the ones to hold down the fort at the casita that had been converted into something resembling a hospital recovery room.

Keeping Annika's presence under wraps was as critical as keeping her alive. The "do not disturb" sign had been hung on the doorknob, and there had been serious negotiations with housekeeping about staying out of the room. Freddy had finally told the cleaners that the person in the room had a case of COVID-19 and was contagious. He had no trouble keeping everyone away after that. By day three, it looked as if Annika was going to pull through from her injuries.

Freddy Kernigan had been able to put his hands on several pints of O negative blood and had transfused Annika. The transfusions had probably saved her life. Freddy wanted to know Annika's blood type so he didn't have to keep chasing down O negative blood, which was always in short supply and always in demand. And it was expensive. Freddy also wanted to know if Annika needed another transfusion.

He had a kit that he carried in his mobile hospital that typed blood and measured a person's red blood count, among other things. He would have preferred to send Annika's blood to a real lab, but somebody would have had to pay for the lab tests. Annika Karlsson Castillo was no more. Annika was dead, and her insurance policy with United Healthcare could no longer be used to pay the medical bills. Freddy felt it was essential to have the test results. The only way for him to find out that information was to draw her blood and test it himself. That is what he had to do and what he did. The situation was complicated. When he got the results of the tests, it turned out that Annika actually had O negative blood. So much for trying to save some trouble and some money. Freddy gave her two more transfusions.

Isabelle had been to the rehabilitation facility in Tempe to visit her friend Pia Karlsson. Isabelle thought, or maybe imagined, that Pia had squeezed her hand when she'd been sitting beside her bed. Isabelle knew Pia was not going to get any better from her second stroke. Pia was on a ventilator. She was unable to breathe on her own. Isabelle was devastated by her friend's deteriorating physical condition. Isabelle had promised to help Annika, and she was determined not to let Pia down. Isabelle was committed to doing everything within her power to make sure that Annika lived. She would do whatever was necessary to deliver Annika to the safe house that Pia had set up for her daughter before she'd had her first stroke.

Isabelle had only an address and the driving directions necessary to transport Annika to the safe place where she would hide out from her abusive husband and his drug crews. Isabelle knew it was a remote cabin, but she knew nothing else about it other than how to program its address into her GPS. Initially, it had not been necessary for Isabelle to know more than where to take Annika. Now Isabelle was concerned about whether or not Annika would be able to take care of herself once she reached her hideout. Would Isabelle have to stay and take care of Annika, and for how long?

Isabelle felt she was under the gun to move Annika out of the Mimosa Inn as quickly as possible and deliver her to the secret hiding place. She hadn't told Freddy Kernigan anything about why Annika hadn't been able to go to a regular hospital after she'd been attacked. Isabelle had not even wanted to tell Freddy Annika's name, but that had been silly. Freddy knew her name was Annika. He didn't need to know her last name. Freddy knew something weird was up, but he didn't ask questions.

Isabelle kept after Freddy, asking him how soon Annika could be moved. Freddy knew that for whatever reason, it was urgent that his patient get out of the casita at the Mimosa Inn ASAP. He'd received the message loud and clear from Isabelle that his patient was in trouble of some kind and had to be moved away from the resort.

Freddy was torn, as were the Ritters, between allowing Annika time to adequately recover and moving her out of harm's way as soon as possible. Isabelle asked Freddy how they would be able to transport someone who was in Annika's condition. She would have to be moved a considerable distance without putting her at any increased physical risk. Isabelle also continued to ask Freddy when he thought Annika would be well enough to get out of bed and take care of herself. Of course, nobody really knew the answers to any of these questions.

In addition to her other serious injuries, Annika had suffered a head injury. Trauma doctor, Freddy Kernigan, had made a decision to put her into a temporary coma to keep her brain from swelling. This was standard procedure for serious brain injuries, and Annika was still unconscious three days after the surgery. No one would know to what extent she had suffered any permanent brain damage until she could be brought out of the medically-induced coma.

Isabelle had promised Pia that she would be sure Annika made it to the safe house. Now Isabelle realized she was going to have to also make a commitment to taking care of Annika until Annika was able to function on her own. Isabelle knew nothing, at this point, about Mona Damours who was waiting in the mountains outside Pinetop, Arizona for Pia Karlsson's daughter to arrive. Annika was in a coma and could not tell anybody anything. Because no one except Annika and Pia knew about Mona, no one had been able to let Mona know that Annika had been attacked or that Pia had suffered a second and probably life-ending stroke.

Mona had expected Annika to arrive sometime on Sunday. On that day, Annika had been undergoing life-saving surgery in a mobile hospital parked in a wash in the Phoenix desert. Mona had no way of knowing that Annika was fighting for her life in a casita at a resort in Paradise Valley. Mona had not seen a Phoenix newspaper or any news report on her phone about Annika's death. Sooner or later, she was bound to see that news, news that was not true, news that had been made up to fool the world and especially to fool Igor Arturo Castillo.

Because Isabelle and Matthew had made the difficult decision that, in order to keep even the smallest hint of Annika's existence a secret, Matthew would have to continue with his hunting trip. Matthew could have been of considerable help to Freddy Kernigan, and Isabelle desperately needed help getting Annika to the mountains. But Isabelle and Matthew decided it was more important to be certain no one knew Annika was a patient at the resort than it was for Matthew to stay and help. Isabelle would have to get Annika to the safe house without any assistance from Matthew.

Isabelle did not want Freddy Kernigan to know where Annika's safe house was located. Both Matthew and Isabelle trusted Freddy, but Freddy loved to talk—especially about his mobile hospital. Isabelle was concerned that he might drink too much at a party one night and decide to tell the story of the patient he had saved with his mobile unit...a patient right here in Paradise Valley. That was already a risk they'd decided to take, but Isabelle was determined that Freddy could not know where Annika would be hiding out in the future. Isabelle absolutely did not want that secret place in the White Mountains to become a part of Freddy's repertoire of stories.

Isabelle needed to talk to someone about what to do. She needed to talk things over with someone she trusted. She trusted her friend Elizabeth, but Elizabeth would not be able to do anything physically to help her move Annika. Elizabeth's disabilities disqualified her from being able to help lift or aid in moving Annika. But Elizabeth still drove.

Elizabeth had worked miracles, despite her disabilities, to save her friend Henley Breckenridge. Elizabeth had brought

Arizona, 2022

Henley home to Paso Robles, California, from halfway around the world, and she had done it all without anyone, except her very closest friends, knowing what she was doing. Isabelle had promised Pia that she would not tell anyone else about Annika's situation. But circumstances had changed dramatically since that promise had been made. Isabelle felt that under the circumstances, Pia would have agreed that Elizabeth could be trusted. Isabelle decided to tell Elizabeth everything and ask for her help.

🌲

Isabelle called Elizabeth and suggested they have dinner together that night. Elizabeth sounded pleased that Isabelle had called. Isabelle told her friend she needed to consult with her about a very serious situation she found herself involved in. Isabelle would explain it all when she brought take-out to Elizabeth's room that evening. It was difficult, but not impossible, for Elizabeth to get to the restaurant at the Mimosa Inn. And Isabelle wanted privacy. A table in the hotel's restaurant would not provide the privacy she felt she needed. She knew Elizabeth loved the food from a certain Greek restaurant that had also been a great favorite of the Ritters during the years they had lived in Phoenix. Isabelle would bring all of their favorites as well as her long list of problems to Elizabeth's casita that evening.

🌲

Isabelle ordered the food and a bottle of Retsina. She had rented a car, thinking she would use it to get Annika to her safe house. After Annika was attacked, Isabelle realized she was going to have to trade the rental car for a van. She would need a van that could accommodate a wheelchair or, heaven forbid, a stretcher. She decided to think about that later. Isabelle put a cooler in the car to keep the take-out food warm, drove across town to Nostimo, and picked up her order. She knew Elizabeth loved Greek food and food from Nostimo in particular.

Isabelle was bringing the fried cheese appetizer that the cook made for special customers only, spanakopita and tyropita, hummus, bread, Greek salads, a triple order of dolmades, a half dozen small meat pies, an order of stuffed eggplant, lamb kabobs, and baklava. Isabelle knew she was ordering too much food, but Elizabeth would enjoy having the leftovers to warm up in the casita's microwave. She would not have to order from room service as often.

Elizabeth almost swooned when Isabelle brought the delicious-smelling food to her door. They had the best Greek picnic ever, and they each had a glass of the Retsina. Neither Isabelle nor Elizabeth had tasted any Retsina in years, and the rough flavor was a shock. They agreed it went down more easily when accompanied by the flavorful Greek food.

After they had eaten all they could of Isabelle's wonderful take-out meal and packed away the leftovers in the mini-fridge, Isabelle told Elizabeth everything about Annika's situation. When she told Elizabeth about her old friend Pia Karlsson's strokes, Isabelle broke down and cried. She scolded herself for breaking down and forced herself to continue. Isabelle explained about El Russo's drug connections and why *everything* about Annika had to be kept strictly hush hush. Even people in law enforcement could not know. Absolutely no one could know where Annika was going.

Isabelle confided to Elizabeth that the FBI did not know who had attacked Annika. Elizabeth immediately understood why it was vital that everyone continue to believe that Annika had died in the brutal attack at the Mimosa Inn. Isabelle pulled no punches when she described how seriously Annika had been hurt. She saw Elizabeth cringe when she told her that Annika was in critical condition at the Mimosa Inn, being cared for by non-nurse Isabelle and flaky Freddy Kernigan. Elizabeth also understood why Isabelle could not ask Freddy to help her deliver Annika to the White Mountains.

Elizabeth had questions. "It seems everything right now depends on Annika's coming out of the coma. When can Freddy make that happen? You need to know if Annika has suffered any brain damage and to what extent she is able to help with her own recovery. I'm not a medical person either, so we have to trust Freddy to let us know when Annika can be moved. I know you intend to trade your rental car in for a van with a wheelchair lift. But can it accommodate a person on a stretcher? There must be such a thing. Your rental vehicle might even have to be an ambulance. I don't know if you can rent one of those, or if they will allow you to drive it yourself. You have to rent some kind of a vehicle that you can drive. You don't want anyone else to know where you are taking Annika, so you alone can drive her there."

Isabelle looked overwhelmed as she considered all these options and the decisions she would have to make. "There's something else. Pia bought a used car, an older Jeep with 4-wheel drive, for Annika to have at her mountain hideout. Apparently there is a garage at the safe house, so the car will be hidden and out of the weather. After she bought it, Pia parked it inside a storage unit—the day before she had her first stroke." Isabelle looked as if she might begin to cry again, but she overcame her tears.

"I think she had intended to drive the Jeep into the mountains when she delivered Annika to the safe house. I don't know exactly what the original plan was. Fortunately, even after Pia had her first stroke, she was able to tell Annika to give me the keys and the instructions about where to find the Jeep. Pia wanted Annika to have a car to drive if she needed it. Maybe she wanted Annika to have a car so she could make a quick getaway in case Igor found her. I don't know exactly why it was so important to Pia for Annika to have the car with her in the mountain hideaway."

Isabelle sighed. "The Jeep is already in the parking lot and has Annika's things in it. But if I am going to take two vehicles to Pinetop, I need somebody to drive one of them up there for me. Can you do that? I know you still drive. We will leave the Jeep at the cabin. Depending on Annika's condition, we will drive back here together in whatever vehicle I'm going to rent. Or, if I have to stay with her to take care of her at the safe house, you will have to drive the van or the ambulance or whatever back here. It will take the entire day to get up there to where we are going to leave Annika and to drive back here to the Mimosa."

Elizabeth wanted to help. "As you know, I still have a license, and I'm a good driver. My problem is getting in and out of various kinds of vehicles. I can probably get in and out of the Jeep, but the van might be tough for me. You might have to get a van with a lift to get me in and out of it." Elizabeth laughed a small laugh. "I'm serious, though, we are going to need a van from some kind of a medical transport company—for Annika and for me. If I have to drive myself back here in the van, we might need a special kind of lift in the van. Do you really think you will have to stay there with her and take care of her? Will you stay there with her until Matthew comes back and can pick you up? This is all getting pretty squirrely."

"The best case would be if Annika is able to take care of herself once she's at the cabin, and I am able to drive back here with you. I will then be on the next plane out of here. I have a couple of clients who are angry with me because I am not in Palm Springs right now, like I promised I would be. The very wealthy can be incredibly demanding. They can be infuriatingly impatient. I have already had to cancel several appointments, and nobody is ever happy to have any kind of an appointment cancelled."

🌲

Elizabeth didn't hear anything from Isabelle the next day, and she was able to throw herself entirely into her mystery writing. She was thankful for the Greek leftovers. She warmed them up in her microwave and had a delicious and quick dinner. The next morning, Isabelle knocked on her door. She was anxious to talk to Elizabeth.

"I have good news and bad news. The good news is that Annika is conscious and does not seem to have any brain damage. She does not remember anything at all about the attack. She remembers putting her computer and her phone into her carryall and heading out the door. She doesn't remember anything after that. She thinks it was Igor who sent someone to kill her, but I told her not to jump to conclusions. She knows not to say anything to Freddy about anything."

"That really is great news. Is she able to get around or stand up or anything? How severely injured is she still?"

"Her injuries are very bad. She may never walk again... her legs have been so badly damaged. Her head wounds seem to be healing more rapidly. She was attacked by a machete or something similar, so she has lots of cuts on her neck and torso. Some of them are very deep. Freddy glued together as many of the smaller slices as he could. He had to put in quite a few stitches, and somebody is going to have to take those out. Wound care is critical, and warding off infection is a big issue. But, here's the other really good news." Isabelle smiled for the first time that morning.

"There is some kind of a woman up in the mountains that lives in the cabin next to the one where Annika is going to hide out. Apparently, this Mona somebody and Pia became fast friends while Pia was organizing the safe house and getting it ready. Mona did all of the work renovating the older cabin where Annika will live. Annika says this Mona person will be able to take care of her. The woman has a satellite phone but doesn't like to use it very often. Annika is going to call her and leave her a message. Pia apparently told Mona everything about Annika's situation, so when Annika can reach her on the phone she's going to tell her everything she knows about the attack and about how the plans have changed. Annika will ask Mona if she's up to taking care of an invalid. Annika is very anxious to get away from Phoenix, and I don't blame her. I'm anxious to get her out of town, too."

Isabelle had a lot of news. "Freddy says Annika doesn't need a stretcher. She will be in a wheelchair when she leaves here. So, I ordered her a new wheelchair from Amazon, and Amazon has promised that it will be delivered later today. It's going to be delivered here...to your casita. I know you already have a wheelchair, but it seemed less suspicious to have the new one delivered to you rather than to me. I hope you don't mind. Annika thinks she can, with Freddy's help, get herself into the wheelchair. That will be much easier to deal with than a stretcher. I am on my way right now to turn in my rental car and pick up the van that has a wheelchair lift. The place where I'm renting the van is going to teach me how to use the lift and how to get a wheelchair-bound person in and out of it. I am planning to move Annika tomorrow. Can you go with me tomorrow?"

"Of course I will go with you tomorrow. We can put my wheelchair into the back of the Jeep. I will have to bring my little steps that I use to get into tall beds, in case I can't climb up into the Jeep on my own. I'm pretty sure I can handle the Jeep, and you will be driving the van back to Phoenix...thank goodness. But this is all incredibly good news. You said there was bad news. What's the bad news?"

"The bad news is the weather. It's November, and we will be driving up into the mountains. We will be going up into the White Mountains, to around seven thousand feet, to deliver Annika. It hardly ever rains in Phoenix, but of course it's going to rain tomorrow...and the next day. So what comes down as rain here at one thousand feet will be snow in the White Mountains. The van I'm renting has the wheelchair lift, and it also has all-wheel drive. That's the best I can do. The Jeep you will be driving has 4-wheel-drive. You won't have a problem, unless it gets really bad. It's supposed to be a two-day, pouring-down-hard rain here. That doesn't usually happen in November here in Phoenix, but it is going to happen tomorrow and the day after."

"What about Matthew and Richard? Are they coming back here? I know quail hunting in the snow...or the rain...isn't ideal."

"I'm a little concerned about that myself. They will be at three thousand feet when they are hunting in the San

Carlos Reservation, so they should get rain. Of course, hunting in the rain isn't any fun either. Matthew finally got a satellite phone after I bugged him about it for years. But it's heavier than a regular iPhone. So of course, he leaves it in the truck when he is in the field. He says he can't handle a dog, a gun, his shotgun shells, and a satellite phone all at the same time. So the phone gets left behind. You probably didn't know that he brought Dixie on the plane with us when we flew here for the reunion. The Mimosa Inn has special kennels for dogs. He left Dixie in one of the kennels, and he went to visit her every day. Actually, he visited her several times a day. He brought her along specifically so she could go hunting with him and Richard on this trip. I thought it was ridiculous to bring her on the plane and all of that, but he was determined that she was going to go hunting with them. So she was here all the time, and now she's gone to the San Carlos Reservation with them. I think Matthew was embarrassed to tell the others he'd brought his hunting dog with him. Of course Richard knew he was bringing Dixie, but Matthew swore him to secrecy."

"Richard never said a word to me about the dog. I had no idea. So they took Dixie with them. But you can't get Matthew to call you back on his satellite phone? I've left a couple of message for Richard, but I know there is terrible cell tower service in many of the places where they're going. I wish they would go down to Wilcox or Sonoita, if the weather is going to be really bad east of here."

"I wish they would, too, but you can't tell Matthew what to do when it comes to hunting quail." Isabelle was anxious to leave to trade in her rental car and pick up the special van. "So, are you still up for this road trip...even with bad weather coming?"

Elizabeth knew Richard would put a big nix on the plan, if he'd been anywhere around to hear about it. Elizabeth was nervous about driving the Jeep in a snowstorm. She felt vulnerable driving an unfamiliar vehicle as well as driving in bad weather. Richard would be furious if he knew what she was going to do. But Elizabeth wanted to help Isabelle, and she wanted to help Annika. "Of course, I'm up for the road trip. I hope we can make it up and back in one day . . . in spite of the weather. I don't do well sleeping in strange places."

"Great. I've got to run now to pick up this special van with the lift and learn to use it. I'll check in with you when I get back. Please send me a text when the wheelchair arrives from Amazon. They promised to get it here today, but sometimes they mess up. Delivering to a resort is probably a little more complicated for them than delivering to somebody's home. If it hasn't arrived by four o'clock, call the lobby. If they don't know anything about it, call me. I'll come by this evening to pick up Annika's wheelchair. I want to get an early start in the morning. I plan to get Annika into the van before dawn. I'd like for you to follow us, but I'm going to text the GPS information to you so you will know where to go in case we get separated. It's less than a three-hour drive one way. But that's in good weather."

"Before dawn is really early for me. I will order a room service breakfast for six in the morning. That's the earliest they'll bring breakfast, I think. Can you push my wheelchair to the parking lot at 6:30 a.m.?"

"I'll send Freddy to push you to the parking lot and help you get into the Jeep. He can put your wheelchair into the back of the Jeep for you. He knows Annika is leaving tomorrow. He's not happy about it, but I think he understands it has to happen. After we leave, he will clear out the casita. He will move out all of the hospital equipment that we don't take with us. He wants to send some things with Annika. I told him neither one of us knows how to start an IV. Annika claims she doesn't need the IV anymore, but she wants us to bring all the stuff that is necessary for starting the IV. So I am packing that in the van. I'll be by later to pick up the wheelchair, and I'll see you at 6:30. Text me if you have any questions."

Elizabeth had a difficult time concentrating on her writing that day. She hoped Richard wouldn't call her. She didn't lie, so what in the world would she be able to say to him if he called and asked her what she was up to. After Isabelle had picked up the wheelchair that Amazon had delivered, as promised, Elizabeth went to bed early. But she couldn't go to sleep. She was anxious about how things would go the next day. She could feel the barometer dropping, and it was dropping quickly. She had always been very sensitive to the fluctuations of the barometer. It felt to her as if this coming storm was going to be a significantly bigger one than the Weather Channel was predicting. She didn't like driving on slippery roads... even at sea level, but who does?

Moscow To Guadalajara

1945–2018

Twenty

Lavrentiy Pavlovich Beria was Joseph Stalin's most powerful and longest serving chief of the Soviet Union's secret police. Beria was Stalin's hit man and was the person who carried out Stalin's most vicious and deadly commands. Stalin appointed him Deputy Premier in 1941. Beria served as the head of the feared and hated NKVD from 1938-1946. In 1946, the NKVD's name was changed to the MVD, the Ministry of Internal Affairs. The MVD was still the secret police of the USSR; it just had a new name. Beria, as the head of the MVD, continued his reign of terror against the people of the Soviet Union until he was executed in 1953.

In 1947, Beria was at the height of his power. That same year, he met Tatiana Volkov who was only seventeen years old. She was a ballet dancer with the Kirov Ballet Company, and when Lavrentiy saw her on the stage, he had to meet her. He went to her dressing room after the ballet. Beria had a wife and a son, and he was completely committed to his Communist politics. He had no time and no place in his life for a mistress. But Tatiana was innocent and beautiful and enticing. She was captivated by Lavrentiy's power and position in the Soviet hierarchy. Tatiana knew how to charm, and she flattered and seduced the older politician. He had to have her, and they began their affair later that evening.

Lavrentiy Beria stole time away from his duties as a leader of the Soviet Union, and he even neglected some of these duties, to spend time with his mistress. He was captivated by the young and nubile Tatiana. She was every older man's fantasy, and she belonged to Beria. He kept her in a luxurious apartment close to the Kremlin and visited her often. By 1949, Tatiana was pregnant with Beria's child. She refused to get rid of the baby and in June of 1950, she welcomed a beautiful female infant into the world. Lavrentiy Beria and Tatiana named their child Irina Volkov.

Having given birth to a child, Tatiana was even more voluptuous and alluring than she had been as a trim and youthful ballet dancer. Beria could not get enough of her. Beria had been Stalin's right-hand henchman for many years. He was cruel and vicious and violent in his job as enforcer. But he never beat Tatiana. He was never angry with her. She always had her way with him. She saw only the best side of this meanest of the mean and powerful in the Soviet Politburo. A mass murderer in every other aspect of his life, he was in love with and adored his mistress Tatiana. He also adored their child Irina.

When Stalin died in March of 1953, Beria, the man who was old enough to be Tatiana's father, if not her grandfather, realized that things were going to change in the Soviet Union. Politicians were jockeying for power in the vacuum that was left by Stalin's death. Both Beria's contemporaries and his underlings in the Kremlin began to treat him differently. These changes in the behavior of others toward him were slight, but Beria was smart and acutely tuned in to political nuances.

He shared everything with Tatiana, and he told her he was afraid he had become persona non grata in the Soviet state. He had been close to Stalin, and when Stalin died, political upheaval was inevitable. Stalin had called Beria his "Himmler." Beria did not know what he had done to deserve the shift in attitude towards himself, but because he had been so close to Stalin, he feared he might be arrested as the efforts to grab power intensified in Moscow. The politicians who were competing for Stalin's job were cleaning house and getting rid of those who had been loyal to evil Joe.

That Lavrentiy Beria had a mistress whom he worshiped was not a secret to his colleagues. They knew where Tatiana and Irina lived. Beria realized that if he was arrested, both Tatiana and Irina would also be arrested and would probably be killed. If and when he lost his power and influence in the government, he would lose his ability to protect them.

After Stalin died, Lavrentiy told Tatiana that in case he was arrested, he had arranged for her and Irina to immediately leave the Soviet Union. He explained to his mistress that because of her relationship with him, if something happened to him, Tatiana and Irina would also be at risk. He told them that if the Kremlin turned against him, both mother and daughter would be in mortal danger. He told Tatiana about the plans he'd made for them to travel to South America where hopefully they would not be able to be touched by the long arms of Soviet Communist power. In secret, he made expensive and elaborate arrangements for his mistress and their child to escape what he was afraid was inevitable and would be coming soon.

He purchased first-class train tickets for them and arranged for their voyage across the Atlantic Ocean. He reached out to people he trusted to help Tatiana and Irina escape with their lives. He laid out for Tatiana in detail the plans he had made for her to survive his arrest and probable execution. Beria provided his mistress and their child with alternate identities. He provided them with the papers they would need to prove they were the imaginary people these papers said they were. He hoped he had thought of everything to save these two people he cared about. He had done everything he could to be certain they would be safe on another continent, and he had sent a great deal of money abroad to provide for them financially. They would have a quiet but comfortable life far from the Rodina.

Tatiana had arranged a small birthday celebration for Irina whose third birthday was on June 26, 1953. The celebration included Beria, Tatiana, Irina, and an older woman who lived in the apartment next to Tatiana's. The neighbor sometimes babysat for Irina when Tatiana and Beria went out for the evening. There was champagne and caviar and roasted chicken. Tatiana had baked and iced a rich yellow cake with sugary pink icing. Irina blew out three candles. Beria gifted his three-year-old daughter an antique gold heart-shaped locket. After the party, the neighbor returned home, and Irina fell asleep in her little bed. Beria and Tatiana made love on the chaise in the drawing room of the apartment. It would be their last time together.

Beria was arrested later that day. He was taken to prison. But he was able to send word to Tatiana that she was to activate the escape plan he had put in place. Tatiana and Irina were to leave Moscow by train that night. Tatiana knew what she had to do. She had her instructions, and she had several sets of papers for herself and Irina.

Beria had told her weeks earlier to begin packing up her things. He had suspected that events would eventually go badly for him. Above all else, he wanted to save his lover and their child, and he went to his jail cell knowing that he had made careful plans for them to escape. Tatiana had packed up her clothes and her other belongings that would fit into suitcases. She was able to pack her jewelry, but she had to leave behind the furniture, the Limoges china, the silver, and most of the other luxuries Beria had provided for her during their years together.

Tatiana used the hair coloring she had secretly purchased a month earlier. Her light red, strawberry-blonde hair would disappear forever. She would dye her hair dark brown. She would still be beautiful, and her hair would still be curly. But she would have to bid goodbye to the Titianesque hair she had been born with. Irina's hair would stay blonde. Tatiana cringed as she cut off her daughter's blonde curls. Irina was going to become Pavel, a young boy, for the duration of the journey to their new home.

Tatiana was running out of time and hurriedly gathered the golden locks she had removed from her daughter's head. She flushed the blonde curls down the toilet. She put the packaging in which her own brown hair dye had been purchased into her tote bag. She could not leave behind any evidence that she had changed her hair color or that Irina's hair had been shorn. Beria had been insistent. Any evidence that they had changed their appearances could not be left behind at the apartment.

Tatiana's lover had explained that his colleagues in the Kremlin knew about her and knew about Irina. They knew where they lived. They knew what Tatiana and Irina looked like. Beria told Tatiana that after he was arrested, men would come to the apartment to look for her and their child. He told them they could absolutely not be in the apartment when these men arrived. Mother and daughter would have to be gone. The men would be coming to kill Tatiana and Irina. When they did not find them at the apartment, they would search everywhere to try to discover where the two had fled. If they found evidence that either one had dyed their hair or that either one had cut their hair, they would have a clue about what the two might look like on the run. This could not be allowed to happen.

All papers that had to do with their new identities had been hidden away in Tatiana's carryall bag for weeks. Beria had provided a set of identity papers for their journey and a different set of identity papers for their new life in South America. Beria had still been an important person in the Soviet Union when he had used his influence to obtain these new identities for Tatiana and Irina.

When the photographs were taken for their new passports and various other identity papers, both mother and daughter wore wigs. Tatiana wore special makeup. Beria wanted both Tatiana and Irina to look, in the new photographs for the new identity papers, as much like they would look after they had dyed and cut their hair. He wanted to be sure that they looked as close as they could to the way they would look they when they were escaping and using their new identities.

When these photos were made for one of Tatiana's new passports, Beria insisted she apply the same makeup she would put on for the disguise she would use on the train ride across Europe and aboard the ship. Tatiana and Irina would travel from Moscow to South America using the identities of Pavel and Olga Lebedev. They would be a young lad aged three accompanied by his great aunt. For that long journey, Tatiana would wear clothes and makeup that made her look much older and much heavier. Tatiana's clothes, hair, and face would transform her into a matronly great aunt in her fifties. She would have to use the makeup and wear the padding she had under her clothes until she was safely in South America. Irina would have to pretend to be a boy with short hair during their escape from Moscow.

Tatiana had protested, but Beria had been blunt. He had told her this was the price they had to pay to save their lives. The disguises were designed to be used during their travels. Beria hoped that by the time they had reached their destination, they would no longer have to wear any disguises. He was sad that no one would ever again see Tatiana's beautiful red hair, but that was the price she had to pay to keep on living.

Beria had provided train tickets for Tatiana and Irina to leave Moscow and travel to Lisbon. From Lisbon, they would travel by ship to South America. Olga and Pavel Lebedev had tickets for first class private sleeping compartments on the trains for the entire trip from Moscow to Lisbon. But they did not have reservations. Of course, Lavrentiy had not known precisely when their escape plans would have to be activated. He had not known the exact date on which they would have to leave Moscow. So it had been impossible to make reservations for compartments on the numerous trains in which they would travel during the nearly four-thousand-kilometer journey from Moscow to Lisbon. Tatiana knew it would be a long and tiring journey.

But she also knew she was very lucky. Few people in the Soviet Union could afford to travel first class and have their own sleeping compartment.

Tatiana and Irina Volkov would disappear forever. They would not be at the apartment when the men from the Kremlin came to find them. There would be no evidence left behind that they had changed their names or their appearances in any way. They would simply vanish. They would begin their long journey on board the midnight train from Moscow to Vienna with fifteen pieces of luggage.

Their train would travel exclusively through the Soviet Union until it reached Vienna. This would be the part of their trip where they would be most at risk. The secret police would be looking everywhere for Beria's mistress and love child. The two would have to stay in disguise and inside their compartment all the way to Vienna.

In 1953, Vienna was still controlled by the four major victorious powers from World War II: the United States, Britain, France, and the Soviet Union. In addition to the train tickets and new passports, Beria had provided Olga and Pavel with the special papers they would need to leave the Soviet Union, travel to Vienna, and continue on their way. From Vienna, the remainder of their train trip would be outside the Soviet Union through Western Europe...from Vienna to Paris, from Paris to Madrid, and from Madrid to Lisbon. Olga had tickets, but she would have to book their accommodations for sleeping compartments along the way as she traveled.

Beria realized that the only language Tatiana and Olga knew, other than Russian, was some French she had learned in school. She would struggle to use her French to negotiate her way as she traveled on the train from Moscow to Lisbon.

Beria wanted her to use her French as much as possible and to completely avoid speaking Russian until she reached South America.

The first-class sleeping compartments were more than a luxury. They were also a hiding place. Beria told his mistress and his daughter that they were to stay inside their train compartment most of the time, even after they had left Vienna. They were not to walk around in the train or talk to any of the other passengers. The fewer people who saw her and the child, even with their disguises and new names, the better their chances would be able to escape successfully. If they had little or no contact with others, the more likely it would be that they would make it to their final destination without being discovered.

Once they left Vienna, they would have their meals delivered to their compartment and avoid the public dining cars on the trains. They were to stay low key all the way to Argentina. The tickets were in their travel names, the same names that were on the passports that Beria had provided to them for their journey across Europe and across the Atlantic Ocean.

Once the two arrived in Lisbon, Beria had arranged for them to contact a trusted ship's captain. The boy Pavel and his great aunt Olga might have to stay in a pensión in Lisbon for a few days or even a few weeks, but the captain had been paid to take them on board his cargo ship and deliver them safely to Buenos Aires. It would be another long and stressful trip across many miles of ocean.

There were adequate, if not luxurious, sleeping quarters on the freighter for the boy and his aunt, who would still be traveling as Olga and Pavel Lebedev. Meals would be brought to them in their ship's cabin. The freighter would make routine stops in Havana and Cartagena before it finally reached Buenos Aires. The two who were fleeing the Soviet Union would follow Beria's advice and keep to themselves during the long ocean voyage of more than ten thousand kilometers, from Lisbon to Argentina.

※

Years earlier Lavrentiy Beria had purchased a small horse ranch in Uruguay. The ranch was several hours drive from the city of Buenos Aires. He had bought the property as a possible future home for himself, in case he ever had to escape from the complexities and viciousness that characterized the politics of the Kremlin. He knew he had committed terrible crimes. He knew that one day he might have to disappear to avoid paying the price for having been Stalin's assassin. He knew that when Stalin died, her might be out of favor under a new regime.

When the time came, the ranch in Uruguay was intended to be Beria's getaway. When he had purchased the ranch, he had done it through a lawyer in the west and a convoluted and obscure process of contracts and corporations. He had set it up so that his own name would never be associated with the property in any way. It would be the perfect place for Tatiana and Irina, who would become Marina and Anya when they reached South America, to hide and live their lives.

Beria had kept a minimal staff at his ranch, while he continued to live in the Soviet Union. Even though he was now in prison, through friends, he arranged for the staff to prepare the ranch and the house that was on it for Marina and Anya. He had already made significant financial provisions for them, and they would want for nothing while they lived on the ranch.

▲

On the day of his arrest, Beria had been able to arrange a last-minute reservation for Tatiana and Irina, who would be traveling as Olga and Pavel Lebedev, for the first leg of their journey, the train trip from Moscow to Vienna. He had also arranged for a hired car to drive them to the train station. It was imperative that they leave Moscow that night. If they waited even a day, it would be too late. Tatiana packed sandwiches and bottled water so they did not have to go to the dining car.

Tatiana struggled to explain to Irina what was happening. She coaxed her daughter into believing they were playing a game, and for their game, Irina would have to pretend to be a boy. Curious about why her mother looked so different and appeared to be so much older and so much fatter, Irina asked her why she was playing dress-up. Irina told her daughter that they were going to pretend to be different people while they had a great adventure traveling on the train and then on a ship across the ocean. Tatiana told Irina she would explain everything eventually, but she insisted that as soon as they left their apartment, got into the car, and as long as they were traveling on the train or on a boat, the little girl must agree to pretend to be a boy, Pavel Lebedev. Pavel would have to remember to call Tatiana "Aunt Olga." If anyone asked him his name, he was to tell them it was Pavel Lebedev.

The journey from Moscow to Lisbon took many days. There was a great deal of changing trains and waiting for the next express train. The two travelers sometimes spent the night sleeping in the train station. Olga had money for adequate lodgings, but sometimes it was easier to stay in the station than it was to move to a hotel for the night.

Olga Lebedev devoted considerable time and energy to keeping an eye out that their many pieces of luggage made the transfers from one train to the next. It was an arduous journey for anyone, but it was especially difficult for a woman with a small child. She had believed Lavrentiy when he said they would be in danger if they stayed anywhere in Europe. She followed his directions exactly and made her way across multiple countries and thousands of kilometers on the train to reach a freighter that would sail from Lisbon to Buenos Aires.

When they arrived in Buenos Aires, they left immediately for the ranch in Uruguay. In Uruguay they became Marina and Anastasia Varvara Baranov. Anastasia would be known as Anya. Worn out from their many weeks of travel, Marina and Anya arrived at the ranch in Uruguay in November of 1953. Only one of her several pieces of luggage had been lost during the complicated journey from Moscow. Marina was exhausted and ready to rest. Everyone on the ranch spoke Spanish. No one spoke Russian. Marina and Anya were going to have to quickly learn to speak Spanish.

Lavrentiy had made an excellent escape plan for them, and Marina had done her best to follow it as exactly as she could. As far as Marina knew, no one had followed them on their journey. No one had found them. At last, she felt confident that no one had been aware of how they had accomplished their disappearance. She also felt secure that no one in their new country had any idea who they were. No one knew of their relationship to the NKVD's Lavrentiy Beria or why they had left Russia.

Beria had been primarily concerned for their safety. He hoped that by the time they reached Uruguay, they would be far enough away from the politics of the Kremlin that no one would know or care who they were. He hoped that their association with him would have become obscured by the distances they had traveled and by their various changes of names. When they settled in Uruguay, Beria hoped that Marina and Anastasia would have little contact with the Russian community in South America.

He had instructed Tatiana that she would have to continue to dye her hair brown, probably for the rest of her life or at least until it turned gray. She could shed her old lady clothes and become a young woman again, but she could never go back to having the beautiful light red hair she'd had during her years living in the Soviet Union. Beria knew that children changed as they grew older, so he was not as worried that anyone would recognize Irina. She would have changed somewhat by the time she reached Uruguay. She would grow up. She would be taller. Her face would mature. Her hair color would change. She would look different every year. If her mother was safe, she would be safe.

Beria had held onto a wild and crazy hope that somehow he would not be killed, that he would escape execution. He dreamed that he might be allowed to emigrate from the USSR to South America. He told Tatiana that his greatest wish was to someday be able to join her and Irina. They both knew this was a pipe dream, but it was the only hope they could hang onto.

It was not until months after his execution that Marina learned of Lavrentiy Beria's death in December of 1953. Marina had learned to avoid other Russians, and she did not speak her native language to anyone. She had not yet learned to read the newspaper in Spanish. Lavrentiy had told her ahead of time that a firing squad would be his fate, but of course they had both hoped that he might be spared. She grieved for the man she had loved. She never married again.

Anya was a spirited child and grew up to be a rebellious teenager. Marina suspected that her daughter had inherited her father's ambition and drive, maybe even his aggressive and domineering personality, his love of danger and violence. Marina was a dancer at heart. She considered herself to be an artist. She wanted to live well and in peace. She had no desire to cause trouble or participate in the wider world. She was content to focus on what happened at her ranch. Anya, on the other hand, was a handful as a young woman, and Marina was often overwhelmed by her daughter's behavior. The two were often at odds. They were very different people. They shared a love of horses and riding and often rode together. Marina was frequently horrified by the chances Anya would take when she was riding. Marina nearly had a heart attack when Anya, at age sixteen, rode through the ranch at full gallop standing on her horse's bare back.

From time to time, Marina had attempted to tell Anya something about the past they had shared in the Soviet Union. She wanted to tell Anya something about her father. She wanted Anya to know that she and Anya's father had not been married, but that Anya had been born to two people who had loved each other and who both loved her very much. She wanted to share with Anya the story of the journey they had made together from Moscow to Uruguay.

But Anya seemed to have no interest in the past. She told her mother she did not want to hear about a man who had abandoned them.

Marina had insisted that Anya learn to speak Spanish as well as Russian. She had forbidden her daughter to speak Russian with anyone but herself. Anya married one of their ranch hands when she was only eighteen. The marriage didn't last, and fortunately there were no children.

Anya graduated from college which she attended in Buenos Aires. During her years living in the city, Anya continued to live her wild life. She was attracted to other Russians and enjoyed the luxurious and decadent lifestyles they lived in the city. Although Anya did not use drugs herself, she became involved with other wealthy Russians in Argentina who were heavily into the drug trade. She hung out in Buenos Aires with other Russian ex-patriots who were unconstrained by the rules and beliefs of communism and socialism.

Those who had left the Soviet Union were delighted to embrace private enterprise with enthusiasm. One of the most lucrative businesses with which they could become involved was trafficking in narcotics. Marina did not approve of Anya's association with these drug traffickers, but there was little she could do to control the behavior of the daughter who had Lavrentiy Beria's blood flowing in her veins.

In the late 1970s, Anya Varvara Baranov met the charismatic leader of the Mexican drug cartel based in Sinaloa. She was already rich and powerful in her own right when she met Ignacio Castillo, aka El Sagrado. Anya Baranov had become an important force within the Russian Mafia in South America. She was smart, and she loved taking risks. She was also ambitious. Ignacio Castillo was her equal in brains, bravado, and greed. They were a natural pair who would, during their years together, revolutionize many aspects of the illegal drug trade.

Over the ensuing years, the Russian and Mexican couple built a drug empire that extended from Mexico across the border into the western United States. The Castillo family already controlled much of the manufacture of drugs in northern Mexico, and through Anya's Russian mafia connections, they eventually also controlled many of the distribution networks in the western United States.

At age 30, Anya became pregnant with Ignacio's child. They named their son Igor Arturo Castillo. Igor was spoiled and indulged. He was also educated and raised to take over the drug empire his parents had built. His nickname was El Russo, a nod to his mother's ethnic heritage. He had been a mean son of a gun from the minute he was born.

The infamous Ignacio Castillo and Anya Varvara Baranov, the so-called Bratva princess and heiress to one of the Russian Mafia's most extensive drug distribution networks in the United States, had achieved wealth beyond their wildest dreams. They lived in a luxurious fortress in Mexico and employed dozens of security guards to keep them safe. But they both died in 2018 when their home outside Guadalajara was firebombed during a Mexican drug war. Their volatile and violent son Igor Castillo had begun to participate in running the drug business years earlier, but when his parents both died in the bombing, he inherited it all. At last, he was unrestrained by his parents' rules and values. His ambition and his aggression now knew no bounds.

> # *Arizona*
>
> *2022–2023*

Twenty One

"*Turo, we need to talk.*" Hector Gutierrez had always called his cousin by the childhood nickname Turo. The name was derived from Igor Castillo's middle name, Arturo. When the two little boys were just learning to talk, Igor was too difficult for Hector to pronounce. He was able to say Turo without any trouble. Ever since, Igor Arturo Castillo had been known as Turo to his first cousin. "I know you are angry. I am angry, too. But are you certain you want to commit to all this killing — to avenge Annika? From time to time, you have spoken to me about wanting to divorce her. You have a serious girlfriend. I know you still had some feelings for Annika before she was killed, but I can't help but wonder if this reign of terror you're getting into is really about your wife. Or is it about an attack on you? We need to decide if all-out revenge is really in our best interests. We've got some very important irons in the fire right now, projects we need to focus on."

Igor Castillo was so enraged; he was not able to hear let alone answer Hector's questions with any kind of rationality. He was not thinking clearly.

Hector continued. "The plans to make our own fetty in the United States are moving forward quickly. But if you refuse to go back into the U.S., that is going to complicate things. We may have to shut down that project. We have product being sent to California and to Arizona, and we need the cooperation of quite a few people to make sure we are able to get all the raw materials together that we need to manufacture the fentanyl. You have to be on site in Arizona to make sure everything comes together there." Hector paused to see if his cousin was paying any attention to what he was saying. "I'm also worried that, if you set out on this mission of revenge, even our own people will become frightened about what is going on and will decide to disappear. We have invested a great many resources in our decision to manufacture fentanyl in the United States, and the profits will be huge."

Igor had a blank look on his face. He didn't seem to hear anything his cousin was saying to him.

Fentanyl usually comes across the border into the United States from Mexico already made into powder or tablets. It frequently comes into the U. S. already mixed with heroin or cocaine. Border Patrol agents and DEA agents were in a never-ending battle of wits with drug traffickers. Those who were bringing fentanyl into the U.S. were constantly devising new and more creative ways to smuggle the drugs.

Specially constructed compartments hidden inside the gas tanks of trucks had always been one of the drug traffickers' favorite ways to hide bags of the deadly fentanyl. In fact, secret compartments of all kinds had been built into vehicles that legitimately crossed the border from Mexico on a regular basis. Trucks bringing furniture and vegetables often had packages of drugs secured in the empty spaces of the interiors of their doors. Spare tires stored in the backs of all kinds of vehicles could be filled with packages of fentanyl tablets. Any place that had empty space inside a car or truck could be used as a repository for bringing drugs across international borders.

There were tunnels that went from Mexico to the United States. It was often very difficult to detect the presence of these tunnels, and many served as busy drug trafficking conduits for years before they were discovered and shut down. In recent years, drug dealers had been using mini submarines that made their way through the waters of the Pacific Ocean carrying drugs north of the border. Drugs were loaded into the mini subs in Mexico and delivered to various and constantly changing remote locations along the California seacoast.

The financial rewards of smuggling even a small quantity of fentanyl were so great, motivation was extremely high to find new and more imaginative ways to move the drugs into the United States. People taped hundreds of fentanyl tablets to their legs, put on a baggy pair of jeans, and walked across the border from Nogales, Mexico to Nogales, Arizona. These amateur traffickers were often caught.

Drug trafficking has always been driven by demand. The demand for illegal drugs drives the drug trade in the United States, whether it is the addict chasing the high that fentanyl and heroin can deliver or the soccer mom craving the anxiety-reducing effects of oxycodone. Demand drives and determines the supply of drugs that are sold inside the United States. If there were no demand and no addictions, there would be no financial reward for smuggling drugs across the border. Given the predilection of so many North Americans to buy and use mind-altering substances, the illegal drug business flourishes. If there is a demand for something, someone, somewhere will always respond to that demand by providing a supply. This is a law of economics.

The ingredients for making fentanyl have in the past come primarily from China. More raw materials for making fentanyl are beginning to be imported to Mexico from India. The components of this man-made narcotic are sent to Mexico where they are combined and made into fentanyl powder and fentanyl tablets. Fentanyl is frequently combined with cocaine and heroin and other drugs. The drug user often doesn't know the strength of the fentanyl he is using. Or, she doesn't know how much fentanyl has been added to the other drugs she uses. They don't know how much fentanyl they're taking into their bodies. Sooner or later too many of them die from an overdose of something they bought and consumed without knowing what was in it.

Because of high demand and because of the huge profits that are to be made, fentanyl traffic into the U.S. from Mexico has increased. There is a certain amount of risk involved with smuggling drugs across the border. Enterprising drug dealers in the United States have figured out that they can make their own fentanyl inside the U.S. There are still many risks, but if the drugs are made inside the U.S. there will be fewer seizures of drugs at the border, fewer confiscations when packages of drugs are discovered in the gas tanks of trucks carrying roof tiles from Mexico to housing developments in Phoenix. To be able to manufacture fentanyl stateside would avoid so many difficult issues for drug traffickers.

El Russo and Hector Gutierrez were already at work setting up their own fentanyl factory in Tucson, Arizona.

The problem they faced was importing, mostly from China, the necessary quantities of the components used to make the drugs. They sought to solve this problem by ordering only small amounts at a time of the major ingredients that are required for manufacturing fentanyl. They ordered one of the components sent to a farm in Bakersfield, California... a town in the central valley where many agricultural products are grown.

They had another one of the ingredients sent to an upscale and unremarkable family home in Tucson. The house was in a neighborhood of other expensive houses. One drug crew member lived there and kept a low profile. He was at the door to pick up the deliveries of the important ingredients when they arrived. The Gem Show was an international event held in Tucson in late January. Quantities of goods from China were shipped to Tucson for the Gem Show. Packages of one of the fentanyl ingredients, disguised to look like semi-precious stones and other pieces of jewelry, were sent to the house in Tucson for the Gem Show in January.

The cousins hired a chemist in Flagstaff to make the third essential component of the drug. The chemist was able to produce small amounts of the necessary ingredient. Hector was working on how to increase his production to sufficient levels. It was a complicated process. They had rented an anonymous warehouse in a commercial area of Tucson. This would become their manufacturing center.

This idea of making fentanyl inside the USA was a new twist in the operation of the usual fentanyl drug trade. Hector was organizing the complicated details, and El Russo was making sure that everyone did as they were told to do. Hector had leased the farm in California and the expensive home in Tucson. He had provided the chemist in Flagstaff with the space and the equipment for his secret laboratory. The set-up was expensive, but the ultimate payoff was going to be huge. Hector had a business degree. He was interested in being a financial success in the drug business. El Russo was less practical. He liked the violence and the power that flowed from his being an enforcer. It took the skills of both men to pull off an operation like the one they were attempting.

Hector saw his cousin's violent anger over Annika's death and his desire for revenge as a threat to everything they had worked so hard to build. Hector was not into revenge and bloodletting. He was into money. He was constantly working to rein in his cousin. Hector had repeatedly counseled Igor about the beatings he inflicted on his wife, Annika. Hector feared that sooner or later, law enforcement would come to the Castillo home. Hector was the one who had found the oral surgeon and brought him to the house to repair Annika's jaw. Hector was the one who had hired the doctors who had tended to the other wounds Annika had suffered at the hands of the abusive El Russo.

Hector knew that if his cousin followed through with the all-out war of retribution he seemed determined to pursue, their entire empire might collapse. They all might die. Hector was going to do his best to keep that drug war from bringing down everything he had worked for. Keeping the unpredictable and volatile Igor Castillo under control was becoming more and more difficult. He was turning into a crazy man. Losing his wife had pushed him over the edge.

🌲

It took several days for Hector to get to his cousin's house in Scottsdale and retrieve the information that was stored in the safe. Hector brought back everything his cousin had told him to find. Then Hector had burned down the house in Scottsdale, as his cousin had asked him to do. It took a few more days for El Russo to get around to checking his various off-shore accounts. He had no reason to think anyone except himself had access to any of them. He took his money for granted. He always had plenty of it, and he had sequestered millions in various bank accounts around the world. He was momentarily consumed with other things.

A call from his accountant prompted him to check his bank accounts. The accountant had received a call from a bank in Lichtenstein that Igor's account had been closed. The accountant was touching base with Igor to ask why he had closed the account. It was a few more days before Igor realized that all of the money he thought he had hidden away had suddenly disappeared. His accounts were empty.

He went crazy again with rage. He blamed hackers. He blamed his enemies, and he knew he had made many of those over the years. He had been so certain that no one, not even his own wife, knew where his wealth was secured. He had no idea that Annika had discovered the combination to the safe and had found his account numbers and his passwords.

Hector had almost brought his cousin under control and had almost convinced him that it was not in their best interests to perpetuate a drug war and a blood bath. Discovering that someone had stolen his money had set El Russo off again. He was more determined than ever to go after his rivals and kill them and their families. Hector knew he was now going to have an even more difficult time convincing his cousin not to declare all-out war.

Twenty Two

Elizabeth had not been able to go to sleep the night before. She was worried about whether or not she would be able to get into and out of the Jeep she had to drive the next day. She was uncomfortable about driving an unfamiliar vehicle. She didn't like the fact that the weather was supposed to be rain in Phoenix and snow in the White Mountains. She was concerned about Annika and wondered if the woman, who had barely survived such a terrible assault, was really well enough to make this trip. Elizabeth finally fell asleep around four o'clock in the morning. Her alarm woke her at five thirty. She had to get dressed and be ready to eat her breakfast which was being delivered at six. She was groggy and not operating on all cylinders when she dragged herself out of bed.

She pulled on a pair of leggings and then the warmest pants she'd brought with her from Tucson. When she had packed for the reunion trip, she'd planned to be in Paradise Valley. She hadn't counted on driving into ice and snow and below-freezing temperatures. She put on a silk t-shirt she rescued from her dirty clothes bag. The next layer was a cotton turtleneck and then a heavy cotton fisherman's knit sweater. She would wear her leather coat that was always warm and top it all off with her plastic rain poncho that folded into its own pouch. She wished she had a more waterproof poncho, but she was thankful she always traveled with the bright yellow plastic square that folded away into such a small package.

By the time she'd put on everything except the leather coat and the poncho, she wondered if she'd overdone it. She could barely move her legs. She felt like a toddler who'd been bundled into a stiff and confining snowsuit. It was the two layers she'd put on her already inflexible legs that immobilized her. She hoped she would be able to climb up into the driver's seat of the Jeep, dressed as she was. She'd ordered a hearty breakfast the night before and was feeling very full after finishing the meal of pancakes and sausage. She felt like a stuffed turkey and wondered if she would be able to move when the time came.

When she opened the door to put her tray outside on the patio table for room service, she realized the rain had already arrived, and it had arrived with a vengeance. This was more than the usual Arizona misting rain or a passing storm. This was a real thunderstorm with pounding rain like the ones that occurred in Ohio and on the East Coast. Elizabeth was used to driving in the rain, but she began to worry again about what this rainstorm would be like when it became a snowstorm.

There was a knock at the door. She grabbed her tote bag and the steps she used to get into the high, king-size bed. She thought she might need the steps to get up into the Jeep or into the van for the return trip. She pushed her wheelchair close to the door and opened it to greet the man she'd been told was Freddy Kernigan. He was dressed in a poncho with a hood that covered most of his face. Elizabeth had never met Freddy, so it didn't really matter that she couldn't see what this man looked like. She thought he was staring at the steps she held in her hands.

"I have to take these steps. I might need them to get into the Jeep."

"I can't hold onto those and push your wheelchair at the same time. You'll have to hold the steps on your lap." Freddy was clearly not into polite exchanges or introductions. He was no nonsense and let's get this done. That was fine with Elizabeth. Isabelle had warned her that Freddy was odd.

It was still dark, and the wind was fierce and blowing sideways. They made their way through the pathways of the Mimosa Inn to the parking lot. Freddy was rushing, which was okay with Elizabeth as her head was already soaking wet. Freddy knew exactly where the Jeep was parked, and Isabelle's rented van was parked next to the Jeep. The plan was for Elizabeth to get into the Jeep and wait for Isabelle to bring Annika out at the last minute, just before they left. Isabelle was confident, she'd told Elizabeth, that she knew how to operate the van's lift and would be able to get Annika safely and quickly inside the vehicle.

Elizabeth did need the steps to help her get into the driver's seat of the Jeep. She was able to do it mostly by herself without assistance from Freddy. He was obviously impatient with her need for the steps and didn't want to waste his time with her. He folded up her wheelchair and chunked it into the second seat. He threw the small set of steps in behind the wheelchair. Then he was gone without a word. Elizabeth wanted to turn on the heat. She was chilled and wet. Isabelle had filled the Jeep with gas but wanted to leave the gas tank half full when they delivered it to Annika's hideout. Elizabeth knew if she got too cold, she would get sick. She turned on the heat.

The rain was coming down so hard she almost didn't see Isabelle and Freddy arrive with Annika. It seemed like it took them forever to get the van's lift working and to load Annika, who was sitting in a wheelchair, into the van. Finally Elizabeth received a curt text from Isabelle that she was ready to leave. The address and the route were already programmed into Elizabeth's phone. She was warmer now thanks to a pretty decent heater in the Jeep. She had a bottle of water in the cup holder, and she was ready to go.

Elizabeth had promised Isabelle she would follow the van as closely as she could. Unfortunately, they were leaving town just as rush hour in Phoenix was beginning. And it was raining. People who lived in Phoenix were used to monsoons in late summer, but they did not have to drive in pouring rain very often. There were several accidents on the roads, including a bad one on the 101 loop around the city. Elizabeth was tremendously relieved when they'd finally left behind the traffic and the complicated highways of Phoenix.

Elizabeth began to relax. She wanted to accomplish this task and get through this trip without an incident. She knew her lack of mobility was something of a liability. Isabelle had needed somebody to drive the Jeep. Elizabeth had been her last resort. Elizabeth had been the last man standing. Of course, Elizabeth was not a man, and she wasn't standing. She was, in reality, the last old lady sitting in her wheelchair. But she was a good driver, and Isabelle trusted her with knowing the location of Annika's secret hideout. She was the only person left who could help Isabelle get Annika out of town. Elizabeth was going to do her best.

The plan was that they would not stop for any reason. There would be no pit stops for the bathroom and no stops to put gasoline in the vehicles. Isabelle thought the van would be able to make it to the White Mountains and back on one tank of gas. But she had not anticipated the traffic and the accidents and the time she'd spent idling while everything on the Phoenix highways had come to a standstill.

It hadn't been easy, but Elizabeth was able to follow the van on Route 87 until they reached Payson. Elizabeth was thankful for the Jeep's 4-wheel-drive and had not felt insecure on the slippery road. As soon as they had entered the Tonto National Forest, the rain had turned to snow. Once the caravan of two vehicles arrived in Payson, the temperature dropped significantly and the snowfall had become a blizzard. Elizabeth was having a difficult time keeping Isabelle's white van in view. There were other vehicles on the road, and in the whirling snow, they all looked white. The altitude in Payson, Arizona was five thousand feet, so Elizabeth knew the snow was only going to get worse as she continued to climb into the Mogollon Rim of the Colorado Plateau. She still had at least two more hours of driving to go, and it would all be in a serious snowstorm.

🌲

Isabelle had been stressed before she'd attempted to get Annika into the van. She was wishing she had asked Matthew to cancel his hunting trip and stay behind to help her with this nightmare. She had been able to operate the lift without any problems when there had been nothing on the lift. She had practiced working with the lift because she wanted to be able to use it efficiently when the time came. She didn't want to waste any time once she had Annika's wheelchair locked in. The longer Annika sat out in the rain, the more likely it would be that she would get sick. Annika's health was already compromised, and Isabelle did not want to make things worse by fumbling around with the van's wheelchair lift while Annika sat in the rain. But the lift did not work exactly the same way when there was a wheelchair on it as it had when it was empty. There had been a snag, and by the time Isabelle had Annika's chair secured inside the van, both Isabelle and Annika were seriously stressed and completely soaked.

For the past few days, Annika had been spending all day every day lying in bed, recovering from the assault and the surgery. Sitting in a wheelchair was tiring for her. The trip to the White Mountains had not yet begun, and she was already worn out. As soon as Isabelle got the van on the road, Annika fell asleep. Isabelle was thankful she didn't have to talk to anyone while she was driving, especially with the rain and the traffic. She glanced in her rear-view mirror from time to time and was glad to see that Elizabeth had been able to stay close behind the van. A couple of times Isabelle thought she'd lost the Jeep in the snarly Phoenix rush hour, but somehow Elisabeth had been able to find her again.

Isabelle was concerned about her patient. Freddy had wanted to keep Annika hooked up to an IV during the drive to the mountains, but Isabelle hadn't wanted to do that. They had compromised with a care package that Freddy put together. He'd put everything necessary to hook up an IV into a large bag. He filled a box with bottled water, energy drinks, energy bars, and Annika's medications. Annika promised to take her antibiotics on schedule and drink as much water as she could. Isabelle made good time on the road once she had escaped from the Phoenix metro area.

Isabelle was worried because Annika had been sleeping for several hours without eating or drinking or taking her medicine. Isabelle had a box of sandwiches she'd ordered from a deli in Scottsdale. She'd been certain that she and Elizabeth would arrive at their destination before noon, and she had intended for the sandwiches to provide their lunch. That was not going to happen now...at least not in the original timeframe.

Isabelle had planned to reach Annika's mountain cabin and meet Mona before noon. Isabelle now had to admit that they were not going to make it past Pinetop and to the cabin in the woods by midday. State road 87 was icy, and the snow plow had not yet arrived to clear the two-lane road. The van had all-wheel-drive, but Isabelle knew the rented van's tires were not new. She didn't know what she could have done about that, but she felt she should have done something.

She knew Pia had put new tires on the Jeep before she'd parked it in the storage facility. Pia had given Annika the rundown on everything she'd taken care of so that Annika would have a safe vehicle to drive if she needed it. Isabelle wished she had spent more time checking out the van. She had been so concerned about the lift; she'd neglected to worry about the tires. The van was crawling slowly. Visibility in the blowing snow was close to zero. Safety, not speed, had to take priority. In spite of Isabelle's best efforts and in spite of her slow and careful driving, the van hit an icy spot, ran off the road, and found itself stuck in a ditch full of snow.

Isabelle knew she would not be able to get the van out of the ditch on her own. Rescue would require a tow truck.

She had a satellite phone, and she could have immediately called for a tow truck. But she decided not to do that. She had gone to such great lengths, and Pia Karlsson had gone to such great lengths, to keep anyone from finding out that Annika was still alive, she could not risk having a tow truck come to get the van out of the ditch. Annika would have to be safely someplace else, far away from the accident in the snowdrift, before a tow truck could be called and the van could be moved. Isabelle decided to call Mona and crossed her fingers that the artist would answer her phone.

Mona had a satellite phone, but she didn't carry it with her or check it very often. Isabelle knew Elizabeth did not have a satellite phone. There was no point in trying to call Elizabeth. The reception for a regular cell phone in these hinterlands was sometimes spotty. Even if she could reach Elizabeth, it would not be possible for the two of them to transfer Annika to the Jeep. Even with Mona and Isabelle and Elizabeth all working together, it might be impossible for them to move Annika out of the van and into another vehicle. Isabelle left a message on Mona's satellite phone. Isabelle's satellite phone told her precisely where she was...as she sat in the van off the side of the road in a snow bank. She would be able to tell Mona her exact latitude and longitude. Mona called her back in less than five minutes. Isabelle explained what had happened. She told Mona that the van was in a ditch and why she didn't want to call a tow truck. Fortunately Mona grasped the situation at once.

"Isabelle, you almost made it. You are only twenty minutes from where I am. As soon as your friend Elizabeth gets here, we will drive the Jeep to pick up both you and Cate. She's Cate now, you know. We can't call her Annika any more or ever again. She is Catherine Murray now...all Irish and no more Scandinavian. We must try hard to remember that."

Isabelle Ritter and Mona Damours had never met. Isabelle was close to panic because she had no idea how they were going to manage to get Annika or Cate or whoever she was safely out of the van. She did not think this was the right time to be discussing Annika's name changes. Isabelle hadn't quite grasped the reason for the name change anyway. If Annika was going to hide out and live in the mountains forever, why did she need to change her name to Catherine?

"You know Elizabeth is in a wheelchair, too. Do you think we can possibly move...Cate...from the van to the Jeep?" Isabelle wanted Mona to realize how many people in this group of women required wheelchairs.

Mona was more positive at this point. "We have to do it. We don't have a choice. I have some ideas. I have had to move quite a few things by myself that I thought were impossible for one person to move, but I somehow found a way to do it. We will have to be creative. I am bringing some ropes and a sheet. Does the lift still work, even though you are in a ditch? It would help us to be able to use the lift to get Cate out of the van. Getting her into the Jeep is where we will need the creativity—and probably the ropes."

"I don't think the lift is going to be any help to us. The side of the van where the lift is located is down in the snow. The van spun around when it went off the road. It's now listing to one side, and the down side that's in the snow is the side the lift is on. I don't think we can depend on the lift for anything."

"You are lucky you weren't hurt when the van went off the road. Is Cate all right?" This was a more serious accident than Mona had realized.

"I'm fine. She's fine. Let's just get this show on the road." Isabelle was cold.

"Once I have seen the Jeep, I will have a better idea about what to do."

"Please let me know when Elizabeth reaches you. I am leaving the engine running now so we have heat. I was trying to save gas because I was counting on driving the van back to Phoenix tonight without stopping again for gas. It doesn't look like that is going to happen now." Isabelle, who was hardly ever in a bad mood, wasn't in a good mood today.

Annika Castillo, now Cate Murray, had been rudely awakened from her slumber when the van had slipped and slid and bumped its way into the ditch. Isabelle explained to Cate what had happened and what she hoped was going to happen...and soon. Isabelle reminded Cate that she had promised to drink water and take her medicine. Cate wanted to help, but she was clearly worn out and in a lot of pain. Cate swallowed her medicine when Isabelle gave it to her and unscrewed the top from a bottle of water. She accepted a sandwich when Isabelle unwrapped one and handed it to her. When Cate tried to eat the sandwich, she was almost too weak to hold it up to her mouth. Isabelle was worried. This trip to move Cate had been risky to begin with. Isabelle had done everything she could to guarantee that the journey would take place under the best of circumstances. The circumstances that had actually presented themselves had been the worst.

🌲

Isabelle's phone rang. Mona was on the line. She and Elizabeth were in the Jeep and on their way to find the van. Elizabeth had arrived at the cabin and had been able to climb out of the Jeep on her own with the help of her small set of steps. Mona had installed a ramp at the cabin in the woods in anticipation of Cate's arrival. The ramp would allow Cate's wheelchair to get from the dirt road onto the front porch and into the house. When Elizabeth had arrived at the cabin, Mona lifted her wheelchair out of the back of the Jeep. Elizabeth lowered herself into the wheelchair, and Mona wheeled her into the cabin and into the bathroom. After a bathroom break, Elizabeth was ready to climb back into the Jeep and retrace her route with Mona to look for Isabelle and Cate and the van.

The year before, Elizabeth had visited the Woodbrier Resort in West Virginia. Richard had called the concierge to arrange for a handicap accessible vehicle to drive Elizabeth and himself from the main resort to one of the other restaurants that was close to the golf course and in a different building. It was not a long trip, but the very small car that arrived did not look as if it could handle a wheelchair. The driver was a confident woman who assured the skeptical older couple that she had transported more the a few wheelchair-bound people from here to there and back in her special car... all without any problems.

The driver opened the rear door and pulled out a ramp. She pushed Elizabeth's wheelchair up the ramp and into the back seat of the car. Elizabeth's face was almost touching the opposite window, but she was in the car. Richard climbed into the back of the small sedan and sat on the seat beside the wheelchair. The driver pushed the ramp back into the vehicle, where it was positioned exactly in front of Richard's face. He couldn't move, and Elizabeth couldn't move. But they got to the restaurant safely, and they were able to successfully exit the car the same way they'd entered it.

They had both survived the trip and the weird entry and exit from the small sedan. It had not been a particularly comfortable or scenic trip, but it had been short. It had definitely been a make-shift arrangement, but it had worked. At the end of the evening, they'd called their driver again. She arrived in no time with her little car and its homemade ramp. Elizabeth and Richard were back at the Woodbrier in a few minutes, and in only a little worse shape from the ride.

The ramp that had been used to transport her wheelchair the year before had given Elizabeth an idea about how to transfer Cate to the Jeep. She explained her plan to Mona before they left to pick up the passengers from the wrecked van. Mona had agreed it sounded like as good a plan as any, and she found a piece of heavy plywood she thought would make an adequate ramp.

Mona loaded the plywood and the ropes and the sheets into the Jeep. They would be ready to implement their plan when they arrived at the ditch. Elizabeth had used her steps to get into the Jeep at the beginning of the trip and to get out of the Jeep when she'd arrived at Mona's cabin. She'd used her steps to get herself into the driver's seat a second time. Elizabeth knew she was tired, but she pushed through her fatigue. She knew the road she had to take to find Isabelle because she had just been driving on it. They were on their way.

Because they had the longitude and latitude, they knew exactly where the van had run off the road. Elizabeth couldn't understand how she'd managed to drive past the van on her way to Mona's cabin without seeing it on the side of the road. Forty minutes later they found the van. Elizabeth and Mona drove by it three times before they found it—almost covered up with snow and hiding in the ditch. The snow was blinding. It was impossible to see anything, let alone something white that was tilted on its side and halfway hidden in a low spot where it had gone into a ditch. The side of the van where the lift was located was buried in several feet of snow. There was no way the van's lift was going to be of any use to them.

Mona was outfitted with boots and a warm parka and fur-lined gloves. Isabelle and Elizabeth had none of these things. The two wives of the Camp Shoemaker reunion boys were wearing sneakers and socks. They had no clothing that was appropriate for being in the snow, let along anything that was appropriate for heavy duty lifting and maneuvering a wheelchair out of a van that was buried in the snow and moving it to another vehicle parked by the side of the road in a snowstorm. Bless Mona that she had thought to bring along two extra pairs of work gloves. At least it would be a few minutes before their fingers began to show signs of frostbite. Elizabeth had put an extra pair of socks into her jacket pocket when she'd left her casita this morning, anticipating that hers might get wet in the snow. Elizabeth and Isabelle were in their seventies. They were not prepared for the cold, wet weather. But they were strong-willed, so maybe, with Mona's help, they had a chance of accomplishing this almost impossible task.

The Jeep was a versatile vehicle, much more so than the old sedan at the Woodbrier had been. The Jeep's seats could be pushed back and folded down to make room for carrying cargo. Mona and Elizabeth had determined that the wheelchair would fit sideways into the space behind the front seat. They had tried Elizabeth's empty wheelchair in the spot and found that it fit. If Cate's wheelchair was no wider than Elizabeth's, their plan might work. Elizabeth drove the Jeep as close to the door of the van as she was able to get it. Mona and Isabelle positioned the plywood ramp to run from the door of the van to the door of the Jeep. Because the van was in a ditch, there was not much difference in the height of the two doors. The ramp was almost horizontal with hardly any incline. This was a good thing.

It was bitterly cold. Elizabeth was now sitting in her own wheelchair outside beside the van. Mona had pushed Elizabeth through the snow so that she was as close as possible to the ramp. Elizabeth was in charge of holding the ramp steady. Isabelle and Mona struggled to open the door of the van that wasn't buried in the snow. The door was frozen closed, but with some effort, they managed to get it open. They had decided it would be safer to take Cate down the ramp backwards out of the van. It was not an easy task to turn Cate's wheelchair around inside the van. It had to be turned around so it was heading in the direction it had to go to get out the door. There was not a lot of room in the back of the van, and it took both women to turn the wheelchair around.

With the ramp in position and reasonably stable, Isabelle pulled Cate's wheelchair backwards out the open door and continued to move it very carefully on the plywood ramp. The piece of plywood was narrow, just a little wider than the wheelchair's wheels. The women secured the wheelchair with the rope in case the wheelchair began to go off the ramp. They moved very slowly, and the wheelchair clumsily and precariously made the trip from the van to the Jeep. There was a jolt when the wheelchair left the ramp and landed on the floor inside the Jeep. But Cate was finally in the vehicle. Her face was pale, and she looked as if she might be sick. Things could be worse. At least she would not freeze to death overnight in a van sitting in a snowstorm in a ditch in the middle of nowhere.

Isabelle and Mona quickly began clearing everything out of the van. They loaded it all into the rear of the Jeep. They would not be coming back to the van. Cate stared out the side window, and Isabelle climbed into the back seat beside her. They left the plywood behind in the snow. They were in a hurry, and it was too much trouble to lift the wet piece of plywood back into the Jeep. All of this was done in blizzard conditions. It was still snowing hard and was growing colder as the sun went down. The wind was fierce and threatened to blow Isabelle and Mona over as they unloaded the van and stowed the gear into the back of the Jeep. Everyone's core temperature was dropping. They worked as rapidly as they could to be sure they had everything out of the van.

Mona was going to drive to give Elizabeth a break. Elizabeth had overextended herself that day and had more than exhausted her energy supply. She was happy to have Mona drive. Elizabeth's wheelchair was stuck in the snow. Elizabeth was able to get herself out of the wheelchair. She put her little set of steps next to the door on the passenger side of the Jeep, and in less than a minute, even though the snow made everything incredibly slippery, she was back inside sitting in the passenger seat. She was becoming pretty good at this. But the wheelchair did not want to move. It was frozen in place. After some work, Mona and Isabelle were able to free the wheelchair from its icy prison. Then it did not want to fold up so they could put it into the back of the Jeep. Finally, Mona lifted the wheelchair into the cargo space in the rear of the SUV.

Cate's wheelchair was wedged behind the driver's seat, and it wasn't moving. Everyone else fastened their seatbelts, and at last they left the snowbank and the van lying in the ditch. They were on their way. It was almost impossible to see where they were going, but Mona knew where she was going and was used to driving in the snow.

Isabelle handed Elizabeth a tuna salad sandwich on whole wheat bread. Elizabeth ate the entire sandwich in a couple of minutes. Isabelle handed her a second sandwich. Elizabeth had eaten nothing since her very early breakfast. It was past four o'clock in the afternoon, and the sun was going down. Their goal now was to reach the cabins before it was completely dark. No one was going to make it back to the Mimosa Inn tonight.

Mona had another piece of plywood ready at the cabin to get Cate's wheelchair out of the Jeep. It seemed easier this time, now that they were not contending with a ditch on the side of the road. There was already a ramp from the ground level up onto the porch of the cabin. Mona wheeled Cate down the plywood ramp out of the jeep, up the ramp onto the porch, and into the cabin. The cabin had been turned into a warm and welcoming home. Cate's mother and Mona had worked together to create this space for the young woman who was on the run and desperately trying to save her life by faking her own death and disappearing.

Mona lit the gas fireplace and pushed Cate's wheelchair close to its warmth. Tendrils of her wet hair had frozen around her face just in the short time they'd been transferring her from the Jeep to the house. Mona brought a towel to dry Cate's hair as the ice melted and dripped onto her clothes. Isabelle wheeled Elizabeth into the house and went back outside to move the Jeep into the cabin's garage. Isabelle unloaded everything from the Jeep, dragged it inside, and dumped it in a corner of the living area of the cabin. She didn't know what else to do with it, and she was worn out, too. Everyone was exhausted and had used up all their energy reserves. Only Mona seemed to have any spark remaining.

Everyone was concerned about Cate. It had been a rough trip for Isabelle and Elizabeth, too, but Cate was the most vulnerable. She had been attacked and had almost died less than a week earlier. She was the one with the wounds that might become infected. Isabelle and Elizabeth made quick trips to the bathroom, while Mona busied herself in the kitchen. Elizabeth collapsed on the couch, and Isabelle made more attempts to dry Cate's hair. She helped Cate take off the wet clothes and found some dry clothes for her in the bedroom.

"I have soup warmed up, and there is toasted cheese bread with butter. I was going to make a salad, but there are plenty of vegetables in the soup. We don't need a salad. Wheel Cate over here to the table. She needs to eat something warm whether she wants to or not." Mona was giving orders. She had prepared beef vegetable soup with rich beef stock and chunks of meat. She had put every conceivable vegetable into the soup and explained that it was her "end of the summer garden" vegetable soup. There were lima beans, green beans, peas, celery, onions, carrots, corn, potatoes, cabbage, and lots and lots of tomatoes. Mona had grown everything in her mountain garden. She'd even grown the basil and the parsley that seasoned the soup. It was flavorful and hearty and warmed the soul as well as the body. Elizabeth and Isabelle each had two bowls. Mona had also made the cheese bread, and it was heavy and dense with extra sharp cheddar cheese. Neither Isabelle nor Elizabeth had ever tasted anything quite like it. Mona admitted it was her own recipe and joined Isabelle and Elizabeth in a second slice of the delicious bread.

"I see that the cabin has a gas stove and a gas fireplace. Do you use propane?" Elizabeth assumed that Mona's cabin as well as Cate's cabin used propane to power a generator. As reclusive as Mona was, Elizabeth was surprised she would allow a propane delivery to be made by anyone to this remote spot.

"It isn't propane. Surprisingly, it is natural gas. There is a gas line to both my cabin and to this one. We both have generators to provide power to the house. The natural gas powers the generators which light the lights. We have everything we need because of that gas line. The gas line was installed many years ago. I can't imagine how expensive it was to pipe natural gas all the way up here, but supposedly the guy who originally built these cabins insisted on having gas for heat and hot water and cooking. I don't know how he did it. I've wondered if he was on the board of directors of the gas company or something like that. He must have had some kind of important position to have had the pull to get the gas line installed.

"When Pia's father bought this property and rented it to me, he assured me he'd had the gas lines thoroughly checked out. Because the lines had been in the ground for a very long time, he wanted to be certain none of them were corroded or had any breaks or holes in them. Safety was important to him, and he had everything repaired. He assured me the gas lines were in excellent condition. Natural gas is a luxury I never expected to have. I converted both the fireplaces, the one in my cabin and the one in this cabin, from wood burning to gas a few years ago. It was becoming harder and harder for me to cut the wood and carry it into the house. Wood-burning fireplaces send smoke up the chimney, and that attracts attention. Gas fireplaces don't put smoke into the atmosphere.

Nobody knows I'm way up here, and that's the way I like it and want it to stay."

Cate had not spoken a word since their arrival at the cabin. She seemed dazed and out of it. Isabelle had been forced to spoon feed her to try to get her to eat some of the soup. She had to be hungry, and she needed to eat. But she had been through the wringer that day and was really too exhausted to sit up in the wheelchair at the table, let alone eat anything. She didn't really have the energy to chew or swallow.

Mona made short work of the dishes. "I really would like to give Cate a shower, to warm her up more than anything. But she has had quite enough hassle for one day. I will make sure she gets a shower tomorrow or the next day. I know how to do that without getting her wounds too wet." She wheeled Cate into the cabin's sunroom. There was an antiquated hospital bed unexpectedly pushed against the wall. Mona pulled it out into the center of the room. "She needs rest more than anything right now." The old-fashioned hospital bed was already made up. Mona lowered it and helped Cate transfer from the wheelchair and lie down on it. Elizabeth and Isabelle looked on in amazement.

"Where in the world did you ever come up with a hospital bed...and on such short notice?" Isabelle had thought about bringing a hospital bed with her but hadn't been able to figure out how to accomplish that. And here was a hospital bed already at the cabin. It looked like a relic from long ago, but it was on wheels and its height could be adjusted. It would serve its purpose.

"Don't give me too much credit. It was already here. Somebody left it in the garage. I knew it was out there, and I'd just never made the effort to get rid of it. I think it's from the 1960s or before. It makes sense that somebody might want to come here to the mountains to recover from an operation or even to live out their final days. The bed itself was dirty and rusted. I scrubbed it down and sanded the rust away in a few places. Somebody had wrapped the mattress in a plastic bag. Hospital bed mattresses are all encased in some kind of rubberized plastic stuff anyway. It didn't really smell bad, but I scrubbed it within an inch of its life and aired it out anyway. When Cate called and told me that she had been attacked, I checked out the mechanism that raises and lowers the bed. With the help of a can of WD40, I decided the bed was worth saving. So I cleaned it up and brought it in here. It's much easier to do wound care, to change dressings on a narrower bed that can be raised and lowered. It was going to be tough to tend to my patient if she was in that double bed in the bedroom."

"You seem to know a great deal about caring for a patient. I know you are a painter, but have you had training as a nurse?" Elizabeth was curious.

Mona was silent for a long time. "I see I have given myself away." Mona was quiet again, as if trying to decide how much to reveal. "I'm a doctor. I graduated from McGill University's medical school...many, many years ago. I did an internship and a couple of years of residency in internal medicine. Then things turned dark, and my life fell apart. I had to disappear. I could not practice medicine anymore because I was forced to live under another name...to save my life. Because I had earned my medical degree under a name I will never be able to use again, I can no longer obtain a medical license...from anywhere. I loved being a doctor, but being forced to change careers presented me with an unexpected opportunity. Painting had always been my passion, my first love. My family did not feel that being an artist was a practical choice. So I went to medical school. When I left my past behind and became someone else, I began to paint again. I found I had talent. My paintings were in demand and sold for high prices. I was able to support myself in my new life as an artist."

Elizabeth and Isabelle were dumbstruck. Mona continued. "If you look for the name Mona Damours as a graduate of McGill, you won't find that name. So don't bother to look for it. It isn't there. That's all you need to know right now." Mona had one more question. "Did you bring the IV equipment I asked Cate to have Dr. Kernigan put in the van? I do remember how to put an IV in a patient. It's like riding a bicycle...if you've done enough of them. I am concerned that Cate isn't eating and drinking. I think she needs some IV supplements. I can hook her up to what she needs. I just wanted the IV equipment from Kernigan, along with plenty of bags of Ringer's lactate. Ordering that kind of medical gear over the internet raises red flags."

Isabelle stared at Mona and then pulled a bag from the pile of stuff they'd brought in from the Jeep. Isabelle handed Mona the bag. "I thought Freddy was crazy when he insisted I bring this along. I told him none of us knew how to start an IV. He said Cate had insisted he send it with her."

Mona expertly sorted out the tubes and clamps from the bag and set up the IV pole and apparatus. She inserted a needle attached to a tube into the back of Cate's hand without making Cate flinch. It was clear Mona knew how to do this. Soon fluids were flowing into Cate's body. Mona checked her patient's wounds. "I will wait until tomorrow to change her bandages. After she has had a shower, I will clean everything up and be sure she hasn't developed any infection. She just needs rest now. This has been a very long and traumatic day for her."

"And I thought I was being so smart, arranging for a rental car on my satellite phone." Isabelle laughed at herself and continued to be amazed at this still beautiful but older mountain woman who had turned out to be a doctor as well as a painter as well as a roofer. "Is there anything at all you can't do?"

"My tennis game is atrocious. But I haven't played in decades." Mona laughed.

The day finally caught up with Elizabeth, and she lay down on the couch. She was sound asleep in minutes. Mona covered her with a blanket.

"Isabelle, let's leave Elizabeth alone to sleep here on the couch. She seems quite comfortable. You take the bed in the bedroom. I have a cot that I am going to set up in the sunroom. That way, I can keep a close eye on Cate. She is still very fragile. I assumed you and Elizabeth will be leaving in the morning. Do you have everything straightened out with the van?"

"The car rental people are going to pick up the van. I told them they'll have to have it towed out of the ditch. Fortunately I paid for insurance on the thing, so I am covered on that. I've rented another Jeep to drive back to Phoenix. I rented a Jeep because I know Elizabeth is able to get in and out of a Jeep. And it has four-wheel-drive. I think it is still going to be snowing again tomorrow. If you can drive us to Show Low tomorrow to pick up the rental, we will be out of your hair right after breakfast."

"I'll be happy to drive you to Show Low. We can leave as soon as you are ready to go in the morning."

Twenty Three

When they left the next morning, it was still snowing. Mona had been up early to shovel the snow so they could get her truck out to drive to Show Low. Mona gave both Isabelle and Elizabeth the number of her satellite phone. She stressed to them that she never gave her phone number to anyone, but she trusted these two women. "I know you care about Cate, and you will want to know how she is recovering and adjusting to her new life. I am happy to talk to you, but please do not share my phone number with anyone else. You may not understand this, but please don't even share it with your spouses." They promised her and looked in briefly on their patient who was asleep in the hospital bed in the sun room of the cabin. Mona assured them that she would take good care of Cate and promised that eventually the woman on the run would be restored to health. "I know the prognosis for her walking again was grim, but I believe I can work with her to strengthen her legs. From what I understand, there is no permanent damage to her spinal cord. She is in good hands. She will be fine."

🌲

It wasn't easy for Elizabeth to get into Mona's truck, but with the help of Elizabeth's steps, they eventually managed. Mona drove them into Show Low so they could pick up the Jeep Isabelle had rented for the drive back to Paradise Valley. Again using her little steps, Elizabeth was able to get herself into the driver's seat of the SUV. Even though the snow was still coming down, the plows had been out that morning. The snow had been plowed from the roads, so the drive from the mountains back to Phoenix was easier, especially compared with their drive the day before. The weather front that had come through and almost finished them off was moving rapidly to the east. All precipitation was supposed to come to an end by the middle of the afternoon.

Isabelle had asked Elizabeth if she would do the driving. Isabelle had impatient clients she needed to placate. She spent most of the drive back to Phoenix texting and talking on her cell phone, reassuring and talking to the rich and famous in Palm Springs and to the woman who was tending the store for her in her absence. Isabelle seemed to be in her element, putting out fires and calming and soothing those whom she had neglected while she had been taking care of Annika Karlsson.

Elizabeth didn't think Isabelle's job looked like much fun. At least that day, it didn't look like fun. But Elizabeth was an introvert. "Do you ever think of retiring? These people sound as if they are incredibly demanding and don't want to wait even a couple of days for you to get back to Palm Springs."

"I think of retiring every day of my life, but I really love what I do. I usually am able to plan more carefully so I don't overload myself with work. I can almost always stay on schedule. I am compulsive about keeping my appointments and delivering goods and services on time. The past week has been an aberration. I keep reminding myself that some of my clients are not used to aberrations and do not deal well with them. They expect me to show up on time when I have made an appointment with them. And really, they have every right to expect that. They expect their furniture and their slipcovers and lamps to show up exactly when they have been scheduled to show up. Sometimes that is out of my control. A few of my clients don't allow for or forgive the unexpected. I usually do have things under control, but who could have imagined what would happen to Annika. Taking care of my friend's daughter, of course, had to take precedence over my business commitments. And who could possibly have anticipated a snowstorm like that in November... or the van sliding off the road." Isabelle already looked tired, and it wasn't even noon yet.

Isabelle continued. "Most of my clients are a pleasure to deal with, but a couple of my more difficult customers are angry because I am still out of town. To be fair, some of these people, some of my clients, have very demanding schedules themselves. Several are celebrities who have made commitments for tours and performances all over the world. They sometimes cannot show up to meet with me on time because of things that happen in their busy lives. But they always expect me to show up on time. Right now, I am very behind with my work. I will admit that I'm stressed. In fact, I am going to have you drop me at Sky Harbor Airport on your way back to the Mimosa

Inn. I have a reservation to fly to Palm Springs later today. Matthew understands."

Isabelle looked at Elizabeth to see if she understood what the plan was going to be. "I hate for you to have to go back to the Mimosa Inn alone. You will have to get yourself and the wheelchair back to your casita. I've already called ahead and alerted them that you will be arriving and that someone will have to get the wheelchair out of the Jeep and push you to your casita. I've made arrangements for the Jeep to be returned to the car rental people. They will come to the Mimosa Inn and pick it up. So you don't have to worry about that. Everything is taken care of. I hope the next few days are quiet ones for you so you can get some work done on your book. I might not have involved you in this mess of mine if I had known the weather would force us to spend the night in the mountains. But I didn't know what else to do. I knew I could trust you, and I knew you would do whatever I needed for you to do to help me. I appreciate it, Elizabeth. If there had been any other way, I would not have asked you to become involved in all of this. I hope Richard won't be too angry with me for imposing on you." Isabelle was feeling a little guilty, but she had a business to run and needed to get back to it. "I have to confess. I actually had a flight to California booked for this morning because I thought I would be back at the Mimosa Inn last night. I've lost another day."

"It's a good thing you are a genius at multi-tasking. I marvel at your ability to keep these people happy over the phone. They sound very exacting and very impatient."

"A very few are difficult and hard to please, it's true. But most are understanding, and the upside is that they are all crazy about my ideas and are willing to pay me big bucks to deliver creativity for their homes. It's a zany life, but I love what I do." Isabelle sent a few more texts. "Will you be okay? I mean, with the valet wheeling you back to your room and taking the car off your hands?"

"I will be fine. Don't worry about a thing. I mostly enjoyed the trip to Show Low and Pinetop, and I loved meeting Mona Damours. She will be more than able to take care of Annika...I mean Cate. I feel very bad about Annika's mother, your friend Pia. I'm glad you asked me to help. I was happy to do it. Now I am ready to settle down in my casita and get some serious writing done. But I may take a nap first. Sleeping on a couch is not my forte at age seventy-eight. I'm going to put the 'privacy' sign on the door of my casita and hope I don't have to see anybody except room service for a couple of days. Don't worry. I'll be fine."

Elizabeth dropped Isabelle at the Phoenix airport and continued on to Paradise Valley. Elizabeth was tired from the unexpected adventure in the mountains, and she was ready to take it easy and do some writing in front of her fireplace. What more could happen to upset her plans?

Twenty Four

The valet who was delivering Elizabeth and her wheelchair to the casita unlocked the door. Elizabeth was thinking only about having a hot shower, washing her hair, and taking a nap. The two-day trip into the mountains, with all of its unexpected complications, had more than caught up with her. The valet pushed Elizabeth's wheelchair into the room. Both the Mimosa Inn employee and Elizabeth were stunned to see that the casita had been turned inside out and upside down. The place was a mess. Papers and other things were scattered everywhere. Furniture was turned over. Someone had been in the casita, looking for something. In fact, that someone was still there.

Before they could really take in what had happened, a man with a ski mask covering his face ran out of the bathroom waving a gun. When she saw the weapon, Elizabeth threw herself out of her wheelchair and onto the floor, hoping to avoid being shot. She crawled behind a chair. The valet turned around and tried to run back out the door of the casita onto the patio. The man with the ski mask fired his gun wildly, aiming it at the valet who was trying to flee. He fired at the ceiling. He fired at the walls. It all happened in the blink of an eye, and Elizabeth could only see part of what was going on from the spot where she was hiding on the floor behind one of the leather chairs.

The intruder was in a panic. He dropped the gun, pushed the valet out of the way, and ran out of the casita. He was gone before Elizabeth could get her phone to call for help. The valet was lying on the floor. His arm was bleeding. His head was bleeding. He appeared to be unconscious, but not dead.

Elizabeth lay on the floor. Her wheelchair was turned on its side. She crawled to the wheelchair. She fumbled to retrieve her purse and find her cell phone. She called 911 and told the dispatcher what had happened and where she was. She told them to send an ambulance—that someone had been shot and was bleeding. The dispatcher told her to stay on the line. Elizabeth put her phone on speaker and crawled across the floor to where the valet was lying unconscious beside the fireplace. Thankfully, he had a pulse. His head wound did not appear to have been caused by a gunshot. He'd probably hit his head when he'd fallen. Elizabeth was able to reach a decorative throw pillow which she used to staunch the bleeding from the valet's arm. She put as much pressure as she could on the wound.

She tried to pick herself up from the floor. She grabbed hold of one of the heavy leather chairs that was next to where the valet lay on the rug. She was able to pull herself up into the chair. She sat in the chair and kept one hand pressed on the throw pillow at the same time. It was easier for her to use her cell phone if she wasn't lying on the floor. She was thankful that the adrenalin rush of the moment had given her the extra strength she'd needed to get into the chair. She knew the adrenalin would vanish sooner or later, but it had been there when she'd needed it.

Elizabeth told the dispatcher on the phone that she was going to hang up. Then Elizabeth called the front desk at the Mimosa. She told them there had been a shooting and to send help to the room. She told them she had already called 911 and to expect the police and an ambulance. She told the management that one of their valets had been shot and was bleeding. She told the woman in the front office that she thought the valet would be okay, but that he needed to go to the hospital ER. She told them her room had been vandalized and that the man who had done it had fled the scene a few moments earlier — after shooting the valet. Elizabeth knew there was no hope that anyone would be able to catch up with the intruder. He would have ditched the ski mask and might even be taking a leisurely stroll on the pathways among the flowers by now, pretending to be a guest at the Mimosa Inn. It seemed like it was taking forever for anyone to come to the room to help.

She didn't think the valet was in any immediate danger. She kept the pillow on his wound. There was nothing else she could do to help him on her own. She looked around the room and wondered how in the world she would ever get the mess cleaned up. The intruder had not taken anything with him, at least that Elizabeth had been able to see, when he ran out of the casita. She knew exactly why the intruder had been in her casita and what he had been looking for. She also knew that what he had come to find was no longer there.

Next she called Detective Cecilia Mendoza who did not pick up. Elizabeth left a short message for the Phoenix policewoman explaining what had happened and asked the detective to call her back. The door to the casita was wide open, and within a minute or two, several of the Mimosa Inn's employees appeared in the room.

Two of the employees knelt down on the floor next to the valet to tend to their co-worker. A third employee stood over the chair where Elizabeth was sitting and asked her if she was all right. "I'm just fine, and an ambulance is on the way...for the valet."

"Your head is bleeding. It doesn't look like a serious wound. Let me find a washcloth and get you cleaned up."

Elizabeth had not realized she was injured. It must have happened when the intruder had run out of the bathroom brandishing his gun and she'd thrown herself out of her wheelchair onto the floor. She must have hit her head on something. The adrenalin began to wear off, and she was already tired from a long two days on the road. When the EMTs arrived they rushed to the chair where Elizabeth was sitting. She was old and looked pale, and the bleeding from her head wound had not stopped.

She waved the EMTs away. "I didn't call you guys for me. I'm fine. I'm old but I'm not really hurt. The man lying on the floor has been shot. With a gun. Take care of him first."

The valet was tended to and eventually taken away in the ambulance. Before he'd left for the hospital, the room had filled up with law enforcement people. Elizabeth was sure the high-end manager and employees of the Mimosa Inn hated it that the police were back again and that another incident had occurred at their fancy resort. Elizabeth hated it too. She had hoped the excitement was finished and had been wishing for some quiet time.

Detective Mendoza arrived and nodded to Elizabeth. The policewoman wrinkled her forehead when she saw the blood in Elizabeth's hair. The detective was taking in the scene and hovered near Elizabeth. She glanced at Elizabeth with curiosity every once in a while. Elizabeth was fading fast in the leather chair, but she and the detective couldn't really talk until everyone else had left the room. Elizabeth wondered if Cecilia Mendoza was surprised that one little old lady in a wheelchair could manage to get herself into so much trouble. Elizabeth was asking herself the same thing.

Elizabeth was already convinced that she was not going to be able to concentrate on doing any writing that night. She decided she would be lucky if she was able to take a shower and get the blood out of her hair. The much-anticipated nap didn't look like it was going to be on the agenda either. Writing was Elizabeth's drug. She loved it, and it made her endorphins flow. Considering everything that had happened, she wondered if she would have a chance to do any writing at all in the next few days.

Most of all she hoped that Richard didn't hear about the things that had happened to her since he'd left on his hunting trip. He said she brought the drama and the trouble on herself and that she should mind her own business. Maybe Richard was right some of the time, but it was difficult for Elizabeth to find a way to blame herself for any of these recent events.

Finally, it was just Detective Cecilia Mendoza and Elizabeth in the room. It was late, and Elizabeth still had not had her hot shower. She realized she was thirsty and hungry, but she felt she needed to talk to the detective first. Elizabeth knew she was not allowed to say anything to anybody about having driven Annika, or Cate, or anyone to the White Mountains. The trip she had taken yesterday and the destination were a secret and would always be a secret. No one could ever learn about the adventure she and Isabelle had undertaken to deliver Annika to her safe house near Pinetop, Arizona.

Isabelle had also asked Elizabeth not to tell anyone that she had ever spent any time away from her casita at the Mimosa Inn. Elizabeth had promised she would pretend she had been in her casita writing for the past two days. She would pretend that she had never left. It was going to be difficult to explain to Detective Mendoza how someone had managed to break into the casita, ransack it, and hide in the bathroom, if she couldn't tell the detective she'd been gone.

"I was out of the room, and the valet was kind enough to push me back here in my wheelchair. As soon as we came through the door, the intruder ran out of the bathroom. He was wearing a ski mask, so I didn't see his face. He had a gun and was waving it around like a mad man. When I saw the gun, I threw myself onto the floor. The wheelchair turned over. That was probably when I hurt my head. I must have hit it on something when I tried to hide behind the chair. I didn't even realize I was bleeding. When the intruder fired his gun, he hit the valet in the arm. He also fired the gun at the ceiling and the walls. It was wild. He dropped the gun and ran out of the casita. I was able to get to my purse and my cell phone. I called 911. I crawled over and checked to be sure the valet had a pulse. I put one of those little pillows over the wound and kept pressure on it to try to stop the bleeding. He didn't seem to be critically injured. I feel bad that I don't even know the man's name, the valet's name. Then I called the front desk, and then I called you. The employees from the Mimosa showed up. The EMTs and the ambulance showed up. The police showed up. Then you showed up. You know what happened after that. Look at this room. It's a mess. I think the manager of the inn told me she was going to send someone over to help straighten things out. Whoever it was who broke in here seems to have left my suitcase alone. Thank goodness for that. He was not looking for clothes or personal items. He was looking for something that was hidden somewhere in the room itself. And you know and I know exactly what that something was that he was looking for."

"Yes, I'm afraid we do know what he was looking for. I am so sorry. I feel like this was my fault... that your casita was broken into again. After you discovered the fentanyl in the ceramic pot, I should have insisted then that you move to a different casita. After we found the drugs, I should have known someone would be back to try to find them or to try to find their money."

"It isn't your fault. I would not have agreed to move to a different casita, even if you had suggested it. I need a handicap accessible bathroom with a roll-in shower or a shower that's easy to get into, not a bathtub. I would not have agreed to move out of this room anyway, so don't beat yourself up over that."

Detective Mendoza looked chagrinned. "I hate to say it, but you are going to have to move out of this casita anyway. I know it will be a great inconvenience for you, but this casita is now a crime scene. This casita has been vandalized, and a man has been shot here. The CSIs have taken a lot of fingerprints, and they have taken away the gun. But it is still a crime scene, and you can't stay here tonight. I have spoken with the manager, and they are moving you to their ultra plush executive suite. It has a separate tub and a separate shower. You will be able to use the shower in that room without any problem. There are actually three rooms in that casita. Hardly anyone ever stays there because it costs $2,500 a night. The Mimosa Inn is going to allow you to stay in the room for free. Your meals will also be free. You will have first class service."

"I understand that I can't stay in this room because it has become a crime scene. I appreciate your finding me another room where I will be able to take a shower. But I am completely worn out right now and really need to rest. If this room isn't safe, when can I move to the other room? I need to lie down. I need to charge my phone. I need to go to the bathroom. I need to have something to drink and something to eat. I'm sorry, but I've had it for today. I want you to catch these criminal drug dealers who are using the Mimosa Inn as a drop for their drug deals, and I want to help you do that. But I can't help you any more tonight." Elizabeth didn't give up easily, but she knew that none of these young people who worked at the Mimosa Inn and none of the young people who were in law enforcement, including Cecilia Mendoza, realized how exhausting all of this was for someone who was almost eighty years old.

"Your new casita is nearly ready, and two people are being sent by the front office to get you settled in the new quarters. One of them will push you there in the wheelchair, and the other one will put your luggage and rollator and other things on a luggage cart and wheel it all over to the new casita. Someone will unpack for you in the new rooms. The Mimosa Inn is sick and tired of seeing me here, but they are concerned about you and want to try to make things up to you. The manager also told me about why they put you in this upgraded handicap room, this room that has now become a crime scene, because the standard handicap accessible room you had reserved was unavailable due to an HVAC problem. She says she had no idea this room was being used as a drug drop. They feel very bad about putting you in here, so they are going to go out of their way to be nice to you. Elizabeth, just sit back and enjoy the executive suite and being pampered."

"Are the people who run this place at least clued in now that their fancy resort is being used to traffic fentanyl? They need to be shocked into acknowledging that, and they need to be made aware that someone who works here has to be participating in what's going on."

"They are on board now... but only after one of their own employees was shot. I also am quite certain that someone on the inside is participating in the drug trafficking. The management blamed the previous break-ins on outsiders and the murder on a domestic violence situation. Now they realize that somebody who works here is involved. Maybe more than one person. They have turned over all their security camera footage to my office. I have people looking through it tonight. At least in principle, the people who run this resort are pretty careful about security. High profile celebrities and politicians and very rich people frequently stay here. You have to be pretty well-to-do to afford even a small casita in this place. Management tells me they have more security around than the guests know about. Quite a few of the groundskeeping guys are also trained as security people. But I have to say that this fentanyl trafficking thing was happening right under their noses and at the same time it was all happening completely under their radar. They had no idea it was going on until the casitas began to be broken into and vandalized. And people started to be attacked."

"I'm afraid my need to have a special shower in a special bathroom may have triggered the chaos to begin with. This casita had not been used for months until we moved in. It's so overpriced. It is even more overpriced than the other casitas. If the management hadn't moved us in here, it would have been business as usual for the drug traffickers. They could have left their drugs or the money in their usual hiding places and come and gone as they regularly do. No one would ever have suspected anything. But when my husband and I moved into this casita, that threw everything off. And, we not only moved into the casita that no one ever stayed in, but I also found the drug stash in the ceramic pot. And you took the pot and its contents away with you. There were no drugs left here for anybody to find, and there was no money to find here... no matter how many times they broke into the room and searched the place."

"The Mimosa Inn realizes that now. That's why they're comping you that outrageously expensive room for the rest of your stay. They know they messed up and were not watching this empty room closely enough." Detective Mendoza paused. "I have to ask you if you think the intruder saw your face before he ran out of here. Did he have time to see you? Do you think he would recognize you? The policewoman paused again. "I am asking you these questions because I am concerned that the intruder might come after you personally. Very big bucks are involved in the fentanyl drug trade. The guy who's lost his drugs is still on the loose, and we don't know if or when we will be able to catch him—or her. If he or she knows what you look like, you might continue to be in danger. You have been in this room for several days. Whoever it is may think you have the drugs."

"Of course I could be in danger. And it doesn't matter if he has seen my face. Think about it. He knows I'm in a wheelchair. I am a very obvious target because of that. I am probably the only person staying at the Mimosa Inn right now that's in a wheelchair. That makes me unique and quite recognizable. Having said that, I don't think I really am in danger. The intruder had his ski mask over his face the entire time he was in the room. He knows I can't identify him. He knows I never saw his face. And, because he didn't go through my suitcase or open Richard's suitcase, I believe he knows we are not involved with the drug thing. I think whoever broke into the room this last time has to be someone who works here. They knew we were given this room at the last minute. This last time, they broke in here in the middle of the day." What Elizabeth did not say was that whoever had broken into the casita for the second time probably knew that Elizabeth had been away for two days. No one had slept in the casita the night before. Elizabeth had slept on the couch in the cabin in the White Mountains. It had to be an inside job for anyone to have known all those things.

"You're probably right. Moving you to the executive suite won't make you any safer, if this is an inside job. But at least you will be out of this room where the drugs were hidden."

"Whoever is after this load of fentanyl knows by now it isn't in this casita anymore. This casita is now probably the safest place at the resort." Elizabeth didn't know a lot about drugs, but she did know that the use of fentanyl was on the rise. "I've read some things about fentanyl and hear about it on the news. My understanding is that it is extremely valuable. Even a small package of this particular drug is worth so much money. Is that what makes fentanyl such a problem?"

"There are many reasons why fentanyl is an enormous and growing problem. No one wants to admit how really dangerous it is and how it is overwhelming the drug trade. The ingredients mostly come from China, but increasingly the ingredients used to make fentanyl are also coming from India. Each step in the fentanyl trade is lucrative, including whoever provides the chemicals that go into making it. The U.S. government has put pressure on both China and India to do something to stop or slow down the exports of these chemicals, but nothing much has resulted from these efforts. The nasty stuff is still being sent, usually to Mexico, in huge amounts.

"The drug is relatively cheap to make. The various components of the drug are sent to Mexico where they are combined and made into powder or tablets... like the tablets that were found in your casita... the ones that looked like kids' candy. Because even relatively small amounts of fentanyl are so valuable, it is easily smuggled across the border from Mexico. Trafficking in fentanyl is very, very big business." Cecilia Mendoza sighed a huge sigh. Both she and Elizabeth were thinking how close to the Mexican border Phoenix was. Elizabeth was thinking that Tucson was even closer to the border.

Cecilia continued. "It's so discouraging. The latest twist, and to make things worse, drug dealers are starting to make fentanyl in the United States. If that becomes routine, there will be no need to smuggle it across the border from Mexico. There will be fewer opportunities to intercept it at the border before it hits the streets in this country. It will already be here. But it's not just where it's made or how it's distributed that makes it so difficult to stop. One of the major problems with fentanyl is that no one knows what the strength of the drug is in any one batch. Fentanyl is often combined with cocaine or heroin or meth. The people who are selling the drug don't know how lethal it is. Those who are buying it and consuming it don't know how lethal it is either. And they die! Because they don't know exactly what or how much they are taking, they die! The fentanyl craze is a horrible invasion, and it's a synthetic drug. Plant-based drugs require land and water to raise their ingredients. Cocaine and heroin are examples of plant-based drugs. Fentanyl requires only a lab in a warehouse. It is easy to make. It doesn't require any land to speak of or any water. It doesn't even required a drug maker with any brains."

"Can you call and see if I can get into my new casita now? I do want to learn more about fentanyl, but that will have to wait until I have eaten something and had some rest. I am very alarmed by these things you are telling me. How can anyone claim that dealing drugs and taking drugs are victimless crimes? I am just completely puzzled by those statements which have been made by those at the very highest levels of our government. So many people who were incarcerated because of drug crimes have now been pardoned and let out of jail. Why is that? I don't understand the logic behind that?"

"Don't get me started on that subject. I may freak out. Let's focus on getting you moved."

"If these break-ins are an inside job, and I think they must be, at least one employee, and maybe more than one employee, is involved. They know exactly what room I am being moved to and exactly where I am at any moment...wheelchair or not. That means I am really not safe at the Mimosa Inn...at all. What do you think?"

"I think we need to get you settled in a different room. You need to take your shower and order from room service. Then you really must get some sleep. I am going to have someone from PPD outside your room all night. I will be back in the morning. We will talk then about what to do going forward. You look completely worn down by all of this. Enough!"

Twenty Five

*E*lizabeth gathered the energy she needed but didn't think she had, to move to her new room. The Mimosa came through as promised and provided a staff person to unpack and help her get settled. The management sent a basket of fruit and two bottles of wine to the room. The room was large and luxurious, as advertised. Elizabeth was glad she wasn't paying for all this extravagance. The large shower had a small barrier that Elizabeth had to step over, but she was able to do that without any problem. And the shower had a convenient bench for her to sit on while she washed her hair. The bathroom was likewise spacious and had plenty of room to move around in with either the rollator or the wheelchair. There was a mini kitchen with a small refrigerator in the suite as well as a microwave and a sink.

Elizabeth washed her hair, put on her last clean sweat suit, and ordered from room service. She dropped off to sleep on one of the room's two queen-sized beds. When her food arrived, she struggled to make herself wake up to answer the door. The waiter set up her dinner on a table in front of the fireplace. Elizabeth was almost too tired to eat, but the sight of the perfectly grilled steak and the crispy French fries on the plate revived her appetite and her energy. She had a glass of red wine with her dinner. When she had finished eating, she called to have her tray removed from the casita.

Her phone was charged by now. She called Richard and left him the message that they had been moved to a larger casita. She said something had gone wrong in the casita where they'd been staying, but she didn't go into details. She made sure to let Richard know that the Mimosa Inn was not charging them for the larger casita. She hoped that by the time Richard had returned from his hunting trip to pick her up to return to Tucson that he would be so impressed with the upgrade, he wouldn't remember to ask too many uncomfortable questions about why their previous room had been declared off limits. Elizabeth knew she would end up telling Richard everything, as she always did, but she liked to time her revelations to catch him in the proper mood. He'd already been grumbling about the cost of the standard handicap accessible casita.

Elizabeth was happy to have a few days to herself. She slept late and had a room service breakfast every morning. She spent most of the days working on her next novel. She contracted with a staff person at the Mimosa Inn to come and push her around the grounds of the resort for about thirty minutes each day. She gave whoever took her on her daily outing a nice tip in addition to paying them for their time. She enjoyed being able to be outside, to go on a tour through the Mimosa's beautiful gardens, and to sit in the sun for a few minutes. She ordered her dinner from room service, and one night she watched an Agatha Christie mystery movie on the room's large flat screen.

On the second day after she'd moved to her new casita, when she was on her daily wheelchair tour of the Mimosa's grounds, Elizabeth thought she saw Detective Mendoza eating lunch on the patio. But Cecilia did not look like herself. Cecilia had distinctive red hair that made her very noticeable. Elizabeth could swear the woman she saw eating lunch was Mendoza, but the woman on the patio had brown hair. Maybe Cecilia was wearing a wig. Elizabeth knew Cecilia Mendoza worked in the homicide division of the Phoenix Police Department. Why would she be hanging out at the Mimosa Inn, wearing what could only be described as a disguise? Was she staying at the resort undercover? This was a mystery Elizabeth wanted to solve.

Whenever there was a knock at the door that she wasn't expecting, Elizabeth experienced a brief jolt of anxiety. This had just begun to happen while she'd been staying at the resort in Paradise Valley. The vacation at the Mimosa Inn had not turned out the way she'd thought it would. There had been much more excitement and much more confusion than she'd expected.

Her phone let her know that she had a text. She glanced at the text, and it was from Detective Cecilia Mendoza telling her she was standing outside her casita and wanted to talk to her. Elizabeth made it to the door with her rollator and smiled to see Cecilia's red hair and Cecilia's face. She welcomed the detective and invited her to sit down in front of the gas fire that warmed the casita on this chilly November morning.

"I really had intended to call or text you, to see if it was convenient, before I came over. Sorry if I'm interrupting the mystery writer at work, but I wanted to be sure I caught you before you left. I remembered you were leaving either today or tomorrow. I have several things I want to tell you about. I think you will find all of my news to be good news."

"You aren't interrupting anything. Richard and Matthew Ritter are returning later this afternoon from a week of quail hunting. We will have dinner together tonight and take Matthew, and his dog, to the airport on our way out of town in the morning. I'm delighted to see you, and I am always happy to welcome good news. Maybe I am turning into an old fuddy-duddy, but it seems like there is less good news lately than there used to be. I hope I'm wrong about that."

"I don't think you are wrong about that, and you are anything but an old fuddy-duddy." Cecilia seemed more relaxed than Elizabeth had ever seen her. She'd always felt the detective was wound up tight and ready to spring at any moment. She was always in a rush, as if she had way too many things to do and too little time in which to do them. Elizabeth was happy to see how attractive the law enforcement officer was when she wasn't stressed beyond belief.

"You look as if you have cracked a case. That's good news. And if it is my case, that's even better news. I've wanted to ask you how that valet who was shot in my casita is doing. I thought you might be bringing me news about his condition."

"As a matter of fact, that valet is an important part of the story I have to tell you. His part in the story is more than that of a valet, and you may be surprised, even shocked, to hear that he has been doing much more than pretend to be a valet here at the Mimosa." The detective paused. She had a lot to tell Elizabeth, and it was complicated.

"The valet who was shot when he pushed you to your room a few nights ago is going to be fine. His arm is healing nicely. The surprising piece of the story is that he was part of the drug ring that has been using the Mimosa Inn as their base of operations."

Elizabeth gasped. "Not that nice, polite young man who pushed me back to my room. He's part of the drug gang? And I was worried because I didn't know his name. Wow!"

"No one was more surprised or upset about being shot that day than the 'nice, polite young man' who was working here as a valet. The guy in the ski mask, the man who shot the valet, was another member of the network that has been working out of the Mimosa." Cecilia was clearly delighted that she had been able to uncover the drug traffickers who were using this famous and historic hostelry as a place to deal fentanyl. "I will tell you everything I can. If you hadn't reserved a handicap accessible room, and if the HVAC system in the standard room hadn't stopped working, we might never have uncovered this well-oiled and sophisticated operation. It was happening right under the nose of the management, and the manager is quite upset that she had not suspected anything at all was going on at her resort. She was completely in the dark. I told her it was a very elaborate and well-run set-up, and I was not a bit surprised that she hadn't suspected anything was amiss."

Cecilia continued her story. "The valet was so angry, and frightened that a member of his own gang shot him, he decided to turn on the others and tell us everything about everybody in the organization. When he realized who had shot him, he couldn't wait to tell all. We lucked out with that. The valet knew exactly who was wearing the ski mask and exactly who shot him. Getting shot pissed him off big time, and he decided to take a plea and come over to the side that has the federal witness protection program. He told us everything...who, how, when, what...and nobody had to ask him why. The why is money! Their set-up was slick and very well organized. The whole thing ran like clockwork, until you moved into the empty casita and upset the applecart. It turns out that something else had actually gone wrong with the drug trafficking arrangements just the day before you arrived here at the Mimosa Inn. There was a new person who made a delivery, a new courier, and he stashed the fentanyl in the wrong place. The new guy was supposed to put the plastic bags of drugs behind that nice pot that was in the niche beside the fireplace. He was standing in for one of the regular couriers, and his English wasn't that good. He misunderstood what he was told to do and thought he was supposed to hide the drugs inside rather than behind the colorful pot. He made a mistake, and then no one could find the score of fentanyl. They were all panicked and searching everywhere. And then something happened to the temporary courier. He disappeared, or he went back to Mexico which is where he came from. In any case, no one was able to find him to ask him where he'd hidden the drugs. The guy at the next level above these guys and gals who actually move the drugs from place to place, was very angry."

"I'll bet he was angry. Did he think one of his couriers had decided to keep the drugs for himself or herself? How many people on the staff here at the resort were involved?"

"I'll get to all of that. There were four people on the staff here who were in on the trafficking operation. Two were valets. One was in housekeeping, and one drove the airport shuttle bus. In addition, there were a number of different couriers who came and went. It was smart to use a variety of couriers, so nobody recognized the same person always coming here again and again. But that was what came back to bite them in the end. They used a courier who didn't know his prepositions. Ha! This was a very complex and very smart set up, and they ran it for a couple of years without anyone noticing what was going on. Somebody made a pile of money out of this one."

Cecilia Mendoza had more to tell. "It was the shuttle bus that was the really imaginative part of the operation. Using the shuttlebus and being able to drive it into and out of Sky Harbor and the Tucson airport and everywhere else it wanted to go was the key. The bus enabled this group of drug dealers to move a lot of fentanyl quickly and on a much larger scale than other smaller groups of drug dealers are able to do."

"I want you to tell me all about it, but I have a question for you. Did I see you eating lunch here one day on the Mimosa Inn patio wearing a wig?" Elizabeth wanted to solve at least one mystery.

Cecilia laughed. It was the first time Elizabeth had ever heard her laugh. "I thought you recognized me. Yes, I was undercover. I stayed here for several nights. My red hair is so distinctive, I had to wear the brown wig. When you went by that day, you gave me such an odd look. I thought you knew who I was, but I could see that the hair color threw you off."

"I was sure it was you, but it wasn't the 'you' I was used to seeing. So you were staying here working on the big drug bust. I thought you were homicide. I'm assuming you have made all the arrests. Do you have the guys at the top, too, or just the peons? I hope that cute, smiley-faced valet or greeter, or whatever they are calling him this week, told you all about everything. Of course, maybe he only knew about the people who were running things here at the Mimosa. Maybe he didn't know about the people who were organizing it all."

"This bust was an all-out effort with quite a few government agencies working on it together. Because you found the pot full of fentanyl, my CSI at Phoenix PD was able to get several fingerprints off the plastic bags. Those fingerprints led us to some bigger fish. Because I was your contact here at the Mimosa and you called me when you found the drugs in your casita, the DOJ and DHS insisted I continue to participate. And, there was the homicide here which we are still working on."

Cecilia stopped talking for a couple of seconds and looked Elizabeth in the eyes. "I suspect that you already know it was an attempted homicide and not an actual homicide. Of course, everyone else thinks it was an actual homicide and that somebody died. That's what we want everyone else to think." Cecilia shifted gears. "Anyway, I was the main person who kept my eyes on the four employees who were running the drugs here at the Mimosa Inn. I had to keep these four in my sights. We didn't want any of them bailing out and going to Mexico or Canada or just disappearing into thin air. That's why I was staying here undercover. We had the FBI, the DEA, the U.S. Department of Transportation, the Arizona Highway Patrol, and a bunch of other people in on this one. It was big. It was a really important bust. Everyone who worked on it was shocked at the volume of drugs that were being run through this resort."

Elizabeth had a bunch of questions she wanted to ask but decided she would let Cecilia tell her story the way she wanted to tell it. "The manager here is angry with herself for not knowing anything about what was going on. But honestly, it was so slick and so few people on the staff here were involved, I can't really blame her for not figuring it out."

Cecilia Mendoza continued. "They have a very fancy van here that is supposed to take people back and forth from the airport. It is really more of a luxury bus than a van. It has leather seats that recline and a bar and serves snacks. It's very plush. It has Mimosa Inn painted on the side. Because this resort has such a stellar reputation, nobody ever bothered to stop it or search it or wonder about its comings and goings. The Mimosa Inn van was allowed to drive right onto the tarmac and pick up cargo. It was allowed to drive right onto the tarmac in the area where the private planes fly in. You can imagine how easy it was to load boxes and suitcases and other containers full of fentanyl on and off that fancy van. Everybody was so used to seeing it, nobody saw it any more. It was just waved through security wherever it was and whenever it showed up. And it was busy all the time. The valets, or greeters, at the Mimosa kept that van going on drug pickups and deliveries all the time."

"I wondered about that. When we decided to have our yearly reunion here, the reservations people told us there was a resort van available to pick us up at the airport and drive us to dinner at other restaurants in the city. That was the manager talking. When we tried to book the Mimosa Inn van to drive us to the Heard Museum and to dinner at Chez Auguste, it was already booked. It was busy every time we wanted it to drive us somewhere. The Richardsons flew into Sky Harbor on their private plane. They tried to get the Mimosa Inn to send the van for them and drive them here to Paradise Valley. But the van was busy of course. The Richardsons ended up taking an Uber to the Mimosa Inn. Now I see why that highly-touted van that was supposed to be available to the guests at the Hermosa was never available to any of the guests. It was too busy running drugs all over the Southwest."

"All the arrests have been made...except for the attempted homicide. We have not wrapped that up yet. The employees who were running drugs here at the Mimosa were pretty anxious to talk. Only one of them was an addict who was getting paid in drugs. The others were getting paid in big money. You don't want to know all those details, but you were helpful to us in two major ways. One was finding the fentanyl in your casita that led to fingerprints. The other was having that 'nice, polite young man' push your wheelchair back to your room. He was so angry when his fellow employee and fellow drug dealer fired a gun at him, he was ready to tell us everything he knew and then some."

"He's the one who's gone into federal witness protection?"

"Yes. I probably should not have told you that. But you were such a major player in this, I thought you deserved to know what happened to him. The others will all be tried and convicted...in a secret court or in a very public trial."

"I guess I got in on some of the excitement, and I guess I should be glad I didn't get in on any more of it than I did."

"If I could have convinced you to move to the Phoenician and if the PPD budget could have afforded it, I would have moved you over there in a minute...out of harm's way. I really wanted you completely away from the Mimosa while we were making our arrests and taking care of business. I was very worried that someone would imagine you knew more than you did and come after you. Just so you know, I've had two people watching out for you day and night...ever since the valet got shot. I don't know if you noticed there's been somebody working on the landscaping around your casita pretty much nonstop for the last three days."

"It seems like there are a lot of landscaping people working around here everywhere all the time...outside every casita. No, I didn't notice anything unusual or realize that you had special surveillance on me. But thanks. I think I was okay, but I appreciate it that you thought to protect me."

Cecilia Mendoza sighed a heavy sigh of relief. "This was a huge victory for law enforcement. We were able to close down a really big drug trafficking organization. It's very important for us, and we are proud of the hard work we did to make it happen. But, because the drug trade is driven by demand, another organization will form very soon to meet that demand. It won't be an organization that operates out of the Mimosa Inn next time. They may not use a luxury transport bus to run the drugs from place to place. But make no mistake about it, another group of dealers will form and find a way to supply what people in the United States want to buy. We have shut things down for a while, but it is only a matter of time until someone else moves in to take over what the Mimosa Inn gang has been doing for the past two years. It's discouraging, but we know it's going to happen. There will be another network in place before too many months have gone by. We have a success, but the bad guys are right on our heels, ready to set up business again. Fentanyl is such a killer, and it is so profitable. Tremendous creativity seems to be drawn to the huge profits that can be realized. Taping the pills to your legs to cross the border, tunnels everywhere, private planes taking off and landing in obscure fields, mini-submarines traveling up and down the coast, a luxury bus from a hugely expensive resort making pickups and deliveries right under the noses of the management of the hotel, the airlines, and others. Our next challenges are drones that fly across the border to deliver their product and the newest trend which is to make the fentanyl inside the United States. No tunnels necessary. No drones necessary. No submarines necessary. It's now homegrown or actually I guess I should say that it's homemade."

"How do you know so much about drug trafficking. I know you are homicide."

"I used to work in drug trafficking. And so many of our homicides these days have their roots in the drug trade. There are people killing each other over control of who is going to make the drugs. There are wars and killings between rival groups who want to distribute the drugs. They are constantly fighting about what the limits of their distribution territories are going to be. We have homicides committed by drug-crazed addicts. We have fentanyl-fueled tirades against enemies, friends, families, and random strangers. We have overdoses that are accidental and some that are homicides. And some that are suicides. It never ends." Cecilia was trying not to let herself become discouraged as she laid it all out for Elizabeth.

"We are also working on the Igor Castillo case. That one is more problematic. He's got a very high profile in both the U.S. and in Mexico. He never does anything himself. He always has his underlings take care of everything for him, especially the dirty work. And now he has disappeared. We don't think he's in the U.S., but at this point, we don't know where he is. We'll find him one of these days, but we may never be able to make any charges against him stick."

Elizabeth had a confession to make. "I want to tell you that I know about Annika Castillo. I know you can't talk to me about this, and I can't tell you all I know about her either. But I know she's not dead. That's all I'm going to say about it. You have been very forthcoming with me, so I wanted to let you know that I am aware that what happened to her was not a homicide."

Mendoza had suspected that Elizabeth knew more than she was saying. "You were helping Isabelle Ritter. I thought you had been gone from the Mimosa for a couple of days. I don't want to know anything about where you went or what you were doing. But I suspected, when your husband and hers went off quail hunting together, that she had asked for your help." Cecilia smiled again. "Enough said. I hope and pray El Russo never finds her. He is pure evil."

"He is indeed. I think she is very safe. Enough said." Elizabeth smiled when Cecilia stood up to leave. "Thanks for everything."

Detective Mendoza wanted to tell Elizabeth more about the person who had tried to murder Annika Castillo, but she did not have much to tell. "As far as who was responsible for the attempted murder of Igor Castillo's wife, Annika, we just don't know who committed that horrible crime. It definitely was two people and maybe three. My personal opinion is that it was people who were in charge of running the drug operation here at the Mimosa Inn who tried to kill her. I think it was probably someone at a higher level on the organization chart who hired those assassins to torture her, to try to get her to tell them what she had done with the drugs. Of course she couldn't tell them anything, no matter what they did to her. So they did their best to kill her. Or thought they did. I don't think any of the killers who tried to murder Annika actually worked here. I think one of their bosses was angry that the drugs had disappeared and that none of his people who worked here had been able to find what happened to the fentanyl. He or she or they may have thought that Annika had found the drugs and was keeping them to sell herself. I also don't think the people who almost killed her had any idea who Annika was. She was staying here under an assumed name, an alias she always used when she stayed at the Mimosa Inn. She even had a credit card in her Mimosa Inn name. She'd stayed here many times in the past, but she never used the name Annika Castillo. If the drug traffickers, either the ones who worked here or the ones who came to torture and kill her, had known she was the wife of Igor Castillo, I don't think they would ever have messed with her. I think going after her was a mistake, an error of judgment on the part of some drug dealers at some level. That's just my view. But I don't have any evidence to back up any of it."

"I don't suppose you will ever be able to solve that one or bring anybody to justice for that awful crime."

"I will update you on what happens with Igor Castillo," the detective promised. "I have your phone number."

Elizabeth was worn out listening to the report about the drug ring that had been uncovered at the Mimosa Inn. She wondered if there was any place anywhere that was just what it appeared to be. She was remembering the incredible secrets that had been kept for so many years at the Woodbrier Resort in West Virginia. And now a huge drug operation had been exposed here in Paradise Valley.

Richard would be arriving back from his bird hunting trip later today. Tomorrow morning they would return to Tucson. It had been another exciting reunion with the Camp Shoemaker crowd. Elizabeth would take her time telling Richard just exactly how exciting it had been this year.

Twenty Six

On New Year's Day, without regaining consciousness, Pia Karlsson passed away quietly at the stroke rehabilitation facility in Tempe, Arizona. The staff had known this was coming, so her death was not unexpected. When she had suffered her first stroke, death had become more of a reality for Pia. She had left specific instructions about what was to be done after she died. Her body was to be cremated. The funeral home that would handle the cremation had already been paid in full for the services they would render. Pia's friend Isabelle Ritter was to be notified. Isabelle's contact information was included with Pia's instructions. Isabelle would pick up the urn that held Pia's ashes. Isabelle already knew what was to be done with Pia's remains. No family members and no friends had been with Pia when she had finally breathed her last.

Isabelle received the sad news that her friend had died by way of a voice mail message someone at the stoke rehabilitation facility left on her cell phone. Isabelle had known for many weeks that Pia would never recover from the second catastrophic stroke she had suffered. Everybody had known that it was just a matter of time until she passed away.

Isabelle consoled herself with the fact that Pia and her daughter had reconciled before Pia had suffered her first stroke. Besides reconnecting with Annika at long last, Pia had been able to help her abused daughter extricate herself from an unhappy marriage. Pia had arranged for Annika to leave the evil man she'd married, and they had worked together to arrange Annika's disappearance. Pia had found and fixed up the cabin hideout for her daughter. Pia had used her computer skills to hunt down Igor's millions. Then she had transferred his money to accounts where El Russo would never be able to find it. All of Igor's ill-gotten gains now belonged to Annika.

Pia had done everything a mother could do to help her child escape certain death. Both Pia and Annika believed that if she stayed with Igor Castillo, she would eventually die by his hand. He was a volatile and violent monster. Pia had saved her daughter's life and left her more than financially secure. Mother and daughter had worked together to make this happen. Pia had convinced her daughter to talk to the FBI and tell them all about Igor Castillo's life as a drug kingpin. Hopefully, the final result would be that Annika's testimony against her husband would be instrumental in bringing down one of the most notorious drug lords in Mexico and North America.

It was months before Igor could be convinced that his now-deceased wife was the person who had cheated him out of his fortune. Igor now knew that before she'd been murdered, Annika had been planning to leave him. She had been able to get into his safe at their Scottsdale home and find his account numbers and passwords. She had stolen the fortune he had secreted away in bank accounts all over the world. Igor had not realized his wife had the computer skills to do all that she had done to get his money. But the money was gone. Where had it disappeared to? Igor flew into a rage every time he had to acknowledge to himself that because Annika was dead, he would never know what had happened to his millions.

When he had first learned of Annika's murder, he had blamed his competition, the rival drug lords he knew wanted to infringe on his drug empire, for her death. He had called for retribution and revenge against his enemies. Then he'd realized that his money had disappeared. The only person who could possibly have had access to the names of the banks and the account numbers where he had secreted his money had been his wife.

Igor's cousin Hector had been the one to figure out that only Annika could have known about the safe, and she was the only person who would have been able to find the combination. Annika was the only person on earth who would have been able to access what was in that safe. When Igor finally realized it was his own wife who had stolen his fortune from him, he went crazy again. But Annika was already dead. El Russo couldn't go after her and kill her for a second time.

Annika's only living relative was her mother. Igor had believed that Annika and her mother were estranged. They had been estranged when Igor and Annika married, and he'd believed they were still estranged when Annika was killed. Igor's cousin Hector had investigated, and he alerted Igor to the fact that Annika and her mother might have reconciled before Pia had suffered her first stroke. Hector had also discovered, when he was gathering information about

Pia and Annika, that Pia had excellent computer skills. Not many people knew this about her, but Hector had dug deep into Pia's past and found that she had developed her abilities using computers and the internet to quite an extensive degree. Hector convinced Igor, and now they both accepted that Pia Karlsson had conspired with Annika and helped her steal Igor's money.

El Russo decided to go after Pia, but when he did, he had to face the fact that Pia was already close to death. He investigated Pia's condition to be sure she was not playing possum with the stroke and pretending to be unconscious. He paid a great deal of money to find out what was happening in the facility where Pia was being cared for. His inquiries assured him that Pia had indeed suffered a fatal stroke and was essentially brain dead. She would never regain consciousness, and it was only a matter of time until she passed away. Igor realized he would never be able to question Pia about the money that had disappeared. He was furious, but there was nothing he could do about it. He decided that Pia would be dead soon enough. There would be no joy in murdering a woman who was essentially dead already.

Because it would be stupid to go after Pia, Igor now found he had no target for his anger. He believed Annika was dead. Pia was almost dead. Because he could not kill the two people he most wanted to kill, his anger was displaced, and he wanted to kill everyone he saw. He was a wild man and growing wilder. It was all Hector could do to continue to talk him down from his craziness.

El Russo had paid an informant who worked in the rehabilitation facility where Pia Karlsson had lived out her final days, and Igor was notified when Pia died. He wondered who would take care of her funeral arrangements. Because Annika was dead, Igor thought there was no one left to settle Pia's affairs. His contact told him that Pia had left a letter with instructions about what was to be done with her body and that she was being cremated. El Russo wondered if anyone would pick up Pia's ashes. There really was no one left to do that. Igor wanted to find out if there were any other distant or previously unknown family members he could go after. Even being able to murder an obscure relative or good friend of Pia's or Annika's would give him some satisfaction. He decided he would pay someone at the funeral home that was taking care of the cremation. If anyone turned up to claim the ashes, Igor would be notified. He would be able to find out who they were. Maybe he would kill them...even though he would be the only person on earth who would have any idea what the motive for the murder was.

Isabelle called and spoke with both Cate and Mona on Mona's satellite phone. Isabelle told them she had been notified of Pia's death. The news was not a surprise to anyone, but even when death is expected, there is still great sadness when one's mother is gone. They decided that in the end it was a blessing that Pia was finally at peace. The plan was clear, and Isabelle told Cate that she would collect Pia's ashes and bring them to Pinetop. Isabelle lived in Palm Springs, California, and she explained that it might be weeks or even months before she was able to return to the Phoenix area and retrieve Pia's ashes from the funeral home in Tempe. Isabelle promised to bring the ashes to Pia's daughter at the cabin. The delay was fine with Cate. She had not yet decided what to do with her mother's remains. There was no rush.

Isabelle was heartened by the news that Cate had recovered as well as she had from the wounds she'd suffered. She would end up with many scars on her body, but she did not appear to have any residual brain damage. She was working every day with Mona to learn to walk again. She had already taken a few steps. Mona had set up a physical therapy program for Cate at her cabin, and Cate was giving it her best effort—to strengthen her legs and to try to get them to work as they used to work. It would be a long road, but Mona and Cate were committed to accomplishing a miracle. Cate would walk again, but she would probably always walk with a limp. She would probably always have to use a cane.

Cate had put herself entirely into the hands of the very competent Mona Damours. Mona welcomed Cate into her life as she might welcome a long-lost daughter. Although they were a generation apart and very different people, they'd had many similar life experiences. Mona would keep Cate safe and teach her how to live so that no one could find her. But Mona worried that in the long run, living in the mountains would not suit Cate. Cate was more of a people person than Mona was. At what point would she grow tired of the seclusion that had been forced on her. At what point would she rebel and decide to go back to the real world, the real world that would always be so terribly dangerous for her to live in.

Even if the FBI was successful and Igor was prosecuted and went to prison for the rest of his life, Cate would still be at risk. As is true for most drug kingpins and mafia dons, they control their networks and do their bossing from prison. Nothing really changes when one of them goes to jail. Igor Castillo would put out a hit on Cate from his prison cell, and she would end up dead. Mona knew this, and Cate knew this. Mona knew she had to impress on Cate how incredibly dangerous it would be for her to try to go back to anything that even remotely resembled her previous life. But would Cate be able to live as a recluse for the rest of her life? Mona had her doubts.

Mona wanted to talk to Cate about her own experiences with domestic abuse, about the reasons Mona had been driven to give up the practice of medicine, her relationships with her family, and her life in Montreal. Mona had never before met anyone she felt would really understand what she had been through and how painful and difficult the choices she'd made had been. She thought Cate was as close to a soul sister in that regard as she was ever going to find. Cate had been through a version of hell similar to Mona's own. They had both been involved with very powerful, rich, and connected partners who would have ended up killing them had they not escaped. Mona felt she could talk openly with Cate. Both Cate and Mona would benefit from sharing their stories.

Nobody wants to talk about domestic abuse. For those who are victims, it is embarrassing and shameful. To admit you were a victim somehow implied that you were, in some way, less than. It implied that you might be stupid or cowardly or a bad judge of character. It implied that you yourself were flawed. It implied that you might be guilty of either provoking the abuse or enabling it. There were so many pejoratives associated with admitting it was happening to you. Those to whom it had never happened couldn't understand.

When Cate had made more progress in her efforts to strengthen her legs and walk, Mona intended to encourage her to take up painting again. She had seen Cate's work and thought she had a great deal of potential. She didn't think Cate would necessarily believe her or listen to her counsel. When Mona had been Cate's age, she had not wanted to listen to anybody but herself.

Twenty Seven

"*I've never really told anybody* the whole story about why I gave up being a doctor and became a painter and a recluse. I hid out in New York City for years, and then I became afraid for my life again. That was when I decided to move to the Southwest, very far away from New York City." Mona paused to see if Cate was paying attention to what she was saying. "For almost all of my life, I have been on the run and in hiding from a man who said he loved me. We were engaged to be married, but he began to beat me, even before we tied the knot. Thank goodness I found out what he was really like before we were legally tied to each other and before we had any children."

Cate had been listening. "I'd gathered from things you've said that you still feel you have to be very careful about never having a public persona. My mother told me the lengths to which you go, with your paintings, to obscure where you are living. She told me about how you drive long distances to send your art work to the gallery that sells your paintings in New York and about the elaborate and many-layered system you have for hiding where the paintings are being sent from. I can only assume from those stories that your abuser is still alive and still actively looking for you."

"You are correct. My abuser is still alive, and he is still looking for me. After all these years, you might imagine that he would have given up and moved on. He's had two wives since he was engaged to me. They both divorced him. He has spent tremendous amounts of money on private investigators to try to find me. He has even used the Royal Canadian Mounted Police to try to find me."

"How could he do that? How could he get the Mounties to try to find you? Is that even legal?"

"My former fiancé was a very powerful man in Canada. His family is enormously wealthy, and they have a long tradition in national politics and in the Canadian military. At one point in his life, my fiancé was an up-and-coming star in the political world. He had ambitions, and years ago, he thought he had the background and the charisma to be elected the prime minister of Canada. Fortunately, he's had to give up his quest for the highest office in the country. His true colors could not be hidden forever, and he inevitably got himself into several kinds of trouble that ended his political career. There is no equivalent of the CIA or the FBI in Canada. The Royal Canadian Mounted Police, the RCMP, is a national police force which investigates federal crimes and handles criminal intelligence. I grew up in Montreal which is in the province of Quebec. Our provincial law enforcement organization in Quebec is the Sûreté de Québec. Many years ago, my former fiancé had the power to have me declared a terrorist. That's the way he has been able to use government resources, and the big guns, to look for me. He put my name on the terrorist watch list and also on the No Fly List. He enlisted the RCMP and the Sûreté de Québec to try to hunt me down. They have never been able to find me, but I am still on the terrorist watch list. This evil man was powerful enough and in an important enough position that he was able to put me on the list and order Canadian law enforcement to search for me."

"Wow. That's really frightening. It's so wrong that he had all that power and influence and used it to try to find you. It was all a lie, and he did it just for his own personal ends. When you have someone like that after you, it's understandable why you've had to stay in hiding all these years and why you are so careful about your exposure to the outside world."

"I am telling you all these things about myself because I want you to know that I understand why you are here. I know what it feels like to have to give up your former life to save yourself. I have been in the same position, and I am still in the same position. I have had to go the same extremes you have had to go to. My real motive for telling you all of this is that I hope you will pay attention when I tell you not to do something that I think will put you at risk. I know the ropes when it comes to staying anonymous. I promised your mother I would help you stay alive. Will you help me do that?"

"I know my mother told you all about Igor and what happened with us. I knew, and my mother also knew, that eventually he would end up killing me. I was so incredibly foolish to have hooked up with a man like that in the first place. It was the worst mistake of my life, and believe me, I've made plenty of mistakes. Igor Castillo was by far the worst of my many horrible choices."

"Many women find themselves in abusive relationships. Most, however, do not have the resources to escape their abusers. They may feel as if they don't have the education or the skills or the ability to earn a living and support themselves or to support themselves and their children. Many stay and eventually die. Others end up in prison because they reach the point where they have had enough and finally resort to killing the man who has been beating them for years. Or, they decide to kill their abuser before he starts in on their children. You and I have been fortunate that we had the resources that allowed us to escape from our abusers."

"But, Mona, the truth is that we have had to pay a terrible price to be able to make that escape. You might even say that we have been *forced* to make that escape. You and I have had to give up our previous identities. You can never practice medicine again, because you can't use your medical license which is in your former name. I went to ASU and studied to be an art therapist. I worked hard to graduate from college and wanted to get a master's degree in my chosen field. I wanted to work as an art therapist and help people in that way. That life is forever gone from me. I have had to give up my previous identity, my name, my home, my relationship with my mother, and my hopes and dreams for the future as an art therapist. I have had to give up everything."

Mona agreed. "I guess you could say that we are lucky that we never had any children with our bad men, but many abused women share offspring with the man who is beating them. Some leave with their children and go into hiding because they fear for their own lives as well as for the lives of their children. But more often, these women who have children stay in the house with their abusers. They may be afraid to leave. They may not know how to extricate themselves from whatever situations they find themselves in. They may be desperate to leave but don't want to leave their children behind. They may not have the financial wherewithal to allow them to get away. You have financial resources. I have been able to make a living and support myself with my painting. Many women do not have the education or the ability to make the break and provide for themselves and their children as single parents."

Cate had never had any children, but she could see the logic in what Mona was saying. "Children complicate things, that's for sure. And you're right, we did not have to consider that part of it when we decided to leave. But I think there is a huge psychological element we've not even touched on. I know I hate to admit failure. I hated to have to admit that I had chosen such a loser for a husband. I hated that I was not able to make him happy, that I made him so unhappy he finally ended up beating the hell out of me. For a long time, I took on the responsibility of causing the abuse. Even when I finally realized the abuse was not my fault, I didn't want anyone to know. I didn't want anyone to know what a bad choice I'd made by choosing to marry Igor. I was ashamed of myself for choosing a man who would beat me up. How could I have been so naïve, or stupid, or clueless, or whatever...to have wanted to marry someone who now wants to hurt me. What does that say about my judgment? What does that say about my ability to perceive what people are like? And, what does that say about my own capabilities as a wife. I can't please my husband anymore. What does that say about me as a woman, as a homemaker, as a lover, as a companion? I think many women don't want to admit that they couldn't make a go of their marriage. They don't want to admit they have failed. So they stay, and they pretend they still have a marriage."

"I agree with everything you've said, Cate, and I see a great deal of myself in what you have described. One thing that has always been hard for me to understand is that some of these women who stay with their abusers actually still love the bastards they're married to, the creeps who are battering them. These women are not saving face or protecting their self-images in their communities. They actually want to be with the abuser. I don't get that. And this very common pattern of behavior with abused women keeps law enforcement from being able to bring charges against the wife beaters. You've seen it and read about it a hundred times. The husband or boyfriend beats up his wife or girlfriend. She calls the police. They come to the house, arrest the husband or boyfriend, and take him away. The police put him in jail. Law enforcement tells the wife or girlfriend she has to come to the police station to file charges against her abuser. The woman changes her mind. She refuses to file charges against him, for whatever reason. She forgives her abuser, and she takes him back, for whatever reason. She wants him back home, for whatever reason. The police have to let him go. And he goes home...to beat her up again at some time in the future. I don't understand how these women can want to stay with their abusers."

"I am disgusted with myself that I married Igor in the first place and that I stayed as long as I did. Once I realized what was going on and gathered up my courage, I decided I'd had enough. I decided to get out. And it isn't easy to get out, no matter what your situation is. I have the whole Russian Mafia thing and the whole Mexican drug lord thing to deal with. That's two entire armies who could be sent after me to either murder me or bring me back to Igor." Cate's shoulders sank when she thought about everyone who might try to find her...if they had any idea she was alive. "I had to kill myself off in order to get away from Igor's world. Nobody should have to do that. I am thrilled to be away, but I should not have had to 'die' to be safe. And, just so you know, I will never allow myself to be taken back to Igor. I will kill myself for real before I ever go back to him." Cate was resolute. It was obvious to Mona that she meant what she was saying.

"Why do you think you were attracted to Igor in the first place? Why did you choose him?" Mona was very curious about how Cate would answer this question.

"I thought he was everything I ever wanted in a man. I was young and clueless. I was estranged from my mother. I was a brat. I had been tending bar to pay the bills, and I was tired of struggling financially. Igor was incredibly handsome, and he had charisma. He turned on the charm with me. He had lots and lots of money, and he promised me the world. At the time, he seemed like an answer to my prayers. And actually, he behaved himself for a while after we were married. We argued about things, but usually I gave in to whatever he wanted me to do. He usually won our arguments. But he didn't start out our marriage beating me."

"What happened? What changed? Why did you finally decide you'd had enough?"

"His violence escalated. I think the novelty of being married to me had worn off for him. He was tired of me. I know he had other women. Maybe he had another one on the string that he wanted to marry. I'm not sure. But his beatings became worse and worse." Cate shivered as she remembered her unhappy life with Igor Castillo.

She continued. "I remember the first time he hit me when we were having an argument. I was stunned. I cried and cried. He said he was so sorry. He apologized on his hands and knees and promised me it would never happen again. He brought me flowers. He bought me a diamond brooch. He took me on a cruise to the Caribbean. He was loving and considerate, and I was again his princess... until he lost his temper the next time and hit me even harder. One time he broke my jaw. And he wouldn't allow me to go to the hospital to seek treatment. He had his cousin Hector find an oral surgeon who came to our house and operated on me there. Igor threatened the doctor within an inch of his life. Igor paid him a bunch of money and told him he would come after him and kill him and his family if he ever told anyone about me or what had happened with my jaw."

Mona decided it was safe to reveal even more personal aspects of her own story of abuse. "I was pregnant with my abuser's child. We were going to be married in two weeks when he beat me so badly I lost the baby. Looking back on what happened, I'm glad I didn't have a child to think about when I decided to leave. I almost bled to death when I had the miscarriage. He'd hit me in the stomach with a fireplace poker. He was so angry, he hit me over and over again with the poker until I was unconscious. I protected my face, so he didn't leave any scars that you could see. Even though I kept him from inflicting any scars on my face, I have scars all over the rest of my body. My father found me half-dead in my apartment and did what he could. He was a doctor, too. He realized I was in grave danger. He drove me across the border to upstate New York for surgery. A physician friend of his in Buffalo took care of me. The doctor in Buffalo didn't report what had happened to the police. He broke the law by not reporting what he'd seen, but he understood what was going on. My father was his friend. He also didn't charge us anything for all the medical care I had to have. I had to have multiple surgeries. I was in the hospital for three months, recovering from my fiancé's attack. I had to have a hysterectomy, so I knew I would never be able to have any children. I never went back to Montreal. My family helped me disappear. They provided me with a new identity and helped me move to New York City. It broke their hearts to have to say goodbye to me. They knew they could not contact me again. They knew the man I had been going to marry would be watching them. They knew if they had any contact with me, they might lead him to me. I was an only child and an only grandchild. I was their future. But if they'd contacted me, he would have found me. As it was, he harassed them for years, trying to get them to tell him where I was living. They never told him anything about me except that they thought I had died."

Cate was quiet as she listened to Mona's story and tried to absorb the impact of what this brave woman had endured. "I don't know what to say. I guess I am just thankful that you and I escaped with our lives. I am thankful you lived to be able to paint your amazing works of art. I am thankful you lived to be able to make a home in your cabin and a home for me in mine. I am thankful you lived so that you could take me in and take care of me."

Cate wanted to tell the rest of her story. "After my jaw was broken so badly and Igor would not allow me to go to the hospital, something inside me changed. I decided I would go to college and get a degree. I'd not yet reached the point where I'd made the decision to leave him, but I knew I needed to have something of my own. I needed something in my life that had nothing to do with Igor Castillo or his big house or his money or his drugs or any of it. I'd always rejected academics in the past. I refused to apply to colleges when I graduated from high school. My mother wanted me to either go to college or attend art school. I rejected both options. When I enrolled in ASU, I loved my painting courses. But it was my psych classes that educated me about what was going on with Igor and with my marriage. My class in abnormal psychology told me all I needed to know about the evil man I had married. I learned about the narcissistic personality and about compulsions and obsessions. I learned about bipolar disorder and about multiple personality and schizophrenia. I woke up to the realization that I was living with a man who could be all of these. I knew I had to leave."

Cate continued. "I gained a lot of insight into myself and into Igor's personality. He has a number of metal health issues, as well as just being downright evil, a thoroughly wicked, bad man. I began to understand the dynamics of what was happening in my marriage. It was my study of psychology that opened my eyes. I think counseling serves the same purpose for others."

Mona nodded her head. "I agree with you that counseling can help some women. But many women can't afford it or are afraid to tell their husbands they are going for counseling. Poor women can't afford counseling, and they are the least able to be able to provide for themselves financially, without a spouse. As we both know, abuse occurs in relationships in all socioeconomic classes. Men of all classes are abusers. Some women also abuse their spouses, but it is usually men who are the violent ones. The very wealthy often get away with their abuse because the women they are abusing do not want to give up their financial security. These women may have become used to a certain lifestyle and don't want to put that at risk. They put up with the abuse because they can't give up the status or the comforts that come with being wealthy. They take the hits because they want to live in the nice house and wear the nice clothes, or they want to continue to send their kids to private school, or whatever. Of course, the dependency thing can happen at any level of society. Even very poor women who are dependent on a vicious husband who has a very low-paying job don't want to lose that financial support. There are so many reasons for staying. Inertia is a powerful thing. It takes a strong and brave woman to leave the danger and the familiarity of abuse."

Twenty Eight

In the early spring of 2023, Igor Castillo was found guilty in federal court of drug trafficking and other crimes. He was sentenced in absentia to ten life terms in federal prison, without the possibility of parole. The evidence against him was overwhelming. Much of the evidence against him was the result of testimony given by Castillo's wife, Annika. She had spent hours giving depositions to the FBI about Igor's activities before she was "murdered" at the Mimosa Inn in Paradise Valley in November of the previous year. The information she had given to the authorities had led to quite a few arrests, even if Igor Castillo himself had not been arrested.

From the information Annika had been able to provide about who had visited her husband, as well as the information found on his computer, quite a few other people who were associated with Igor's drug trafficking organization were convicted and sentenced. Many of the underlings were found, arrested, and imprisoned. But El Russo could not be found. He had disappeared and was believed to be living incognito somewhere in Mexico. Rumors abounded that he was living under another name; that he'd had plastic surgery and looked nothing like he'd looked previously; that he had died; that he had turned state's evidence and entered the U.S. government's witness protection program. There were many other rumors... some that could possibly be true and others that were so outlandish as to be impossible.

Detective Cecilia Mendoza called Isabelle Ritter periodically to keep her up to date on the status of the cases against El Russo. Isabelle wanted Igor Castillo to be locked up in prison for the rest of his natural life. If he was never able to get out of prison, Isabelle imagined that Annika Castillo might be able to worry less that he would find her and kill her. Isabelle hoped that she might eventually be strong enough to leave her mountain hideout once in a while. But as long as Castillo was on the run and running free, Annika, now Cate, would have to stay hidden and watch her back every day of her life.

Isabelle was angry that Igor Castillo had not been arrested. She had hoped the depositions Annika had given to the FBI would be sufficient to indict and convict the man. And they had been. The trouble was that he had disappeared. It was as if there had never been a court case, as if there had never been any convictions. Igor Castillo might have to be careful, because he was a wanted man, but in fact he was free as a bird to do whatever he wanted to do. There was no comparison between the life Igor had in Mexico, even with a price on his head, and the life that Annika was forced to live to protect herself from her former husband.

Isabelle was enraged deep in her soul at the lack of fairness in life. Why did the bad guys get to live it up like kings and their victims had to hide themselves away? Isabelle agreed with Detective Mendoza that he was probably hiding out and living it up in Mexico. That was El Russo's home. His first language was Spanish. He had property in Mexico. He loved the food. There were people in Mexico who were willing to protect the violent and wacko murderer.

Isabelle was trying to disengage from her fury at what had happened to Annika Karlsson and what had failed to happen to El Russo. She felt powerless to do anything, and in fact she was unfortunately aware that she was completely powerless. At least she could console herself that she had been able to help her friend Pia and had successfully participated in saving Annika's life. She had made sure that Pia's daughter made it to the safe house in the mountains. She had one more duty to Pia, to deliver her ashes to Annika. Isabelle finally made the trip to the funeral home in Tempe in May, months after Pia had died. Annika, now Cate, had said there was no rush. But Isabelle knew she would not be able to put this sad chapter in her life behind her until she had fulfilled her one last promise to Pia.

🌲

Isabelle flew into Phoenix and rented a car. She wanted this last mission she was on for Pia Karlsson to be no more than a two-day trip. Isabelle was a very busy woman. She had to get back to her business in Palm Springs, but first she needed to do this one last thing for her friend. She had called the funeral home in Tempe and told them when she would be arriving to pick up Pia Karlsson's ashes. Pia had died in January so there was some confusion. But the ashes were located, and the funeral home was expecting her. The funeral home knew they were not to turn the ashes over to anyone but Isabelle Ritter.

Isabelle did not know, of course, that one of the employees of the funeral home was being paid by Igor Castillo to report to him if and when anyone came to the funeral home to pick up the ashes. That employee was being well compensated for just keeping her eyes and ears open. She had been promised a bonus if she gave Castillo the information in time for him to have someone come to the funeral home before the pickup. So many months had passed, the employee thought she'd missed her opportunity to collect the bonus. But one day, she overheard a conversation between two colleagues that someone was finally coming, at long last, to pick up Pia Karlsson's ashes. Families usually picked up their loved one's ashes within days of the cremation. Hardly any of their clients stayed around for as long as Pia Karlsson had stayed around. Igor's spy at the funeral home was able to find out the exact day and time when Isabelle was supposed to arrive.

Igor never imagined he would hear anything from his snoop at the funeral home. He had completely forgotten he was paying her. In fact, he wasn't paying her. Hector, Igor's cousin, was taking care of the payments to the snoop. When Igor received the call that someone was arriving to pick up Pia Karlsson's remains, he was shocked. He'd never expected anyone to pick up the ashes. He didn't think his former dead wife had any living relatives or friends who would bother with Pia Karlsson. He wanted to go to Tempe himself and see who this person was. He wanted to decide if this person was worth killing. He was curious.

At the same time, he knew he would be putting himself at tremendous risk if he went back into the United States. He knew he had been convicted of numerous drug crimes in a U.S. court. He knew that United States law enforcement would love to get their hands on him. He knew he ought to stay out of the U.S. But he couldn't stay away.

Igor's cousin, Hector, was busy setting up a fentanyl manufacturing operation in southern Arizona. The new wave of fentanyl trafficking was to manufacture it in the U.S. and avoid all the hassle at the border trying to smuggle it in. Hector was living temporarily in Tucson where he was buying supplies and renting the properties he needed for his elaborate drug scheme. Hector was getting all of his ducks in a row.

Igor called Hector and told him he was coming to Tucson. Tucson was not that far from Tempe. Igor planned to stay with Hector and drive to Tempe to get a look at the person who was picking up Pia Karlsson. Igor knew the name of the woman who was picking up the ashes was Isabelle Ritter. He had no idea who Isabelle Ritter was or what connection she had to Pia. Igor knew she wasn't a family member. She was not even a distant cousin. Igor's people had researched Pia and Annika's background thoroughly. Isabelle Ritter's name had never come up. Igor was curious about what this Isabelle Ritter person would do with the urn of Pia's ashes. It was a mystery Igor wanted to solve.

Hector told Igor not to come to the United States. Hector knew all about Igor's legal status and urged him to do the sensible thing and stay in Mexico where he could not be touched by U.S. law enforcement. But Hector also knew that his cousin Igor was strong willed, determined to do whatever he wanted to do, and loved to take risks. Hector knew he was not going to be able to talk Igor out of coming to Tucson. But once Igor was in Tucson, Hector thought he might be able to convince his cousin not to go to Tempe.

Hector wanted to maintain a low profile, as he was just getting the fentanyl manufacturing operation off the ground. He did not want Igor coming to town and causing trouble. Hector knew his cousin well and knew he could go nuts at the drop of the hat and mess up everything Hector had been attempting to create.

🌲

Hector and Igor argued. Igor was set on driving to Tempe the next day to see Isabelle Ritter for himself. He had Googled her and found she was an interior designer who owned a store in Palm Springs, California. He had not been able to figure out what her connection was to Pia Karlsson. This piqued his curiosity. He wanted to see what the woman looked like, and even more importantly, he wanted to know what she was going to do with Pia's ashes. He intended to follow Isabelle from the funeral home until his curiosity was satisfied. Hector told Igor he was a fool to come back into the United States. Hector told Igor he was even more of a fool to try to make contact with Isabelle Ritter and follow her someplace. Hector knew this idea of Igor's was at one extreme on the crazy spectrum.

Their argument became heated. In the past Hector had almost always been able to talk his cousin down from his stupidest ideas. That was not going to happen this time. After Hector had objected to his going to Tempe, Igor became even more determined to follow through with his risky and dangerous plan. Hector didn't very often lose his cool, but this time he became furious with Igor over his irrational desire to track the woman who was picking up Pia Karlsson's ashes. Igor's wife was dead. Her mother was dead. Who cared what happened to the ashes?

Hector had invested a great deal of time and money in his homemade fentanyl operation. He was almost on line for production. He could not take the chance that Igor would blow it all to smithereens. Hector was fed up with Igor's craziness. He'd reached the end of his patience with his cousin. Hector planned to tie Igor up and keep him as a prisoner, albeit temporarily. He didn't want to hurt Igor. He just wanted to keep him from driving to Tempe. If he could keep him tied up long enough, Igor would miss his chance to intercept Isabelle Ritter and follow her and the ashes.

Hector decided he was going to strike while Igor was sleeping. It was early on the morning Igor was planning to drive to Tempe. Hector had the plastic handcuffs, and he silently let himself into Igor's bedroom. He intended to put the cuffs on Igor before he was fully awake. Bus Igor was a light sleeper, and he heard Hector coming. They struggled. Igor kept his gun under his pillow. Hector had brought only the plastic cuffs. Igor was not going to let himself be restrained by anyone. He drew his gun from under his pillow and shot his cousin, Hector Gutierrez, in the face.

Igor was a madman. He had shot and killed the only person in the world who cared about him, the only person in the world he'd trusted. Igor left Hector's dead body in the bed. He dressed and shaved and drove to Starbucks for coffee and pastries. He drove to the funeral home in Tempe and waited in the parking lot for Isabelle Ritter to arrive. Igor knew what she looked like from the picture she had posted on her business website. He had brought his gun with him. He had decided that he didn't care who she was or what relationship she had or didn't have with Annika and Pia Karlsson, Isabelle Ritter was going to die today.

Twenty Nine

Isabelle arrived at the funeral home at the appointed time, said a few words to the people who had handled Pia Karlsson's final requests, and carrying the urn that held her friend's ashes, returned to her car. She put the urn on the passenger seat. She planned to have one last conversation with Pia while she drove to the cabin near Pinetop, Arizona.

She would remind Pia of the fun times they'd had together when they were young and studying at ASU. She would remind Pia how lucky she had been to reconcile with Annika before she suffered her first stroke. She would praise Pia for the efforts she had made to rescue Annika from her abusive husband...including finding and furnishing the cabin in the woods. She would tell her friend how proud she was of the brilliant and almost magical financial manipulations she had undertaken to steal Igor's millions and transfer them secretly to Annika. She would congratulate both Annika and Pia on the assistance they had given to the FBI that had resulted in Igor's conviction and multiple life sentences. She would give thanks that Annika had lived through the assault she had suffered at the Mimosa Inn and had been able to make it to the hideout in the White Mountains. She promised Pia that she would pray for Annika's continued safety and for her long-run recovery. She promised Pia she would pray that Annika would someday be able walk again. She told Pia what a wonderful mother and friend she had been.

Igor followed Isabelle Ritter when she left the funeral home's parking lot. He could not imagine where she was going. He had driven and driven and driven. At first he'd thought they were headed for Phoenix, but they had looped around the city and headed northeast. He was tired from his early morning start. The reality of what he had done to his only friend, his only family, had begun to work on his psyche. He was angry, and Isabelle Ritter was a slow driver. Her driving was making him even angrier. He wanted to get this over with. He wanted to shoot her and be done with it. He wanted to go back to Mexico.

When she turned onto a dirt road outside Pinetop, Arizona, he wondered if he should continue to follow her. Igor had taken Hector's car, and he'd had to stop for gas. He'd lost Isabelle Ritter momentarily but had found her again on the road to Show Low. He decided he would follow his quarry, but at some point he would probably have to park the car and continue on foot. Isabelle was driving even more slowly and carefully on the dirt road up into the mountains. She turned off onto a very narrow road that was almost a footpath. Igor decided they were nearing the end of the road, wherever that was, and he pulled the Lexus over and parked it. He set out on foot to discover where Isabelle was taking the ashes.

He was careful not to be seen. He intended to take a couple of quick shots, make sure Isabelle was dead, and then go back to the car. He was not at all expecting to see what he saw when he turned a corner in the road and saw Isabelle sitting on the porch of a rustic cabin. He was stunned to see three women sitting there together. There was one woman on the porch he didn't recognize. But one of the women on the porch was in a wheelchair, and that woman in the wheelchair was the woman Igor was married to. He had believed for many months that she was dead. She had been murdered in Phoenix at the Mimosa Inn. But here she was. Annika was alive and sitting on a porch in the middle of nowhere in a wheelchair. He could not even begin to get his mind around why she happened to be there, why she was not dead, why she was in a wheelchair, or any of it.

His plan had to change. He didn't really care about Isabelle Ritter. The person he really wanted to kill was his wife, Annika. She had betrayed him in so many ways. He would finally have his revenge. Seeing Annika and being slapped in the face with the reality that she hadn't died, shocked him out of his angry craziness. The cold, cunning, and sometimes logical killer inside Igor Castillo took over. He had to know what she had done with his money. Rather than shoot her outright, he would torture her and force her to tell him where she had hidden his millions. Then he would kill her.

His plan was to hide in the woods and watch the cabin until Isabelle Ritter left. He would shoot the other old woman who was sitting on the porch. Then he would tie Annika up and torture her until she told him everything he wanted to know. His day had been made. He was not going to kill a woman he didn't know, a woman who would have no idea why he was killing her. Instead, he was going to kill his wife who had betrayed him and left him. She had been responsible for his having been convicted of many serious crimes. She had stolen his money. He was ecstatic that he was going to be able to remake his life and finally take Annika's from her.

He hid in the woods beside the cabin and watched the three women have lunch at a small table on the porch. It was May and it was chilly. But the sun was shining. They laughed and talked and ate sandwiches and potato chips. They drank lemonade and iced tea with fruit in it. They ate homemade chocolate chip cookies. He wished he could hear what they were saying to each other, but he kept telling himself that he would soon enough be back in control of everything.

Isabelle Ritter finally said her goodbyes to Mona and Cate and left the cabin. What Igor didn't know was that when she drove away from having lunch with her friends, Isabelle became suspicious of the car she saw parked alongside the dirt road. She got out of her rental car and walked over to the black Lexus that had been abandoned within a few hundred yards of Mona's cabin. It was empty but unlocked. She opened the passenger-side door and tried the glove compartment. It was also unlocked, and the registration was inside. The car was registered to Hector Gutierrez.

Isabelle Ritter knew exactly who Hector Gutierrez was, and she knew that Annika and Mona were in terrible danger. She immediately sent Mona a text about Hector and told Mona where his Lexus was parked. When she received Isabelle's text, Mona was instantly on guard. She'd not heard the name Hector Gutierrez before, but she carefully read the text in which Isabelle briefly told her that the owner of the Lexus was Igor Castillo's cousin.

Mona was sufficiently alarmed to hear that someone so close to Igor Castillo was so close to her cabin. Whether it was Hector or Igor or both, the driver had left his car within a few hundred yards of her home. Where was the person who had been driving that car? Mona could only assume that whoever had driven the car and left it on the road was now somewhere near her cabin. She knew that Annika was in danger from whoever had driven the Lexus up into the mountains. The driver of the Lexus could have come this far with only one goal. That goal was to kill Annika.

Mona texted Isabelle and told her to get back into her rental car and leave the area immediately. She told Isabelle that she would handle everything and make sure that Annika was safe. She told Isabelle never, ever to speak of the Lexus or who owned it. That part of the day had never happened. Isabelle texted back that she understood. She returned the registration to the glove compartment of the Lexus, got back into her car, and burned rubber to get to Sky Harbor Airport in Phoenix. Isabelle was gone.

🌲

There was one rug in the main room of Mona's cabin. This was the room where Mona painted. She pushed Annika's wheelchair from the porch into the cabin. "Don't ask any questions. You need to do exactly as I tell you to do. I will explain everything to you later. Just trust me for now." Mona pushed the wheelchair close to the rug and pulled the rug aside. There was a trap door in the floor. Mona opened the trap door and pulled Annika from the wheelchair. Their physical therapy sessions had strengthened Annika's upper body and core, as well as her legs. She was able to help Mona lower her into the small space hidden below the floor of the cabin. "Don't make any noise. Whatever happens, don't open the trap door until I come and open it for you. Whatever you hear, stay where you are and stay quiet." Mona closed the trap door and arranged the rug back over it.

Mona went quickly to her bedroom and returned to the main room with a heavy blue and white shawl and her handgun. She put the shawl around her head and shoulders and sat in Annika's wheelchair. Then she waited.

🌲

Igor had seen the older woman he didn't know push Annika's wheelchair into the cabin. He decided it was time to act. He quietly crept close to the cabin and took off his shoes. He tiptoed up the steps onto the porch, pulled his gun from his jacket pocket, and pushed open the door. He was going in with guns blazing. They would have no idea he was here, or any idea that anybody was here. He would kill the older woman and then he would start in on Annika. When he pushed open the door, he saw only Annika seated in the wheelchair.

"Where is she? Where is the old lady that takes care of you? Tell me right now or I will shoot you." Igor was on another rampage.

Mona shot the gun out of Igor's hand. The gun fell to the floor. Mona was a crackerjack markswoman. She also shot Igor in both wrists for good measure. He fell on the ground screaming. Mona threw off her shawl and stood over the mewling Igor. "I know who you are, and I have been waiting for you to show up on my doorstep. I am going to shoot you. My motivation is to rid the world of scumbags like you are. My other motivation is to kill a man who abuses women. You think you are a monster, but in fact you are nothing but a sniveling little worm. This is for Annika and for every other woman who wanted to kill her abuser but didn't have the chance. But this is mostly for me. Goodbye El Russo." Mona double tapped Igor in the forehead. It didn't matter where the wounds were. It only mattered that he was dead. Where Igor was going next was to a place where no one would ever find him in a million years.

Mona had counted on Igor being alone. If he'd brought Hector or someone else with him, they both would have come through the door of her cabin at the same time. Mona intended to kill whoever was with Igor immediately and then shoot Igor's gun out of his hand. She wanted the chance to let Igor know why he was going to be a dead man. Igor had come alone. She would have only one body to bury.

Mona went to her garage for a tarp and an old rope. She searched Igor's pockets for the keys to the Lexus. She stuck her gun, the one she had used to kill him, into Igor's coat pocket. She retrieved Igor's shoes from below the steps of the porch. She wrapped Igor and his shoes in the tarp and secured it all so he would not fall out. She wiped the blood off the floor. She filled a bucket with water and scrubbed the floor until it was clean. Mona carefully picked up the gun Igor Castillo had held in his hand when he'd entered the cabin. Igor had dropped it on the floor. Mona used a paper towel to put the gun in a Ziploc bag. She put the Ziploc in the bottom drawer of her chest of drawers.

Then she wound the rope around the body and the tarp

and pulled Igor towards the door of the cabin. In addition to the steps, there was a ramp from the porch to the ground. Mona had installed the ramp at her house so that Annika's wheelchair could easily make it onto her porch. Mona pulled Igor's body down the ramp and pulled it behind a bush. Her adrenalin was pumping, and she wanted to take advantage of that while it lasted. It would eventually give out, and she would not be able to move Igor's body after the adrenalin surge had passed. She had to get rid of him now.

Mona hurried on foot as fast as she could down the road to where Isabelle had told her the Lexus was parked. Fortunately, Isabelle had paid attention and followed directions. Neither she nor her rental car were anywhere to be seen. Mona had the keys. She got into the driver's seat of the Lexus and drove the car the rest of the way to her cabin. This was going to be the difficult part of the job. But she had been able to move a washing machine from a truck into her house. She had loaded furniture into places she'd never thought she would ever be able to move it. She had moved two refrigerators and at least one couch. She knew physics, and she knew how to use ramps and primitive pulleys and ropes to move and lift things. She had furniture dollies. She was strong.

She managed to get Igor, wrapped in the tarp and the rope, into the back seat of the Lexus. It was a sloppy job, but nobody except Mona would ever see any of this. After she had maneuvered Igor into the car, she drove the car until it was out of sight of the cabin. She did not want Cate to see what she had done. She did not want her to see the body or the car or anything about what Mona intended to do to dispose of Igor's corpse.

Mona went back to the house. Her adrenalin was fading

fast. She had to get Cate out of the hiding place under the trap door. She pulled the rug aside and raised the door. Cate was sitting there still as a stone and absolutely terrified. "I did exactly as you told me to do. I know what happened here. I know what you did. I don't know how you did it, but I know I am finally safe."

"I don't have time to talk to you now. I have things to do, but I promise I will tell you everything that's happened." Together they got Cate into the wheelchair. Mona got a bottle of water out of her refrigerator for each of them. Mona handed Cate a large chocolate bar from her cupboard and took one for herself. "I'll be back in about an hour. It will be dark soon, and I have some things to do before the sun goes down. Put a bottle of champagne in the refrigerator, thaw two of those Porterhouse steaks from the freezer. Take out whatever vegetables you want to eat and put two big baked potatoes in the oven at five o'clock. I will make a salad and take care of everything else when I get back."

It was chilly in the mountains in May, especially when the sun went down. Mona put on her parka and her work gloves. She grabbed a shovel from her garage and threw it into the back seat of the Lexus with Igor. She drove the car back towards the main road and turned onto a long-abandoned mining road that nobody knew anything about. The entrance to the mining road was so overgrown with vegetation, it was almost impossible to see. Mona knew exactly where she was going to put Igor. The hole was already there. In fact, the hole had been there for decades. Someone had begun to dig silver or some other valuable metal out of the mountains. It had not been a particularly productive project, and after a few years the surface mine had been abandoned. Just like the big dig in Bisbee, no one had bothered to fill in the hole. Mona had run across the abandoned surface mine during her walks in the area. Even though she was certain that no one would ever "just happen" on this place, she worried that the holes which had been left uncovered were a hazard. She had occasionally begun to fill them in. It was a tiresome, exhausting, and thankless task, and Mona didn't come this way very often.

Today she was grateful that all the holes had not yet been filled in. She was going to take care of one of them this evening. She parked the Lexus as close to the grave site as she could manage. She pulled Igor out of the back seat of the car. She unwrapped the rope she'd wound around him and the tarp. She pulled the tarp to the side and went through the pockets of the corpse. She decided there was nothing of value in his wallet other than a few hundred dollar bills. She removed his identification, which was actually in a false name. Mona put the fake identification and the money into her own pocket. She wrapped the rope around Igor and the tarp for the second time and pushed the trussed up turkey into the hole in the ground. It was a very deep hole. She shoveled dirt on top of the body. She pushed whatever she could find into the hole. She gathered pieces of wood, dead leaves, dried vegetation, and all kinds of debris and dumped it into the hole. She finished filling the hole with more dirt. She dug up a few bushes she found nearby and topped the grave with those. When she was convinced that no one would ever in a million years be able to find Igor's body, she turned her attention to the Lexus. She had to make that disappear, too.

There was a creek a few miles away from the cabin that might work for disposing of the Lexus. Mona knew the creek was unusually deep for a small body of water. If she could somehow manage to get the Lexus into the deepest part of the creek, no one would ever be able to get it out again. She would only be able to accomplish this part of the disappearing act after dark, and it would have to be done very late at night. There might already be campers in the area. It was May, and people began to come to the mountains in May. The Arizona desert could be very hot at lower altitudes in May. People were already on their way to escape up into the mountains to get away from the heat.

Mona was eager to give her report to Cate. Although Cate already knew what had happened, it was a life-changing report. "You never have to worry about Igor Castillo coming after you again. You are free of that burden and free of Igor forever. You had nothing to do with what happened to him. You did not see him here. He was never here at all as far as you are concerned. Don't worry about me. I'm old. The older I get, the less 'life in prison' sounds like a threat. I propose a toast to accomplishing impossible tasks, to realizing one's fondest hopes and dreams, and to freedom." Mona filled their glasses with the bubbly wine and clinked her champagne flute against Cate's. They were having a wonderful celebratory dinner. Mona had taken half a Reine de Saba flourless chocolate cake from her freezer for their dessert. She'd been saving it for something special. This night was special.

Mona was completely out of energy and was pushing hard to celebrate. She wanted Cate to remember the dinner and the champagne and the chocolate cake rather than remember being pushed into a tiny space underneath a trap door where she'd had to be absolutely silent for more than an hour. Mona wanted Cate to celebrate that she was now free of her abuser rather than think about the shots that had been fired and the words that had been spoken and everything else that had happened in order to accomplish an extraordinary feat.

Mona considered how much more to say to Cate. "I was always an introvert. Not everyone would have been able to live this life of a hermit as I have been able to do. I suspect that you are not as much of an introvert as I am. I wonder if in the long run, you will be able to tolerate this solitary existence."

Neither woman was accustomed to drinking champagne, and Mona used her last ounce of energy to push Annika back to her own cabin. Annika was now able to take a shower on her own and get herself ready for bed. It was a slow and difficult and even a painful process, but it was important that Annika learn to take care of her own needs in this way. She would sleep well that night.

Mona didn't try to finish cleaning up the kitchen. Steaks cooked on the grill outside and baked potatoes in the oven did not leave any pots and pans. Cake from the freezer, likewise, left relatively few dishes behind. She put the food away. What had not been cleared from the table could wait until morning. Mona needed to get some rest before she struck out again on her mission to get rid of the Lexus. Fortunately the car was black so it would be discreet and difficult to see as Mona drove it to its final resting place later that night.

Mona knew the campground and the area around the creek. She came to the park during the off season when no one else was willing to venture into the snowy, cold mountains. She knew where the deep places were located in the lakes and the creeks. She knew the ideal spot where she would try to force the Lexus to drive itself into the water.

She hoped there would not be any campers nearby to watch what she was going to do.

There was one campsite in use, but their fire had gone out. It seemed that the people who were camping there had called it quits for the night. Mona was taking a chance, getting rid of the car with people around, but she wanted to finish this before morning. She had already wiped the car down to get rid of any fingerprints, and she was wearing gloves. Mona drove the car over the rough ground and stopped it as close to the edge of the cliff as she could. She found a stone and wedged it into the space on top of and beside the gas pedal of the Lexus. Once she put the car into drive, she hoped the stone would keep the gas pedal down until the car had driven itself off the cliff and into the creek. She hoped the car would hit the sweet spot, the deep spot in the creek, and sink forever into the depths. If the Lexus didn't go down deep enough into the creek, a dry summer or a curious swimmer might sooner or later reveal its secrets. Mona couldn't let that happen.

Mona didn't think the sound of the car's engine or the huge splash that occurred when the Lexus hit the water had awakened the nearby campers. Her missions had been accomplished, and now all she had to do was find the strength to get herself back to her cabin. Home was six or seven miles away, and she only had her own legs and feet to take her there. Mona lay down on the ground to get some rest before she began the long walk home. She woke before dawn and pushed herself to get back to her home, unseen by anyone in a car or on foot. She'd never been as happy to see her little cabin in the woods as she was that morning.

It was a new day for Cate. Mona knew the young woman still had a long recovery ahead of her. Only Hector Gutierrez really knew about Annika's relationship with Igor Castillo. Would he come looking for Annika? Would he come looking for his Lexus? Would he come looking for his cousin, Igor? For the time being, the two women would have to continue to keep to themselves. Mona doubted that anyone knew Igor had driven Hector's car into the mountains. But there were surveillance cameras everywhere these days. Who knew what anyone knew? Sometimes it seemed to Mona that now everyone knew everything about everybody.

Thirty

Isabelle Ritter had driven hard and fast and made it to her flight out of Sky Harbor. She was lucky she'd not been stopped for speeding. She had still been shaking when she'd returned her rental car, and she hoped no one had noticed. She was still shaking when she got on the plane for Palm Springs. The flight would take just a little more than an hour. She would be home soon and safe in Palm Springs.

When she reached the Phoenix airport, she'd sent a text to Mona asking her if she and Annika were all right. Her text had been a cryptic one, in case things had gone badly and someone else had taken possession of Mona's phone. Isabelle hoped that neither Igor nor Hector would ever read her text. Allowing herself to imagine what might have happened after she had made her desperate escape from the White Mountains, she also hoped that law enforcement would not read her text. She had not yet heard anything back from Mona. She had to put her mobile phone on airplane mode when her flight took off for Palm Springs.

🌲

It was several days before Hector Gutierrez's body was found in his Tucson home. He was a single male who lived alone. His work habits were random. He was living in a house that was rented under a name that was not his own. One of his associates had repeatedly called and texted Hector. Hector had missed meetings and hadn't let anybody know he wasn't coming. This behavior was uncharacteristic for Hector, and eventually one of his colleagues went to his rental house. The colleague found Hector dead in the bed in the guest room.

Hector's associate hurried to check the house for drugs and for incriminating paperwork. He gathered a few papers that he thought might name names or reveal other details of their illegal activities. He was relieved that Hector had not kept too much evidence in his home about what they had been doing. One reason Hector lived in the rental house was to receive packages sent from abroad. These packages contained essential supplies and ingredients for the fentanyl Hector was hoping to make. Fortunately Hector didn't keep these packages at the house but immediately transferred them to the warehouse where the drug was being made.

Because of the nature of the businesses that Hector was involved in, his work colleague did not want to call the police from his personal cell phone. It was almost impossible to find a pay phone anywhere. The unfortunate colleague who had discovered the body thought seriously about not calling the authorities at all. He thought about leaving the body where it was and letting somebody else find it. In the end, he purchased a cheap prepaid phone to report the murder. He told the Tucson sheriff's office where a body could be found. He threw the phone down a storm drain after he had reported the murder.

Hector had been in charge, the director of the ambitious project to try to manufacture fentanyl in the U.S. When Hector was murdered, the project came to a halt. This was good news, in a way, for law enforcement. Hector would not be making his fentanyl in Tucson. But somebody else would be starting up their own project, probably sooner rather than later, and they would be making the drug inside the United States. The new entrepreneur would find a way to import the ingredients, either from China or from India. They would rent a space and make the powder and the pills. They would no longer have to worry about smuggling the drugs across the border. Because the fentanyl business was so lucrative, many other drug dealers would get into the business. If one network got busted, another one quickly came together to take its place. It was a constant fight for law enforcement to keep up with the new drug lords and their new ways of making a fortune.

Hector Gutierrez's murder was investigated by the local police in Tucson and by the FBI. Detective Cecilia Mendoza from Phoenix homicide was called in as a consultant. She had been instrumental in bringing Hector's cousin, Igor Castillo, to justice, albeit in absentia, and getting a conviction against him in a U.S. court. Basic CSI work showed that Igor Castillo's fingerprints and DNA were all over Hector's house. El Russo had definitely been there, and it looked as if he had killed his cousin. There was no gun found at the scene. Hector's black Lexus was missing. Detective Mendoza and everyone else assumed that Igor had shot Hector and stolen his car. A BOLO went out for the Lexus, but not a single sighting of the car was ever made. Likewise, no sighting of Igor Castillo was ever made after he had murdered his cousin.

Those who were familiar with Igor Castillo and his cousin Hector were surprised that Igor had killed his cousin. Igor had finally gone over the edge. Law enforcement assumed that Igor had taken the Lexus and driven it back to Mexico. Because it was assumed that Igor had probably gone back south of the border, they searched for the Lexus on traffic cameras that showed the roads south of Tucson. They found nothing. A couple of traffic cameras showed what might have been the black Lexus driving on the complicated highways that twisted and turned around the Phoenix metropolitan area. But so many people in Phoenix owned a black Lexus, who could tell one from the other? Those sightings were dismissed as unrelated to Igor Castillo because they put the Lexus north of Tucson. Because everyone was certain that Igor would have been heading south to Guadalajara, no one followed up on the sightings of the black Lexus in the Phoenix area. Nothing having to do with Igor Castillo or with the black Lexus, was ever found. Cecilia Mendoza believed the Lexus had been cut up and sold for parts in Mexico. Wherever it was, it was long gone. And wherever he was, Igor Castillo was also long gone.

News about Hector Gutierrez's murder eventually made it onto the news. People had heard of Igor Castillo, but Hector had made an effort to stay out of the public eye. It was not a long-running news story...just another drug dealer killed by another drug dealer.

But Mona and Annika, now Cate, noticed the story and were stunned. Cate had not expected that Igor would murder his cousin. Isabelle was also shocked when she learned of Hector's death. Mona had let Isabelle know in a very circumscribed way that Igor Castillo was no longer a threat to Annika Karlsson. No details had been shared, and that was fine with Isabelle.

Isabelle received a phone call from Sidney Richardson who was looking for someone to help out with reservations, emails, and phone calls at the resort that she and Cameron were developing in Arkansas. Sidney wanted to hire somebody smart and somebody she could trust. Isabelle had not had anybody to suggest to Sidney at the time. Now Isabelle wondered if and when Cate Murray recovered sufficiently from her injuries, would she be able to help out at the resort? Would Cate have any interest in such a position? Would she be afraid to leave the security of her mountain hideaway? Did she feel safe enough yet? Was she ready to reenter the world and have a job interacting with other people?

Epilogue

Genetic genealogy has revealed to us the truth of who we are and what we have been doing.

If someone was able to get hold of Mona Damours' DNA, they might have learned that her grandfather was murdered in the Katyn Forest of the USSR in the spring of 1940 at the beginning of World War II. Mona's grandfather was a physician and a member of the Polish military reserves who were called up to defend their country in 1939. He was arrested for political reasons and sent to a prison camp in the Soviet Union. In April of 1940, Mona's grandfather and most of his fellow POWs from Soviet Camp Kozelsk were taken to the Katyn Forest and murdered by the Soviet Union's NKVD. The atrocity was erroneously blamed on the Nazis for fifty years.

If someone had taken one of the DNA samples that Igor Castillo left behind at his cousin's rental house in Tucson, Arizona, they might have found that Igor, on his mother's side, was related to Stalin's henchman, Lavrentiy Beria. Beria, one of the most violent and deadly killers of the Communist era under Stalin, was Igor Castillo's maternal grandfather.

An even more historic example of revenge could be recounted. One might even call it justice. A murder that took place half a world away in a forest in the Soviet Union in 1940 might be said to have finally been avenged, admittedly in a very small and very personal way, more than eighty years after the fact, in another forest, in the White Mountains of Arizona. Enough said. Or maybe not.

WHEN DID I GROW OLD?

When did I grow old?
    It is now so still around me.
    When did all the noise turn to quiet?
    The cacophony of busyness that engulfed me
        for so many years, has subsided.

When did I grow old?
    Did it happen slowly as the years passed by?
    Did it happen as I filled my time with immediacy…
        moving from one crisis to the next?
    Did it happen all of a sudden when I found I had to use
        a cane to get up and down the steps?

When did I grow old?
    Did I fill those years that passed with goodness and giving
        and love?
    Did I spend too many days in anger and hoping for retaliation
        for things in life that didn't go my way?
    Did I spend too many hours organizing and cleaning and
        worrying about my material possessions?
    How much time did I spend shopping? Sorting out
        my closet?

When did I grow old?
    Was it when I learned that I was deaf in one ear
        and there was no help for that?
    Was it when I realized there were so few days ahead
        and so many already gone?
    Was it when I accepted that I would die?

When did I grow old?
    Was it a gradual process as the hairs on my head
        one by one turned white?
    Or did it happen overnight? And what night was that?
    Was it when I became a grandmother?

When did I grow old?
    Did I spend this precious time I have been given
    To make a difference?
    To make the world a better place?

When did I grow old?
    Is it today when I know that however this life was spent,
        it cannot be respent?
    It was what it was...
    Full of imperfections and mistakes and trying hard
        and often struggling and falling short
    And full of joy and good luck.

When did I grow old?
I just don't know.
Or, maybe I'm not old yet.

MTT 5–7–2014

Author's Note

The Katyn Forest Massacre is a true event. It happened in the USSR in the early spring of 1940. My first real introduction to this atrocity came when I watched a movie on my Kindle a couple of years ago. **The Last Witness**, directed by Piotr Szkopiak, was released in 2018. I was stunned, and I was intellectually and emotionally shocked when I understood the story this movie had to tell. I recommend the movie to anyone who has any Polish heritage as well as anyone who has an interest in learning more about this genocide committed by the Soviet Union during World War II.

After watching the movie three times, I read two books that gave more factual details about this event that happened so very long ago. The truth was covered up for decades. These books are:

Death in the Forest: The Story of the Katyn Forest Massacre
The author is J.K. Zawodney
The Kindle edition was published by Pickle
Partners Publishing.
The original manuscript was published in 1962.

and

A Death in the Forest: The U.S. Congress Investigated the Murder of 22,000 Polish Prisoners of War in the Katyn Forest Massacres of 1940.
The author is Daniel Ford.
Published by Warbird Books, 2014.

Both of these books are compelling non-fiction accounts and tell the detailed true story of the Katyn Forest Massacre. I urge anyone who finds this story as riveting and powerful as I found it, to read both of these books which can be found through Amazon.

My account of the event is a summary gathered from a number of sources, including the movie and the two books listed above. ***The Wells of Silence*** is a book of fiction, and chapters 16, 17, and 18 are included in the book to provide background only. The characters in chapters 19 and 20 are fictional.

The accounts of this event touched me deeply. The atrocity itself is incredibly disturbing. Just as disturbing is the way this atrocity was lied about, ignored, and covered up. At first I was angry that the truth had not been allowed to come out during the war. Then I tried to put myself into the shoes of those who were making decisions about the conduct of the war. I tried to understand the necessity and the logic behind the lies and the attempts to bury the story of Katyn.

I was born in 1944 and am a proud war baby. My father served in the South Pacific during World War II, and all of my male uncles, who were of appropriate age at the time, served in either the U.S. Army or the U.S. Navy. We are a very patriotic family. Discussions around the dinner table as I was growing up were often about the war and the fallout from decisions made by those who had led our country during the war. My family spoke often with disgust about the betrayal of the Yalta Conference and Franklin Roosevelt's "giving away the store" to Joseph Stalin.

After many months of trying to sort this out in my own mind, I am less angry about why Allied leaders knew the truth and pretended otherwise. The only thing that mattered in 1943, 1944, and 1945 was to defeat the Adolf Hitler Devil. Roosevelt and Churchill determined that we needed the Joseph Stalin Devil on our side in order to do that. And maybe we did. If accepting the lies about the Katyn Forest was the price we had to pay to defeat the Nazis, I suppose it was worth it.

What is not as easy to understand or to forgive is the lying and the cover-ups that occurred after the war was over. Even when the Communist Soviet Union became our avowed and mortal enemy in 1948 with the beginning of the Cold War, the lies and the denials about Katyn persisted. NATO was formed in April of 1949. The countries of NATO continued to ignore what had happened in 1940 in the Katyn Forest. It was not until 1990, when Mikhail Gorbachev admitted Soviet culpability for the killings that the truth finally came out. The Berlin Wall came down in 1989. The Soviet Union fell in December of 1991. The last Soviet troops left Poland in 1993. The movie *The Last Witness* was not produced until 2018.

Henrietta Alten West

COMPLETE BIOGRAPHIES
of the
REUNION CHRONICLES
MYSTERIES CHARACTERS

MAIN CHARACTERS

The following extensive biographies are those of the characters who appear in all of the Reunion Chronicles Mysteries. These include Richard and Elizabeth Carpenter, Gretchen and Bailey MacDermott, Tyler Merriman, Cameron and Sidney Richardson, Matthew and Isabelle Ritter, and J.D. and Olivia Steele. ***The Wells of Silence*** is the fifth book in this series.

In the previous four books, I included these extensive biographies in the text of the manuscript. For readers who had read all the books in the series, rereading these lengthy descriptions of the characters became tedious and annoying. I have received many suggestions about to how to give readers background on the characters but not put these biographies in the story itself. I decided to include the complete biographies at the end of the book, but not to include them within the pages of the manuscript. Hopefully, the action will flow better without these interruptions. But following is everything new readers need to know about the main characters in the series.

H.A.W.

RICHARD AND ELIZABETH CARPENTER

When Elizabeth Emerson was a senior at Smith College in Northampton, Massachusetts, the CIA was actively recruiting from the Ivy League men's schools and from the Seven Sisters women's colleges. The spy agency had decided women had good brains after all and made good analysts. The CIA was especially interested in hiring economics majors because they'd found that people who understood economics had analytical minds, were able to process information in a systematic way, and could reach conclusions and solve problems. The CIA was not looking for covert operatives when they interviewed the college seniors. They were not hiring women to wear the classic fedora and trench coat spy outfit, lean against a lamppost in rainy, post-war Vienna, and wait for a rendezvous with a Russian double agent. The CIA wanted desk jockeys.

Elizabeth, an economics major, was of the duck-and-cover generation and had lived in the shadow of the Cold War all her life. She was intrigued by the pitch from the CIA and decided to look into what would be required for her to pursue a career with The Agency. She went to the initial meeting on the Smith campus and then made the trip to Boston with three other women from her college class. In Boston, the four were given a battery of tests, designed to evaluate their abilities to do the work the CIA would require of them. This was the first step in the application process. Those who passed the initial tests would be given more tests, some interviews, and then perhaps the offer of a job in Washington, D.C.

Elizabeth scored "off the charts" in the inductive reasoning part of the testing. Only one other person in CIA recruitment history had ever scored higher than she did in this one very important area, critical to the kind of work the CIA needed doing. Although she had never realized it before, Elizabeth was told she could read and evaluate vast amounts of material in an incredibly short period of time and come up with an accurate analysis and conclusion. The testing people made a big deal over her, and this embarrassed the somewhat introverted Elizabeth. They singled her out, and she didn't like it. Since she'd never known she had this special skill, she wasn't that impressed with herself. She wondered what all the fuss was about.

Elizabeth had been seriously dating a graduate of Princeton who was now a first-year medical student at Tulane. Elizabeth was in love, and she thought Richard Carpenter was, too. It was 1966, and women married young. It was early in the women's liberation movement. Not all women, even very well-educated ones, had careers. Many became housewives and mothers. Elizabeth had always been very independent, but she couldn't imagine her life without Richard. Richard was not enthusiastic about her pursuing a career with the CIA. He didn't really understand that she wouldn't be in any danger, sitting in an office in Langley, Virginia, reading newspapers and looking at data sets. He wanted her with him in New Orleans, although he'd not yet asked her to marry him.

When he did pop the question, Elizabeth said yes. They would be married that summer. The CIA was disappointed when Elizabeth turned down their offer of a position as an analyst. They pulled out all the stops and harassed her mercilessly for the remainder of her senior year. They played the "serving your country" card and everything else they could think of. Elizabeth did not waiver, and she and Richard were married in August. She got a job teaching in the New Orleans public schools, and the CIA became a distant memory. But the CIA kept its eyes on her, and years later when she decided to change careers, they welcomed her with open arms.

After she left New Orleans, Elizabeth went to graduate school. After spending two years on the faculty at the University of Texas at El Paso, she took a position teaching economics and economic history at a small college in Maryland. She was pressured to change a grade so that a failing student could become a "C" student. The student, who had not put forth any effort whatsoever in her class, had to have a "C" in order to maintain his eligibility to play basketball for the college team. The academic dean leaned on and threatened Elizabeth. Because she was only a part-time professor, the dean told her she could easily be fired from her position, if she didn't do as she was told and change the grade.

Elizabeth refused to knuckle under to the threats and gave the student a "D." He had barely made the "D" and had just escaped failing her class by the skin of his teeth. After she'd turned in her grades, someone went to the registrar's office and changed the student's grade from a "D" to a "C." The young man never missed a step or a dribble on the basketball court because of his failing academic work. Learning and getting an education had proven to be an afterthought, or given no thought at all, when it came to qualifying for a sports team.

Elizabeth thought she could hang on to her job, but she decided she did not want to be a part of the rotten system any more. She'd always known academia was fraught with politics, corrupted by competition to get ahead of one's colleagues, and filled with bloated and narcissistic egos.

She decided life was short, and she didn't have to play the stupid games required to succeed in the university arena. She didn't want to be around the grasping and ambitious meanies any more.

She decided to take a job that she'd been offered years earlier. She made some phone calls and began the difficult task of hiring babysitters, drivers, and a housekeeper. She made complicated arrangements for her duties at home to be taken care of when she was gone. She began to build her cover story, that she was taking a research position at the Wharton School in Philadelphia. It was a three-hour commute one-way to her new job, and she would be away from home a couple of nights a week, sometimes more. It was a big commitment, but her new boss was willing to work with her to maintain the illusion of the imaginary job she supposedly had at the University of Pennsylvania. She was a valuable commodity, and the CIA helped her manage her home duties and her non-existent position in Philadelphia, as she committed to the more dangerous job she'd really been hired to do.

Most of her work was in Virginia, using the skills she'd demonstrated when the CIA had wanted to hire her as an analyst years earlier. Occasionally she had to make trips overseas. None of her family or friends ever doubted for a minute that she was working at the Wharton School. They thought it was odd that she was gone from home so much, but by now, two of her children were away at boarding school in New England. Only one daughter was still at home. No one, not even Richard Carpenter, was allowed to know what Elizabeth did when she was out of town.

It was a rocky period in the Carpenters' marriage. Richard was consumed with his work as head of the surgical pathology department and clinical laboratory at the local hospital. He participated in the children's activities whenever he could, but he was pretty much oblivious to Elizabeth's needs at this time in their lives. He was angry that she wasn't around all the time, as she had always been before, but he was so preoccupied with his own career, he only noticed she wasn't there when something went wrong.

Richard Carpenter had risen to the top of his career and was the main partner in his pathology group, Richard Carpenter, M.D., P.A. He had done his internship and residency at the University of Pennsylvania, and during those years he'd had the opportunity to work with Philadelphia's medical examiner. In addition to spending his days accompanying the Chief Medical Examiner on his rounds, Richard had done moonlighting for the medical examiner's office to earn extra money. The young doctor became a skilled and convincing expert witness. He was a favorite with prosecutors because juries loved his boyish looks and earnest, honest voice. When he was on the witness stand, members of the jury believed everything Richard Carpenter, M.D. had to say. If he gave evidence against someone in a murder trial, that person was always convicted. Vance Stillinger, M.D. was the Philadelphia Medical Examiner, and Richard Carpenter M.D. became his golden boy.

Carpenter's testimony had sent a number of very bad guys to prison. The child molesters, murderers, drug dealers, and drivers who had committed serial DUIs all should have known it was their own behavior that had caused them to be convicted. But bad boys and girls always want to find someone other than themselves to blame. Carpenter became a lightning rod for their anger, and some wanted to blame the blonde, cherub-faced scientist who had so convincingly swayed the juries that had convicted them. Occasionally, a defendant would shake his fist at Carpenter when he was on the witness stand.

Once a man stood up and shouted threats at Carpenter after he'd given his expert witness testimony. The defendant, who had been resoundingly drunk when he'd crossed the highway's median strip and run headlong into a van full of children, said Carpenter had misrepresented his blood alcohol level. The driver of the van and four of the children had died, and the defendant was sent to prison for many years. The drunk vowed that when he got out of jail, he would hunt down Carpenter and kill him and his family.

Elizabeth Carpenter had just come home from the hospital after giving birth to the Carpenters' second child. Law enforcement took the threats against Carpenter and his family seriously, and until the convicted criminal was sentenced and safely locked away, the police kept a guard on Carpenter's rented house in the Philadelphia suburbs. Elizabeth wondered who would be there in a few years to watch out for her family when the man was released from prison.

Stillinger tried to convince his protégé to stay in Philadelphia and become a forensic pathologist, but Carpenter owed Uncle Sam two years of his life, serving in the U.S. Army. Furthermore, Carpenter had educational debts and needed and wanted to earn some money. He wanted more income than the salary of an urban medical examiner would pay him, and he didn't want to live in a city. The Army sent Carpenter to William Beaumont Army Medical Center in Texas for two years, and from there, Carpenter took a position at a hospital in a small town in Maryland where he built a successful pathology practice. He still testified as an expert witness, but the threats that had come his way when he was at the Philadelphia Medical Examiner's Office were long-forgotten. The question was, had the men he'd helped send to prison forgotten him?

BAILEY AND GRETCHEN MACDERMOTT

Bailey MacDermott graduated with an engineering degree from the University of Arkansas. He was hired by IBM directly out of college, and because of his outgoing personality and gift for gab, he quickly became one of Big Blue's best salesmen in his region. But Bailey was an independent guy, and he felt as if he was being smothered in the corporate world. He'd been selling computer systems to the oil industry, to help them with payroll and inventory and to keep track of where their oil was coming from and where it was going. Bailey let a couple of his clients know he was interested in making a change, and within a few weeks he had a job offer from a major oil company. He submitted his resignation to IBM and left his job in Chicago. Houston was calling, and Bailey was ready to conquer the oil business and earn some big money. Soon he was flying back and forth from Houston to the oil-rich kingdoms in the Middle East. Before long, he knew the countries and who the movers and shakers were in the world's wealthiest oil-producing nations.

When the Shah of Iran fell, the world, and especially the Middle East, was turned upside down. Previously ignored actors on the world's political and economic stage were on the march, and a few days after the hostages in Iran were taken, the U.S. Department of Defense was knocking on Bailey's door. He was a patriot and agreed to work with the DIA, one of the pentagon's spy agencies.

At first, he just met with other Americans in Riyadh and other Arab capitals. He carried the packages and papers these agents asked him to take back with him when he flew home to the U.S. Then he was asked to meet with foreign nationals and accompany them to safe houses. Once, in Lebanon, he had to rescue an American who was in desperate shape, running from Hezbollah, and suffering from serious gunshot wounds in his leg and thigh. Bailey drove the man to the airport in his rental car and slipped him aboard the oil company's plane. Bailey's assignments became more and more complex and more and more dangerous. He told himself he was doing all of this because he was helping to fight terrorism, but he also loved the rush he got from taking risks.

After a particularly harrowing mission, Bailey had to take some time off from his regular job with the oil company and from his special work for the DIA. He spent a month recuperating in Paris. He slept late and ate well. He also met and fell in love with an American woman he met at the Rodin Museum. Bailey had gone there to learn more about the sculpture. Marianna Archer was at the museum posing for magazine photographs. She was a gorgeous redhead who earned her living as a highly-paid model wearing the latest in trendy clothing. She was doing a photoshoot for an American fashion magazine and was dressed in very tight stretch stirrup pants, enormous earrings, and a sexy faux suede off-the-shoulder top. Bailey stumbled into the room where Marianna had her arms draped around *The Thinker*. That day Bailey completely missed seeing Rodin's most famous work of art, but he couldn't take his eyes off Marianna as she pranced and posed around the naked man made out of bronze.

It was the 1980s and Bailey MacDermott decided he had been a bachelor long enough. Marianna was a lonely ex-pat living in France, and she quickly succumbed to Bailey's warm and friendly personality. They spent a lot of time at her apartment getting acquainted, and before Bailey's month of vacation was over, the two were married. It was probably a mistake for them to marry, even under the best of circumstances. The complexity of their work lives and the travel both of their jobs required meant they spent a lot of time apart. Their time together was frenetic, and they never had a chance to really get to know each other.

What Bailey didn't know about Marianna was that she was manic-depressive, a mental illness that has since been renamed "bipolar 1 disorder." If she stayed on her meds, Marianna was mostly fine and a lot of fun. When she went off her meds, all bets were off. When they returned to the U.S., she realized she was pregnant. Bailey and Marianna's son was born in Houston, and Bailey was beside himself with joy. Marianna, on the other hand, fell into a serious postpartum depression. She reached the point where she didn't want to get out of bed at all.

Bailey and Marianna eventually divorced. She ceded custody of their son to Bailey, but Bailey was juggling too many things. He told the Department of Defense he wasn't able to work for them anymore, and he quit his job working for the oil company because he didn't want to travel all the time. He began dealing in oil futures and was incredibly successful. He made a lot of money, but at this time, the best part of his life was that once he settled down in Dallas, he was able to make a home for himself and his son.

Before he met Gretchen, rumors flew that he had married again twice...in haste and then quickly divorced...twice! He didn't like to talk about what had happened in his love life during this period, and no one wanted to ask. It was clearly a painful subject for Bailey.

Gretchen Johanssen technically worked in human resources, but she was one of those people who was so competent that, wherever she worked, she eventually took over running much more than the HR department. She was petite and fit, and her good looks and style attracted attention. Once you got to know Gretchen and once you had worked with her for a while, because of her extraordinary competence, you forgot how small she was. Her abilities and her organizational skills belied her size, and she took on a significant presence in any room where she worked or spoke.

Gretchen had married twice and had two wonderful sons. She adopted and raised a foster daughter. Her daughter was still in graduate school, but after her second divorce and after her sons were launched, one into the military and the other to college, Gretchen decided to take a job with an international financial group. She had always wanted to travel and was excited to be sent to run the HR department at her company's office in Zurich.

As always happened when Gretchen arrived on the scene, her ability to get things accomplished was immediately recognized, and she took on more and more responsibilities, above and beyond her HR duties. She always attracted attention at a board meetings. When she made an outstanding presentation to a group of international businessmen, the head of one of Switzerland's wealthiest and most secretive banks noticed her. He wanted to date her, and he wanted to hire her to work for him. He offered her a salary three times what she was earning in her current job. She agreed to take the lucrative position as his special advisor, but she never mixed business and romance.

The Swiss banker was smart enough to agree to her terms, and Gretchen spent several years making top-level decisions in the arcane world of Swiss banking and international finance. She became fluent in German. She met arms dealers, heads of state, assassins, movie stars, Russians and Saudis, and people she was sure were mafia figures or drug dealers or both. She helped her employers invest their clients' riches. She knew the identities of many who had secret money and needed to conceal it.

When one of her ex-husbands was murdered, Gretchen returned to the United States. Her son who was a Navy Seal, was involved in an almost-fatal car accident, and Gretchen wanted to spend time with him, helping him heal and boosting his spirits as he recovered. She was an accomplished corporate executive, but she was first and foremost a mother. It was while her son was recovering the use of his legs at a rehabilitation center in Texas that Gretchen met Bailey.

Bailey volunteered at the VA hospital where Gretchen's son was going for physical therapy. Bailey still made deals of all kinds. He had branched out from oil futures into commercial real estate, and it seemed that whatever he touched turned to gold. Volunteering to work with military personnel who were trying to get back on their feet was Bailey's way of giving back. He loved his work, but he loved working with the disabled vets even more. He spent time with Gretchen's son almost daily, and it was the young Navy Seal who introduced Bailey MacDermott to his mother.

Bailey and Gretchen had both been burned in the marriage department. Neither one was looking for a spouse. Each of them was happy living alone, but as they spent more and more time in each other's company, they realized that they they loved each other and wanted to spend the rest of their lives together.

Gretchen took a job with a company in Dallas, and in no time, she had, as she always did, made herself indispensable to her new company. She was the kind of employee who quickly became critical to any organization. When she mentioned the possibility of retirement, she was offered a large bonus to stay on for two more years. At the end of those two years, when the subject of retirement came up again, she was offered an even larger bonus, if she would just stay on a little longer. She might never retire because she was making too much money just by mentioning the word "retirement."

Bailey had moved into doing deals in international real estate, and this new clientele sometimes presented challenges. There were language barriers, although most people involved in the upper echelons of the business world spoke English. There were cultural differences, especially when it came to determining what was legal and ethical and what was not. Most of his clients were legitimate buyers who actually wanted to own a warehouse in Hong Kong or Mexico or an apartment building in Singapore. But a few clients who contacted Bailey were interested in buying real estate for the purposes of laundering money.

The schemes the money launderers devised were complicated and slick. Bailey found himself involved in a couple of these transactions before he caught on to what was happening. When he realized what these fake buyers were up to, he had to say no. He refused to participate in any money laundering intrigue. More than once, a disappointed money launderer had threatened Bailey's life. Bailey loved the rush and the risk of doing high-flying business transactions, but he definitely did not enjoy having a loaded gun pressed against his head. When one of these crooks tracked him to his home and threatened him, Bailey and Gretchen had to move to a different house. Bailey learned to be more discreet, but it was impossible for him to give up the thrill of making a deal. Now he was always wary when he took on a new client. Even as he entered his eighties, he was a vital and busy wheeler-dealer in the financial world.

TYLER MERRIMAN

Tyler Merriman was a high school football star. The Air Force Academy recruited Tyler to play football, and he played for one year before he was sidelined by a shoulder injury. Tyler stayed on and graduated. He subsequently earned an MBA from Stanford. He became a pilot for the United States Air Force and spent ten years flying military missions for the USA. He never talked about the years he'd spent in the USAF, but his closest friends speculated that he was flying the Lockheed SR-71, "the Blackbird" spy plane that supposedly had the capability to see the numbers and letters on the license plate of a car parked in Red Square. When anyone came right out and asked him if he'd flown the Blackbird, Tyler would hum a few bars of the Beatles' song of the same name and smile his enigmatic smile. If he had flown the Blackbird, he would have been able to see everything and everybody from way up there. But he would never tell.

Tyler had married, briefly, when he was in the military, but his wife was young and somewhat spoiled. She resented the time Tyler spent away from home, and they divorced when they'd been married for less than two years. Tyler moved to Northern California after he left the Air Force. He built a commercial real estate empire and became a wealthy man.

Tyler dated well-known and glamorous women — movie actresses, anchorwomen who appeared on national television, and female politicos. He was very good looking and a much sought-after bachelor, but he successfully avoided the altar for decades after his first marriage ended.

Tyler Merriman had been smart and lucky in his business dealings, and he was a consummate athlete. He bought a condominium in Telluride, Colorado so he could ski for several months in the winter. Because he was such a skilled and outstanding performer on the slopes, it wasn't long before he was hired as a ski instructor. His time was his own, and he arranged his schedule so he could spend most of the winter in Telluride. He found he loved teaching others to ski. Tyler had his own plane and flew around the country to check on his commercial real estate empire. He hiked and biked and ran, and he even sometimes played squash, when he couldn't be outdoors. Tyler was a very active guy. He decided he wanted to be closer to his condominium in Telluride and eventually relocated from California to Colorado.

Tyler had been attending the reunions for years and looked forward to seeing his old friends and their wives and girlfriends. He'd never brought a date or a partner to one of the events until he'd met Lilleth Dubois when he was in his early seventies. They'd had a long-term relationship, and Lilleth had attended several of the Camp Shoemaker reunions. Tyler wasn't sharing the details of their break-up, and no one was asking any questions. But Lilleth and Tyler were no longer a couple, and Lilleth would not be attending any more reunions. Tyler was still athletic and energetic. He was still a force on the ski slopes and in other demanding athletic arenas. Who knew what the future might hold in terms of romance for Tyler Merriman?

CAMERON AND SIDNEY RICHARDSON

Cameron Richardson had always loved to build things. From the time he was a child, he'd been taking things apart and putting them back together again. He loved to tinker. He loved to invent. He liked to change something, even just a little bit, to make it work better. That was the way his mind worked. There were stories of the rockets he and a friend had constructed and tried to launch; they were just in junior high school at the time. There were stories of gunpowder explosions in the woods and the resulting craters in the ground. Of course he would study science when he entered the small, exclusive southern college. He transferred to a university with an engineering program for his last two years, and upon graduation, he was immediately recruited by IBM.

Mastering the technology of computers opened up a whole new world to Cameron, and it wasn't long before he was out on his own, inventing and tinkering and making things better. He built an innovative and tremendously successful computer empire. Then he built a second revolutionary electronics enterprise. The man lived to challenge the status quo, and his head was always in the future.

Cameron's businesses dealt with enormous amounts of data, and thanks to computers, this data could be accessed relatively easily. It made him millions. It was inevitable that the U.S. federal government would, from time to time, come asking for help with something. Cameron was a straight shooter, a good guy. He was an entrepreneur of the first order, but he was also honest through and through his character and soul. He would not knowingly do something that was illegal or wrong. Sometimes he helped out the feds, and sometimes he didn't. He knew how to say no, even to

Uncle Sam. When he said yes, it was never for his own gain but because he felt a patriotic duty to lend his expertise. He helped crack the cell phones that led to the arrests of terrorists. He helped out whenever he felt it was the right thing to do. He didn't want his part in any of these operations to become public, but there were some people who knew he had been instrumental in tracking down and gathering evidence on the bad guys. The question was, did any of the bad guys know that Cameron Richardson had helped to finger them and put them away?

There was no question about it. Cameron had information on everybody and everything. He didn't use it for nefarious purposes, but he did have it. Anybody who knew what his companies were all about knew he had the goods, and the bads. Anyone who has achieved the level of success that Cameron had, and anyone who has made the hard decisions about everything, including personnel, has acquired some enemies along the way. Because Cameron was a fair and benevolent boss, he'd made fewer enemies than most, but he had appropriately fired the dead wood that unfortunately but inevitably turned up, from time to time, among his employees. He'd made some people angry. He was cavalier about his own security, but his second wife Sidney worried about him.

Cameron had married for the first time when he was just out of college, and he'd married a woman several years older than himself. His friends had been puzzled about the union that, to those on the outside, seemed unusual. Were these two well-matched? Did they have anything at all in common? The guys loved their buddy and accepted his marital decision. Sometimes, love is strange. The marriage produced two children but eventually came to an end. The failure of the marriage wasn't anybody's fault.

After being a bachelor for a few years, Cameron met the love of his life. He had made his fortune and his reputation, and he finally had the time and energy to invest in a relationship. Sidney Putnam insisted on it. She let Cameron know that, to make their marriage work, he needed to listen to what was important to her and spend time with her. He was wildly in love with Sidney, but she refused to marry him until he learned that she would be an equal partner in their marriage. She was not a back seat kind of woman.

Sidney's first marriage had also ended in divorce. She had one son, to whom she was devoted, and she'd been able to remain friends with her first husband, her son's father. Most people can't achieve this almost impossible feat, but Sidney had people skills that most people don't. Sidney had been the runner-up in her state's beauty pageant for the Miss America contest. She'd always had the looks, but more importantly, she had the smarts—of all kinds.

Sidney's most outstanding way of being smart was her gift for reading people. Her uncanny ability to know when someone was lying was an asset when she worked as a consultant for the Texas Department of Criminal Justice. She was the prosecutor's secret weapon. She consulted on jury selections and sat in on law enforcement interviews with suspects and witnesses. She was never wrong in her assessments. She didn't necessarily tell the authorities what they wanted to hear. She told the truth. And sometimes, nobody wanted to hear the truth. Sidney demanded that her assistance in criminal cases remain confidential, but she was almost too good to be true. Eventually, what she could do leaked out beyond the walls of the justice department, and she knew being exposed could put her in danger.

Her ability to vet people was invaluable to Sidney when she started her own business. As a single parent, she needed to support herself and her son. With her business, You Are Home, she identified a need that existed and built a business that responded to that need. Her first clients were corporations that frequently moved their employees from place to place. Corporations arranged to move their employee's household goods and paid for the packing and moving and unpacking. The gap in these employee benefits came when the wife, and it usually was the wife back in the day, had to put it all away and set up the new household. The husband, and it usually was the husband back in the day, was off doing his corporate thing, and the wife was at home with the kids, trying to find a place to put their stuff in the new kitchen and the unfamiliar closets.

Sidney's company was hired to come in and put their household goods away where they belonged. Her well-trained employees would organize the kitchen, at the housewife's direction, but with suggestions from the experts about the best kitchen logistics to make it fully functional. They put shelf paper in the drawers and on the shelves. They put away everybody's clothes—organizing, folding, and hanging everything in the most efficient and easy-to-access way. You Are Home would arrange for a room to be painted and would bring in other professionals to position furniture to its best advantage and hang art work. Sidney was good at this, and she taught her carefully-selected employees to be good at it, too. She charged high prices for her services, but there was a huge demand for what she was selling. Her company grew rapidly. She was a very successful entrepreneur in her own right when she literally ran into Cameron Richardson in a restaurant.

It was an expensive steak house in Fort Worth, and Sidney was there having lunch and closing a deal with a corporate client. It was summer, and she was dressed in a stunning white designer linen dress. She had a white cashmere cardigan sweater over her shoulders because the air conditioning was turned up so high in the steak house, to counter the July Texas heat.

She got up to go to the ladies' room, and a tall, good-looking man didn't see her making her way through the tables in the dark, wood-paneled restaurant. The man pushed back his chair and stood up from his table with a large glass of iced tea in his hand. He ran straight into Sidney and spilled the entire glass of tea all over her dress, cashmere sweater, and expensive white high-heeled shoes. They were both stunned. He looked into the bright and beautiful eyes of the woman whose clothes he'd just ruined and couldn't turn away. To say it was love at first sight on his part would probably be the truth. She was angry that her outfit had been spoiled, but Cameron Richardson was so gracious about sending a car to drive her home to change her clothes. He insisted on paying for dry cleaning and replaced the clothes that could not be saved. Sidney had to soften her annoyance.

She had no idea who Cameron Richardson was, and they'd had several dates before Sidney fully grasped the extent of Cameron's wealth and success. Sidney was not looking for a relationship of any kind at this point in her life. She had a business to run and a child to raise. She was incredibly busy. But Cameron always went after what he wanted, and he usually got it. He went after Sidney like nothing he'd ever gone after in his life. Cameron pulled out all the stops to court the independent and strong-willed Sidney Putnam.

The more she got to know him, the more she realized that Cameron was not only a success. He was also a kind and caring human being. She finally had to admit to herself that she'd fallen in love with the man.

MATTHEW AND ISABELLE RITTER

They met in New Orleans when he was a fourth-year medical student at Tulane and she was a freshman at Newcomb College. They both had roots in Tennessee, albeit at different ends of that very long state. Their first few dates had serious relationship written all over them. Isabelle Blackstone was considerably younger than Matthew Ritter, but he was committed to being eternally young and worked out every day to stay that way. They made a handsome couple. Isabelle was blonde and beautiful, and Matthew knew she was the one.

He was in love, but he wasn't ready to settle down. He had places to go and people to see. He had an internship and a residency to do, and he had signed up to fulfill his obligations to his country by spending two years working for the United States Public Health Service. She had just finished her freshman year in college. Matthew was moving on to California for his internship, the next chapter in the long quest to become a urologist. Would Isabelle go with him or would she stay in New Orleans?

In the end, she decided he was worth it. She would transfer to UCLA and complete her undergraduate studies there. Her parents were not happy when their nineteen-year-old daughter told them she wanted to leave Newcomb College and move to California to complete her degree. But they trusted her and agreed to pay her tuition in California. She was an excellent student and worked hard to graduate with a dual degree in psychology and sociology.

Isabelle and Matthew married after Isabelle finished her undergraduate studies, and they moved to the Phoenix area where Matthew served his two years in the Public Health Service, working on what was then called an Indian Reservation. While they lived near Phoenix, Isabelle earned a master's degree in clinical psychology at Arizona State University in Tempe, Arizona, and she later opened her own counseling practice in Palm Springs, the same year Matthew joined a thriving urology group in that California city.

The professional corporation Matthew Ritter joined was the leading group of urologists in Southern California. Movie actors and other famous people from Los Angeles drove to Palm Springs for medical care, especially when they had an embarrassing problem they didn't want anyone in L.A. to know about. Matthew was bound by the Hippocratic Oath and the covenant of professional confidentiality not to talk about his patients. And he never did. He kept many confidences about highly-placed people in all walks of life. As well as the Hollywood crowd, he treated wealthy businessmen and politicians, including two governors of Western states, several United States senators, and assorted congressmen and judges. His group was known for its medical expertise as well as for its discretion. Matthew knew many scandalous things, secrets quite a few famous people hoped he would carry to his grave. He would, but did they all trust that he would always abide by his commitment to confidentiality?

Isabelle likewise knew her clients' secrets. She was an effective therapist and a warm and caring human being. Her patients loved her. She had a successful practice within a year of hanging out her shingle and had to begin hiring additional counselors to join her. There was a lot of money in Palm Springs. There were also some very large egos in residence, a not unexpected circumstance, as the very successful wanted to live, vacation, and retire in this golf course mecca that was reputed to have more sunny days than any other place in the United States. There was a great deal of infidelity, and many people came to her with problems that were associated with their addictions to drugs and alcohol. There was domestic abuse, and women, who did not want to be seen in public with a black eye or a broken arm, left Beverly Hills to hide out and seek counseling in Palm Springs. Isabelle listened and dispensed advice to the rich and famous.

Isabelle was sometimes called to testify in court, something she hated to do. She didn't like to break a confidence, but she was legally bound to respond to a subpoena to appear in court and to testify honestly when questioned under oath. She had almost been called to testify in the extraordinarily high-profile murder trial that involved a very famous football player and his second wife. Everyone knew the athlete had been beating his wife on a regular basis. He'd finally killed her and was on trial for murder. Isabelle thankfully hadn't had to testify in that case. But there were other cases where her testimony had resulted in an unstable parent being denied custody of their child or children in a divorce. She had received direct and very personal threats as a result of some of these court cases.

She had struggled to work, at least part-time, while she raised the couple's two children. Isabelle had household and babysitting help, and she spent as much time in her office as she could. She knew she needed the stimulation of doing her own thing while dealing with diaper changes, wiping down counters, making endless peanut butter and jelly sandwiches, and driving her children to their after-school activities and numerous sports events. When her children graduated from high school, Isabelle realized she was burned out being a clinical psychologist, and she began to look for a new and less stressful career.

She found her next identity as an interior designer and owner of an elegant high-end shop that sold European antiques, lamps, and other wonderfully beautiful and expensive accessories for the home. Isabelle's store, Blackstone White, immediately became everybody's favorite place to find the perfect piece to make a room both interesting and classy.

What Isabelle had not expected was the extent to which being an interior designer and a store owner would call on her skills as a therapist. People came into the store to talk and sometimes to cry. Her clients had a great deal of money, but they did not necessarily have lives that included much happiness or contentment. Isabelle was a good listener. She was patient and kind. People she barely knew poured out their hearts to her. If a husband was laundering money, his wife might express her disgust or her fear about his activities to Isabelle. If a boyfriend was involved in the drug trade, the girlfriend might confide in Isabelle. There were plenty of mafioso living in Palm Springs.

Isabelle sometimes helped a client disappear. It started with a woman who was a prolific shopper and regular customer of Isabelle's. The woman came into the store one day, terrified that her husband had sent his henchmen to kill her. She begged Isabelle to allow her to hide in the storage room at the back of Blackstone White. Isabell trusted her gut and helped the woman lie down, well concealed, behind a pallet of oriental rugs. Sure enough, two greasy looking tough guys with tattoos all over their arms arrived at the store, and without asking, burst into the store and searched high and low for the gangster's wife. Isabelle was frightened, but she was also angry. The mobsters were unable to find Isabelle's client, and as soon as they'd left, Isabelle called the police. She reported the two for coming into her store and turning everything topsy-turvy and for searching her property without her permission. She knew nothing would come of the police report she'd filed, but she felt she had done the right thing.

Isabelle hid the frightened woman in her own home for several days and then drove her to Mexico. The woman had a secret bank account in L.A. and hoped to start a new life south of the border. The incident had been terrifying, but Isabelle had found a new calling. She was now an interior designer, store owner, and rescuer of the abused. It was a lot to take on, and Isabelle often asked herself if she had merely traded one stressful job for another even more stressful job.

The interior design part of her business was booming. Isabelle had excellent taste. Everybody wanted her to design the addition to their house; consult with them about the space planning in their new kitchen; and do the paint, curtains, and new furniture in the family room renovation. She had more business than she could handle. She spent a lot of time in clients' homes and often drew on her counseling skills to settle disputes within these families. The husband, who was paying the bill for the redecorating project, didn't like white walls. The wife, who would be spending most of her waking hours in the room, wanted only white walls. He dug in his heels. She refused to talk about it. The interior designer/marriage counselor came to the rescue and often brought a compromise and reconciliation. Isabelle wondered how interior designers without experience in clinical counseling were ever able to accomplish anything.

Isabelle saw and heard many things she'd never wanted to see or hear. She kept her secrets, but she sometimes worried if an angry father, who had been denied access to his children because of his mental illness or his drug use, would remember her court testimony and come after her. She worried that the women she'd helped disappear would be found. Would the assistance Isabelle had given to rescue and hide these victims be exposed? Would an angry abuser hunt her down?

J.D. AND OLIVIA STEELE

J.D. Steele had been an athlete and a scholar in high school before he matriculated at the University of Oklahoma. He was handsome and outgoing as well as smart. He joined a fraternity and dated many women, but he also managed to make good grades, at least good enough for him to be admitted to the University of Oklahoma College of Law after he finished his four undergraduate years. After law school, J.D. fulfilled his obligation to Uncle Sam and was stationed in El Paso, Texas with the JAG Corps.

J.D. had always wanted to be a prosecutor. He had a strong sense of right and wrong and wanted to help make sure the bad guys were found guilty and put in jail. He would devote twenty-five years of his life to this cause, and he became a legend in Tulsa legal circles. His specialty was trying the most complex and difficult criminal cases, including murder, rape, and drug cases. He was a relentless defender of justice and a dispenser of appropriate punishment. He was always prepared and performed brilliantly in front of the jury. J.D. seemed to thrive on convicting the worst of the worst, and he could count the cases he'd ever lost on one hand!

J.D. and his first wife were married just after they'd finished college. They were both very young, and neither of them was ready for marriage. The two had almost nothing in common, and after less than a year, they realized their union had been a mistake. They had no children and few assets, so their divorce was relatively amicable. They remained friends.

After his divorce, J.D. became one of Tulsa's most eligible bachelors and was quite the man-about-town for a few years until he met Signa Lindstrom. It was a love match, and they married and had twins, a boy and a girl. Signa had her pilot's license and loved to fly. Both of their children had graduated from college when Signa was killed in a plane crash. She was a passenger in a friend's private plane. J.D. was devastated and terribly angry. He was convinced that if Signa had been flying the plane, there would not have been an accident. He didn't handle his enormous grief well and vowed never to marry again. He resigned abruptly from his job as an assistant district attorney, abandoned his beautiful Art Deco mansion without even cleaning out the refrigerator, told no one except his grown children goodbye, and left the country for French Polynesia.

This was where J.D.'s life and marital history became murky. Some say he married again on the rebound...two times! But no one is really sure whether he ever married again at all, or if he did, whether it was once, twice, three or even four times. Rumors flew, and J.D. wasn't talking about it. It didn't matter. J.D. never went back to Tulsa, and his house was sold. He eventually returned to the United States, and with the money he had saved, combined with an inheritance from his now-deceased, well-to-do parents, he bought a trucking company. The company's headquarters were in Missouri, and J.D. bought a condo in St. Louis.

He'd never thought he would enjoy anything as much as he'd enjoyed being a prosecuting attorney, but he found he loved running his own transportation empire. He was good at logistics and good with people, and RRD Trucking made him ten times more money than he'd ever dreamed he would make in his lifetime. He bought a cattle ranch. J.D. liked to travel to Washington, D.C. to lobby his legislators in person about transportation and agricultural issues. It was on one of these trips to the nation's capital that he met Olivia Barrow Simmons.

Olivia Barrow had been a cheerleader and her high school's homecoming queen. She was beautiful and outgoing. She was the prettiest and the most popular girl in her school, and she was also very smart. She was the valedictorian of her high school class. After graduating from the University of North Carolina with a degree in mathematics, Olivia moved to Washington, D.C. where she shared an apartment with three other young women. Olivia had landed a job as a cypher specialist at the National Security Agency, so she wasn't able to talk to anybody about what she did at work.

Because Olivia was so attractive and had such a winsome personality, the NSA quickly identified her as a person who could represent the agency at Congressional hearings and other official public events. She always had all the answers, and although she would rather have been spending her time working on the complicated puzzles, mathematical constructs, and computer coding she loved, she was happy to be the pretty face of the No Such Agency. It was during one of her appearances before the Senate Select Committee on Intelligence that she was introduced to Bradford Simmons, the youngest man ever to be elected to the United States Senate. He was from Colorado, and he had a reputation as a womanizer.

Once he'd laid eyes on Olivia, there was no one else. She was young and vulnerable and flattered that a United States Senator wanted to date her. The women with whom she shared her apartment were envious and urged her to continue going out with Bradford. Olivia was eventually persuaded by the young senator's attentions, and within eighteen months, they were married. Olivia was devoted to her work and insisted on keeping her job at the NSA. Olivia and Bradford had three children, and Olivia chose to stay married to the senator until all three had graduated from college. Simmons had continued his womanizing behavior all during their miserable marriage, and Olivia had finally had all she could stand of the ridiculously handsome and adulterous cad. She divorced him and took him for everything she could get in the divorce.

Olivia vowed she would never marry again, and she focused her life on her children, her grandchildren, and the career she loved. Olivia had a very high security clearance and was a valuable employee at the NSA. Nobody could ever know exactly what she did, but whatever it was, she was very, very good at it. She knew lots of secrets about everything and everybody, but she was a person of the highest integrity. No one ever worried that she would suffer from "loose lips."

Many eligible bachelors in the nation's capital wanted to date her, but she was done with men...or so she said. Even in her late fifties, she was a beauty. She was a fascinating conversationalist, and everyone, men and women, wanted to sit next to her at dinner. It was at one such dinner party, hosted by her best friend, that Olivia was seated next to J.D. Steele. The two hit it off immediately and were roaring with laughter before the main course was served. The hostess, who had known Olivia for decades, had thought J.D. and Olivia would appreciate each other's company, but she'd greatly underestimated the enormous amount of fun they would have together. For Olivia and for J.D., there was nobody else at the party.

They were inseparable from that night on. J.D. bought a townhouse in Georgetown and courted the woman who had swept him off his feet. He had never expected to fall in love like this so late in life, but he adored Olivia and didn't want to be away from her. Olivia was just as shocked to find herself head over heels in love with J.D. She liked men, but after her disastrous marriage, she wanted nothing more to do with romance. But these two were a match that was destined to be. They had such a good time in one another's company. Each of them had a wonderful sense of humor, and they could always make the other one laugh. Even their very skeptical grown children had to admit it was a beautiful thing to behold.

It was Olivia's idea to move closer to where J.D.'s business had its headquarters. The couple bought a house in St. Louis. She hated to leave her job at the NSA, but it was time to retire. Because Olivia insisted on spending one week out of every month near her children and grandchildren, who all lived in the Northern Virginia, Maryland, D.C. area, they kept the townhouse in the District. This was fine with J.D., and he usually came East with her. They traveled and enjoyed their lives. In spite of love and compatibility, Olivia was skeptical about marriage for many years. She didn't see why it was necessary. J.D. finally convinced Olivia that being married would not be the kiss of death, and they ended up tying the knot when they were both in their late 60s.

Acknowledgments

Heartfelt thanks to my readers and editors. I couldn't have done this without you. Thank you to the photographer who always makes me look good, Andrea Burns, and to Jamie Tipton at Open Heart Designs. Jamie puts it all together for me. I am nothing without Jamie. Thank you to friends and fans who have encouraged me to continue writing.

About the Author

A former actress and singer, **Henrietta Alten West** *has lived all over the United States and has traveled all over the world. She writes poetry, songs (words and music), screenplays, historical fiction, spy thrillers, books for young people, and mysteries. She always wanted to be Nancy Drew but ended up being Carolyn Keene.*

More Books By
Henrietta Alten West

I Have a Photograph
Book #1 in the The Reunion Chronicles Mysteries

Old friends gather in Bar Harbor for a reunion. They've made it to age seventy-five this year and are ready for a party. Who knew that their annual celebration of camaraderie, food and wine, laughter, and memories would turn into an adventure of murder and revenge?

Released 2019, 277 pages Paperback ISBN: 9781953082930
Hardcover ISBN: 9781953082947 ebook ISBN: 9781953082923

When Times Get Rough
Book #3 in the The Reunion Chronicles Mysteries

In spite of the COVID pandemic, the Camp Shoemaker yearly reunion was being held in Paso Robles, California at the elegant Albergo Inn. Kidnapping and torture were on the program. The group once again rallied to save a fellow guest at the Albergo and a physician whistleblower from Hong Kong who had been targeted by Chinese Communist agents operating inside the U.S. Then these seniors had to scramble to save the lives of two of their own.

Released 2021, 352 pages Paperback ISBN: 9781953082077
Hardcover ISBN: 9781953082060 ebook ISBN: 9781953082084

Preserve Your Memories
Book #2 in the The Reunion Chronicles Mysteries

After surviving the previous fall's harrowing adventure in Maine, the Camp Shoemaker group of friends has gathered at the fabulous Penmoor Resort in Colorado Springs. In this sequel to *I Have A Photograph*, unanswered questions are addressed, and complex Russian connections become clear.

Released 2020, 362 pages Paperback ISBN: 9781953082015
Hardcover ISBN: 9781953082008 ebook ISBN: 9781953082022

A Fortress Steep and Mighty
Book #4 in the The Reunion Chronicles Mysteries

The Cold War is hot again. The audacious plot to assassinate a powerful world leader will keep you on the edge of your seat. Bogged down in an endless war, will Russia's Hitleresque president decide to use nuclear weapons to achieve his objectives? Forces are at work to bring him down. The world holds its collective breath as the threat of global annihilation looms. This thriller, the fourth book in the Reunion Chronicles Mysteries series, reaches into the future with an outrageously bold plan.

Released 2022, 378 pages Paperback ISBN: 9781953082190
Hardcover ISBN: 9781953082183 ebook ISBN: 9781953082206

Available in print and ebook online everywhere books are sold.

MORE FROM
LLOURETTIA GATES BOOKS

CAROLINA DANFORD WRIGHT

Old School Rules
Book #1 in the *The Granny Avengers Series*

Marfa Lights Out
Book #2 in the *The Granny Avengers Series*

MARGARET TURNER TAYLOR
www.margaretttaylorwrites.com

BOOKS FOR ADULTS

*Traveling Through the Valley
of the Shadow of Death*

I Will Fear No Evil

Russian Fingers

BOOKS FOR YOUNG PEOPLE

Secret in the Sand
Baseball Diamonds
Train Traffic
The Quilt Code
The Eyes of My Mind

*Available in print and ebook
online everywhere books are sold.*